THE
BODY
IN THE
CLOUDS

a novel

ASHLEY HAY

WASHINGTON SQUARE PRESS
—
ATRIA
New York   London   Toronto   Sydney   New Delhi

WASHINGTON SQUARE PRESS

ATRIA

An Imprint of Simon & Schuster, Inc.
1230 Avenue of the Americas
New York, NY 10020

First Washington Square Press/Atria Paperback edition July 2017

WASHINGTON SQUARE PRESS and colophon are registered trademarks of Simon & Schuster, Inc.

For information about special discounts for bulk purchases, please contact Simon & Schuster Special Sales at 1-866-506-1949 or business@simonandschuster.com.

The Simon & Schuster Speakers Bureau can bring authors to your live event. For more information or to book an event contact the Simon & Schuster Speakers Bureau at 1-866-248-3049 or visit our website at www.simonspeakers.com.

Manufactured in the United States of America

10 9 8 7 6 5 4 3 2 1

Library of Congress Cataloging-in-Publication Data

Names: Hay, Ashley, author.
Title: The body in the clouds : a novel / Ashley Hay.
Description: First Washington Square Press trade paperback edition. | New York : Washington Square Press, 2017.
Identifiers: LCCN 2016057143 (print) | LCCN 2017004232 (ebook) | ISBN 9781501165115 (softcover) | ISBN 9781501165122 (eBook)
Subjects: LCSH: Life change events—Fiction. | Self-realization—Fiction. | BISAC: FICTION / Literary. | FICTION / Historical.
Classification: LCC PR9619.4.H38 B63 2017 (print) | LCC PR9619.4.H38 (ebook) | DDC 823/.92--dc23
LC record available at https://lccn.loc.gov/2016057143

ISBN 978-1-5011-6511-5
ISBN 978-1-5011-6512-2 (ebook)

Praise fo

"Exquisitely written ar
limpid and deep as the
book's characters and just as teeming with vibrant life. Ashley Hay's
novel of love and pain is a true book of wonders."

—Geraldine Brooks, Pulitzer Prize–winning
author of *The Secret Chord*

"*The Railwayman's Wife* is a fine evocation of place and time—a
vivid love letter to a particular corner of post-war Australia. Ashley
Hay writes with subtle insight about grief and loss and the heart's
voyage through and beyond them. It's a lovely, absorbing, and
uplifting read."

—M. L. Stedman, author of *The Light Between Oceans*

"After wowing European audiences, this book is coming stateside
to dazzle you . . . Beautifully written, and featuring some excellent
passages about writing and reading itself, this book will have you
feeling every emotion at once."

—*Bustle*

"Ashley Hay weaves a moving tale of love, loss and hope."

—*Us Weekly*

"[Hay's] prose style is simple yet vivid, and her insights on bereave-
ment and moving forward are wise. Perhaps most impressive is her
portrayal of the human predicament, the notion that one's heartfelt
hopes are sometimes crushed against the rocks of reality."

—*Star Tribune*

"This story is a study in emotion: grief, hope, love, redemption, and yearning. The prose is so elegant that it seems to glide."

—Historical Novel Society

"*The Railwayman's Wife* is a beautifully attentive study of what comes after—after a funeral, after a war—and Ashley Hay is a wise and gracious guide through this fascinating territory. This is a book in which grief and love are so entwined they make a new and wonderful kind of sense."

—Fiona McFarlane, author of *The Night Guest*

"A literary and literate gem of a book that leaves you with a set of emotions that I suspect last for a long, long time."

—*Psychology Today*

"Multilayered, graceful, couched in poetry, supremely honest, gentle yet jarring, Hay's thought-provoking novel pulls you along slowly, like a deep river that is deceptively calm but full of hidden rapids. Much to ponder."

—*Kirkus Reviews*

"Significant moments are described with astoundingly solid writing, and the coastal setting is beautifully depicted. Previously released to critical acclaim in Australia in 2013 and a 2014 winner of the Colin Roderick Prize . . . , this second novel from Hay is the kind of slow, ruminative, evocative story that will appeal to devotees of literary fiction."

—*Library Journal*

"This thoughtful, elegant portrait of lives turned inside out and finding the way forward from despair is sure to find a place in the hearts of its audience."

—*Shelf Awareness*

"Hay delicately threads together the lives of a widowed librarian, an unproductive poet, and a guilt-ridden doctor as they grapple with life after loss in post–World War II Thirroul, a small seaside village in New South Wales, Australia."

—*Coastal Living*

"Hay has lovingly crafted a poignant, character-driven novel filled with heartache and hope, which is transferred to the reader through lyrical prose, poetic dialogue and stunning imagery."

—*RT* Magazine

"*The Railwayman's Wife* uses beautiful prose and empathetic characters to tell a story of both hope and heartache."

—*BookPage*

"In this poignant rumination on life, death, memory, dreaming and the anxious spaces in between, it's hard to find fault with a single one of Hay's words, which speak to and provoke our deepest desires for literature to transform and heal us."

—*Sydney Morning Herald*

"Hay handles the delicate progress of Ani's return to the world with sympathy and toughness; she is an author in whom intellectual scope and empathetic imagination are not separate activities but two sides of the same coin. . . . recalls the sour-sweet best of Michael Ondaatje's fiction. Another author, Ford Madox Ford, began his *The Good Soldier* by claiming, 'This is the saddest story.' It isn't. That title rightly belongs to *The Railwayman's Wife*."

—*The Australian*

ALSO BY ASHLEY HAY

FICTION

The Railwayman's Wife

NONFICTION

Museum (with Robyn Stacey)

Herbarium (with Robyn Stacey)

Gum: The Story of Eucalypts and Their Champions

The Secret: The Strange Marriage of Annabella Milbanke and Lord Byron

AS EDITOR

Best Australian Science Writing 2014

For Les and Marilyn Hay

In Breughel's *Icarus*, for instance: how everything turns away
Quite leisurely . . .
. . . the sun shone
As it had to on the white legs disappearing into the green
Water; and the expensive delicate ship that must have seen
Something amazing, a boy falling out of the sky,
Had somewhere to get to and sailed calmly on.

—W. H. AUDEN,
"MUSÉE DES BEAUX ARTS"

That they have some idea of a future state appears from their
belief in spirits, and from saying that the bones of the dead
are in the graves, but the body in the clouds: and the question has been asked, do the white men go thither?

—GOVERNOR ARTHUR PHILLIP
TO LORD SYDNEY, FEBRUARY 13, 1790

THE
BODY
IN THE
CLOUDS

Into the Blue

FROM ABOVE, from some angles, it looked like a dance. There were men, machines, and great lengths of steel, and they moved in together, taking hold of each other and fanning out in a particular series of steps and gestures. The painters swept their grey brushes across red surfaces. The cookers tossed the bright sparks of hot rivets across the air in underarm arcs. The boilermakers bent to the force of their air guns, rivets pounding into holes, and sprang back with the release of each one. The riggers stepped wide across the structure's frame, trailing a web of fixtures and sure points behind them.

From above, from some angles, it looked like a waltz, and a man might count sometimes in his head to keep his mind on the width of the steel cord on which he stood, on the kick of the air gun on which he leaned, on the strength of the join created by each hot point of metal. To keep his mind off how far he stood above the earth's surface. One, two, three; one, two, three—there was a rhythm to it, and a grace. They were dancing a bridge into being, counting it out across the air.

Halfway through a day; brace, two, three; punch, two, three; ease, two, three; bend, two, three; and it was coming up to midday.

It was one way to keep your concentration. Here was the rivet, into the hole, a mate holding it in position, the gun ready, the rivet fixed, the job marked off. And again.

Brace, punch, ease, bend—the triple beat beneath each action tapped itself out through your feet into the steel sometimes, and other times it faded under the percussive noise of the rest of the site.

Perhaps that was all that happened; perhaps there was a great surge of staccato from another part of the bridge and he lost his place in the rhythm. Lost his beat, lost his time. Because although he bent easily, certain of what he was doing, when he went to straighten up, his feet were no longer where they should have been, his back was no longer against the cable of rope the riggers had strung into place. When he straightened up, he was in the air, the sky above him, heavy with steel clouds, the water below, an inky blue.

He was falling towards the harbor—one, two, three.

And it was the strangest thing. Time seemed to stutter, the curl of his somersault stretched into elegance, and then the short sharp line of his plunge cut into the water. The space too, between the sky and the small push and pull of the waves: you could almost hear its emptiness ringing, vast and elastic.

On the piece of land he liked best, the land near the bridge's southeastern footprint, Ted Parker looked up from patting the foreman's dog and saw—so fast, it was extraordinary—a man turn half a somersault and drop down, down, down into the blue. The surprise of witnessing it, of turning at just the right time, of catching it, and then his head jarred back, following the water's splash almost up to the point where the fall had begun. All around, men were diving in—from the northern side, from the barge where Ted should have been working, from the southern side where he stood.

In they went, and down, and here was the fallen man, coming up between their splashing and diving. The top of his head broke through the water and the miracle of it: he was alive.

Along the site, men had stopped and turned, staring and waiting. On the water, people bunched at the bow rails of ferries and boats; a flutter of white caught Ted's eye and was a woman's white-gloved hands coming up to her mouth, dropping down to clutch the rail, coming up to her mouth again. He could almost hear her gasp. And it seemed that he could see clear across the neck of the harbor too, and into the fellow's eyes—so blue; Ted was sure he could see them—blue and clear and wide, as if they'd seen a different world of time and place.

He thought: *What is this?* He thought: *What is happening here?* And he felt his chest tighten in a strange knot of exhilaration, and wonder, and something oddly calm—like satisfaction, like familiarity.

At his knee, he felt the butt of a furry head as the dog he'd been patting pushed hard against him.

"You're all right, Jacko," he said, turning the softness of its ears between his fingers. "Just a bit of a slip somewhere."

Dawes

AT THE height of summer, the ocean a rich blue under a rich blue sky, King George III's eleven British ships plowed one last path. Leaving the disappointment of Botany Bay—where was the fresh water they'd been promised; where was the grass?—they passed two unexpectedly arrived French ships, and turned north along a coast with rose-gold sandstone cliffs, high dunes, and scrubby heathland. Four leagues on, they turned inland, catching at the hidden entrance of another harbor and sailing into the body of the land itself. It was the southern summer of 1788, and they had disappeared from any place that existed on any Admiralty map. The ships slid silently into this New Holland, this New South Wales; their passengers wondered what might happen next.

Before this, the only white that had glanced at the blue of this harbor, the blue of this sky, had come from clouds, from flowers, from feathers. Now a procession of chalk-sailed boats moved slowly westward, quite small against the size of the shore, the trees, the rocks. From above, they were scrubbed lozenges of wood topped with squares of canvas pinned and floating. From below, they were dark oblongs, obscuring some of the light, the sky, the day. From the cove where they anchored, they were a new world, tacking and curving. The flour, the blankets, the piano, the plants, the panes of glass, the reams of paper, the handcuffs and the hundred pairs of scissors in their holds—what they held of these things was all there was of them here.

Their cargo included a thousand-odd people—some two hundred marines and officers to take care of some seven hundred convicts; an even five dozen officers' wives and children. And this augmented by an ark of five hundred animals. They were here to establish a colony, an outpost of the British Empire. They were here to establish a prison, an outpost of Newgate or the convict hulks that floated on the Thames. So far away, they were here to settle the mythical antipodes, literally out of the world—as the old sailors said of such low southern voyages. They were here, on the whole, to either guard, or to be guarded.

But one man—twenty-four-year-old Second Lieutenant William Dawes from Portsmouth—had plans beyond that. Championed by the Astronomer Royal, William Dawes had also been dispatched to scan the skies and the stars, to look for a comet. Praised for a facility for languages and natural history, William Dawes aspired to astronomy, to botany, to meteorology and cartography. He wanted to know what was here. He wanted to see everything. He wanted to learn new stories.

It was midday, and in the captain's quarters at the back of the ship, he paused in the middle of winding the clock. A fine-featured young man, his eyes bright and his brow almost always dinted by a frown of concentration, he was especially charged with the care of this expedition's astronomical instruments, like this beautiful silver-backed timepiece. Which accounted not only for the frown, but also for an occasional straightness of the back, and an occasional pleased smile.

Through the wrinkled glass of the cabin's windows, he watched another of the fleet turn and settle, and he squinted against the flash of her sails, the rush of white movement as they were hauled in. The hard sun made it dazzling. Outside the door, the sentry scuffed his feet and coughed, waiting for the task to be done: when the clock was wound, the watch could change. Clearing his own throat in return, Dawes looked down at the instrument in its cushioned box, his sight dull in the dim cabin after the shine of the world outside. He blinked, recovering its shape, its white face snowier, cleaner than any sail and ringed with elegantly black Roman numerals that marked minutes, hours, days. It was a beautiful thing, this clock, and it had made its own momentous voyages. Sometimes Dawes, daydreaming, wished it had been able to record what happened in those seconds, not just count them out. Then he could have seen its long and far travels with that great mariner, James Cook. "My never failing guide," Cook had called it, and it had even marked off the last hour, last minute, last second of the great man's life—was said to have stopped at that moment. Imagine a clock that could show you what had happened in that then, that there, as clearly as its casing showed you the edge of your face, as its numbers showed you the when and where of your position.

It was midday, and probably the first time any kind of "midday" had been marked here, thought Dawes. There it was, so simply done: another place, fixed into the world's twenty-four hours of time, fixed into its web of longitudes. He rubbed at the clock's silver, bits of himself reflected in its surface: the hair, the face, the deep bright eyes, and the dint pressed above them. He smiled. Here they were then, after all this time. There was a shout and a splash outside; one of the sailors must have gone out of the rigging. He gave the clock an extra rub with his sleeve, and set it back into its box.

"Here we are, then." His voice echoed a little in the room.

On the deck, under the sun, Dawes took his bearings—the coast four or five miles out to the east; the harbor's water heading west along some unknown course. All around the cove tall trees jostled for space, some with subdued green leaves hanging straight against the colors of their bark, others with wide shiny leaves spreading from wide, dark branches to make canopies of damp-looking shade. Below these, the different greens of ferns, grasses, heaths, low brush mixed among themselves, offset here and there by the bright feathers—scarlet, green, blue—of some quick bird surveying the British arrival.

Twenty-four hours, thought Dawes, *and the first of you will be shot for our collectors.*

Below the birds' movement, a shuttle of luggage and people was making messy, busy progress, oars hauling weight through the water and landing one thing on top of another, random and haphazard. *It must have been so quiet here this morning.* The Governor's dogs and the parson's cats made their contesting calls above shouts of instructions and misunderstandings, questions and decisions. Things would be determined today, in a hurry and for half a reason, and that was how they would be fixed and set. At least time had arrived, pinning the ship and the clock and this new port back to the faraway reference of England with lines of mathematics and measurements, as certain as if the two pieces of land were floating safely together in a bathtub of water.

Dawes took a deep breath in and held it, his shoulders back and his body straight as he heard his name called—"Lieutenant Dawes, I need you here"—and made for one of the jolly-boats and the short trip to land.

"What do you think, sir? What'll happen here?" one of the ship's mates called down to him as the little boat began to pull away.

Dawes waved at him, smiling. "Anything you like, Mr. Southwell," he called. "Anything at all." It was one thing to come into port somewhere, to struggle with new words, to find your way among new streets, to bow at ladies with different hairstyles, different dresses to any you'd seen, to worry down a dinner of some meat you couldn't quite place. It was another to come into an anchorage like this—no buildings, no systems and, on the few people who had been seen, no clothes. There were already complaints about what little headway Britain's implements could make against this forest, yet trunks were beginning to fall, gashes of space were beginning to appear among the branches, and the beginnings of a camp, a settlement were being made. Dawes could feel the look of the place, the way it had been until now, dropping away like the edge of a precipice while all that it might turn into rushed in at him. He grabbed the dinghy's edge to steady himself against it.

He saw her then, a young girl sitting cross-legged on the cove's western shore: still, dark, watching, and he raised a hand to her, repeating the wave he'd given a moment before. It was hard to tell, beneath that brilliant sun, if she saw him, let alone if she waved back.

His ambitious imaginings of the settlement's progress, its future state, folded in on themselves like an umbrella and he trailed his fingers through the water, its cool wetness shutting up his fancies and dropping him back into somewhere practical, somewhere useful. Looking around, he began to visualize the line of the cove from east to west as it would be drawn for a map. From above, the headland where the girl sat was held firm by a ridge along its spine, set here and there with tall red-trunked trees and squat grey undergrowth. Below this, the cove's western edge ran almost precisely south to north, one indent like a semicircle and then on to its end, a snubby stub, almost square, and set as perfectly north to east as the edge ran south–north. *A nice finish to a drawing*, thought Dawes, *like a flourish at the end of a signature.*

He looked at his fingers, paler beneath the harbor's blue; he watched the surface of the water rise and roll a little just ahead of the boat's movement. From all around came a full buzz like summertime crickets, so loud that he thought for a moment it might be a different kind of silence, not insects at all, and he brought his gaze back down from its practiced bird's-eye view.

The line of foreshore he'd been studying was so still, so empty, that he wondered if the girl had been there at all.

Perspective was always tricky when you crossed water towards land. As a small boy, making his first flailing, splashing stabs at swimming with his father, Dawes had realized that the smaller the vessel in which you headed for shore—your body was the smallest, then up through rowboats and dinghies to the grandeur of ships with multiple masts—the larger and more looming the shoreline would look. This shoreline, though, had seemed as big from the deck of the ship as it looked now from his squashed spot in the boat, and he suspected that if he had been scooping his way through the water himself, swimming in towards its flats, it would have looked just the same. There was some trick here, whether it was to do with the thick-set trees, the dazzling vastness of the sky that made everything beneath it sit forward like a prop on a stage, or some other proportion of light and space at work, like the innards of a telescope. There was no question that the trees were thick; from between them the pale canvas of one or two tents glinted like a chandelier's light, or a jewel in a buttonhole. And there was no question that the sky was huge.

His frown deepened. He had the strangest sense he'd seen this place—or at least a place like this—before. Behind closed eyes, he tried transposing the topography of other ports he'd visited, the lip of the coast where he'd grown up, onto the shape he'd just traced. He shook his head a little, as if that might loosen a memory. The mystics would say he'd dreamed of coming here, and maybe they were right. Waiting through the long slow sail, waiting before that for the order to leave: in all that time a man could conjure up a lot of ideas of where he might be going. As he opened his eyes he caught the edge of a bird's dive down into the water, but by the time he'd turned to see it emerge, even the rings made in the water by its plunge had settled completely. He'd need more time to work out the perspective of this place.

"You're for the maps, Lieutenant?" he heard behind him, and he twisted around towards the question. "They're after starting on the harbor's chart as soon as possible." It was Watkin Tench, lieutenant from the *Charlotte*, his face flushed above his red coat. "I think there's a suspicion that some of those little inlets and promontories might start shifting around if they're not immediately pinned down onto paper."

The two men smiled; they'd struck up a conversation before the fleet had sailed from Portsmouth, had eaten together with Dawes's father once or twice, had hailed each other in Madeira, in Rio, on the Cape as they could. They'd exchanged books. Dawes to Tench, the *Original Astronomic Observations* made by the astronomer on Cook's second voyage. ("Not much of a narrative," Tench had grumbled, flicking past the briefest of introductions to its pages of measurements. "At least you'll know what I'm trying to do out there," Dawes had said to excuse his choice.) Tench to Dawes, *Gulliver's Travels*, which Dawes had opened below decks as the first swells of the voyage broke against his ship's wooden walls. *Having thought long and hard*, Tench had written on the flyleaf, he considered this *the one book you must have by you as you travel to the antipodes*—and he'd slid a marker into the pages that told of Gulliver's own last, brief trip to New Holland. Dawes had smiled—a ridiculous thing. And on deck that first night out of port, the first pages of *Gulliver* fresh in his mind, he had looked up to catch the edge of a single shooting star.

All the astronomy in the world, and a thing like that could still look magical.

"Like Gulliver's floating island of Laputa," said Dawes now, looking again at the harbor, at its islands and beaches, pleased to already have one arm of cove etched—however lightly—across the surface of his mind. He'd been particularly taken by the book's flying island, its course determined by a band of governmental astronomers who turned it this way and that by adjusting a lodestone buried deep within its observatory. "It does have a chimerical feel," he conceded, "although this light is so clear, so bright; everything should be well and truly fixed by that." The men at the oars smirked at each other as they pulled—pair of loons, in their scarlet.

"Well," said Tench, ignoring the grimaces, "it will be nice to see you ashore, sir. A quiet week, I hear, before they get the women landed; we should toast this beginning sometime in between, and find you the best place for your instruments." The crates holding William Dawes's purpose—instruments for an observatory, for sighting and measuring, quantifying and calculating—were somewhere deep in a hold; he didn't like to think about what might have been piled in on top of them. "All this sky and land to measure," said Tench. "Got your eye out for a baseline? Your feet ready to stride?"

Watkin Tench, whose father had been a dancing master, found it slightly comical that a man might count his steps—one, two, three—to measure and map a piece of ground. "If you're counting your steps, you should be dancing," he'd said, threatening the studious and careful Dawes with a turn about a dance hall first in Portsmouth, then in Rio, then in Cape Town. He'd failed to persuade him each time. Still, he was adamant, he would see William Dawes dance yet.

Dawes shook his head; his feet took days to settle to steadiness when he came off a ship. Like Tench, he'd seen action against the French off the coast of America, but he'd taken a hit, and the injury had left him with the limp he blamed for his awkward transitions between sea and land. A limp was one reason he'd avoided Tench's dancing; a solemn way of working another; a complete inability to dance the third. "Baseline to run straight past the Governor's house, I'd have thought," he said. "Wherever they decide to put that."

"Very wise, Lieutenant. And what do you make of our new home?"

But Dawes could only repeat the shake of his head; the brilliance of the sun, the impossibility of arriving after a voyage of some eight months, and that heightened sense he'd had that they were off the maps, beyond finding, at least for the moment.

"We are out of the world, sir, as the sailors would say. Well and truly somewhere new now."

Their four hands braced against the boat's sides as its bottom scraped the mud, Tench quickly on his feet and onto the sand to turn and steady the boat for Dawes.

From beyond the beach came the noise of ax-heads against wood, of arguments and complaints, of orders and reproaches, and a glossy black bird sailed overhead, the ends of its wings stretched taut and pointed against the sky and its call clear and melancholy. Dawes followed its path. *I know of nothing that sounds like that*, he thought—*nothing in the world*. He turned a little further, his hand grabbing for something stable: whatever the trees were, whatever the birds were, whatever these waters were. *I don't know where I am.* But it was exhilarating, not disorienting. Not even frightening.

He balanced himself carefully, feeling the usual resistance of his stiff left leg against the eagerness of his right one. It was his habit now to keep his balance on his good leg and step out with the awkward other one. But as he put his hand on Watkin Tench's shoulder and steadied himself again, he felt his good leg move forward instead and plant itself, his first footprint, on wherever, whatever, this place turned out to be.

Ted

IT WAS not how his mother had wanted it to turn out—the mines, she'd hoped, would keep him close to home—but Ted Parker had dreamed of working this job since he was a kid and the newspapers started writing about what it might look like, when it might start. From his bedroom window, at night, he'd watched the moon lay down a thick, bright bridge of light across the ocean, and when he closed his eyes he'd seen that bridge translated, luminous and elegant, to the middle of the city up the coast. He dreamed of all the shapes it might take, all the noise its creation might generate. He dreamed of working on its deck, its beams, on its foundations, anywhere. In the best dreams, though, he was soaring above it, silent like a bird, or, later, with the purring engines of an aviator's plane. To be on it would be one thing, but to be up above it again—there was a thrill in that, an anticipation, that the boy could hardly put into words. If he could get to the city, if he could be part of it, who knew what might be possible?

By the time the tenders were awarded and the project was fixed—a baseline designated to ensure that the two perilously suspended halves would meet; a particular arch chosen to be beaten out across the air for a particular amount of money—by the time the land had been blasted and reshaped to take its weight and its spread, his mother had given up trying to talk him out of going. She'd worry about him, she said, if he ended up hung out over the water with next to nothing to hang on to, and if his father had been alive he'd surely have put a stop to it. But she'd sat through enough breakfast recitations—maybe steel, maybe concrete, maybe stanchions, maybe suspension—that she stopped suggesting the pits, the trains, the delivery job on offer from the local grocer.

On the night before he left at last to try his luck with Sydney's big bridge, Ted woke suddenly from the darkest part of his sleep, his fingers working at the edges of his bedclothes and his heart racing. He lay still, found the layer of silence that held the sound of the ocean as it folded itself against the sand, and tried to find his way back into his dream. There'd been noises, shouting, the usual busyness, and then something had grabbed at his throat, taken his breath away, cut off his own shout. All he could recover was a sensation of shock, of escape; he didn't want to think about what it might mean.

"Bet there's only a few will have come as far as you for it, love," his mum said at breakfast, folding paper around a packet of sandwiches.

But of course men had come from everywhere for it, nothing unusual in Ted's coming at all—although nobody else he met admitted to dreaming about it, or mentioned the alchemy that seemed necessary to ensure that the two halves, inching out into open space high above the water, would meet up one day, solid and sure, sometime in the future.

He was young then, just fourteen—though "fifteen," he'd said, off the train and with sandwich crumbs sticking to his sweater. They told him he needed to be twenty-one to work on the arch, so he took whatever bits and pieces of jobs he could to keep himself nearby: days carting bricks away from houses that had been demolished, days down in the deep cavities that would hold the bridge's southern footprints, days on the ramp that would become its approach. But always he was some way away from the bigness of being on the thing itself. He didn't really mind; near enough, he reckoned, was good enough, and he got to see it creeping and creeping, a little farther every day. He got to see its routines and rhythms, to hear the percussion of it coming together. And some days, when the light was right, he thought he could see fragments of it sketched against the sky, like a blueprint sitting beyond the busy movement of the men up in the air.

The first time he'd come to the city, at seven years old, he'd followed his mum through quiet, dark offices. It was about the war, that Great War, about his dad, and it was the first time too that Ted had understood his dad wasn't coming home. After hours of sitting on a hard-backed chair in a hallway, his mum had grabbed his hand and walked him fast out of the building and into the light, up this street and down that one, so jerky and erratic that he wasn't sure she knew where she was going. She'd stopped at last by the water, sitting herself down on its very edge with her feet dangling, like she was seven years old herself. She'd talked to him about the war, about its ending, about the men waiting to come home, about a great wave of sickness—she'd said "flu" but he heard "flew" and had an image of lines and lines of men flying against the clouds, trying to get themselves home. "Because he's so far away," she'd been sobbing by then, "and there's no chance they'll bring them back to bury them." He'd lain back on the wharf, patting at the hem of her coat now and then, looking at the shapes the clouds made against the sky. There was a ship in one. There was an alligator in another. There was a tall man running with his coat flared out behind him—and Ted could remember thinking that maybe it was his dad, trying to run around the world and fly home.

That old wharf had been eaten up by the site's comings and

goings, but Ted wondered if that was why he loved that particular spot, the place that would take the bridge's southeastern weight; if that was why he still sat there, whenever he had the chance, and looked up into the sky; if that was why he loved the bridge itself: for the idea that he might be able to get higher, or that his dad, still running, might find it and be able to climb right back down to earth.

Really fifteen, then sixteen, seventeen, Ted took the shifts he could get and slept on a cot on his gran's veranda. It was not too bad, out on the coast, and not so different from the place he'd grown up in a hundred miles south. He could keep an eye on the sea, on the gulls and the waves and the other things he liked about the land's shore. The sound the water made, and the nights when the moon rose clear and huge up over its horizon, the light glowing and so thick that he had no doubt he could step onto it and walk out forever. He'd thought about it, stepping off the boardwalk, pushing into the water and out through the surf, fully dressed, all the way beyond the breakers. A daft thing to do, he knew, shaking his head at himself, and he stayed on the shore, leaning back to pick out the few stars his dad had taught him, the Cross, of course, and Sirius, the Dog Star. He always hoped for a meteor before he got too cold and had to head home.

"He's a funny thing," said his gran to his mum, "down the beach at all hours for the moon and whatnot."

She suspected there was a girl, but Ted hardly knew how to talk to any he met in daylight, let alone in the dark of an evening and waiting for a moonrise. He didn't mind dances, and the city ones were better than the ones back home—more girls to choose from so they were less likely to remember you and chase you down the next week. But he liked the pictures better, and sang their songs under his breath whenever he did find himself walking some girl home, for want of anything to say. There was an Al Jolson one he loved: "I'm sitting on top of the world." He hummed it almost daily to himself. He never dreamed of the girls, although he dreamed of the dancing sometimes, the bridge almost always, and whatever it was that had woken him so sharply, so shockingly, the night before he came up to the city still came to him, some nights, and shook him out of his sleep. He could pick the where of it now, if not the what: in the dream—in the nightmare—he was standing near the harbor's edge where his mum had taken him after the war; standing near the harbor's edge where one of the bridge's four huge feet now pushed up from deep inside the ground. On some weekends, or after a shift if the light was still good, he'd wander down there, thinking about his dad, wondering what it was he saw in that instant before he was awake.

It was there, one day after work, that he met Joe, both of them crouched down and staring out towards the water, just a few feet away from each other in the dusk. Joe saw him, called out, getting his question in first, "What you doing here, mate?"

In the fading light, Ted started at the voice and thought, for a moment, that he was looking across at some vision of his father: the man's hair, the man's bearing, even the sound of his voice was somehow familiar. He made up a line about waiting for someone who obviously wasn't coming, standing up and stretching as if he ought really to be giving up, heading home. But, "How 'bout you, then?" he heard himself ask instead.

"First site I worked on down here," said Joe, stepping towards him with his hand out. "Joe Brown. I've seen you here sometimes. You always waiting for someone who doesn't come?" His smile was friendly, not teasing or accusatory, and Ted smiled back. "No, no," said Joe, "I like it here too when there's not so many people around. It's a good spot to sit and watch."

Ted nodded. "My mum brought me down here when I was a

nipper and we sat for hours." It felt like enough of an explanation to get him around the lie of the friend who never arrived, and Joe smiled again, acknowledging that.

"What about a drink then?" he asked, turning away from the water and up towards the city. Ted paused, taking one last look at how much the two halves of the arch had grown that day, before he turned as well and followed Joe up the hill and around to the pub.

His glass cold between his fingers, Ted studied the other man in the pub's light. Joe was taller than him, and older, but had the same bright grey eyes as Ted's, the same fine blond-brown hair, the same slender frame, the same wide, friendly smile. Not his dad, exactly, but maybe like the reflection in a mirror that could show him what his dad might have looked like in a different world. Joe was talking about his own first day working on the bridge, back when the earliest excavations were being made, the earliest gashes hewn into the rocky ground.

"They used to bring dignitaries' wives down to look at the holes we were digging," he said, laughing. "Very polite about it, they were, but you had to wonder what excitement they thought they were going to see." He drained his beer, inclined the empty glass towards Ted. "Although we did dig up some fine stuff, old buildings and bricks, back from the convicts—made you realize how busy that place's been the past hundred and something years, with soldiers and ships and coming and going. You know they had astronomers down there, years ago, on the lookout for comets. What a job that would've been, eh, Ted?" He paused then, lost in some middle distance for a moment. "The missus," he said, blinking at last, "says I spend too much time looking back there—looking in the wrong direction." He took the full, frosty glass Ted held out, and raised it in a cheer. "But you work on it too, don't you?" Nodding back towards the site.

"Whenever I can, here and there," said Ted. It had been harder the past year, with more men hunting for work and fewer shifts offered to each to try to spread the work around.

"Come talk to a mate of mine tomorrow," said Joe, "who owes me a favor. We'll see what we can do."

Early the next morning he was waiting for Ted, as he'd promised, steering him towards the foreman as though Ted was his oldest friend, to see what jobs might be on offer.

"Be grand to be up in the air," said Ted, taking in the line of the bridge, the two curves firming against the sky. He still hadn't made twenty-one, but he was sure there were a lot of blokes fudging things like this to get themselves some work.

Joe's arm swept out at the twinned arches as if they were his old friends too. "You're as bad as my wife," he said, "hankering after putting your feet where thin air should be. Makes no sense to me unless I'm being paid to do it." He shook his head. "The way your toes ache at the end of each day from clinging on up there. There are some say it's easier as you go . . ." He shook his head again. "There are some who go up the first day, turn round and go straight down again and never go back. Dunno what stopped me doing the same—apart from the pay packet at the end of the week." He laughed. "So where are you staying, mate?" And offered a room just like that—"Well, a veranda, really, but glassed in, and with a comfy spot to sleep." A stop or two on the ferry and much closer than Ted's gran's out at the beach, and it was Ted's for the taking, he said, once they knew about a job.

"What about your missus?" asked Ted.

"Glad of the company," said Joe. "She's greedy for stories about this place—you'll see what I mean. Besides . . ." He paused. "Someone else putting in, you know; it all helps."

Around them, the day was already busy, men making dark shapes against the metal, dark shapes against the sky, their hats like bits of punctuation. The noise was tremendous. Ted had never got his head around the mechanics of the thing, even after all these years. How did you get up there—and how did you stay up? How did you hear what anyone said? How did you brace yourself against the high clear space you had to stand in, move in, work in? It was amazing. *Top of the world.*

The foreman clapped Joe on the shoulder, asked after his wife, looked at Ted—"I'll see what we can do"—and then at his sheets, his vacancies. There was work on the water, he said: someone was wanted for the barges that ferried the men about, the barges that ferried the pieces of bridge to the point where they could be hoisted into the sky. "Okay, son?" Shifts, shillings.

A hand held out, Ted shook it, and that was that. He was a proper part of it at last, even if he had to keep looking up.

The particulars of the thing: scores of men in the shops, on the ground, on the water, on the structure itself, fitting, bracing, heating rivets, driving rivets, driving cranes, rigging, painting, cutting, finishing, moving, yelling, running and flying up into the air as each section was winched into position. Across to the north from Dawes Point, the real center of activity thumped and hummed in great sheds, built where rocks had been blasted away—the first assault of noise the project had made on the city, years ago now—and where each piece was brought as close as possible to its final shape before it was let outside and moved along to fit into the bridge that was growing. Shading his eyes against the morning sun, Ted was sure he could see the walls of the shed pulsing with everything that was happening inside them. *Sitting on top of the world.*

Ferried out to the harbor's center then for the first time, he looked up again, noted how far the south side had inched ahead of the north, as if it was showing the way, lighting a path. It still felt as if chance, or alchemy, was more likely to make the two halves meet than any effort of lines and math and angles. But at least it was getting closer now, the southern end moving towards the point that would take it as far as it could go, the northern end catching up, catching up. It had taken just two years for the arch to get this far.

And then, thought Ted, *it'll look like a rainbow*. A rainbow—his head, his shoulders, his chest shuddered, as though, his mum would have said, a goose had walked over his grave.

"Here," he heard someone call, "take that end and bring it round." And that was it; he'd begun.

Joe talked most of the way home, onto the ferry and up the river a way, and then a walk with a "Right here" and a "Left here, mate," and Ted almost at a run sometimes to keep up. "So that's that, mate, you're here now with a solid job and a place handily close—left again, mate, and we're almost home." A tidy garden, thick with roses that his mum would envy, and the stairs up onto the porch glaringly clean.

"Rolling along," he sang softly, "just rolling along."

The front door was open, showing a hallway that ran right through to the back. More green there, and the late day's light brushing it golden like the moon on water. Looking down for the first step, Ted caught the edge of a shape, something dark, as it moved across the lit tunnel of the house's passage. When he looked up, the light was clear again, unimpeded.

"Around here for your things." Joe's boots were off—Ted struggling with his balance and his laces—and he padded through the house to a louvered room with a cane lounge, a knitted blanket, a couple of cushions, a book splayed open and facedown.

"The missus," said Joe. "Always reading something."

Gulliver's Travels. His mum had read it to him when he was a kid, all the little people and the big people and the faraway places and Laputa, the flying island—he'd loved that; never more embarrassed than the time he asked his teacher, fanning the pages of the classroom's atlas, why he couldn't find Laputa on any of the maps. He blushed again thinking about it now.

"Us in there," said Joe, gesturing to one of the windows that gave onto the veranda, "and a bath at the back. I need a wash." He went through another door with Ted, still holding his bag, in his wake. Cold water into a basin and a big cake of yellow soap on the side. "It's the worst part of the gig, that you bring it home every day," said Joe, rubbing up suds. "Not so much as a tub to get the muck of it off your arms, and you're scratching the bridge off your skin and out of your ears and from under your nails until bedtime." Joe had his face, his arms, covered in lather as he looked up and caught Ted's eye in the mirror.

"Joy," he said, but it wasn't the soapy water, his clean hands. It was his wife, standing in the bathroom doorway behind the two of them, a clean towel held out towards Ted. "This is Joy," said Joe. And the woman smiled.

"It's getting so dark these evenings," she said. "Come into the kitchen for some tea when you're ready." And then, turning to Joe, "Let's hear what stories you've brought for me today."

Dan

AS THE great wheel swung slowly towards the top of its arc, London sprawled away, a mess of roofs and shadows with spots of light coming up here and there as the daylight faded. So many people, so many stories: Dan liked how easy it was to disappear into the city's multitudes. He liked that the sheer mass of it still let him feel separate, invisible, even after a decade.

In one of the wheel's glass pods, he steadied himself against the handrail and looked carefully along the curve of glass as it moved through the air. He could manage the inevitable rush of vertigo if he stretched his gaze incrementally; look all at once and he'd swoon. But there was the sky, there was the horizon, there were buildings and trees and then the river below, punctuated by its bridges—Vauxhall, Lambeth, Westminster, the rail bridge into Charing Cross, Waterloo Bridge beyond that and, around the sweep somewhere, Blackfriars, the fine line of the Millennium Bridge and Tower Bridge with its famous opening arms all farther downstream. Dan liked the slightness of the Millennium Bridge, so fine it looked like it had been drawn onto the city in the palest of pencil. He liked the buttresses and ridges that held Waterloo Bridge in place—so plain above, with elegant and gliding curves beneath.

After more than ten years, he thought, these two bridges were probably the shapes in London he knew best, yet he still wasn't confident he could have drawn them from memory. How many pylons? How many arches? He could never remember.

"What time did you say you'd booked the restaurant?" Behind him, Caroline rested her chin on his shoulder, its movement tapping a rhythm into his flesh as she spoke. "Did you get a chance to check that everyone had the details?" Dan's gaze shifted from the world outside to their reflections in the glass. He saw his own face: skin speckled from too much Australian sun years before; dull brown hair that used to lighten in those summers; eyes an indeterminate color with more lines and creases around them now, and around the corners of his mouth too. *At least the suit's sharp*, he thought, brushing imagined dust from its shoulders. They'd looked out of place, him and Caroline, in their city suits, queuing for the ride with tourists in zip-up jackets and sneakers.

He was heading for forty, and the idea made him pull up his shoulders, pull in his stomach. When he stood like this, he was taller than Caroline, and she would lean her head more often against him. When he slouched, she stood taller and apart. She was younger than him, five years or so, and her face had the smooth whiteness of English summers. He was never certain about the color of her eyes—they seemed to change from blue to green—but he knew perfectly the texture of that pale smooth skin. "Like rose petals," he'd said the first time he touched it. He still remembered the way her smile had spread then. Five years ago—she was as old now as he had been when they met, as if she'd caught up. He watched as she tucked her pale hair neatly behind her ears: she did this whenever she wanted him to concentrate on what she was saying.

"Sweetheart? Did you check everyone knew what time to come? I can message them now . . ." Her fingers were already tapping her phone: she knew him too well. "Hopeless, Dan, you're hopeless."

She shook her head as she clicked her phone off and put it back in her bag. But she smiled, resting against his shoulder again, and he reached across to grab her hand.

"Look at the lights, Caro," he said. "I can't believe it's taken me so long to come up here."

"That would be because it's such a touristy thing to do. And because you hate heights, Dan, which begs the question why you wanted to come up here at all." And her voice was different then— frustrated, or maybe tired. It had happened once or twice these past few weeks, and out of nowhere, it seemed to Dan, so that he was never sure what had caused it. And it passed, it always passed: now Caro squeezed his hand a moment, and leaned in while she scanned the view below. "Still, it's your birthday." And she kissed his cheek so suddenly that he recoiled a little, startled, and wished that he hadn't. He heard her inhale, too slowly and for too long, before she spoke again, but she said nothing about his recoil, just: "How high do you think we are?"

"One hundred and thirty-five meters," he said promptly, and was relieved when she laughed.

"How could you possibly know that?"

"It's a meter higher than the bridge at home—it stuck in my mind when I read it."

She shook her head, laughed again, but the sound was a little forced. "That bloody bridge. It's always on your mind, isn't it— home?"

The night they'd met, camping in Kent with a bunch of mutual friends, they'd watched the stars twinkle, counting satellites, listening to the big silence and feeling like they were the only people on the face of the earth. There was a village a mile or so away. His hands pulling the warmth from a mug of tea, he'd told her stories from the other side of the world, his home—nothing stuff, he thought, that just about anyone must know. But she'd listened to them as if he was the most exotic creature she'd ever met. He'd told her about his city, Sydney, and the places on the harbor where the old bush still grew down to the shore. He'd told her about the birds that laughed, the birds that shrieked, the birds that called and yodeled. He'd told her about Sydney's big bridge, like a rainbow of steel. And she'd laughed and said that she thought he was in the business of money, not poetry.

The warmth of that laugh: he'd felt it infusing him, and so he'd kept talking about Sydney's light, Sydney's space, about the best place, at the foot of the bridge's southern pylons, to sit and gaze at the view. He'd told her stories about the bridge being built, about the men who'd made it. He'd told her about the men who'd lost their footing, slipped, and perished. And he'd told her about one man who'd slipped and dived into the water and come up "alive, marvelously alive." Her eyes had shone with the miracle.

"What a fabulous story," she'd said. "Where did you hear it?"

"I know the man who did that," he'd said. "It's my—he's my grandfather—well, my . . . I grew up with that story." He'd taken a mouthful of tea, so hot it felt dry in his mouth, and then he'd swallowed and said, "Like flying." But she'd heard the swallow as "I', *I like flying*, and said yes, she did too. He didn't correct her. And the story wasn't his grandfather's—it was Gramps's, Charlie's grandfather's, the closest thing Dan had to a grandfather but not, as Charlie liked to remind him, actually his.

But Caroline had looked so pretty, so attentive in the firelight, Dan would have said anything to keep her there. And his city, Sydney, had rebuilt itself in his memory as he trawled it for more stories to tell her. Which were mostly Gramps's anyway. His stories were the ones Dan carried with him. When he'd left home and come away, he'd told himself it was because he wanted to find some of his own stories for a change. But it was still Gramps's stories that he told. They were adventurous. They were seductive.

And if knowing a man who could fly couldn't get you a girl, then what could?

"I want to go there sometime," Caroline had said at last. "People are always going, aren't they—they just buy a ticket and that's it—but it seems so impossibly far. A whole day of flying." And before he could wonder if he should offer to take her, she'd leaned in and kissed him and he'd felt her petal-soft skin for the first time.

"Like rose petals, like a white rose."

Through the glass, now, he watched the planes heading towards Heathrow. It still amazed him how many you could count, load after load of passengers flying out, or flying in, or flying home. Nine, ten, eleven; it was the wrong time of day for them to be coming from his side of the world. Antipodean planes mostly landed in the mornings, arriving with each new day. He followed the line of one jumbo down and down towards the airport—too fast; his stomach turned and he felt his throat tighten.

Seeing him tense, Caroline brushed her hand along his arm, held it over his hand, tight, on the rail. "This thing you have about getting up above cities," she said. "Makes no sense if you really do have a fear of heights." And although she smiled, it sounded for a moment as if she might not believe this to be true of him anymore.

"And would it have been so much trouble to check that everyone knew about tonight?" She let out a long sigh. "It's not that hard to call people, you know."

"I like trying to work out how cities go together," he said, ignoring her last sentence and kissing her cheek to compensate for flinching earlier. "And you have to admit I've taken you up some pretty good towers over the years." He looked down at London. "I still can't fit all these pieces together, and I've been here—" He shrugged, unsure how it could have been ten years.

Caroline shrugged in return, staring into the fading colors of the day as her frown deepened.

"Look at that cloud," said Dan quickly, turning her towards the one tiny shape that glowed gold with the last sun. "It looks like there's a light inside it." But she shook her head as her phone began to beep with returning messages.

He let her go, surveying the sky while her fingers tapped again behind him. His cloud was an island marooned in a vast sea, and below it, like an underscore, ran a streak of vapor from a plane, its hard line just beginning to soften.

He leaned forward, his thumb rubbing the palm of his other hand until its skin felt warm. The way that one little cloud caught the light. Dan shifted his head from one side to the other, trying to decipher its shape. It was strange that it seemed so familiar. Could a cloud look familiar? Could you have déjà vu looking at a cloud? He turned towards Caro to ask her, but she was looking down, as if she was trying to work out how long it would take to reach the ground.

"It's all right," he said. "It won't matter if we're a bit late—it's my birthday, after all."

"It's a bit rude," she said. But she was beside him again, her pale hair spreading across his shoulder. "Looks like a comet's tail," she said at last, nodding towards the blurring line of vapor as it caught the last of the sun's light.

"That bloody comet," he said, hoping she'd laugh. The night they'd met, she'd seen a comet, picture-book perfect and sitting low along the horizon. "Look," she'd said, pointing, "look, look out across from that tree." He'd looked, looked out across from every tree, but he hadn't seen it. Part of him, he suspected, hadn't believed it could be real. Shooting stars and satellites were one thing, he'd teased her later, "but who gets a comet on their first night together?" And she'd teased him about looking in the wrong place at the wrong time. "But I was looking at you," he'd said, laughing.

So when she told people the story of how they met, she talked about the comet. When he told people the story of how they met, he talked about how surprisingly cold a spring night could be. He did wish he'd seen it: it made hers a better story than the one he told.

And she did laugh now, catching at his hand and kissing it. On the pavement below, a set of couples twirled and turned, dancing to music that Dan and Caro, sealed in their bubble, couldn't hear. The brightness of the women's skirts flared against the solid dark of their partners' suits. Alongside, on the river, a small boat pulled away from a wharf, the white trail of its wake surging wide as it picked up speed.

"Why aren't there more boats on your river?" Pointing down, Dan traced its path along the glass.

Caroline's finger followed the same line. "I suppose the tubes and the buses are faster, and go where people want them to go." She paused. "There must be some ferries, though—I remember going on one, out to Greenwich, when I was little." She spun towards the east, as if she might see the very boat itself, still plying the Thames. "We went to the observatory, so many clocks and telescopes, and we stood with our feet on either side of the prime meridian." She wiggled her shoes further apart, as if the line now ran through the middle of the wheel's cabin. A playful thing, and Dan reached out, grabbed her hands, and stood with his feet opposite hers, mirroring her position.

"The east and the west," he said. "When I was little, I could never get my head around any of those lines, the prime meridian, the dateline, how something could be one thing on one side of it and another on the other—east or west; today or tomorrow. I couldn't imagine that it was possible to actually straddle one of those lines without fracturing yourself somehow. And the way this one little place somewhere in England dictated where everything was and what time it was there. Must have been funny in places that had just been going along before that, thinking they knew where they were and what time it was, then they found out about Greenwich."

"I'll take you there sometime, satisfy these touristic urges of yours," said Caroline. "You can see if you do break in half with one foot east and one foot west." Craning her head back, she watched the cabins above as they slid across the sky, everything turning gently towards the ground. "This reminds me of that ride at Disneyland, the Peter Pan one, when those little chairlifts sweep you up and over the streets of London."

"That would be too touristy even for me," said Dan. "Although I suppose I should go to the French one while I'm here—be silly to be so close and not go, wouldn't it?"

A pause, a beat too long, then, "Sure, Dan," said Caroline, but with that weariness, that tightness in her voice that made her sound like another person.

He looked at her quickly. He winced: there it was again. *Did I say something wrong? Have I forgotten something else?* He waited for her to smile, to come back, to say something light, or warm. But she stood apart on the other side of the car, rubbing the skin around her eyes, and silent.

Overhead, his cloud had changed from a glowing gold to the kind of golden-pink that belonged in an old Italian painting.

"Look at it now, Caro," he tried, but she shook her head.

"Hopeless, Dan, you're hopeless," she said again, her back turned as she looked down the river towards Greenwich and its magical line of longitude.

~

Stepping out of the quiet bubble of glass, Dan heard shouts and laughs, horns and cars, and then the surge of a tango starting somewhere and he swung Caroline out along the length of his arm and back in again before she had time to speak. There was a stark coldness in the air: it was October, the time of year he most registered the weather. Where he came from, his birthday fell on the cusp of summer, and he'd never adjusted to these autumnal birthdays.

The music soared, and as he dipped Caroline fast and low for its finale, he heard shouts of encouragement in his own accent. There were three of them, their faces and hands brown, their backpacks scruffy, and their jackets emblazoned with the familiar slogans of surfing. Yes, he thought, he'd come to London on the easy conveyer belt of travelers like these ones, a few years out of uni, wondering what to do. Some were stayers, some were goers, and some, *like me*, he thought, *are drifters*. He liked the sound of that; it was more romantic than saying you were a banker.

It was an easy story to tell.

The music finished, and he held Caroline close for a little of the silence.

"I'm sorry I didn't ring everyone, and I know we're going to be late," he said at last. "Let's get a cab instead of rushing." And he grabbed her hand and began to run—half a pace, and half a skip— smiling as she smiled. *Saved by a tango*, he thought. If he was lucky, he would think of enough things to keep her giggling. He hailed a cab with a flourish, swinging the door wide as Caroline slid inside.

"I know," she said, "you love these things, with the true passion of a man who believes they only exist in movies."

He breathed out. It was all right—she was laughing. And she was right: black cabs had an impossible glamour. He could ride in them every day and they'd never feel ordinary. The car sped through the dusk, across the river, and into the maze of streets that still disoriented him.

"What do you want for your birthday?" asked Caroline, tucking her hair behind her ears.

"This," said Dan. "This'll do."

"Nothing else?"

"I like this, just how things are. A cab, a restaurant, the view . . . you."

She smoothed her skirt and turned to look out the window at the lights they'd just floated above. And when she turned towards him again, her face was tight and her cheek was striped with the wet track of one tear.

~

The street was quiet when they left the restaurant, and Dan felt himself dozing in and out of wakefulness as their train rattled through its tunnels. Caroline was quiet, and he wondered whether he should ask her about her tears in the taxi, or whether to pretend he hadn't noticed. He closed his eyes and saw a series of images like stills from a suite of dreams: the garden where he grew up, the stars the night he met Caro, the view of Sydney from beneath the bridge—he could feel the wind there, smell the salt coming in from the ocean. When he opened them again, he was sure he saw their station just pulling out of view and he leapt up, grabbing Caroline's hand.

"What are you doing? We've got two stops to go yet." She shook herself free from his grip.

He felt his face go hot and red; he hadn't blushed in years. It made him feel young, and silly, and embarrassed. For a moment he disliked so much that she'd made him feel this way that he found himself disliking her. It was a new feeling, sharp and nasty, and he wanted to shake it as far away from himself as possible.

They were going to his place, a smart flat to the east—Caroline's was a smart flat in the southwest—and as they came out from the Underground a car flicked on its headlights, dazzling them both for a second so that they fumbled for each other's hand, warm and steadying. Dan's eyes flared with the bright shapes left behind, and he breathed out, felt better.

"It was a nice night, Caro."

"It was," she said. "Your friends are nice."

It had never occurred to him that she didn't think of them as her friends too. Dan felt a shiver of cold, and exaggerated it, shaking his shoulders with a cartoon noise.

"Brr, what's that thing about a goose walking over your grave?"

"Well, it's a cold night," said Caroline, sharp again. "Must be time for you to complain about how cold your birthday is on this side of the world. You've only got a few minutes left before it's not your birthday anymore—or not in Greenwich Mean Time." And although she smiled, she pulled away from him, shuffling her hands into her pockets.

Inside the flat, he let the door click shut behind them and crossed the room in the darkness, pulling up the blinds that had obscured the view of the river, the city, the lights.

"I brought you cake," said Caroline suddenly. "I dropped it in this afternoon—it's in the fridge. And there are candles. Do you want me to fix it for you? I can make some tea."

Dan squinted as yellow light spilled from the open fridge. He sometimes felt uneasy when she'd been in his flat without him, although he had nothing to hide.

"No, no, you stay there—I'll bring it in."

It was a gorgeous cake, rich and chocolatey, and iced on top with a blue-green globe of the world, Australia at its center.

"You're lovely, Caro," he said, swiping a little of the chocolate from the edge and licking his finger. "I like the decoration."

"Had it done specially for you." He heard her shoes thud onto the carpet, one after the other. "It seemed appropriate."

The candlelight made their shadows bounce on the walls as he carried the cake across the room. They sat side by side on the floor, the cake and its tiny spots of light, then the view and its larger ones through the window. Neither spoke as they cut and ate, licked their fingers and drank their tea.

Finally she said, "There's a message on your machine. Charlie rang when I was here with the cake, but I didn't like to pick it up."

"Charlie," said Dan. "She never forgets a birthday." On one of Dan's walls was a huge print of Sydney's harbor that Charlie had taken, all blue water and golden light. Caro and Dan turned to look at it at the same time.

"You know, for ages I thought she was your sister," said Caro, and Dan shrugged.

"So did I, when we were little." For years, it seemed, he'd not been sure if they were related or not. She was the closest thing he had to a sister, just as her grandfather was the closest thing he had to one of those as well. Like patchwork, as Gramps liked to say, these people without enough people around them: Charlie had needed a mother and a sibling, and there were Dan and his mum on the other side of the flimsiest of fences. "Meant to be," said Gramps. Four palings knocked down and the union was achieved; the kids were only four or five at the time.

"The way you talked about her, and you've her picture on your fridge, not your mum's. You're lucky I'm not the jealous type." Caro pulled her fingers through her hair, erasing what was left of the day's style.

"She's like a sister, Caro. You know that: I've told you. Charlie didn't have a mum, and I did; I didn't have a grandfather, and she had Gramps. Neither of us had dads. So we just sort of . . ."

"Merged," said Caro. "I know. I like the story. But still . . ." She reached out and cut herself another slice of the cake, picking little pieces from it and eating them delicately. He'd never seen someone make a piece of cake last so long. Shaking the last of the crumbs from her hands, she patted her hair. "I just wonder sometimes, if you're really so close to your mum, and to Gramps, why do you go on living here, and how long are you going to stay?"

Dan leaned forward, working fragments of icing free of the cake. *How long are you going to stay?* He felt uneasy, immediately defensive; he'd meant it in the cab when he'd said he liked things exactly how they were.

"I was thinking about it tonight," he said at last. "I was thinking about how some people come and stay, and some people come and go, and some people come and just drift, don't really know what they're doing."

"Neither here nor there," said Caro.

"I guess. I liked the sound of drifting. It sounded . . ." But he balked at the word "romantic." He took a deep breath. "What makes you ask?"

She shook her head. "Nothing—it's not anything. It's just, you know, we've been together five years now, and I've hardly even spoken to your mother. She must think I'm some figment of your imagination. We don't live together, which is fine, fine—" She patted the air to stop his sentence, whatever it might have offered or defended. "But we don't even talk about it. And you, you talk about your side of the world all the time—all the time, Dan—and I wonder whether that's because you do want to be there, but something's stopping you. And I wonder whether that something is me."

She paused, worrying at a thread on the edge of her skirt until it came loose. "You're still such a tourist here, you know. When I first met you, I thought you must have only just arrived, the way you spoke about everything. I thought you were always comparing things because everything here was new. But it's not that. You say you can't piece London together, but we go anywhere else and you've got it memorized in a morning. Here, I don't know, it's like you can't be bothered." She shrugged: he'd never seen her look so sad. "I just think you should work out where you want to be . . .

Do you live here? Are you just visiting? Do you want to go home? We talk about going there, and then we never go . . ."

Dan closed his eyes, trying to trace the path overland between his flat and the city, his flat and Caro's, but there were too many blanks and elisions. It was nothing—it was only because he didn't drive here, and hardly ever walked anywhere either. Caro was making too much of it. After all, as long as he knew where she was, he didn't mind not knowing how the city's other bits and pieces connected. He couldn't imagine any sort of London without her. He wondered if she knew that.

That look on her face—tired, and forlorn: the last thing he wanted was to be the cause of that. He glanced about, searching for something he might say or do to recover her brightness, and across the room, his answering machine blinked. Charlie—he'd missed her birthday again this year, and only remembered his mother's because Charlie had reminded him. And Caro's birthday? It was just after Christmas—was it the fourth? The fifth? His lovely Caroline.

"Sometimes," said Caroline, when he didn't speak, "I think that you do want to go home—you do want to go. You just don't want to go with me."

Charlie, his mother, and Gramps: his tiny pool of people. Caroline's family ran away in all directions—siblings, second cousins, great aunts. They were like London; you could disappear into their numbers, and Dan liked that.

"Of course we can go home," he said at last. "We can go this Christmas, if you want to. I didn't know it was such a big thing for you."

"It's not." Caroline was standing now, but awkward. "It's not really anything to do with it. The point is where *you* want to be. Here or there. Not just for some little piece of time like Christmas."

Her skin was almost luminous in the darkness. She was beautiful, he thought. It still astonished him sometimes.

"I don't know," he said. "And it's not that I'm indifferent. It's easy to be here because I am here, but—" He shrugged, adding too quickly, "And you're here, Caro, of course." She frowned. "Sorry," he said, "I didn't mean—"

She shook her head. "It's all right. It's just . . ." She took a deep breath and sat down again, close enough that their arms were touching. After a moment she took his hand, lacing her fingers between his. "Tell me a story now," she said. "Tell me the story about the man who could fly."

"I don't think—it's late, Caro. We should get some sleep."

And then she was standing, her shoes on, feeling for her coat, her bag, almost before he'd had time to regret his refusal.

"I'll get a cab," she said as he began to apologize, to protest. "And you should get some sleep, you're right. See which side of the world you dream about. I bet I can tell you that even before you close your eyes." But she leaned down, kissed him gently on the top of his head. "I'd like to be able to think about what happens next in this story," she said, and her voice now was wistful.

He stood up then, followed her to the door. "Stay here," he said. "Don't go off and get a cab—it's too . . ."

"It's too late," she said, but she smiled. "Don't worry, this isn't the end of the world. I've just had enough for tonight. I'll talk to you tomorrow." And she was gone, pulling the door shut quietly behind her.

What did he want? Not this, he thought, not going off in the middle of the night. He knew he should go after her. He remembered Gramps, the last time he'd seen the old man before he came to London, saying, "You're a good boy, Dan, but don't be careless," and nodding towards Charlie. Dan had smiled, and hugged him. Him and Charlie together somehow, that wasn't the story—he knew that. Nor was it what Gramps had meant.

As he turned away from the door at last, his phone began to ring.

"Caro?"

"Hey—no, Dan; it's Charlie."

"Charlie! Did you ring earlier? Caro said she thought she heard a message."

"She did—I did."

"You know it's after midnight here—what are you doing calling?" Charlie could operate in four time zones in her head; she was not a person who accidentally rang in the middle of the night.

"I—well, it's your birthday, and . . ." The line went so quiet Dan thought it might have dropped out until Charlie said, "It's Gramps. When I rang before I was at the hospital with him. They're saying it doesn't look hopeful, Dan . . ."

"Charlie, I'm sorry—I didn't . . . I wish I could . . . what about Mum?" A sudden fear, new and shocking, that one day Charlie would ring to tell him there was something wrong with his mother; the possibility had never occurred to him before.

"Your mum's been with us all day—she's worried about him too. I mean, he's such a good age, you have to . . . But he just looks sort of small, and he's not talking very much which, you know . . . Anyway, I said I'd ring and tell you."

And for the first time, the world felt big: the shrunken version of phones and email and fast flights ballooning back to its thousands of kilometers of vastness.

"Do you want me to come home? Does Mum want me to come?"

"Your mother always wants you to come home, Dan. It's been ten years, mate, and you're terrible at even calling. But look, it's a long way." She was back to her pragmatic self.

"I'll see what I can do about work, about coming. But Gramps'll be all right, Charlie. He'll be fine. You know, he's the man who can fly." And he laughed into the line's silence before he heard Charlie take a deep breath.

"You should get some sleep," she said. "I'm sorry I called so late—I did it without thinking." He heard her swallow, and swallow hard again. "And I guess I'll ring you when I know . . . when I know what's happening." She said goodbye then, and the line clicked.

In Sydney, thought Dan, it would be late in the afternoon. The sky would still have all its color, and Charlie would be sitting by a window somewhere, watching the light change, thinking about her grandfather. *Tired*, thought Dan. *I've never heard her sound so tired.* He rubbed his hair, hard. *No—idiot.* It was morning in Sydney, already morning. She was ahead of him. Always ahead of him. He pressed at the side of his head with the palm of his hand. He'd think about it all in the morning.

Still in the darkness, he watched the lights through the window—points of blue, green, orange, and red, and then the yellow-white of ordinary lights in ordinary rooms like his. A floor of lights went off in one building across the river—maybe its cleaners had finished for the night—and a single light went on in another; maybe a phone had rung there too, or an argument had just finished, or someone was just getting home. Dan reached for his phone, got halfway through dialing Caro, and then hung up as the light across the river clicked off again.

So many lives, he thought. *So many stories.* Above the lights and the buildings, the flare of the city obscured the stars.

Dawes

IN THE darkness, away from the bustle and mess that constituted settlement, William Dawes tipped his head back towards the night so that his silhouette showed a nose pointing straight up, and then one long line—chin, throat, neck, chest—running down towards the ground. His face, spare at the best of times, pared itself back to skin and bone when pulled taut like this, and what little fleshiness did sit around his cheeks, under his chin, disappeared against his skeleton. His hair was clammy with the sweat of a long and busy summer's day, and the air was so heavy it might itself have been sweating, although the occasional puffs of wind that reached across the water from the south were cooler now, already touched by the smell of rain.

From the camp, a little way off, came great shouts and screams—he paused, waiting to hear laughter, but there was none—and the gashes of orange and red bonfires threw darker shadows onto the night. Their burning wood crackled a staccato percussion under voices calling, voices singing.

"And we won't go home until morning, we won't go home until morning, we won't go home until morning—" this last word stretched to a perfectly timed ritard "—until the break of day."

But this was home now; here they were, and almost two weeks into it.

The air above growled with thunder and a new whoop went up from the camp: "Come on, come on." William Dawes shivered. He could see the lightning in the south, and the storm was on its way.

He wasn't sure that he was meant to be out on the point alone, but then he wasn't sure that he wasn't meant to be there either, and that idea had propelled his feet away from the tents and the noise and on around the waterline to this sandstone bluff. The last of the convicts had been brought ashore during the day—less attention paid to unloading most of them than to the unloading of stores of food and paintings and books, the piano, the chickens, the hatchets, hoes, and spices. Now, among the fires and before the storm, everyone was getting down to the business of being on land, some of them for the first time in years.

Two weeks ashore, but the ground was still strangely mobile under Dawes's feet as if the dirt was pitching and rolling to match remembered waves. He'd watched other sailors, other officers, getting about in other ports, but he'd never picked the ducking and weaving in anyone else's steps. A week usually, before the length of his stride clicked into regularity and he could begin to walk easily, to pace out accurate measurements. Until that happened he considered his idea of how far it was from one place to another as vague as anyone's.

Walking through the dark brush—sneaking through the dark brush—had been even worse; with every twig that snapped, every stone that turned and clattered, every shadow that rose up in front of him, his breath quickened and his throat tightened. This darkness seemed darker than any other darkness he'd moved through. A tree with two branches perpendicular to its trunk loomed up and was a superior officer, ready to question who he was, what he was doing. A rock with round edges was a convict crouched ready to jump and strike at him, to take his red coat and his purpose. He heard breathing from behind one clump of ferns—was that the flash of someone's eyes?

There was no moon. A new moon, the thinnest line, had set with the day's sun. Now clouds, laden with light and sound, raced up the coast towards him to dim the stars as well. The Cross, low and near the horizon, had been swallowed by the storm; so had the opalescent glimmer of the Magellanic Clouds. He tipped his head back further. There was Sirius, his star and his ship, still directly overhead; there was Orion; there were Castor and Pollux, the twins of Gemini, hands joined through one shimmering light.

Let it rain, he thought simply; to be wet, to be washed, to be cool and clean—that would be happiness. He shook the stiffness out of his neck, his shoulders, and lay back on the ground, ready now for nights and nights of stargazing from this place. Mr. Halley, Mr. Herschel, Mr. Dawes, famed for their observations of the night skies, famed for their acquaintance with comets; that was how it would be. He would see planets from this place; he would see transits and meteor showers and all manner of amazing things. He would set up his clocks and his instruments and he would make his name incorporating this place into the knowledge of the world, the knowledge of the heavens.

A great crack of thunder, and the camp cheered and applauded. Nice to be away; nice to be set apart a little; nice to be alone. He would propose this spot for his observatory in the morning; he was just above the sandstone ledge where he'd seen that girl sitting—watching him, he thought—as he came ashore. No sign of her since, but then there'd been not much sign of anyone apart from the increasingly familiar faces of the thousand-odd available British. And this was a perfect place for watching, a perfect place for waiting—unseen from what was becoming the main body of the camp.

This new place was settling, onto the land and onto its maps.

Already the shallows between land and water had been converted into fine black lines on white paper, names suggested here and there—Sydney Harbour, Port Jackson—and these sketches had been replicated, spilling out from the magic nib of Dawes's favorite instrument, the pantograph. He loved the way the pantograph's point ran across a map painstakingly measured and deduced—all the chains and baselines and steps and angles worried into the unique single-line signature of somewhere—to create a copy of it, perfect, under the instrument's other leaded point. It was as easy and as fluid as if some new version of the place was making itself then and there. It was like being up with the birds, watching the land appear below with another turn, another curve, another rise, another river; the invisible becoming visible. Straining towards the darkness, Dawes rubbed his eyes hard until sparks flared behind their lids. He'd been staring at those fine black lines too long.

His eyes closed, their sparks dulling and fading, and he breathed in time to the sound of the wind pushing through the tall trees on the ridge behind him. Whether it was the months at sea, whether it was the newness, the difference of these trees, the sound was different here—softer, and differently shaped somehow, but as if the wind was something solid that could be glimpsed as it moved and not just when it disturbed branches and leaves. He squeezed his eyes tight for a moment, opened them wide, and the sky had been swallowed by layers of thick velvet that turned a bruised purple-green against pure white sheets and lines of lightning. The brilliance was almost directly on top of him when the rain came at last, its smell sweet and its drops heavy and round. He opened his mouth and felt the water against his tongue, his lips, his forehead as he pulled at his coat, his shirt, stuffing them underneath the dry ledge of a rock.

More thunder, more lightning, and the rain pelted down, flicking so hard against his bare white skin that it almost stung. He rubbed the wetness across his arms, his chest, his face as if he was in a tub of hot water with a great cake of soap. The first lick he took across the back of his hand tasted like the ocean's salt and the weeks at sea; on the fourth, the fifth, the salt was gone and he was sure the water was sweeter than anything he'd tasted before. He cupped his hands and their hollow filled in a moment. He drank in the rain, puffing his cheeks out and swishing the liquid from one side of his mouth to the other before he swallowed. *So sweet*, he thought again, laughing at the memory of the last water he'd taken unexpectedly. Climbing the mountain behind Cape Town with John White, the surgeon, they'd carried no water and found themselves licking the only available dampness out of a brackish muddy pool.

"Piquant," Mr. White had said, as if he'd just been offered the finest wine. Dawes could still taste its dirt in his mouth every so often, even these three or four months later.

"Piquant," he said now into the night.

As he stood, his trousers, soaked through, clung fast to his shape and little pockets of air tickled his legs, his ankles as he eased their material away from his skin. Too late to take them off, but it would have felt so good. His body stretched and arched, anticipating the next burst of light, the next crash of sound, and then his arms were reaching as high as they could above his head and he was shouting nothingness under the weight of the thunder.

It was better than happiness; it was ecstasy.

Around him, the lightning cracked in three dimensions, tracing a secret map of trails that ran out east towards the ocean and on from this coast to the Americas, out west towards whatever lay between this meager nest of tents and this continent's own far-off westerly limit, and up and down between the sky and the ground. It was a grid of pinpoints, if only he knew how to connect them, and what those connections would reveal.

Another flash, and a tree exploded up near the camp. The cheering stopped, and the sound of pigs squealing and sheep bleating rose above the clamor of the rain and the calls. *More*, he thought, *let there be more*. And another bolt came, the screams timed so precisely to its light that he knew someone had been hit, had been knocked down. Should he put on his shirt and his coat, run up and see who it was, if he could help? A great sheet of lightning opened out across the sky and he crouched down again to take in the full reach of its movement. Nice to be alone.

Through the next hour and the next, the storm surged and tossed, the wind driving the rain hard onto the harbor's surface. Leaning against the trunk of a tall tree, Dawes watched the heavier showers scuttle towards him, pocking the black of the water. There were so many darknesses in this night: the water was a different dark to the cliffs that blocked the harbor from the ocean out to the east, and the sky—with the clouds, and then again as the storm sped north and the stars reappeared—was a different dark again. The celebrations he'd escaped had died down a little, but shouts and shrieks still burst out every so often. He hadn't heard or seen a single nocturnal animal this night, but they were probably steering well clear of the ruckus too. Nor were there any other spots of fire around the harbor's edge. A woman's voice cut across the night, her gasp and her curse closer than he expected, and he started, shifting further around to the point's northern face. The breeze had dried his skin; his body's warmth had almost dried his fine trousers, and he wrapped himself back into his shirt, into his coat, and tried to curl against the roughness of the sandstone. The last of the day's warmth was still tucked into it, and his eyes closed.

What could you tell about a place in a week, a fortnight? That the wood from the trees was difficult to manage; that the parrots were beautiful, easily shot and preserved; that there were curious insects crawling around too—some already caught and pinned. That the water carried sound loud and clear to the shore so that Dawes, on the point, had heard Dan Southwell, on the *Sirius*, doubled over with laughter at the sight of the Governor's French cook coming ashore—"Out of the boat and running clear across the water, look at him, trying to get to the land"—as clearly as if they'd been standing next to each other. That the leaves of the trees, bent to make their thick flesh crack, had a sharp, astringent smell; that burnt skin peeled away under the still-burning sun. And that there were other people somewhere around, people who sometimes said, "*Wo-roo wo-roo*," and seemed to mean by that, "Leave this place, go away." People who sometimes couldn't tell if the British were male or female. ("Drop your trousers, sir," someone had commanded, and some obliging young marine did.) People who sometimes accepted beads and bits of looking glass; people who sometimes took the hands of the British soldiers and danced with them on the beach.

Watkin Tench had regarded this last development as almost too good to be true. "Dancing, of course there should always be dancing, and if I couldn't get you near to it in Portsmouth, Rio or Cape Town, Lieutenant Dawes, then I'm very pleased I shall be able to offer it to you here." Interrupting himself with a full, round laugh. "Not quite the style I had in mind, sir, but not so challenging that you'll lose your footing and get flustered as I suspect you would otherwise do. Hands together, round and round . . . even you should be able to manage that." Laughing long and loud again.

In the damp night, the days playing over in his mind with the sound of Tench's laughter and of feet scuffing circles in the sand, Dawes couldn't have said if he was awake or asleep. But he was sure he saw a girl next to him in one last blast of lightning, her face leaning close to his, and she seemed to start and jump away when he stirred and reached out a hand as if to ask her to dance, here, now. Still young, her eyes were bright against the darkness of her skin and the darkness of the night. And he was certain, for no reason, that he was seeing up close the face of the girl who'd watched him arrive.

Sitting up to look at her, he woke himself properly. But there was nothing there, no one. The wind had dropped so completely that he held his breath for a moment, waiting for even a single leaf to move. Away in the north, the thunder mumbled. He had no idea how long he'd been lying down, but his legs were stiff and his guts cold from the last lingering damp of his trousers. Standing awkwardly, he heard something splash out in the water, and a man's snore closer still. And there, a dozen paces away or so, was a fellow in a red coat—or rather a fellow with a red coat, the red coat pulled across the huddled body of a young woman. Her pale hair was pushed back from her face and she looked as comfortable as if she'd been tucked into a feather bed. *What are you dreaming? Where have you gone?* wondered Dawes, and was sure he saw the girl smile in reply.

The strange intimacy of watching somebody sleep—he'd watched over his father one winter, the older man coughing and shaking. Sometimes sleep looked like happiness, and sometimes it looked so much like death that you wanted to ruffle the covers, drop the pitcher and wake the person back up into life. But no matter how well you knew them, sleeping minds were even less penetrable than waking ones, pressed into pure dark stillness or off adventuring in a thousand unimaginable places. The girl turned a little, her face glancing against the sleeping man's shoulder, and he flinched and turned away from her; it was a mean movement, even if it was unconscious. *Let her wake first and leave,* thought Dawes. There were so few places to avoid that uninterested shrug among so few people.

Moving along the track then he realized he was counting for the first time since he'd arrived—a dozen paces: forty-two feet. His land legs back at last, he strode towards the tents, all intent and certainty compared to his furtive dash to the point earlier. The tree that had been an officer was just a tree; the rock that had been an ill-intentioned convict was just a rock. He was in control, on the job, and ready to quantify everything that presented itself. Half a mile from the point to the settlement, almost on the nose.

William Dawes turned and looked out across the rough-hewn clearing; snores from tents here, snickers there, and unmistakably quick and carnal breathing still pulsing and pushing from others again. The men and women had found each other then—he could smell the stickiness of sex against the wake of the storm and the messy mash of mud and muck around his feet. And there was the tree that had been hit by lightning, splintered and fractured with the disaster of a stock pen that had been staked out underneath it. *Our first night all together here*, he thought, *and we're losing animals and gaining people*, and he froze as one of the youngest boys from his ship dashed out of a tent and across the grass, whooping.

Later, under his blanket, Dawes remembered the toast Tench had wanted to propose to these new places, these new acquaintances. How tiny and civil that would have been against the last night's bodies, its abandon. Closing his eyes, he saw the face of the girl on the point, the girl he'd seen or dreamed. He couldn't tell if it was lightning or daylight, but she seemed surrounded by brightness, almost luminous, with a great curve of black above her where the sky should have been. And behind her—he heard himself snore as he tried to turn his head to see it better—something like a bird began to swoop and dive, down towards the harbor's deep black-blue.

⁓

There were things that it was important to say—things it was important to do—when you were making up a new piece of empire on the underside of the world.

Weddings were a good start. Seven couples lined up and much was made of fine examples and healthy morality, particularly in the wake of the storm and the physical melee that had taken place under cover of its noise and confusion. But it was also important for the Governor to stand, at the end of the spate of marriages, and make clear the colony's position on bread and wine. In this place, he announced, there was no such thing as transubstantiation; the bread and the wine of religious communion were always just bread and just wine, at no point turned into the literal body and blood of Christ. There would be no such magic, no such miracles. This had to be stated, and stated publicly; there was still some rancor among the Catholic convicts that they'd been transported without a priest and confessor, and it would do no good if they fell to practicing their superstitious and transformative beliefs while no one was paying attention. Things like that could undermine a place as it tried to find its feet. Things like that could be perilous to order and advancement. The Governor's voice whistled a little on words like "transubstantiation"—he was missing a front tooth—but everyone stood still enough, and looked at their feet and the dirt beneath them, and the sanctity of the moment was preserved.

Yet at the base of his own quietly religious soul, it seemed to Dawes that if ever there was a venue for transformations, this might be it. Another week on, and the place itself stood so remarkably altered. There were more tents between the trees, the Governor's portable canvas house sat larger and more sturdy, and the new leaves of the British-born plants were trying to make their way in newly regulated rectangular beds where everything had grown unchecked and untrammeled before. Coffee, indigo, the cactus that would deliver bright red cochineal from its bugs—these were the things expected to thrive. And now the year itself was turning towards what should be its autumn, while local leaves still sat greenly on their trees and only Dawes's thermometer gave any indication of the seasonal transformation that must have been happening, in some other, less obvious way, all around them.

"Should we cheer for the newlyweds?" asked Tench mischievously after the vicar had given the final benediction.

"We should cheer as much as possible," said John White, "or it'll be groans of God give us strength." He'd have had more time for discussing the intricacies of bread and wine if he could have made anyone talk to him about where he might find some fresh vegetables, now that he had more than a thousand bodies ashore to care for. Yes, those vegetable beds were pressed with seeds and new green had sprung up here and there. Early sprouts looked promising, but even in the short time since "taking this place on for the empire," as the surgeon, an eyebrow raised, liked to put it, so many of those little leaves and buds had withered and failed, peas one week, cabbages the next.

"Anyway, marriage is as beneficial for the body as it is for the heart—do them all a power of good," the surgeon added. "I should have doled out a measure of lime juice for their wedding breakfast."

"A delightful memory for them," said Tench. "A lovely thing to think of through their years together." Here they were, this group of men, learning each other's tempers and humors, learning the footfall of one from the footfall of another, learning each other's stories. It was less cozy to think that this would be the size of their company for who knew how long—just these men, just each other, and whatever the dimensions of this place proved to be. William Dawes had already calculated that the indigo-blue hills to the west were at least forty miles distant, if not fifty, and that distance had begun to feel as far as it was possible to imagine to men who only weeks before had managed always to keep in mind the thousands of miles that lay between the wake of their ships and England.

"To the newlyweds, then," said White. And the men cheered, almost seriously, each one with a wedding day to remember cast straight back to it. "And how's your locket, Lieutenant?" The surgeon turned to one of the younger men, who might not have wanted the entire company to know that he carried a portrait of his wife on a necklace of ribbon, that he kissed it every night, and so fervently that he was afraid of wearing the image away altogether. But there seemed no use denying it, and he ignored the snickering to announce that it would be his own wedding anniversary in a month or so, and he hoped they would all toast the happiness of his marriage then.

White slapped him on the knee. "That's it, sir—don't let them mock you," as if he himself would have been the last person ever to mention the matter in public.

"I'm sure most of us have a locket, one way or another," said Tench, but gently. "Some keepsake to hold as a little piece of the rest of the world." He had his own memento of his father, dead four years ago, almost to the day, and he nodded his head to acknowledge him under this vast new sky.

"I dream less of her now," the young man with the locket confessed, as if there was some relief in saying anything aloud about his wife. "And sometimes I'm afraid when she turns to look at me she'll be one of those intemperate hussies we brought out here."

"That's the way of it," said the surgeon. "That or these tales I already hear of convicts taking up with the Indians, however many beads and mirrors that might be worth." He took a deep breath. "Although I suspect such encounters are taken more than exchanged." He turned back to the young man. "But not to worry, you've got your little picture to remind you of the right face, whoever you wake up with"—and a great "ho" of merriment surged over the young man's outrage that anyone could suggest such a thing.

A little apart from the group, William Dawes smiled sympathetically. "When I woke this morning, just for a moment, I couldn't remember my father's face—it was only a moment, but . . ." He raked his fingers through his thin hair; the moment had been breathtakingly unnerving. "Be thankful for your locket, Lieutenant. I'm sure you will see her properly a while yet."

The young man blushed, Tench coughed, and the surgeon puffed his cheeks full of air and held it there. "If it's seeing things properly," he said, "I was coming back from visiting the Governor this afternoon, and a woman stopped me in a state of some distress:

51

said she'd seen an alligator running between the tents, and that it was the second one she'd seen in a fortnight."

"An alligator?" Dawes shaded his eyes with his hand, trying to see the surgeon's face more clearly. "What kind of an alligator?"

"A fourteen-foot one," said John White, "as opposed to the eight-foot animal she'd seen the week before last. A very sane woman, I'd say on the whole, but she was adamant about this."

"I think it would be quite comforting to see an alligator at the moment," Tench said carefully. "Almost everything we see is so new, at least an alligator would be a thing we might find somewhere else, a thing from some known part of the world."

"I'm not sure I'd like to find one getting about in my tent, sir," said the surgeon. "And certainly not one that ran to fourteen feet."

"True, but I had one of your birds laugh at me for the entire duration of my shave this morning," said Tench. "And a creature that laughs is a disconcerting thing. I'm still not clear on how kangaroos might be put together, and why they jump, and I don't even want to think about the size of the creatures that make those hisses out in the darkness every night. At least I know what an alligator looks like. And at least it wouldn't laugh."

"I heard Lieutenant Dawes say this would be a place where anything might happen," someone said, looking to Dawes for confirmation. "I heard about that alligator the other week too, but I didn't think it sounded comforting. I just figured it was the next strange thing to turn up here, like the hand and arm."

A hand and an arm washed ashore; the surgeon had spent hours poring over them, trying to explain whose they were. Ultimately, though, all he could say was that they had belonged to a white person—and he wasn't even sure if it had been male or female. And no one seemed to be missing them that he could see.

As the young sailor said, they were just the next things to appear, as if people had been more or less expecting the unexpected since they'd reached their antipodes. Take the two French ships that had appeared at the heads of Botany Bay precisely as the British fleet made to decamp north to Port Jackson: the extraordinary coincidence of their intersection, and that strange do-si-do of maritime might. It almost belied Dawes's own sense of being out of the world, knowing that the French were just a few miles away, as usual, even closer than the distance they usually kept across the English Channel.

"A place where anything might happen," Tench mused. "That should keep us all in good conversation for as long as we've only ourselves to talk amongst. Not to mention being rich fodder for all our literary aspirations." Watkin Tench, like the surgeon, belonged to the band of men who had sailed with publishing contracts in their portmanteaux and hoped to write up the days, the birds and animals, the potentials and disappointments of this place, novel as it was and unrepresented in their catalogs of natural history. "You should be writing yourself, Lieutenant Dawes, what with your appointments with comets and stars."

Dawes smiled. There'd be no shortage of material, he suspected, but perhaps one of time. "Maybe a miscellany," he said, "or something along the lines of the French encyclopedia."

"You might be our antipodean Dr. Johnson," the surgeon boomed, slapping his knee at the thought. "You could start with alligators, then bits of bodies, comets . . . and with the fertility of imagination that our convicts already display, I warrant you'll have all manner of exciting entries—there'll be gold and dragons claimed in this place before we're six months landed, if that's not what the alligators are already."

"The antipodean Dr. Johnson." Dawes smiled again and made to take his leave. "As your publishers all know," he said, shifting the balance of his weight away from his frail leg, "it's none of it real until it's written down and read in London."

Ted

WHEN TED and his mum, or Ted and his gran, sat down to their tea, the space between them held salt and pepper shakers, a dish of butter, and the clatter of cutlery and plates against a scrubbed wooden table, the wide pages of the day's newspaper. Neither asked the other what they had done during the day, assuming that they already knew, and their quiet rhythms of different chewing tended to fall in time before the meal was halfway through.

When Joe and Joy sat down to their tea, there was a white cloth across the table and the space around the chewing was filled with the busy darts of their conversation. The butter dish was exactly the same as his mum's—and this was the first and, Ted was afraid, possibly only thing he could think of to say.

"It must be strange being underneath when everyone thinks of being up," said Joy. "If I worked there, I'd want to be up—up as high as I could."

"It's Joy's heart's desire," said Joe, "that I'll sneak her up there one night, show her the city from up in the sky." But he shook his head, pushing potatoes onto his fork with his knife. "My grandad, another Joe, he was always superstitious about women getting in to where he worked."

"He was in the mines, love," said Joy—the exchange had the feel of something repeated over and over—"and if women going *under* the ground is bad luck, then women going so far *over* the ground should be . . ."

"Positively beneficial?" suggested Ted. It was one of his gran's favorite phrases, although she usually attached it to hot milk if you couldn't sleep, or a flannel tied around your throat if you had a cold coming on, rather than the idea of climbing a great metal ladder up towards the clouds.

"Positively beneficial," said Joy, smiling, and she reached over and patted his arm so that he flinched a little, the red rushing up from under his shirt—back in school, asking the teacher where Gulliver's flying island was in the atlas. "A fellow two streets over snuck his wife up the other week; he said there was another fellow who took a girl up there and convinced her to marry him while she was looking at the lights and the view. You see, Joe, you could get me to agree to anything if I was up in the air."

Joe shook his head. "I don't need to change your mind about anything, love," he said peaceably.

His cutlery suspended over his plate, Ted looked from one new face to the other: it seemed impossible that this time last week he hadn't even known they existed. Joy's hand was on Joe's arm now, her knife laid down, her fork poised in midair too. They were both tall, like Ted—"a bit stringy," his gran would have called it—but the light made their heads shine blond where Ted's usually blond hair seemed darker and all bristle. And their eyes, their brown skin, their slender arms and fingers looked like they might have come from one person, not two different people. He shifted the fork in his hand so his grip matched Joe's, matched Joy's. The way she was looking at him, her eyes bright, her face expectant.

"You'll have all new stories for me, with that whole different perspective on it to him"—nodding towards her husband—"won't you, Ted? Down there on the water, while he's up in the clouds."

Swallowing hard, wondering what to say, Ted caught the smallest movement of one of Joe's fingers underneath his wife's arm, soothing, stilling. Somewhere, a long time ago, he'd seen his dad do that with a dog that was turning itself inside out with barking. But in the instant of remembering, he couldn't recall his father's face at all, and put his knife down to feel for the wallet in his trousers. His dad's picture was in it and he could rebuild the bones, the glance of that face, for himself. His fingers made out the leather rectangle, and his body relaxed a little, registering a new ache in his legs from learning to stand on top of the harbor's turning tides. The beginning of the day felt as far back as history. This was a whole new world.

"Just a blur at the moment," he said at last, self-conscious in the face of her enthusiasm and wishing he had some better story to tell. He'd leave the talking to Joe tonight; he'd concentrate tomorrow, bring her something then.

"Have you got a sweetheart then, Ted?" Joy pushed the potatoes towards him, the gravy jug in its wake.

"Well . . ." He scooped a potato onto the plate, measured a dollop of gravy. "You know." Looking at Joe but nodding towards Joy, the way he'd seen men do when there were secrets to be kept, things best left unsaid. "I suppose, with the moon and everything, and if you'd been dancing . . . sometimes walking home you might see a shooting star."

"You can't get a better end to a night than a shooting star," said Joy. "We used to walk down to the water every night when we first came here, in case we saw one. We should go again, love. Ted could come with us. I was always happy with a star, but Joe's one for comets—a much bigger ask." She smiled at her husband. "Although one's bound to turn up some day. For you and your old astronomers." Her fingers linked through her husband's without either of them seeming to notice.

The clock on the mantelpiece chimed, and she pushed her chair back from the table. "Some of the men come round," she said. "Did Joe tell you? A few beers and a few stories—maybe we can see about the stars another evening."

In the backyard, on the steps, on the grass, the men settled like a tableau from an old painting, fragments of sentences sitting against the click and fizz of opening beer bottles, as if no one could get beyond the shortest comment or observation until they'd taken a good few mouthfuls. A line from the newspaper; a joke from the radio; they jostled and settled and took their first sips with the first flight over the South Pole ("And I reckon that's better than Kingsford Smith," Ted heard one man mutter to Joy as if it was a treacherous suggestion), some calculation that proved the earth was billions of years old—"more than 1.8 billion," specified another voice—and news of a meteor that had slammed into South America like millions of tons of dynamite. This last made Joe pay particular attention. "Blood-red sun and a sound like artillery shells," said someone.

Where Ted grew up, a phrase like that would loop the conversation straight back into the war, but in this new world someone said instead, "The size that sound must've been, when you think about how far away you could hear them blowing up the north shore's cliffs for the bridge."

Here, it always came back to the bridge, always came back to the work—and how grateful they were for it against the price of butter, the price of steak, and the lines and lines of hopeful workers that Ted had stood in for years, turning out earlier and earlier to see if there was a chance of a shift for the day. It was something, he thought, to lean back against some permanence. But underneath the drinking and the banter sat other topics—things about the scale of the job, how impossible it was, how dangerous. Like the danger in trusting that two metal arms would meet high over the water thanks to the columns of sums done half a world away in London and a spider's web of surveyed lines and angles held on a separate sheet of paper. Like the dangerous sparks of those smaller bits of riveting, red hot and shooting through the air from cooker to boilermaker like shrunken stars. Like the way the two halves of the arch swayed and swung from their pivots to the south, to the north, when the wind came in hard from the east, from the west, closing down work for fear the men would all be brushed off, shaken free. But as close as anyone got to poetry was some mention of the trails left by boats overnight and in early mornings, still visible on the harbor when the first men went up for the day.

Do they dream about it? thought Ted. *Do they dream about climbing high above it, about how it will look the day it's done? Do they ever dream things that leave them panicked and breathless?*

He was starting to think his dream must be about falling. He was starting to feel a little less afraid of it, now he knew he'd stay down at the water's level, safe on his barge. Because these blokes were all walking in the sky, in the clouds, in the air. *No wonder*, thought Ted, *they tell so many stories about getting to work rather than being there*. Feet on the ground, they were holding on to the idea of their feet on the ground—the idea that they'd been there, that they'd be there again.

"You could hear it from ours and we're an hour's walk away, as I well know," said someone, "although I heard some chap in the shop say he was walking two hours in and two home."

"I used to walk in from my gran's some mornings," said Ted. "Two hours that was, to queue for a shift." And suddenly it was a competition: who'd come farthest, been highest, or pissed the greatest distance (with an apologetic mumble to Joy), or run the fastest on the steel.

One bloke thought to tell a good story about riding all the way up from Gippsland to Sydney, which was thousands of miles, he was sure, and probably would have been thousands more again if he'd told it later in the night with a few more beers. But then another bloke had walked clear across Russia from somewhere near Moscow to the oriental coast. That was half the world, he said, and here he was.

"But you didn't walk all that way specifically to be here," protested the boy from Gippsland, wanting the primacy of his ride established. "You walked all that way, sure, and found a boat, and sailed down to Sydney, and got yourself this work, but you didn't make the trip for it, did you?"

"I would've," said the man, who had a heavy accent. "This is the sort of place a man would come half the world for." And he took a big swig of beer, to cover up almost saying something about beauty.

"No matter how far you walked, mate, and no matter how far you rode," suggested another voice, "I'd beat you both hands down running along that span."

The running had always intrigued Ted whenever he looked up into the sky; the way men's feet must have molded themselves to the new surfaces so they didn't fall. *It's acrobatics*, he thought, *or a ballet*, the troupe of men perched in their crepe-soled shoes, their rubber-soled shoes, gripping edges and walking narrow lines. And it must have changed how they stood on the ground too, changed the whole set and bearing of their bodies, the way the work itself hardened different muscles and strengthened different postures. That new tiredness in his legs from standing on the fluid movement of the barge—how long would it be before he took on some new shape to accommodate that?

Sitting among the men and their stories, Ted listened to a well-practiced loop of the job's conditions: no washrooms, no locker rooms, no tearoom or canteen for your lunch, no five minutes on the job to rinse the grime off your hands at the end of the day—if you wanted to do that sort of thing, you did it in your own time. "And if you're up on the top, and you need to . . . well . . ."

"If you need to go," another voice said at last, "well, by the time it hits the water it would've disintegrated—there'd be nothing left. We're over four hundred feet up at high tide. So you do your business, and by the time it's halfway down it'll have dispersed. Some blokes," another apologetic nod to Joy, "do it in a brown paper bag and let that go over the edge."

Up there, in his top-of-the-world air? Ted shook his head at them, which only encouraged them.

"Mate of mine says they—you know—on them shovels they use for feeding the fires to cook the rivets. Do their stuff on that, throw it off, cook the shovel clean, and then do their sausages on it for lunch. Handy piece of equipment, they say."

"Another bloke says he did his in a bag, folded it up, and threw it over. And as soon as he let it go, the bloody thing opened up, and went round and round and round and fell straight onto the top deck of one of the ferries. Bit of a shock for the passengers to have that fall out of the sky, I reckon."

"I'm up on the arch with Kelly the other day," another speaker began. "You know Kelly—big bloke, a boilermaker." The man's voice was excited with the new story he had to tell. "And we're talking this, that, nothing and the cricket—and he drops his spanner right into the harbor, stands there watching it fall all the way down, as if he half expects it to flip over and fly back up into his hand. It breaks the water with an almighty crack and he turns to me and says, 'I suppose another man'll be going over there one of these days, like that spanner.' I said, 'Don't be so damn silly'— sorry, Joy."

Joy smiled and shook her head, encouraging the man and his telling of this story.

"'Don't be so damn silly.' He dives on weekends, you know—one of those clubs with springboards and what-have-you. And I watch him looking up and down, and I keep an eye on him now. You don't want to go saying that sort of thing on a half-made bridge."

A long silence in the darkness, cut by the sound of a cigarette's smoke being puffed into rings.

Then Joy coughed a little, pulled her cardigan tighter around herself, and said, "Someone was asking about Nipper's wife the other day. Came into the shop and asked if I knew how she was." The silence thickened.

Swallowing the cold beer, Ted saw Joe's face tighten and frown. "Nipper Anderson?" he said, misunderstanding Joe's pause. This was a story he knew, a story he could tell. "I heard about that, how he went in and the people who dived in to fetch the body found it stuck as if it was sat down in mud." He caught his breath. He felt his hands go sticky, rubbed them hard against his legs.

"Steady, Ted," said Joe. "Steady, mate, there are blokes here that were doing that diving." But someone else had already picked up the recitation.

"It was my first day up there, you know, getting the feel of it. One of the riggers was calling out, 'Look at this place, over here, and the mountains over there, and there's a ship coming up the harbor.' Some of the blokes were joking around, saying they hoped the bridge would keep him on when she was done, so he could call all the attractions for people walking across underneath. Good bloke, the rigger, and his malarkey was nice to keep your mind off where you were, what you were doing, before you started to look around."

A deep breath—punctuation. "The clouds look really white, when you're that bit closer to them. And the noise, strike me, the noise was big: air guns and cranes and steel bashing steel, and rivets sizzling to white hot, everyone shouting, needing this, doing that, and underneath it all this huge noise that's the machines in the workshops below. And I heard someone say, so clear, 'Righto, Nip, let's take another purchase.' This was some bloke, just talking to Nipper."

Another pause—the man might as well have been on a stage, spotlit. He held the audience in the palm of his hand, no matter how many times they'd heard this story before. Leaning forward, Joy's face was taut, her eyes shining.

"Young bloke—just married, someone said—and his brother worked on the site too. Nipper had spoken for him to get a job, and they'd made him ambulance officer. Ambulance officer—you wouldn't believe it. Anyway, his mate calls for another grip, and then there's this noise, sharp. It's a spanner bouncing off Nipper's mate and jarring on the steel, and it's hit Nipper's mate because Nipper's dropped it. And Nipper's dropped it because he's lost his footing. His mate's hanging on to him, his mate's hanging on. He's got him by the foot, and he's holding him—and it looks okay, looks okay. This Nipper, he's only a little thing, looks like his mate'll hold him.

"And then the mate's holding a sandshoe, that's all, just a pissing little sandshoe—sorry, Joy—and I'm standing there looking at the shoe and counting, waiting to hear a splash like a clap of thunder. Dunno why I didn't hear anything. Someone's shouting, 'Get yourself straight.' And there were men running down off the bridge, down to the water, and they were diving in, going for the body, three or four of them. Him—" pointing to a man on the bottom step, who raised his hand, "and him." He pointed to another farther out on the grass, who nodded. "These men diving down, coming up, shaking their heads.

"And no one said anything—do you remember? No one said anything at all." He took a long puff of his cigarette, and stubbed it out in the dirt. "Then the whole site cleared, and we went home."

He wiped one hand across his eyes. "Bloody Nipper. You don't need a first day like that, Ted, I'll tell you that, mate. I'll tell you that."

In the silence, Ted chewed at his lip and thought of the line he'd always had ready against his mum's fear, his gran's, that someone would give him his job up in the air and he'd end up tripping, falling down and down. "If you started to fall, it'd feel like flying for a second, wouldn't it?" But what did he know? If some dream could make you feel so thick and anxious, what could you say about finding yourself in a real moment like that?

"Time, gentlemen," said Joe, and the men stretched and stood and headed into the darkness, calling their good-byes to Joy, nodding to Joe as he corralled the beer bottles into a crate. Ted could hear Joy inside the house, humming, could hear the stove being stoked and the kettle being filled. But as he turned to go in, Joe caught his shoulder.

"Those stories, the ones like Nipper," he said, his cigarette smoke hovering like a cloud in the glow of the house's lights, "she takes them on, you know. She makes a lot of them, feels them keen and deep. I try to . . . well, it's better to keep it a bit light and easy, isn't it, mate?" And he clapped his hand onto Ted's shoulder again as they stood a moment, like the younger and older version of the same shape, the same stance. "Anyway, good you could meet the neighbors. They're good men, good nights." And he flicked the smoldering butt of his cigarette in a high arc through the air beyond the reach of the bright windows and into the garden's blackness.

Ted watched it rise and peak and fall, dropping down in the dark green somewhere like a lost rivet that had somehow worked itself away from its steel and followed these men home.

Dan

TURNING FROM the front door of his building, Dan saw something flare just beyond the corner of his eye—turned again and saw a man walking away as his cigarette butt rolled towards the gutter, its end glowing red. The morning was grey, skittering towards winter, and as the cigarette disappeared into the grating of a drain, Dan paused a moment on the gutter, wondering where it might end up, swirling below the streets towards a river, a sewer. At home, in Sydney, some grates had signs that told you which body of water the drain led to. Drop something here, it would end up there. There was probably a map that showed these tracks and all these veins, these arteries, clogging slowly, silting up.

He buttoned his coat and began to walk to the station. He was dull with the heavy, vaguely nauseous feeling of not enough sleep—his mind had spent the night working its way around the triangle of Caroline, of Charlie, of Gramps, and the morning seemed littered with traces of each of them: a woman on the other side of the road had Caro's hair; a woman pausing on a street corner raised a camera to her eye as Charlie would; an old man sat on a bench in one of Gramps's cardigans, working on a crossword.

The sun pushed through the layer of clouds for a moment,

catching the bright color of a front door, the metallic sheen of a car, the rainbow of flowers in a florist's barrow—yellow gerberas, blue hydrangeas, the orange-and-blue flames of birds of paradise. He remembered them from childhood. A wave of perfume reached him: roses, three buckets of white roses, and he swerved towards the cart, caught by their sweet smell. Caro. He'd missed her beside him—spent an hour after Charlie's phone call tossing up whether to follow Caro across London. There was Gramps to think about too, and Charlie had sounded so far away. And Caro had never looked so sad. Caro. He'd buy her a bunch of those roses, take them to her at lunchtime, he thought, swapping a crisp ten-pound note for the bouquet. Their perfume was thick as he cradled them in his arm. *She'll like that, she'll be pleased*, he thought, then he frowned: *She'll be astonished.* He couldn't think of the last time he'd bought her flowers, yet it felt such an easy thing to pause, to buy, to carry.

Farther along, he stopped at the stall where he always stopped, picked up a newspaper, folded it and tucked it under his arm before he realized he had no change in his pocket, and now no money in his wallet. The cash machine was two blocks away.

Every day for eight, maybe nine years he'd come to the same place and bought the same paper, exchanged a few words with the man in the kiosk.

"Tomorrow? I've got no money on me," he said, and was walking away as he heard the man say, "I can't do that."

Dan turned. "Sorry?"

"I don't do credit."

"But you know me—I've been coming here for years."

It was obvious from the blankness of the man's face he had no idea who Dan was.

Dan shook the folds out of the paper and put it back on the pile, as red, as self-conscious, as if he'd been caught trying to steal it. It was the second potent blush he'd had to endure in less than twenty-four hours, and he was sure everyone walking past was staring at him. "Jesus." His embarrassment turned to anger. He shouldn't have bought the bloody flowers.

His skin was cool by the time he got through the ticket barrier and onto the platform, but he sidled a little farther than usual into the crowd of people, farther into the mess of men in suits and women in optimistically light dresses, as if he didn't want anyone to notice that he was holding a bunch of roses instead of his paper.

A deep breath in—"Fuck it"—and he started to scan the billboards and posters on the other side of the tracks to find something, anything, that he could read while he waited—anything to distract him from thoughts of what to do, of Caro, of Charlie, of Gramps, even just for a moment. He read about travel insurance, about car insurance, about some new credit card that promised the world. The message on the indicator board clicked over; the train that had been two minutes away would now be arriving in eight minutes' time, and a heavy sigh rattled along the platform. Dan moved a little farther down. There was an alcove cut into the wall just beyond the vending machine. Eight or nine years of being at this station almost every day, and he'd never noticed it before. It was just deep enough to conceal a man, and carefully tiled like the walls around it; you could step in there and disappear.

Farther along, he passed a woman with a huge bunch of white roses, exactly like his—the fragrance doubled as he passed. Two small children were holding hands and dancing, singing "Ring-a-ring-a-rosies," while the woman—presumably their mother—stared absently across the empty tracks. "We all fall down," and they did, their mother suddenly loud and sharp about the "muck on the floor and dirt on your clothes and mind the edge, please."

But then she saw Dan, saw the flowers he held, and smiled. *Makes me look like a nice person*, he thought, noncommittal.

He moved farther on again, wondering if it really mattered if he didn't read the paper. He'd have a look at the headlines when he got to work. Anything he needed to know—currencies, mergers, government decisions—someone would tell him. Maybe he didn't need to bother with a newspaper at all. Although he'd miss the crossword, and the football; you had to read the paper on a Monday to see what had happened with the football. Still, it felt liberating now and he rocked back and forth on his feet, staring at the middle distance of the station wall. *Or I could buy one of those daggy crossword books like Gramps used to have.* He snorted: *Fuck, I must be getting old.* One hand pushed into his pocket, the other clutching the roses, he rocked a little more and thought about Gramps, wondered how he was doing. Ninety-four, ninety-five . . . *He might even be ninety-six this year.* All the things Dan had thought about since Charlie rang, but now, as he closed his eyes and tried to remember the old man's voice, the space inside his head was silent, empty, and he stared at nothing, trying to rake up the memory.

Somewhere in his flat, in a drawer or a cupboard or a coat pocket, he had the old man's watch—huge and silver, a pocket watch, for heaven's sake, rather than anything as modern as a wristwatch. Gramps had given it to him when he went away overseas, and he could still remember how furious Charlie had been; it was the only time they'd fought.

"He's my grandfather, Dan," she'd snarled. "My bloody grandfather, not yours, no matter how much he wants to think we're all just one family." But, "You just take bloody good care of it," she'd said at last. "Maybe you'll feel like returning it to its rightful owner one day." He should have sent it back to her, he thought now, even if she'd forgotten about it. He let out half a laugh. Not Charlie. Charlie wasn't one to forget things. Even if she made jokes about her lousy memory turning her into a photographer, "so I can pin things down."

He shifted the flowers to his other arm, registering a single drop of water as it hit his shoe. Maybe he should start buying his paper from the supermarket instead of the kiosk. He watched another droplet hit his shoe. That was an extra half a block's walk, and he knew he'd never do it. He'd be back at the kiosk tomorrow, handing over his change. It was always easier to keep doing what you were doing, like it was always easier to stay at a party than think of the next place to go—even if that next place was home.

It had never occurred to him before that this might mean he ended up staying too long. Whatever Caro would make of that.

The wall he was staring at, he realized then, was almost completely blue, a huge reproduction of a photograph, all sky and water, on which was traced, with the lightest black line, the famous and familiar frame of the bridge in Sydney. The bridge that Gramps had put at the center of so many of his stories—all the boys coming in to work on it, to beat it into being, and the danger and the daring of it all. Dan and Charlie curled up next to him on the sofa, one on either side, staring at the pictures of the men so brave, so delicate up in the air, with nothing to hang on to and the water a long way below. Dan and Charlie laughing at the formality of the ones in suit coats, in hats. Gramps coaxed into telling the best story of all: of the day he'd found himself falling from the thing; how he'd flipped in the air to enter the water, elegant and purposeful; how he'd emerged, the only one to manage it, "marvelously alive, my dears, marvelously alive." Dan could remember how carefully he'd listened to that story when he was young, and even not so young, so caught up in its telling that he felt sometimes he must have seen it himself.

It was strange, now, seeing such a familiar landmark in such an incongruous place. He looked at the poster more closely, wondering how long it had been there, opposite this unfamiliar part of his platform. He'd never found a piece of London's skyline that made him breathe out and smile a little, like he was doing now—not even its bridges could do that for him, no matter how nice it was to mooch around them, watching the water, the light, under their vast shadows.

Maybe this is homesickness, he thought suddenly. Maybe Caro was right and it was time to decide where he wanted to be. Maybe Gramps was the excuse he needed to go home, to see what was there now. *And of course I have to see Gramps, if Gramps is going to . . . if anything is going to happen.*

He shifted the roses in the crook of his elbow and felt one of the thorns drive hard into his flesh. As he looked down from the big blue picture to see if his finger was bleeding, he saw something fall through his peripheral vision, so fast it threw him off balance.

He looked up. There was nothing there. He looked down and the roses glistened, pale and smooth.

Truth and innocence, that's what white roses meant, Gramps always said. But what had the old man's voice sounded like? Dan tilted his head to one side, to the other, as if the lost sound might shake itself loose and roll into his ears, but nothing came and he felt his eyes drawn back to the blues in the billboard. They were hypnotic, their brilliance distracting his gaze from the ad's words, bright and white, over the top. Something about tourism, he supposed. He stepped closer to the blue, not noticing the nothingness beyond the tips of his shoes, the edge of the platform, until he felt a tug on the back of his coat, heard a woman's voice, sharp—"Hey, what are you doing?"—and he felt the red rise up in his face. She thought he was going to jump.

"No, no, it was the picture, I wanted to see if—"

And the woman stepped back, blushing herself—it was the mother with the bunch of roses. They stared at each other uncertainly.

"I just thought, how awful," she said, "to be holding such beautiful flowers and then . . ."

There was a rush of noise from the tunnel and they both turned towards the train. Dan felt the surge of air it pushed before it, cool on his face. The bridge, the sky, the water disappeared behind the line of carriages, and the doors clattered open. He stepped aside, his head down as the platform began to clear. He was last onto the train, and his heart was pounding as he sat down.

Leaning back against the window as the doors shut, he caught the radiance of the photograph's blue again. That was it: it was an old one of Charlie's—he'd been with her the day she'd found the place on the shore where the angle between her lens and the bridge reduced its famous curve to almost nothing. "Airy thinness," her grandad had said when he saw it. "Like gold to airy thinness beat." And there was Gramps's voice at last.

It was funny that he'd never walked far enough along the platform to see that picture before. "Never been in the right place at the right time, then, have you, boy?" Gramps would have said. He wondered how long it had been there, waiting for him.

He'd ring Charlie when he got to work, and then he'd book a flight. He needed to see Gramps. And Caro was right. He needed to go home.

He was at work half an hour before he realized he'd left the roses on the tube.

Dawes

CERTAIN STORIES were important to tell—certain things were important to do—when you were establishing yourselves in a new piece of the world. And if it was important for the Governor to confirm the impossibility of miracles, particularly in the matter of bread and wine turning into the literal body and blood of Christ, then it was also important for him to transplant some sense of the recognizable, the known, through the bestowal of rather grand names. The town they were making, he had proposed, could be Albion, in Cumberland County: an old name for England and the name of a far-off English county, stuck directly onto somewhere unknown, unexplored.

Their faces lit by irregular firelight beyond the canvas hospital, Dawes, Tench, and White tried to think of some reason that earlier Albion, that earlier Cumberland, might have influenced their Governor. "A hankering for sausages," suggested White. "A hidden idea of Utopia," suggested Dawes.

Watkin Tench dismissed the two of them as men of appetite and ideology respectively.

"I like the poetic jab of Albion—Francis Drake gave the west coast of America New Albion; you can even see it on Gulliver's maps," he said, smiling at Dawes, "but Sydney Cove, New South

Wales, that's more workaday, more like it. I reckon they're the names that will go back around the world—although I'm favoring Port Jackson at the moment in my version."

"And mine," said John White, another man with a publisher. "Albion reminds me of Milton," he went on, "and I wouldn't want to give him too much credence until we work out if we're paradise lost, or paradise regained. I'd wager lost—another batch staggered in this morning." A ship, sent northeast for turtle meat, had arrived back turtle-less, and some of the convicts were failing so fast that their punishments had been deferred until they were hale enough to bear them. That was hunger.

William Dawes could mostly distract himself from the emptiness of his own stomach with the busyness of his days. But there was a lean, scruffy look to most people now—someone had even suggested joining the natives in their nakedness for want of tailors and drapers. You couldn't let yourself think it would be that bad, thought Dawes, not after less than six months; not yet.

"It's a fine night out there on the harbor," he said, in an attempt to steer the conversation into calmer waters. Beyond the shoreline, the moon nipped at the dark harbor's movement.

"Finest and most extensive harbor in the universe," commented White.

"That's how you've put it?" Tench brushed a bug from the back of his hand. "I've given it 'superior in extent and excellency' to anywhere else we've been—but the universe is a big claim to make."

Three sets of eyes looking out to the cove, the thin mark of light across its surface. Three ships had sailed for China too, off to fulfill their tea contracts, and the calculations running around the settlement in their wake had been palpable. Fewer ships meant more people who'd need to be left behind if a decision was taken to give up, to sail away. Or more people dead in the meantime and fewer to make the voyage.

The French had already sailed on, but not before Dawes had gone down to visit them, spending a strange day discussing scientific matters with their astronomer.

"A slightly discomfiting thing," he had said to Tench on his return, "to find yourself discussing experiments on gravity and the latest calculations of the moonrise with a Fellow of the Parisian Academy beside a barren bay in the antipodes."

Stranger still, although Dawes had not told Tench of this, that the French astronomer claimed to have found a rosebush, a white rosebush, growing back from Botany Bay's shoreline among a nest of banksias and gum trees. A creamy English rose: it had to be a fantasy, or a mistake.

"It's a year ago they gave me instructions for the clock," said Dawes now, pouring another nip of rum for Tench, for White. "A year ago we stood in the cabin with the Governor in Portsmouth and took our lessons on when to wind it and how many of us must pay attention to ensure it was done." The noise of it, its tick, its tock, and the opulence of silver case, white face, in the middle of this hasty nest of canvas and bobbing ships and uncertainty; this was soothing to think about sometimes.

"You know a batch of men walked over to Botany Bay the other day in case any British ships had come in, thinking to find us there. Can you imagine? A flotilla of storeships seven miles away, us with no idea they were there and them with no idea where we were. Thinking us lost, disappeared, like those early Virginians."

A joke between them, when they'd met. John White, the surgeon, so concerned with keeping together the bodies and souls of as many as possible, and not doing too badly given the lack of almost everything he might have thought necessary for the task, such as malt, blankets, vegetables, tea. It was Tench who'd first wondered if White knew he shared his name with a settler from two hundred years before, who'd taken a hundred folk across the Atlantic from England to settle Roanoke, a New World place. Realizing too late how much their supplies were wanting, he'd sailed back to England, thinking to replenish and return. He'd left a grand-daughter in Roanoke, just days old, England's first American-born child. But there was a war, and his ship was commandeered when he reached home, and it was three years before he returned. It was the day that should have been his granddaughter's third birthday, but he'd found no one, not a soul, not a body, not a sign, not then or later—just intermittent rumors of Indians with pale blue eyes; Indians who could read the Bible.

"And of course, Francis Drake's supposed settlement at Albion disappeared from the face of the earth as well," said Tench now in a morbid tone, kicking at the embers of the fire. "We really are laying the worst omens on this place."

It was all about waiting, thought Dawes, and at least he could enjoy the happier anticipation of seeing one of the comets pre-dicted by the great Mr. Halley streaking gloriously across the sky, while everyone else focused on the slightly less predictable arrival of the British storeships that would come, should come, might come, must come, answering their wants and shortages and anchoring them firmly back into the world. *Still floating*, thought Dawes, *like Laputa. We can't think of ourselves fixed here until our presence, our activity, our needs are acknowledged.*

The thought felt weightier, more ominous, as the surgeon said, "I wonder if we're getting closer every day to those pale-eyed Indi-ans here," and stared gloomily at the fire awhile. "But then," after a mouthful of rum, "we're a thousand bodies to that hundred, sir, and the world is a more possible place than it was two hundred years ago. And rocks were painted to our south, I'm told, giving clear directions of where we are and how to find us, should anyone come looking. Should anyone come."

"Painting the rocks, us and them," said Tench, gesturing out towards the darkness that held their still-elusive neighbors and the figures they made—animals, men—around the rocky foreshore of the harbor. Dawes had found some below the point where his new observatory was growing.

"Painting the rocks, I like," said the surgeon. He'd spent the morning with the body of a convict whose forehead had been fatally split by a rock—a different attack to the handful of spearing injuries he'd already inspected. "That's a dozen convicts run off into the wild to try to find their way somewhere, and another run off with a spear in him. One I'm still trying to piece together and another two to be buried—and all this," he scratched at his forehead, "while I write shopping lists for currants and spices and the Governor thinks of the grand town he'll build."

"Perhaps you have to admire a man who can think of boulevards and fancy names in the face of spears, and hunger, and finding oneself out of the world," said Tench.

"Out of the world," said Dawes. His head tilted back, a reflex: even in the middle of the day he found he tipped his head back to check, to see, just in case his comet had come. Still early yet of course, but you never knew. "Out of the world," he murmured, and drained his glass as if it was a toast. "Two plans to finish before morning, gentlemen, so . . ." He stood up, excusing himself, and left them staring at the orange of the fire's flames, the white of the moon.

Because if the Governor had fancy names in mind, he had topographies in mind now too, and it fell to William Dawes to create this future on land and on paper for him. It fell to Dawes to survey the ground on which the Governor's vision would come into being, and to lay out the place that the Governor imagined.

In the mornings he paced out narrow tracks that carved through the bush and wide reaches of ground for putative buildings. In the afternoons, he drafted their shapes and curves into the roadways, the blocks, the Governor wanted, marking out their land as if these constructions might begin at any moment. ("Never mind," as Tench observed, "that our more cynical residents reckon a population ten times the size we've got couldn't get the place he wants built with ten years to do it in.") Dawes paced and pegged, counted and sketched, heading in from the harbor over tussocks and hummocks and running slopes and steep climbs, feeling the shape of the land beneath his feet, and counting out his paces—three and a half feet, then another three and a half feet. The Governor envisaged a wide square, like a piazza, leading down to a quay in the cove, its space offset by the tall importance of a cathedral. The Governor envisaged boulevards two hundred feet wide, and generous space around the buildings that would abut them. The Governor envisaged permanence, elegance, organized success.

He was about the only person who did.

But in some chill mornings, Dawes could stand a minute, his eyes following a tiny track, felling trees here and there, shifting boulders, smoothing bumps and inclines, pulling up grass, and laying down wide grey flagstones. If it was quiet, he could think, *Yes*, and see his new road running away into the future. If the morning was harsh, if he could hear only shrieking and crying, if there was the sound of someone being struck, someone being forced, then he would blink hard, try again and think, *No, not here. I can't see how that would happen.*

Mostly, though, he wiped his hand across his eyes, looked at the mess of scrub and scar in front of him, and thought, *Maybe. I suppose some of this might come to be here. Maybe.* He'd expected it to feel more glorious than this, the settlement and establishment of a new place. But it was only activity: lists and maps and tasks.

"Extent of empire," Watkin Tench had commented sarcastically, tracing a finger along one of the Governor's desired streets, "demands grandeur of design."

Now, his candle burning late, Dawes drew up the Governor's dreams of a quay here, a plaza there, the cathedral shifted and expanded to become even more prominent (the vicar claimed to be going deaf from preaching out of doors). Later, among the snores, he pulled out a clean sheet of paper to copy down the few meteorological observations he'd managed to make in between the plazas and promenades—of cloud cover, of the winds; his instruments were still boxed up. Then it was another fragment of shoreline for one of the many maps prepared for sending, with the longitude and latitude marked so clearly and carefully on each: here we are, if you're coming, if you're looking.

Never enough hours; never enough light. And when the candle began to sputter, he reached for a chipped metal canister tucked at the back of all his books and papers. Twisting its lid free, he shook it gently and watched as the browned and wizened petals of a white rose sprinkled across a possible street map of Sydney-town, and a column about clouds.

A rose dropped by a lady in Portsmouth more than a year ago now—a lady who had wished him well and said she'd wait to hear from him. Miss Judith Rutter. The petals his secret keepsake, his secret souvenir. And if it was easy at three in the morning to be assured of a lady's interest, to be still awake at four made it simple to think of walking those seven miles overland to Botany Bay to pick a bloom from the improbable rosebush the French astronomer insisted he'd seen. Once or twice Dawes had even stepped into the night, intending to set off, before some thought—or sound: a sentry's call, a nocturnal hiss—sent him back. Once he thought that, purely in the spirit of botanical inquiry, he might ask that party of men going over to the bay to check for British ships if they would bring him some specimens. He imagined his voice at its most authoritative: he'd need them to bring him something complete, "a flower, stem and leaves." But he'd said nothing, and they'd mentioned nothing—and at four in the morning that only made him more certain that the plant was there, within his reach, with sweet new roses ready for his collection. However familiar he now found this branch, that voice, a beard, this was still a place where impossibility became the very thing you expected. An alligator, a human hand, a rosebush among the gum trees.

Dear Miss Rutter, he practiced in the depths of the darkness, *I write to you from a place where cats have pouches and jump, where birds laugh and shriek, where it's as reasonable to see alligators running between tents as it is to see a human hand in the water—even as we call for our tablecloths to be removed before we're served fruit.* He stared at the darkness, picturing the constellations above him here, and above Judith Rutter's roof in Portsmouth. Outside, the sentry's step; the sentry's call.

Dear Miss Rutter, I have calculated the position of this harbor to be 33°52'30"S 151°20'E. It is a fine wide place—it is safe, snug, say some, and best in the universe, say others. On a clear day its water is a rich, deep blue and its sky is high, clear, and bright, another shade again. We are hungry, and we wonder what is happening in the world and when we will be part of it again.

Somewhere nearby, an owl made its doubly round call, and Dawes turned on his side, sounding its syllables: *oo-ooo, oo-ooo*. There were consonants tucked in there too, but he'd have to hear them again to decipher them.

Dear Miss Rutter, If I could describe to you the bits of beauty of this place, among our mess and our hunger and our arguments and our terrors. The blue of the water, the blue of the sky, the warmth of the rocks when the sun hits them and the same warm rich colors in the bark of our trees. A yellow parakeet, a red one, fly past and call— brilliant. I am measuring time and space and can already see every turn and tuck of some of this land in my mind's eye, as if I was up there with the parakeets. Yet some people even now wish this place might be given up and we might sail that long way home. Nothing grows. We are waiting.

Conjuring up one of the Governor's grand avenues, he could picture a house to one side, a room or two, and a garden—roses—some time off when the place was firm and sure. He could picture a school; perhaps he could come back, could teach here, could bring with him Miss Rutter. *Mrs. Dawes.* He closed his eyes, slept at last, so close to the sunrise whose moment he wanted to record—time, weather, wind. Another set of facts securely pinned down. Another piece of this place clarified and caught by the reliable words of science.

Ted

"WHAT WORD would you use to describe it then?" Joy was opening the front gate, leading them in from another night's unsuccessful search for her shooting star, Joe's comet. "If you could only give your bridge one word, what would it be?"

Once, when Ted was little, a magic show had stopped a night in the local hall, surprising his mother with balls conjured from behind her ears, and a flower from the sleeve of the man who lived four doors down.

"What I liked best," said Ted, his hand on the gate's catch, "was a trick he did with a great big horseshoe magnet, the way things flew in towards it. He let me have a hold of it afterwards—I was running around the hall trying to pick up anything I could." He cupped his hands together, a rough approximation of a horseshoe—a rough approximation of an arch. "That's what it is, magnetic: pulling us all in to itself and keeping us close by."

Joy smiled. "I like that," she said. "I like that story best." She was leaning back against Joe now, his arms around her like the sleeves of an extra sweater while his hands rubbed together and then rubbed their warmth into hers. Her breath hovered in the air after her words—Ted imagined its little mist taking on the shape of letters. Then, "Let's get in out of this chill," she said, stepping out of the embrace. "There's some cake."

If the bridge was like a giant magnet, charged up and pulling its workers and other devotees in from all over the city, then it was pulling in a great band of chroniclers too. Artists—photographers and painters in the main—were relinquishing every other subject for this one, even before it reached its whole, perfect shape. Which comforted Ted: he wasn't the only one who found the process so attractive.

"Even the clergy are seduced," said Joe the next morning as they went in for their shift. "One fellow, a vicar from the north side, takes a picture of its progress from his window every morning. You'll see him around sometimes—our mascot padre, some of the blokes call him. Seems a nice enough chap, although he does seem to confuse rivets with God in terms of what's holding the thing up." He paused a moment, seemed to hesitate a little. "He's made a book out of some of his pictures. I was thinking of getting it for Joy, but I don't know. She makes—you know, like Nipper, she makes a bit too much of things sometimes, takes stories on a bit too hard, and I don't know whether it would keep her mind off getting down to the bridge itself, to have all these pictures of it, or if it would just make her think about it even more." He lit himself a smoke, drew a breath. "Anyway, anyway," his voice bustled on, "if I don't get this one for her, there's bound to be another one later."

A buzz, high in the air, interrupted him, the two men stopping to stare up towards the plane, thin against the brightness of the sky. "There's photographers talking their way onto those too," said Joe, "coming at us from all angles, and we're not even done yet. And then there are the government blokes, and the magazine blokes, all crawling around it and over it and nearby and snapping away. And women—I heard there are women setting themselves up with paints and what-have-you around its edges. Of course I can't tell Joy that, or that'll be her next plan, suddenly taking up drawing."

They stood a moment, Ted, at least, imagining Joy with a blank pad of paper and a handful of pencils, striding through the mess of the site and up, straight up and onto the arch. He wondered what she'd see, what she'd draw.

From above the bridge came the purr of another plane's engine, and they watched it make its way towards the city from the west.

"And after I get up there," said Ted, watching as the plane cut precisely through the narrow gap still waiting to be filled in the bridge's arch, "the next thing'll be a ride in a plane. That'd be something, Joe, up there, under the clouds. Even the bridge'd look small from up there." He'd dreamed of its shape from high up in the blue, dreamed of the line it would make across the water and how high you'd have to be to make that line no more substantial than the thin mark of a pen.

"Up in the clouds, eh?" said Joe, cuffing him, but gently. "Lots of blokes got their chance for that in the war, and it got a lot of them killed too." He shook his head. "Get this job done and I'm happy to stay on the ground forever. You can keep your loop-the-loops." But Ted heard, as he walked away, that his friend was whistling a familiar song: "I'm Sitting on Top of the World."

He hummed the tune's next phrase, but quietly, very quietly. Here he was: rolling along.

～

"You're lucky to have found yourself such good friends," Ted's mother said when he went down to see her the next weekend, bursting with talk about Joe and Joy, about their house, their backyard full of stories. "I thought you'd be all full of your barge and your nice new job, but you haven't stopped about your lodgings since you got here. Nice to be closer than you were at your gran's,

I guess, and nice for a change." She pushed a plate of biscuits and a cup of tea towards him, poured some tea into her own saucer to let it cool. "And what about your bridge?" she said. "Will it hold up long when they're done?"

There was a critical moment with biscuits. The moment when they were so perfectly soft they squashed warm and soggy against the roof of your mouth had to be balanced against the moment later when they folded and melted into a sludge at the bottom of your cup. Ted concentrated on the science of it, thinking about the size of the bridge compared to the smallness of everything in his mother's house.

"It's funny," he said slowly. "It looks really big from far away sometimes, and really small up close. Then other times I'm right underneath it and it's the biggest thing in the world. Sometimes it looks heavy, and then sometimes it looks like all the bits of it are very fine somehow, like they might snap away in the wind. Joy says it's the light—I don't know. But it's tricky."

"Tricky like you wouldn't trust it to take your weight?" His mother, not a small lady, had a fear of weak wooden veranda slats, of rickety chairs, of stepping or sitting on something and feeling it fall away underneath her. "Or tricky like newfangled?"

"Tricky like you might catch it changing, from thin to thick, big to small, if you could just look at the right time." He stirred another spoonful of sugar into his half-drunk tea. Joy had talked about watching shifts end, watching the men come down out of the sky, watching the bridge's frame settle into stillness, "as if it had given itself a shake and got rid of all these things that had been clambering about, hanging on." Just this past week, the bridge had tried to shake itself free at the wrong time; one of the men working with the rivets, high up and straight over the place where Ted's barge was parked, had lost his grip and made to follow Nipper Anderson down through air and water into that thick, banking mud. But the hose of his air gun caught somewhere and held him on, like a harness—which wasn't a story, thought Ted, that he needed to share with his mum. He'd spent days wondering what the man had felt, had seen, in the instant of falling before he was jerked back up like one of those new American yo-yos. He'd spent days wondering if it was a sensation like this that woke him up, startled, from his uncaught dream. Joy had spent days imagining it was Joe, even Ted—"either of my boys"; curled up and anxious in the face of what hadn't happened.

"Anyway," back in the kitchen, back with his mum, "the arch is so close now. It's like someone's inking it in really slowly, and sometimes when you're standing somewhere on the shore and you look up in a hurry, it seems as if the two pieces have already met, while you weren't looking."

"I heard they were doing all the sums for it in England," said his mum, "which sounds a bit daft. I'd have thought you'd do better to have men making their sums where they can see the thing. I don't like a bridge I can't trust, and I don't trust a bridge made by people who can't see it."

"You just have to think it's magic, Mum, like the way it's a great big curve made out of all straight pieces."

But she shook her head. "Your fancy imaginings. I trust a boat," she said. "I might just stick with ferries if I ever need to cross that water."

Catching the train back up to the city, Ted wished he'd done better at making her like it—or at least making her think it was a good thing. Maybe if he took her a bit of steel next time, something with weight she could feel. Maybe if he found her a photograph. He leaned his head against the carriage window, pressing hard to stop it bouncing with the train's jolts and rattles. He'd get a photograph. And he'd stop talking about it shrinking and growing, coming and going.

Back at the house that afternoon, walking down the hall and into the kitchen, he called out his hellos to no answer. In the middle of the table sat a heavy book whose leather cover was embossed with gold. *Parables of the Sydney Harbour Bridge* by the Reverend Frank Cash, that enthusiastic vicar Joe had talked about who leapt out of bed every morning to take a photograph of the bridge. Here was his book, his thoughts about engineering, about steel, woven around bits of scripture and morality, and his pictures all the way through. Ted traced the word, *Bridge*, in its title, before flicking through the pages and taking in sentences at random.

This, the greatest and most important work of its kind undertaken by man, he read, *and it displays outwardly, with most shining light, a faculty which men often call* reason, *and others call, the image of God . . .*

Outside, a cloud passed in front of the sun and a black bird, the tips of its feathers held out like fingers, swept into the backyard with a hard, scraping cry. Ted shivered, pulled his coat around him at the neck, the way Joy held her cardigan tight against drafts and bad thoughts, and the cloud passed.

The bridge as an image of God. He tapped his fingers across the words. *Reckon this bloke dreams about it,* he thought. What had Joe said about making a bit much of something?

The Bridge is truly sacramental. It displays, against our southern sky, day by day, a further and progressive visible expression of faculty, which can be seen and known, in no other fashion. And in proportion as the steel tracery webs out fascinating figures amidst the fleecy clouds (so lofty it would seem), so there will be displayed outwardly *for our delight, more and more of the invisible originative faculty of man.*

"Sacramental." Ted sounded out the syllables. Funny word. He wasn't even sure it belonged in the sentence. He'd probably never paid enough attention on Sundays, but wasn't it something to do with communion, the wafers and the wine, something to do with divinity?

Skipping across a page here, a chapter there, he saw deckways and girders, cranes and pylons, blessings and panoramas. *A very real analogy exists between the Main Arch Span of the Bridge, and the span of life allotted to man . . . and . . . I (a steel member) make a fine sight, shining red in my red coat of paint, and as the creeper crane hoists me from the barge in the stream—*

That's me, thought Ted, *that's me.*

—I am always the admiration of thousands of eyes . . . and . . . Every construction, every building made by man, casts a representation of itself when it comes between a light or the sun, and any other body. And man, in his imagination, peoples worlds, both visible and invisible, with shadows . . . and then, *On Falling Off.*

Ted smoothed the pages back, pressing a little too hard into the V of the spine as the door swung open and Joy's voice called, "Anyone here?" She came into the kitchen where Ted stood.

"It's beautiful, isn't it?" she said, taking the book from him and cradling it a moment before she leafed through to its introduction. "'The Rev. Frank Cash can claim to be the only person outside of those connected with the bridge, to have unlimited access to the work,'" she read aloud, "—lucky bugger—'and in seeking his information he has shown a complete disregard of personal risk.

"'The "Mascot Padre",'" she read on aloud, running her finger down the list on the contents page, turning first to the chapter on rivets, then to the chapter on the divine city. "'I am not sure which aspect people will wonder at most on the first crossing,'" she read, "'the strength of the structure, or the beauty of the outlook.'"

"I tried to talk to my mum about it being . . . you know, beautiful," said Ted, unwrapping the bag of biscuits his mum had sent back with him, "but she was just worried that it might fall down. It's a nice book though, and handsome."

"From Joe," said Joy. "More stories, more pictures—I think he thinks he can buy me out of wanting to get onto it myself. But it does feel a bit . . . well, it does feel a little bit like rubbing it in."

Ted fiddled with the lid on the biscuit canister, unwilling to side with one over the other.

"I mean, it's lovely," said Joy. "It's lovely, and must have cost him . . . well . . ." She set two teacups, two saucers, ready on the table. "But these photographs are beautiful, and it is a handsome book. And he must know I'll get up there one day, somehow. I'm sure of that—I've got to somehow." Her fingers were tense against the book's open pages; her voice sounded tense too.

Ted poured the boiling water into the pot, listened to the sizzle as he set the kettle back down on the heat, opened the stove and threw in another handful of kindling, another couple of dried-out orange rinds—Joy loved the smell they gave the fire. *Makes a bit too much of things*, he remembered again and, watching her fingers clutch fast at the surface of the book, he saw something of what Joe had meant.

"I thought I'd go in and watch them close up the arch," she said then, her voice steady again. "Joe reckons it has to be soon. Then I thought, you know, I could try to draw it or something, and then no one would mind that I was there. One of the blokes says there's a few women around the site now, trying to draw it. I wonder where you go to see what they make of it, how they see it, after they've finished." She poured tea, then milk, spooned sugar, and stirred the two cups, her eyes focused on the nowhere of halfway across the kitchen floor.

"Maybe it is something about beauty," she said at last. "Or maybe because it feels miraculous." And she picked up one of the cups, blew gently across the surface of the tea. "So big for this place, sometimes it feels like it's shrinking everything else, pushing it down towards the ground. It's like those folks who built the amphitheater on the harbor to watch the heads and wait for their savior to walk through. I went, you know, for a while, went and waited—not Jesus, it turned out, but a very nice young man from India. Joe doesn't like me talking about it, but it was lovely to sit by the water and watch the light change. And why not wait for a miracle, if you've got the time?" She blew again across her tea, watched it lap against the rim of the cup. "Anyway," she nodded to Ted across the table, "at least I've got two of you to wheedle stories from now."

Ted fiddled with the cuffs of his shirt. "I reckon—I don't know, but I reckon everyone's paying attention to it," he said at last. "Just some of them don't know how to talk about it. And I reckon everyone, if they were really honest, everyone wants to get up in the air. I do, out there every day on the barge. I mean, the men are great and the pay comes, and I love the water, diving in some days off the edge of the workshops there with some of the blokes and we swim round . . ." Their bodies so small and pale in the darkness of its great big shadow. "But then Joe talks about the things they can see from up there—how far, out to the ocean and out to the mountains and the city shrunk to roads and rooftops underneath. I'd like to see that." Daring himself. "I'd like to be brave enough to climb up too."

She poured more hot water into the teapot and set it between the two of them. "Then we'll go," she said. "We'll nick off one night and we'll get up there and see the stars and the moon and the whole big city. What do you reckon, Ted? Do you reckon we could?"

It was infectious; it was a dream. He nodded and laughed, thinking it would never happen. He patted the cover of the Reverend Cash's book. "We'll read this up like a guidebook, and we'll be right. He's been up there hundreds of times."

"We could go now if Joe wasn't on his way home," said Joy. "But I'll get the soup on instead." And she laughed herself.

It was ridiculous; it was all a bit of fun. He watched as she picked up the book and hugged it. And he said, but quietly, when she was almost out of the door, "Do you dream about it, Joy? Do you ever dream about it?"

She stepped back into the kitchen, the book held tight. "I used to dream, when Joe started up there. I used to dream he'd fall off, and I wouldn't know what to do with myself. Nipper's wife, you know, they say she had to go into some kind of hospital. That'd be me. But the dreams stopped, and he got on all right, and I fell in love with it, started trusting it. That last bloke, caught by the strap—it shakes me up, but I do trust it, and now I reckon I think so much about it in the day, I can give myself the nights off."

And Ted smiled. Not like him at all, then.

~~~

He came across one of the bridge's artists the next morning—a lady with a big block of paper propped up in front of her and her eyes, narrowed, flicking up and down between the steel and the page, the steel and the page. She was sizing up his bridge, her mouth screwed up as tight as her eyes, as if she was trying to suck in the essence of the structure somehow and didn't much like its taste. She was shaded by the dome of a large black umbrella, its shape, its darkness a misplaced refraction of what she was trying to draw.

She was not, he reckoned, in a particularly picturesque spot, pressed so close to the concrete road that would carry trams and traffic up and across the water. He stepped forward, trying to see what she was doing.

Her page looked impossibly small for its subject, covered with diagrams that looked more like the workings he'd sometimes fancied he could see inching ahead of the thing itself. Thick red lines divided the rectangle into a grid, with pencil marks to indicate the shapes and angles of this big body of steel. Some sections were buffed in with shading; some had notes about colors. And down at the bottom, dwarfed by the arch, sat small houses and other little buildings—too insubstantial, surely, to anchor it all to the ground.

But the magic of it: she'd made it still and permanent while the thing itself kept growing new sections, bustling with movement. And the extra magic: she'd caught one of those spots where it looked as if the two arms of the arch had already touched—a private preview of the moment everyone was waiting to see.

"It'd be something to be able to do that," he said at last, poking his finger at the page and embarrassed when he touched it. He leaned in, anxious that he might have not only smudged the paper but somehow smudged the real structure as well.

"You can always try," the woman said, her words drawn out and distracted by her task. "You could get yourself some pencils."

"I thought of that—not me, but my friend Joy. I reckon she'd be able to draw it from memory, straight off." None of this blocking in and planning, he thought. Joy would make one big confident line straight off and there it would be.

"Well, do that," said the woman, her eyes busy again with their quick up-down shuffle. "Was there . . . ?"

And Ted said, "No," and then, "Thank you," and went down the hill to the workshops, his barge.

At the end of the week, he thought, he'd buy Joy a packet of pencils and a notebook. Her bridge, he reckoned, would be drawn more delicate, more . . . There was a poetic word on the tip of his tongue, and he trawled through the crevices of his memory as the morning sun rose higher.

"Gossamer," he said at last and aloud, surprised by the strange shape of rarely spoken syllables. Gossamer and *gold to airy thinness beat*. He laughed at himself—he'd caught the edge of the Mascot Padre's poetry. Must be something from back in school.

Dawes

IN THE early-morning sunlight the web shimmered and glistened like a handful of jewels. At its center, heavy among the delicate dew and the strong strands of silk, sat the spider, still and waiting. Heading up from the observatory's point, William Dawes found the web strung across the pathway; heading in the opposite direction, the surgeon found it also blocking his track; and the two men looked at each other across the gossamer as if they'd found some great strong wall between them.

"A big belly on that thing," observed the surgeon from his side of the spider, "and it looks like it's walked against wet whitewash— see the markings on its legs?"

Leaning forward, Dawes pressed his finger against one of the web's strands, testing its tension, its strength. He pulled his finger away as the strand snapped, and stepped back to watch the spider register the break, the tear. "The colors, once you start to look at them," he said. "And you have to get them down to so few words to describe them for entomology: white, brown, black." He was talking more to the spider than to John White, and White, stepping forward, bent over to address the spider too.

"And you're tricky things to keep once we've got you," he said.

"It'll probably be a box of dried-up thorax and legs that gets back to London, and the gentlemen there will have all the fun of working out which piece goes with what—which is how it looks like the kangaroo was put together in the first place." He crouched in towards the spider's movement. "I wonder if you'd wait here till this afternoon, my friend," he said to it. "I'll be back with a vial and we can begin our acquaintance." He stood up. "On which matter, I saw one of your fellow gentlemen, clearly hungry for some new acquaintance, dancing with a kangaroo last night. It had its paws around him like an embrace, and round they went and round."

The spider moved along its web towards the breach made by William Dawes's finger. *That will be Tench's next suggestion*, thought Dawes flatly. *He'll see me dancing with a kangaroo.*

"Your spider seems amenable to waiting for you," he said aloud, watching the creature's movement. "More interested in assessing the damage I've done, I guess." And the repair work was already underway, a new line reaching from one disconnected point towards the other while the two men watched from their respective sides of its bridge. They stood so still in the face of this activity that the camp seemed to fall into silence. William Dawes moved first, the straightening of his body in its red coat making such a gash of movement that John White too pulled himself up sharp, as if he'd been called to attention. He coughed then to cover his startle.

"They call you an ingenious sort of observer, Lieutenant Dawes, sir," he said. "How go your own collections and observations of the beasts around this place? How goes that cyclopedic project of yours?"

"Most of my time is taken up with time," said Dawes. "The clocks, you know, and the skies, and the weather, and waiting for my comet. I expect it soon. I do keep an eye on the plants though; I've got a pile pressed and drying for when I'm settled down there"—waving his hand towards the point where his observatory was coming into being—"but no time to look at them closely . . ." Dawes trailed off as the spider moved lightly back towards the center of its web. "The best I can hope for is to gather it all together later." He laughed. "What we're all trying to do here, I suppose. And now there are the surveys, and the maps, none of which get us any closer to clearing or building . . . It would be easier if we could weave a place out of our own kind of web, like this creature. Spin a church one morning, some barracks after lunch, and a good new hospital for you, sir, through the following day."

John White laughed, the noise round and loud against the moment's quietness. "A church made of gossamer," he said. "That would be a pretty thing. And it'd probably last longer than the mud and the timber we're building with at the moment."

"Or a bridge," said Dawes, arcing his arm across the harbor's blue water. "Imagine that, catching the light . . ." Dawes half closed his eyes, seeing a near enough suggestion of silky struts and stanchions through their lashes. "Only don't mention it to the Governor or he'll have me surveying the lines it would need to get it off the ground."

They both laughed then, their heads bowing towards each other over the web and taking care not to interfere with its silk. William Dawes imagined the spider, its various eyes watching two big fleshy shapes coming in towards it, blocking its light, its sky. Did it feel threatened? Did it feel anything? He imagined their heads nodding from above; his automatic vantage point, up in the air and configuring coastlines and prospective streets. That would give the best view of two men, stopping suddenly, leaning, concentrating, and then making the courteous bob of one of Watkin Tench's dances—step together, dip, step apart—with the thin sheet of spider's silver suspended between them. Above, a kingfisher let out its raucous laugh—noisier and rounder than the surgeon's—and Dawes wondered if it had been watching their heads too.

"They do make me smile, those birds, with their big voices and their furry chests," said White. He'd had one shot not many days before, and it lay skinned and scrubbed on one of his benches— a fine specimen of these birds that had laughed at him over the months. He'd found himself earlier that morning stroking at the softness of the buff feathers under its throat and talking to it quietly. Setting off along the path—the wrong way, away from the town—it was only Lieutenant Dawes he could have hoped to meet for his next conversation. And here he was, with the spider, and the laughing, their own and that of the boisterous relative of his precious dead bird.

"Were you coming to see me, sir?" Dawes asked. "Was there something you wanted?"

The surgeon cleared his throat and frowned, and his pause lasted so long that Dawes wondered what he might say next. But it was nothing of soft feathers or a yearning for conversation.

"Just vegetables," he said at last. "I've more and more patients in dire need of something fresh. I thought you might see something, some plant, some tree—anything that might feed us—when you were out and around with the surveys. If you could look while you're . . . if you might already . . ."

Dawes shook his head. "Although to be honest, sir," he said, "with all the measuring and mapping I sometimes think I could walk past a banquet and not notice it, and I must be the only man here who thinks that." Every second exchange around the cove conjured an imagined menu or a remembered taste, while people sat down to meal after meal of salt rations—and were issued less and less of those. They were a study of waiting, as Tench said, and none much better at it than any of the others.

The surgeon winced. "I cut a man open when he died the other day, and there was not a blessed thing in his stomach—not a thing. I stood there with Tench staring at this great gaping emptiness as if it was the worst kind of monster. The Indians are starving now too, you know, all of us hungry together. And then that earthquake: a more superstitious man—and we've too many of those—could have thought it the end of the world. What do you think, Lieutenant Dawes? How long do you think it will be before they come?"

Tucked somewhere in his mind, William Dawes had a table of calculations of the different days on which ships might appear; it followed the same kind of logic as the numbers that predicted the arrival of his comet. The first letters begging supplies had been sent back almost before the fleet was out of sight of the English coast, so the ships acquitting those lists might have arrived quite quickly in the fleet's wake. The next waves of letters, sent from the ports at which the fleet had called, would have needed more time to make the journey back to England—a few weeks from Tenerife, four months from Rio, six months from Cape Town—and then the furnishing of their provisions, and then that eight-month sail to this deep, far south.

But even with the most imaginable slowness, the most tardy set of merchants requisitioned for supplies, and even with the most generous calculations of the time and space involved in the journey between England and Port Jackson, it felt reasonable to hope that at least one ship bearing some answer to all those requests might have made its way up the harbor by now. Still, as Dawes knew, the math of the situation could spin on for months to come yet, the only other possibility being that nothing was coming at all. And that was an unsayable thing, at least for now.

"It must be soon, sir," he said. "It must be soon."

"There was a fellow had me in fits last night making up newspaper stories of the ways we'd been lost," said the surgeon. "Gales of wind sinking us and cliffs of rocks striking us and the convicts rising up and running off with us and a hundred other ways to our destruction. But on we go, on we go, unless all those things have already happened and this is some strange Irish limbo." John White laughed. "I swear there'll be mutiny among the women if they don't get a proper pot of tea soon." And his own lips smacked together once or twice, for sweetness, so that Dawes knew exactly what he'd been thinking.

"I could put a kettle on, sir," he said, "but I've only got the local stuff."

The surgeon shook his head. "No," he said, "I'll get back. I don't know if I could bend low enough to get under this spider without upsetting it, and I would like to find it here again this afternoon. Nice to see you, Lieutenant; always nice. And if you do come across any creatures, any plants, that you've no time to make your own study of, you know where to find me." He waved his arm with the kind of flourish that suggested that location was a manor house at least. "I'd say the door is always open but, you know . . ."

"The canvas flap," said Dawes and they laughed again, the kingfisher joining in. These birds always sounded to Dawes as if they were working their way through vowels, performing a series of exercises before singing, perhaps, or mounting a play in a hall with bad acoustics—their series of long *aa*s, and short *oo*s, and the hammering *e-e-e*s. He found his own mouth following the shape of their calls and considering which other letters he'd need from his own alphabet to transcribe them precisely. Another thing for his records.

The bird reached the stanza that was almost pure gurgle and stopped suddenly, ruffling its feathers and tilting its head to one side. Another pause, another shake, and it was in the air, its wings beating it up higher and higher into the sky, and then stretching as it glided out across the water.

"'For how shall we sing the Lord's song in a strange land?'" murmured the surgeon. "I'm on the psalms again, God help me," he said briskly. "One a night, but don't tell the vicar—he takes it as a sign of more religion when it's really just a sign of nothing else to read." He tipped a small salute towards the bird and watched as it soared and climbed, dipping to begin a huge sweeping curve. Around it came, its body solid against the light of the sky like a mark on a musical score and then thinning down—lighter, lighter, lighter—as it turned, until it disappeared altogether for a moment, invisible against the blue.

"That, that," said John White. "I remember the first time I saw that happen when I was a boy. I thought it was magic."

"It was a pale seabird out over the water at Portsmouth," said Dawes. "I watched it disappear and I thought my father had made it happen somehow, like a trick." The light and movement of an illusion.

The beat of a wing, and the bird was dark again against the air.

"I always think I should applaud," said the surgeon, sighing. "All right then, and good day to you, Lieutenant Dawes. If you're coming along the path, could I ask you step around my spider? I'll be back to look for it later." And he turned and headed away.

Dawes watched as the kingfisher looped up towards the clouds, and around—visible, visible, invisible, visible. How fast would a man have to move, and in what sort of light, what sort of space, to manage a moment of disappearance? Here they were, collecting all sorts of information about samphire and spiders, about wind and weather, when maybe they were in the time and space for questions like this.

He rubbed his eyes. He'd hardly slept the night before, trying to trick his mind towards sleep by separating the settlement's layers of nighttime sounds. At the base of it all was the water against the rocks; high above everything else the hiss and growl of animals busy in the treetops and the undergrowth. And between that, the occasional call of the sentries, the regular tick of his clocks and watches, and the soft padding of feet—human, he thought, rather than animal—making stealthy, nocturnal visits to the camp. Perhaps it was their elusive native neighbors, thought Dawes, come to see if the white men hungered, if the white men dreamed, if the white men disappeared somehow in the darkness, like a bird against the sky at that one moment of its trajectory.

He rubbed his eyes again; he needed more sleep. Maybe he'd take his copy of *Gulliver* along to the hospital, in case the surgeon wanted a change from the psalms. Last night he'd read again of the astronomers on Laputa, guiding the island's flight with the lodestone at the center of their observatory and taunted by fears of a fiery comet streaking down and striking them from the face of the earth. *Which is all we need*, he'd thought. His own dreams, when he did sleep, flared with fire that dropped from the sky, so close, so close to where he lay, sizzling to nothing in the harbor's water when he rushed to see its splash—his own comet, he presumed, or something unknown out in the night.

The sooner the real comet comes, he thought, *the better.*

Pulling himself up onto the rocky ledge that moored one end of the spider's web, William Dawes stepped carefully over its anchoring line and jumped down on the other side, heading for the bustle of the rest of the camp and its smells of cooking. That thing with the bird, it was all a trick of the light; look at anything from just the right angle at just the right moment, and you could thin it down to insubstantiality. That was probably what the black men were doing in the darkness of their visits, calculating the angle at which you could look at the disturbance the settlement had made so that it disappeared altogether.

The kingfisher landed back in the tree from where it had started, its tail neat and its feathers snug around its body. There was no hint in its shape, its still sitting, that it could fly at all, let alone that it had been in the air, and briefly of it, just a moment before.

Dan

AS THE plane turned onto the runway and began to pick up speed, Dan leaned back against his seat, closed his eyes, and saw quite clearly the shape of a man flying across the face of the sun. Somewhere, as far back as childhood, he'd started thinking about Icarus whenever he was in a plane that taxied, accelerated, and pushed itself, and him, up into the sky. It was a strange thing to think of, let alone a habit to have kept up; it must have been from one of Gramps's tales, one of the early drawn-out stories around which he and Charlie had built their ideas of truth and certainty. If Gramps said that if you watched a bird carefully enough, you might just see it disappear, like magic, against the sky's blue, then it was so. If Gramps said that the Harbour Bridge was magic too, that the great big curved thing was "made entirely of straight pieces, my dears, entirely of straight lines," then it was so. If Gramps said it was possible to fly there—"Not in an aeroplane, no, Charlie, but straight out from the deck of that bridge and down into the deep water"— then it was so. And if Gramps said that a young man called Icarus had once escaped from a prison on wings made of feathers and wax, then even when Dan's world had solidified into currencies and trades, the last traces of the story were still lodged firmly enough in

ASHLEY HAY

his imagination to be triggered by a jumbo's thrust of acceleration, its sudden push up towards the clouds.

"Still a bit of poetry in your mercenary soul, isn't there," Charlie would have said.

And maybe he always thought of Charlie too, because there she was, in his mind's eye, looking exactly as she'd looked the last time he'd seen her, years ago now. He couldn't see himself, but he could see that she was sitting in the day he'd left home. She was sitting where they'd sat on the harbor's edge, as if she'd been there all the time, if he'd thought to look.

Stretching his arms, Dan looked along his row; there was an empty seat next to him, then a woman with her eyes closed. Beyond her came the thin public space of the aisle, and then a family sitting father, child, child, mother, across to the next aisle. On the other side of the plane, a woman, an empty seat, and a man leaning forward to look too—just as Dan was—so that for a moment he thought he was looking at a mirror somehow, the reflection ruined only by the asymmetrical family in the middle. Dan rubbed his hands across his eyes as the man at the other end of the row pulled a book from the seat pocket, and the illusion was broken. The plane lifted itself free of the ground, and Dan cupped his hand around the little screen in front of him. Thousands of kilometers to go.

Whereas Caro was probably almost home by now, clattering back to the city, her lap full of the replacement white roses he'd bought her that morning. "I'll ring you, or I'll text," he'd said, and she'd hugged him and said, "No you won't: I know you. Just go and see. Go and see how your Gramps is. I'll talk to you when you're back again." She'd seemed happy he had a reason for going that wasn't about her. So he'd kissed her, brushed his fingertips across her cheek, and walked through customs with his senses full of the flowers, their texture, their perfume. Ten days he'd be gone; he wondered if the roses would last that long.

100

"I lose all sense of time on planes," said the woman on the aisle, tilting her own screen to read the distance. "It can say fourteen hours and I can know how long fourteen hours is in a regular day, but time feels all different when you're just sitting here hurtling along, doesn't it?" She held out her hand. "My name's Cynthia," she said.

"Dan," said Dan. No one had ever introduced themselves to him at the beginning of a fourteen-hour flight before. It felt ominous.

"Don't worry," said Cynthia, "I'm not going to talk to you all the way home. You are going home, aren't you? I just think it's really strange that we'll spend all this time so close to each other, and you'll clamber over me for the loo, and we won't even introduce ourselves."

"I always find it really hard talking on planes," said Dan, and he hoped he sounded firm. "Really hard to hear over the engines—you know, all that noise you forget about as soon as you're back on the ground."

"That film they made about the American plane that crashed into the field on September 11," said Cynthia, raising her voice a little. "Did it have that kind of furry noise underneath all the sound track stuff, or did they mask it all out?"

"I never saw it," said Dan. He hoped there was nothing else to say, watched as she opened a shiny magazine.

"A clairvoyant once told me I was going to meet the love of my life on a plane," said Cynthia. "But then I went back to her a couple of years later and she said I was going to die in a plane crash. It made me a bit doubtful about flying for a while. I think that's why I started to introduce myself to people when I was up in the air—to feel a bit more at home in case she was right the second time, and to keep my options open in case she was right the first."

There was nothing to do, thought Dan, but smile, nod, and find something to read—in a hurry. He put his hand into his bag, his fingers working through shapes and textures: a pullover, a plastic water bottle, something smooth and round—he groped at it and saw Gramps's watch, shining and lovely in the palm of his hand. He smiled. It was nice to be traveling with it again. But as he pulled out the first book his fingers found—his journal—he realized that the book he'd meant to bring was still sitting at home, next to his bed. Fourteen hours with someone who consulted clairvoyants, and no book. The watch smooth and cool in one hand, he pulled a pen from his coat pocket with the other. Beneath his feet, he could feel the sharp angle of the plane's ascent.

"Of course, I'm married now," said Cynthia, "so you don't need to worry about that."

"Just about the dying then," said Dan.

"Sorry?"

He shrugged. "It is really hard to hear, isn't it?" There was something wrong, he knew, in not wanting to keep the conversation going, like the rudeness of getting into a cab and not wanting to talk to the driver. "Sometimes I think I must be going deaf," he said, an arbitrary and untrue excuse. And he creaked open the pages of the empty book. Even so far into the year, with another almost in sight, nearly every page was blank.

At the beginning of every winter, every year he'd been away from home, Dan had gone into a big bookshop in the city and chosen a journal for the imminent new year. He'd taken it home, shrink-wrapped in plastic, and he'd put it carefully on the table next to his bed. On New Year's Eve, he would unwrap it and write all his details onto the first page: name, address, passport number, work email, his mum's number on the other side of the world as the one to call in an emergency—he read the number slowly now and wondered what Caro would have made of that.

On New Year's Day, he'd open the book, uncap a new pen, and try to think of something to write about the night before. He'd try to think of one observation, of one line that was beautiful, or unexpected, or generous—something worthy of being the first sentence in a whole new year. Gramps had opened the first year after the war by telling Charlie's grandmother how lovely it was going to be falling in love with her again. You could build a family, a history, on a story like that. It was the kind of line he must have worked on through the deathly mess of the years they'd been apart.

Dan never came up with anything like it. And after an hour or so, he'd leave the top few lines blank so that he could fill in his great sentence later, and then start a bullet-point list of resolutions. Call Mum once a week. Go to the gym. Save more money. One year, more hungover and tired than usual (one of the boys had put a company credit card down for the bar tab; it had been a big night), he'd written more extreme promises. Propose to girlfriend—he couldn't remember now if he'd even had one when he wrote that, let alone if it was Caroline. Go to Antarctica. Run a marathon. And at the end of the list, the usual: call home more often, call his mum, call Charlie. He hadn't done any of those things. He never kept any of his resolutions, and only rarely got around to writing anything in the journal again for the rest of the year, although sometimes, late on a Sunday night, he felt that he ought to. Gramps would have insisted. "Keep your stories, boy, remember what you're doing and where you are—it's your immortality." But the books stayed blank; the days slipped by. He never ran a marathon or proposed to anyone. And he called home as infrequently as ever.

He blamed the time difference, the amount of time his job consumed. He never really meant to let his silences run so long, always felt at least a little guilty when he found a message from his mum, wondering why she hadn't heard from him in so many weeks. But their conversations were so desultory, he thought—he was in his routine, she was in hers. What was there to say, other than that he was still on one side of the world, and she was still on the other?

His record of calling Charlie was even worse—partly, he told himself, for want of exciting things to tell her, and partly, he assured himself, because she called him so infrequently too. "You get to the end of the day," she'd say in their sporadic calls, "and, well, you know." Besides, his mum told each what the other was doing. He could believe they were as close as ever.

Staying at Caro's place half the week was another excuse—no matter how many times she offered her phone. "I'll call later, I'll call tomorrow," he'd say, and she'd shake her head and shrug. She could talk to her mother three times before lunch, could text people without even looking at the keypad. Had she meant it about not calling her? Dan was never sure about things like that.

On the screen in front of him, the little aeroplane inched out of England and on towards Europe. Dan clicked the lid on and off his pen a few times. *I'm flying home,* he wrote on the first line of that day's page. His writing was awkward and irregular, like it still belonged at high school. He made another dot of ink on top of the full stop and watched as it flared across the paper. What next?

The aeroplane on the map nudged a little farther across the solid green lump of land. He wrote: *I tried to call Charlie and she wasn't home. I left messages.* He frowned. *I asked after Gramps. Gramps would know what to write on a page like this. The aeroplane on the screen is too big for the land it's flying over. We'll be on the other side of the world in less than a day. The woman next to me thinks she's going to die on a plane. They should give you a clock and a compass when you board. Caro will be home by now—I can't remember the last time I traveled without her. I can't remember the last time I spoke to Charlie properly. I can't remember what Gramps looks like—what he looked like when I left. I don't think I even have a photo. But I'll be home tomorrow, on the other side of the world.*

He stared at the next block of blankness, willing it to fill.

Next to him, Cynthia had taken a book out of her bag too, moving her feet—in bright red socks—onto the spare seat between them. She held the book out at arm's length to read, the way Dan's mum did. Dan thought, *She must be older than I think she is.* He thought, *I wonder if Mum's got glasses by now.* It was a book of instructions for writing a memoir, and she was underlining things with a pencil. Above their heads, the seat-belt sign flashed on, and a disembodied voice told them they were heading for some turbulence.

"I'm sure it won't be today," said Cynthia, without looking up from her page.

Once, years before, and before Caroline, Dan had looked out of a plane's window on his way to Greece and seen the Matterhorn, perfectly clear and familiar among the Alps below. Its rocky faces had gleamed and sparkled in the sun and there was snow glistening on its peak.

Gramps had a terrible story about the seven men who'd first climbed to its top; how four of them, roped together, had fallen to their death on the way down. "Men will do anything," Gramps had said, "to get up in the air."

But what about all the people who've hiked to its summit after that? Dan had wondered, gliding above it, *trying to get close to the sky— and here we are whizzing over the top. Easy.* He'd meant to write to Charlie about seeing it; he thought that later on his holiday he'd even bought a postcard of a white building against a blue ocean to hold the story. But he knew, as he looked out through the window at the bank of clouds below, that if he dug down far enough in his bag he'd probably find the card, still blank and scrunched into an inside pocket with a few Mythos bottle tops and a hotel receipt. Funny, the things you never got around to doing. Now Caro wrote all the postcards when they traveled. Sometimes he added *and Dan* on the bottom. His mother called it carelessness, laziness, but Dan, if he thought about it, suspected that Charlie not only heard any news he'd told his mother, but that she still heard, somehow, every story he meant to tell her. When they were kids, they'd made tin-can telephones to run through the fence. One Christmas, Gramps had bought them walkie-talkies. Charlie in particular had loved the idea of making words move through air—she wanted Dan to leave his walkie-talkie on in his room while his mum read to him, so she could hear the stories too. Her mum had died, she pointed out with the child's pragmatism she would never lose, and she only had Gramps's voice left for storytelling.

The plane shuddered, Dan's stomach lurching with it as his fingers tightened around his pen. It didn't bear thinking about, the power of the air, if it could hurl a jumbo jet up or down or from side to side so casually, so easily. The plane jolted as though its nose was falling forward, and a woman hurrying along the aisle grabbed at the headrest of Cynthia's seat, and clutched her hair by mistake.

"*Izvi'nite, pros'tite*," said the woman, patting at Cynthia's head and slipping into the row of seats in front of them. Cynthia smiled at her, accepting the apology.

"Did you see them boarding the plane?" she said to Dan. "Russian, I think, and the old man isn't well. The crew didn't want to let him on without a doctor's certificate or something—they were just in transit, apparently, and trying to get to Australia. He's supposed to have some operation there. He was in a wheelchair. It must have been before you got on. Must be her father."

Dan leaned his head against the window, craning to see the old Russian man she said was in front of them. He could see a little bit of skin, very papery and pale, and thin hair that looked colorless rather than anything you'd call grey or blond. The woman's face came into view; her smooth cheek and her eye were disproportionately large somehow. *Must be something to do with only seeing part of her*, thought Dan. She picked up a face washer and dabbed at the old man's skin, murmuring gently. The tone of her voice didn't change, didn't waver as the plane made another sudden jolt, although Dan saw that she held the cloth above the man's forehead a little longer, waiting for the strange air to pass before she tried to touch his skin lightly.

Outside the window, the clouds were so thick that the world below had disappeared and Dan was sure that if he'd been able, somehow, to step through the side of the plane and into the cool, white silence, they would be solid enough for him to stand on.

For years, when they were little, he and Charlie had daydreamed about cloud-walking, begging Charlie's grandfather again and again for stories about making the bridge up in the air, up in the mist, up in the blue or white sky; for stories of planes flying through clouds, later, during the war. They imagined stringing tightropes between hot-air balloons; they imagined diving into a big tuft of white as if it was the local pool. They imagined being able to sculpt the soft whiteness into statues, mazes, whole cities of buildings. Dan shook his head: crazy-kid things to think of. That cloud he'd seen from the Eye on his birthday, he hadn't even been able to decipher its shape. Yet lying on the grass unraveling the clouds had been part of every weekend, every holiday, every late summer evening after school. *Primary school*, he thought now. Surely they'd outgrown that sort of thing by the time they were in high school and mapping out their lives. "All I want," Charlie would say at the end of every fantasy, "is to put my hand out and grab a great big chunk of white." And then they'd argue about whether it would be wet or dry, hot or cold, until Gramps shut them up with stories about coaxing planes through white banks that loomed solid and cold—"towering cumulonimbus with spikes of ice at the top," he said. They were the worst; the coldest and the worst. Dan shivered now; those spikes of ice, and how big were the clouds through the window if a plane, so big itself, felt small against their billows and curves? The floor, the ceiling, jerked up and bounced down again, and he heard Cynthia swear under her breath.

Surely not today, he thought, but some part of him didn't feel sure enough.

Outside, one of the clouds had taken on the colors of a complete circle of rainbow. Dan smoothed his hand over the page in his journal and tried to draw its shape, marking in the divisions for the seven colors that he remembered from school, red through to violet. He couldn't remember the last time he'd seen a rainbow, let alone flown past one, and he wished he could have made the picture in his journal look nicer than a blobby shape cut by black lines with the names of the different colors written in. A few years ago Charlie had sent him a postcard of a perfect white cloud haloed by a rainbow. He'd read the message three times before he spotted the credit along the bottom. It was one of her photographs. *Where are you?* she'd written. *I'm making more pictures and wishing I could show them to you.* And she'd copied a couple of lines of a poem *by one of the world's other Dans—if you've still got time for that sort of thing with your busy job and your mysterious Caroline.* The lines written carefully in her neat handwriting:

> *My failing:*
> *To see similes, cloud as something other.*
> *Is all inspiration correspondences?*

He wondered if he'd ever replied, ever acknowledged that the card had come. Yes, it was so easy to put off getting in touch with someone when you knew it could be as instant as email, as a phone call. This rush around the world used to take six weeks, six months. Now, he was one hour down; only twenty or so still to go.

He flicked through the blank pages of the journal again, thinking about Charlie's cloud photo. The last series of her work he'd seen, she'd placed photographs of old weather records against photographs of the same days in her year—23 October 1789: *At 10, a shower of small rain.* 23 October 2002: *Dust storm on the edge of Sydney.* She was just as delighted when the days' temperatures and tempers were completely different as she was when the weather repeated itself across the centuries.

"But what do you think it means, if they're the same?" he'd asked her. "What do you think it tells you?"

She said, "It tells me something nice about time, that sometimes it folds one way and something repeats, and sometimes it folds another and you end up somewhere different, with something new. It's not science, Dan, it's poetry."

She hadn't sent many pictures after the cloud—the occasional photo printed on a rectangle of glossy white card, announcing an exhibition; the odd one torn out of a magazine. And she always wrote across the middle of the images in thick black pen—*It'd be nice if you were here*, or, *I thought you'd like to see where this ended up*—so that he wanted to tilt them to make the black words slide onto the floor and leave the picture clear. He should have gone home for one of her shows—Caro always said she liked the pictures.

"Do you know what the weather's been like back in Sydney?" he asked Cynthia, to compensate for his earlier evasiveness, and she shook her head. "It was a great day when I left—blue sky without a cloud. Be nice to land back into a day like that."

"You've been away a long time?" she asked, and as Dan nodded, he realized he had forgotten how Sydney's streets fitted together, forgotten the series of steps and turns you'd need to get from the main railway station down to the bridge. All jumbled now, like London. *I should tell Caro*, he thought. *Might make her smile*. Still, he remembered its sky, its big blue sky. He remembered Charlie turning her face up to the warmth of its bright sun—when they were kids, when they were grown up, when he was leaving.

He looked down into the clouds, now far beneath, and his eyes closed against the light. In a backyard on the other side of the world, he and Charlie used to lie and watch the jets draw their trails of vapor high across clear skies: yellow-orange at dawn, white at noon, red sometimes at dusk—maybe that was what had made the sky from the Ferris wheel feel familiar.

"Imagine if you were living two hundred years ago and you saw something like that in the sky," Charlie would say. "Imagine. You'd think it was God or something, wouldn't you?"

Dan took a drink from the flight attendant, took too big a mouthful, and turned back to the window. From nowhere, below, he saw the huge silver body of a plane with a dark blue tail—he could see its insignia quite clearly—as it cut at right angles across his plane's trajectory. His mind stammered. How big was a plane? How close must it be if it looked that big, took that long to pass by his window? A hundred feet or so? But that couldn't be right. He could see the color of the pilot's hair—"Fuck me." Should he tell someone? Had anyone noticed? Should it be there? Should he be there?

Cynthia yawned and turned the page of her book. The picture of the clouds below, framed by the window, was clear again.

He finished his drink in three gulps, holding the last mouthful against his teeth, his cheeks, scanning the horizon for anything else that might appear. It was unnerving enough when you saw other planes, made miniature on other far-off flight paths, but this . . . He shivered. The rush in the airport, all the people queuing with bags, their shoes off to be x-rayed, and the screens and screens of departures, the endless abacus of flight numbers. It didn't bear thinking about, how many planes were being kept apart, kept in the illusion of a pristine empty sky, at any one time. How many people were moving so far up above the earth, between somewhere and somewhere else.

He uncapped his pen. *A plane just cut underneath us—close enough for me to see the pilot's head and the name on the tail. No one else seems to have noticed. I wonder where it was heading. I wonder whether we were in the wrong place, or it was. I wonder how long it would take people to realize if we disappeared up here.*

I'm going home.

Dawes

IT WAS an extraordinary cloud, long and narrow and very straight, as if a stripe of color had been erased from the blue or a line of longitude, cutting perfectly from north to south, had been drawn onto the sky's curve. William Dawes stared at it for a while, watching as it began to blur, as it faded to let the sky's blue through more and more brightly until, in the end, there was only a sky so clear that he wondered if he had imagined it.

He shook his head and came back to the industry around him, the last tweaks and tightenings of the frame for his roof, the last securing of his rounded timber walls. They seemed so sturdy, but the surgeon said ominously, "Just something for them to find ruined when they come looking for us and find our place abandoned like my namesake's Roanoke."

Shading his eyes now, Dawes held on to optimism. Yes, the Governor had said, his observatory would be built—and yes, it would be built on the point Dawes coveted, the point he had called, with the Governor's permission, Point Maskelyne, in honor of the Astronomer Royal.

The little promontory of land was changed beyond measure, bits hewn out and leveled, and the grasses and coverings pulled back to show more and more gashes in the soil. Here were walls. Here was the break for a door. Here was a snug and solid space. And leaning against the trunk of one tree that rose up farther along the ridge was the great white square of canvas that would stretch across the frame for a roof, ready to be rolled back on its casters, ready to open his room to the stars. It was something, in this place, to watch the quickest pencil sketch become an edifice, and in only a few months—particularly when all the other surveys and designs he'd made for the Governor's Albion had so far come to nothing.

"Lieutenant Dawes, sir?" The voice came from down by the shore. "These rocks, sir, very flat—are they the kind of thing you want to fix the clock into place?" The man was kneeling on the ground, his hand smoothing two big rectangular slabs of stone like a merchant displaying a fine piece of silk.

Dawes crouched down, almost tipped off balance by the sudden movement of the man spitting at a fly that brushed near his lips.

"Fish?" said the man, and smelled his fingers. "These rocks smell like fish, sir."

"Maybe they were used for cooking," suggested Dawes, running his own fingers across the rock's grain, bringing them up to his nose. It was definitely fish. He corrected himself. "Maybe they are used for cooking," he said. "We should leave them, I think."

The man shrugged; if it meant he was going to have to chip away at another couple of lumps of stone, he wasn't happy. But as he stood up, his shrug froze, and his eyes narrowed. At the water's edge stood two girls, their dark skin shiny and their eyes wide and clear. The man tensed, cursed, and spat again. There was no fly near his mouth this time, but a convict had been speared the previous week, and had died, and Dawes saw the reckoning in the man's eyes; there was no use in pointing out that another native had been killed by the settlers as well.

"Gentlemen," said William Dawes, "we have some visitors."

"Probably them that went after a catch of our fish—probably cooked it down here right under your nose, sir." The spitting man tucked a snarl around that short final word.

"They're starving," said Dawes quietly. "They're hungry, like us. Now please, we need to . . ." He took a step towards his visitors, and wished he knew some of their language, but his only options—wo-roo wo-roo, meaning "go away," or kangaroo, for that strange hopping beast—seemed unhelpful. He tried "Good morning" and "Thank you for coming," but the words hung unacknowledged in the air. The girls stood, still and quiet.

If only he could convince them to accompany him up to the camp, to meet the Governor, to see the smallness of what they were doing. And of course it was small—a barren patch rubbed here and there, the line for a roadway nothing more than a paced-out suggestion between two points. If England summoned them home tomorrow, Dawes thought sometimes, the land would swallow any trace of them in no time, leaving only strange come-and-gone shadows in the stories these natives told. If he could tell these girls anything, he'd tell them this. "The size we look," he'd say, "we're nothing really, even with the noise and the mess we make. We're incidental."

He took another step forward, patting his chest. "Mr. Dawes." The girls patted their own chests and said, "Mr. Dawe," swallowing the last letter. Dawes smiled. He tried "Welcome," his hands spread wide in greeting, and again they repeated it. He tried "Good morning" again, with the same result.

"What about a tune, sir?" called someone else, pushing in front of the man who'd cursed and spat. "They like a tune, I heard." And he started to whistle. The girls smiled, pursed their lips, and began to whistle the tune in his wake, out by a bar or two, and out a note or two from each other, like some discordant round or a persistent echo. And then more of the men followed them into the beginning so that the point filled with whistles, chasing each other through phrase after phrase of the song "until the break of day." A cheer, and a whoop, and Dawes was clapping too.

Stepping towards them, he held out his hand—"Good morning," he said again—and one of the girls, the younger, stepped forward, took his hand and held it as they stood, their eyes, their faces, their bodies so close together that each could see the breath in the other's chest.

"Good morning," she repeated, and she held out her other hand. They made a cross now, like the makeshift stretcher that might carry a wounded man—left hand holding left hand, right hand holding right. He could feel her skin underneath his thumb, and it was as soft as his fragile rose petals had been long ago. It took all his concentration not to stroke the skin a little, to investigate its texture. A moment longer in the still silence, and then the whistling started up again and the girl, smiling, began to turn in a slow, careful circle. She was dancing with him, turning him around and around in time to the whistling.

Dawes laughed—dancing at last, and where was Tench?—and held his visitor's hands more tightly. Around they circled, around they went, all the men whistling and stamping, and the landscape spinning by in more and more of a blur as the song quickened, her steps followed it, and his steps followed hers. He heard the tune pull up grandly for its climax, and smiled. The water, the sky, the blocks of brick for his walls, the trees across the harbor; around they went in a loop. And as the whistling stopped at last, as the two dancers stepped back and broke their grasp, both stumbled a little.

The girl regained her footing first, her feet moving easily through some extension of the dance. But William Dawes tripped on his stiff leg and fell, his weight hitting the shallow water of the shore with what sounded like the most disproportionate crash, almost thunderous. He looked around him, expecting to see the ripples, the bubbles, the white foam of some greater disturbance, but its blue surface was almost perfectly still.

The girl was staring too. He heard her say a word that sounded like *man*, and he wondered if she was trying to say something about him, or perhaps about whatever had happened behind him somewhere on the water. But it was a rounder sound—"*Mawn*," she said, "*mawn*," flinching a little even as she offered him her hand and pulled him up from the ground. The whistling, the cheering, the clapping had stopped. *What next?* thought Dawes. *What now?* She let go of his hand.

Her face frowned then, creasing itself first into a question, and then into something like fear or terror. She shivered, as if the warmth had gone out of the day, and Dawes realized that the sun had indeed disappeared behind some large, grey cloud blown in from nowhere. But she shook herself at the end of the shiver, as if she was shaking something out of her fingers, her hands, her wrists, and they stood facing each other, as awkward as any two people after a dance.

"*Mawn*," she said again, her right arm reaching towards the sky and its hand, fashioned like a beak, swooping down then and worrying at her throat, her neck. She pointed across the water as if she too had expected to see something else breaking through its surface. "*Mawn*," she said. "*Mawn*, Mr. Dawes"—but it sounded like a question. She stepped back, her thumb rubbing the lines and creases on her palm as if he might have left some trace of himself on there. And then she patted her hands together and smiled, a wide, warm smile.

Behind him, something unsettled moved among the men, and he wondered how to end this, to turn them back to their purpose. Then he saw her raise her hand and realized she was holding it out to shake his. "Mr. Dawes," she said again, gripping his fingers and stepping in to pat at his chest. She gestured to her friend and they were gone, darting away over the rocks to the west.

He looked up towards the sun, clear again, wondering what it was that had fallen from the sky and made such a noise in the still water. If this light could trick you, maybe the air played tricks with the sound. But he still had the sense that he'd just missed seeing something, might at least have caught a glimpse of it from the most peripheral corner of his eye.

"Come on, gentlemen," called Dawes. "Let's get this up." He scooped up the pale bundle of canvas like a week's worth of the white tablecloths on which the officers still took their meals. And as he gave the word for it to be shaken wide and free, a puff of the harbor's breeze arched his roof into a dome before it settled flat and taut across the struts of its frame.

That new invention the French astronomer had extolled, the day they'd spent talking beside Botany Bay. That exciting new device—"Created by a Frenchman, of course, Monsieur Dawes"—a balloon, that could take you up into the air and across the sky—"So thrilling, Monsieur Dawes, to be above the clouds"—and he'd skated on through all the studies of electricity, and of optics, and of the atmosphere itself that such an invention might make possible. "All sorts of experiments with falling bodies, not to mention the balloon's great use for topographers and cartographers, monsieur." It was here, he had confessed, that he was thinking most of this New South Wales and of William Dawes in it. "The space so large, and your capacity to explore it so small. They will want surveys. They will want maps. They will want to know what is here, what is there, and what is in between. Think of all you could do, monsieur. Think of all you might see." And the Frenchman had swept his arms out in a great flourish, upsetting a sheaf of papers. "*Magnifique!*"

Yes, thought Dawes, as his balloon settled down into the roof it was supposed to be, *magnificent*. It would be something to be up above this place, to see so easily all the pokes and pinches of the harbor and its tributaries, to see all the way out to the hills that set their high blue line along the western horizon.

But a balloon, of course, was folly. Even having an observatory was unlikely enough given that the vicar could only wonder aloud when someone might begin to talk of making him a church and the higher-ranking officers had started to quibble about the canvas they were living under. He'd do better, Dawes suspected, to wish for his balloon to make an impossible and unexpected appearance like one of the surgeon's alligators, or the Botany Bay rose.

Later, his instruments ashore and unpacked—one quadrant, three clocks, one sextant, one barometer, two thermometers, a protractor, and the precious pocket watch with sweeping second hand that had belonged to the Astronomer Royal himself—William Dawes felt completely arrived.

Inside his snug new room, he let out a long breath. Waiting to get here, waiting to find a space for his observatory, waiting to raise its canvas. And now, here he was, the man put forward for this expedition for having *several languages and a good knowledge of natural history*. A man charged with supervising the skies. And a man with his own room built in the perfect spot for watching, for observing, for recording what might happen in this new part of the world.

~

Settling himself outside, the dark harbor before him, the dark sky above, Dawes jostled his head, his body so it rested straight and firm. Eyes open, just a little more than usual, a little wider. This was his first night of watching, and he was back in the exact spot from which he'd watched the high-summer storm. Six months ago now, that cataclysmic arrival.

The night was still, cold; it was winter, and the crispness of the air seemed to make the stars glisten and pulse a little more. Everything was where he now expected it to be: the Cross moving up to the center of the sky from the southwest, big bright Vega out to the northeast, and Jupiter almost directly overhead. How amazing it would be if his comet came on this first night. How amazing; how miraculous. He pulled a sheet of paper and a pencil towards him, ready for whatever might transpire. Here he was, the night and the sky and a column of calculations that said this much-anticipated comet might be near—start scanning, start looking.

A star fell towards the east, and something shrieked from a tree nearby. Dawes's right hand fiddled with the pencil; he scratched at the ground with his left. The pencil's casing was smooth, the leaves his left hand found were smooth too, but neither were close to the velvet of holding the girl's hand and dancing around. He could still see the shape her mouth had made as she smiled and took her leave; it was so long since he'd had anyone new to look at.

Strange, the new stories that were surging around the camp. It wasn't daytime alligators people believed they'd seen darting between their tents now; it was dark people, sneaking in at night, creeping between rows of sleeping bodies and—who knew?—stopping to stare, patiently and for a frighteningly long time, at those closed and unaware eyes. Now it wasn't only Dawes who thought he heard their footsteps: his theory about those noises—about which he'd never spoken—had spread like contagion through the settlement. It was as if the sleepers feared their dreams might be sucked out and violated, as if some part of their soul had been made off with like a precious piece of clothing, a hoarded mouthful of food.

The Governor had received the reports of these nocturnal visits, listened to them, noted them among his papers, and declared that they were *only the effect of imagination.*

The sky above him still and settled, Dawes let his own thoughts wander a little.

Dear Miss Rutter, I imagine you sitting with my father, taking a cup of tea in one of my mother's cups. I imagine the rosy brown liquid being poured, its smell as you bring it up to sip it—its heat, its sweetness—and the sound, like a bell, of your spoon set down against your saucer.

Dear Miss Rutter, We often think of tea over here. There's a local leaf that we pretend will do, but the color, the flavor, the scent: all are wrong. Snakes and lizards are regular dinner stuffs now. And more ships have gone; only three remain from the eleven that were our world, that could take us away as reliably as they brought us. The ships have discharged one cargo—our settlement—and sailed north to collect the next one—sweet Chinese tea—to carry back to you. And we are left here, brewing new leaves in kettles and trying not to notice the harbor's emptiness.

Dear Miss Rutter, In the sky above is a set of stars that might be a teapot. The surgeon says some of the women are coming close to mutiny for want of a cup of this beverage. A native girl came to my observatory and I danced a little with her, down on the shore, around and around. There was a great crash in the water at the end and she gave it a name, like "man" or "mawn," although I have no idea what it might have been.

Dear Miss Rutter, I cannot imagine with what words they talk about us, what words and names and stories.

Arching his neck, Dawes tried to ease his shoulders, his arms, out of their cramped position. Overhead, the stars flickered and pulsed. They looked nothing like a teapot—he knew that—but it was a thing to think. Of course there was no letter to Miss Rutter either. Perhaps there was no longer even a Miss Rutter. There was no sign of his comet, even though some part of him had believed that it would appear on the first clear night he had an observatory. He would look up, and there it would be. Still, it was a glorious sky, and more familiar now too; he knew where to look for what, a whole piece of the world's night etched onto his brain. This point too was familiar, and the dips and turns of the harbor's coves. Things became what you expected to see so quickly, in the end.

Inside, preparing to sleep, he picked up a pile of pages, tapped them into alignment, and found himself checking again the different workings of where his observatory actually sat on the face of the earth: 33°52'30"S 151°20'E according to one calculation, about a mile out from that according to another, and perhaps as far off as 33°51'10"S by another reckoning.

Perhaps, he thought, yawning, *it's actually floating around somehow, unmoored and mobile like Gulliver's island of Laputa or one of the Frenchman's balloons.*

Ted

HE CAME up to the front of the house, his head full of the swirling couples he'd just seen at the pictures, and for a moment the turn of her movement matched the turn of some remembered dance as it whirled through his mind. The two doorways between them framed her—the mottled greens of her dress, the woolly green of her cardigan, against the greens of her grass, her flowerbeds—like a painting. He paused, looking and listening, but there was no sound in the house. A kookaburra chortled from the street lamp above him.

Stepping onto the front veranda, Ted's feet landed naturally on the boards that would not creak and he felt some different sense of belonging. Another step, then he eased open the fly-screen door and paused again. Along the hall and out in the yard, Joy was bending down for something and for a second he couldn't separate the green of her clothes from the green of the garden—it was as if she'd disappeared. The screen door snapped shut behind him, and she stood up at the noise, seeing his shape in the hallway. One hand waving, the other full of flowers, she called something that he couldn't hear. But he smiled, waved back, and pointed towards the bathroom, miming the water, the soap.

She was arranging the flowers—white roses—in a bowl when

he came out, and she held them up for him to admire. "I said, we've got our chance," she said—no hello, nothing small about the day. "Joe's gone to help someone with a move; won't be back till tomorrow. Smell these." She took a deep breath, her nose close to the petals. "Aren't they beautiful? We had these at our wedding; they always make me smile."

Ted leaned forward, breathed in. There was something like vanilla in the fragrance, something almost smoky, and something that felt like satin in his nostrils. He touched one of the blooms, and a petal came away in his fingers—it was like velvet, and so soft it felt wet somehow.

"The crunch if you bit into one—would it be more like an apple or a pear, do you think?" asked Joy, pulling a petal from another bud and rubbing it between her own thumb and forefinger. "Terrible if they didn't taste as good as they smell." She set the vase down in the middle of the table, brushed her hands against her skirt, and smiled at him. "So we'll go to the bridge tonight?"

He felt his guts twinge and tighten, and he grabbed at the back of a kitchen chair. "Back tomorrow," he heard himself say, "of course—and the move. I should've offered to help." Joy was smiling, almost laughing. He'd never felt more terrified in his life. Imagine ever saying he wanted to sneak off and do such a thing, let alone that they would go together. His mind skittered through a thousand things that might happen, that might not happen, that might go wrong, to pull up against one solid fact: he wasn't even sure he knew how to get onto it. His fingers worked at the softness of the rose petal; it was creamy, comforting. "Well then," he said at last, "I suppose we'll go after tea."

"It'll be magical," she said. "It will be perfect." She looked as if she might clap her hands. "Really, it will be the most amazing thing to do. Standing up there, up in the air: I can't tell you how many times I've thought about it."

Up we go, thought Ted. *Top of the world.* He closed his eyes as she ran through her plans: they could catch the ferry in, walk through the Rocks, climb up from the south.

"We'll need to take a bone or something for the dog," he said. "There's a dog, Jacko, at the south end and I've only met him once. Hear he barks like billyo, but . . ."

"I'd give up a chop for that," said Joy. "And there's a nice one here ready for him."

She's not going to let us out of this, thought Ted. "Joy," he began, but she turned and put her finger to her lips.

"Shh," she said. "It's terrifying. But think of all those people who've snuck up before us. Safe as houses, they all say, and I know the way—Russian George told me. It'll be fine. Come on, come on."

There were so many things that could go wrong. It might not be fine. And when Joe found out—when Joe found out. Ted practiced the words in his mind: *We just wanted to climb it, Joe, you know we did, and we . . .* He'd be saying this when they were safely at home. And of course Ted was dying to get up there as well. To walk up that big metal frame, up into the sky and the clouds and the stars. He took a deep breath, flicked the rose petal out through the open window, and squared his shoulders again.

"After tea," he said, "we'll get the ferry." He could hear her humming as she went back into the yard—humming his song. *I'm sitting on top of the world . . .*

Rolling along, he thought to himself, but he couldn't manage the tune. *All right then.*

⁓

This is what I'll do, thought Ted, trying to convince himself that the nervousness he felt was excitement, not fear. *I'll go out through the front gate and I'll tell myself that it's just like looking at the stars.*

I'll get onto the ferry and I'll tell myself that it's just like going in to work. I'll walk through the Rocks and I'll tell myself that it's just like going for a drink. I'll get onto the site and I'll tell myself that it's just like going to see the foreman. I'll get onto the arch and I'll climb along the cords. I won't think anything. I won't think about anything. And when I get to the top—

Joy, with her coat on, was already on the front path. "Let's go," she called, and it occurred to Ted that if he walked slowly they might miss the ferry. But his pace sped up to match hers. He was sure he was going to be sick, sure something bad was going to happen, although he wasn't sure he wanted to think about what the bad thing—the worst thing—might be. *The worst thing would be getting caught.* Which he knew wasn't true.

From where they stood on the ferry's deck, the boat seemed low in the water, as if they were closer to its surface and skimming along. It made the foreshores—the bays, the coves, the walls they passed and the wharves—look so much higher, more looming, more imposing.

"Isn't it wonderful?" said Joy. "Isn't it wonderful to be out on the water at night? Don't the lights look pretty?"

The voids between the house lights, the streetlights, seemed darker, more menacing than usual. This must be how burglars feel, how murderers feel, *how lovers feel*, thought Ted, and blushed, as if even thinking the word was somehow dangerous, somehow sneaky. In the darkness, he could see Joy's silhouette leaning towards the water as if she was urging the boat on. Ted sat back a little as the ferry cut under the space the bridge would soon entirely fill, took in the diminishing slice of sky that still gaped between the arch's disconnected arms.

"It looks a lot higher at night," he said. But Joy was smiling, still smiling, and she tied the knot on the scarf that covered her hair a little tighter as she tilted her own head back to take in its size.

"It's all right," she said, "I'm terrified too. I'm just imagining that we're walking out to look at the stars." He wondered about taking her hand, as if he was just helping her to step over something, or helping his mum up some stairs—and as he thought about this, she reached over and took his. "The worst part is going to be not telling everybody—we'll keep it our secret, won't we," she said, but it was a decision, not a question. "Are you ready?" And the ferry pulled in.

The old stories Joe loved about this place. The first Englishmen sitting, watching, and waiting—and his astronomer, staring at the stars from the place where the bridge sprouted now. And then, later, the dark lanes and alleyways that ran away from that piece of land; men disappearing into tunnels that snaked beneath them and waking up to find themselves on a ship and away across the ocean, indentured. That was its history—sailors, stars, and convicts chained to walls. Digging the first great holes for the bridge, Joe had found bolts in a wall where he was sure those convicts must have been chained, the way the caretaker's noisy dog was chained tonight. The darkness felt heavier again.

There was the hole in the fence, just like they'd been told. There was Jacko's kennel; Joy had the chop out of the bag and in front of the dog before he could make a noise. There were the cranes and the barrows and the scaffolding and the cables and the rubble—and the pylon rising up towards them, pale and enormous like the way he imagined an iceberg. They were running fast by the time they reached the first section of steel, pulled up hard against it, panting. Joy eased her fingers out of Ted's grip; his hand was stiff from holding on, sweating from fear, from exhilaration.

"I don't think we should stop," he said between breaths. "I don't think we should think about this." And he went up the first ladder as easily as if he was going onto a roof after a missing ball. Hand over hand; foot after foot; his eyes on the rungs and his heart pounding. He cleared the first climb and straightened up for his first step onto the line of the arch, that magical curve made of so many straight parts. "Step onto the rivets, feel them under your feet, and kind of brace yourself against them—you can do it better in bare feet, I reckon." He wondered where the certainty, the authority in his voice, came from; pictured Joe, with his shoulder under a wardrobe or a sofa somewhere.

All I have to do is get her home, he thought, trying to reassure himself. Joe must have known Joy would seize this moment. He must have known he was giving her her chance.

She was there, right behind him, her shoes in her pockets and her feet steadying themselves, beginning to grip.

"It's wider than I imagined, even when Joe said how wide—and it's solid. Come on, let's go." She reached out for him and he caught her hand again. "Let's go, come on: we've got to get higher, higher up."

One foot, then another; one step, then another. It was a still, clear night, just the thinnest sliver of moon making the thinnest gash in the black sky. Ted kept his eyes on his feet, one arm out for balance, one hand behind for Joy. Another step, another step—he wished he knew how far they had to climb, or had any sense of how far they'd climbed already. Then the gradient eased and changed under his feet and he slowed down, cut his steps in half.

"Joe says they'll lay steps along the edge," he said, for want of something ordinary to say. "I guess everyone'll be scurrying on up then."

The metal was cool under his feet, the knob of each rivet pressing into his skin like a marker. In front of him—ten or twelve paces—the color of the darkness changed. That was all there was. He stopped, lowered himself onto his haunches, and sat down; felt Joy easing herself down beside him. His knees were shaking, every nerve in his legs, his toes, his body tingling, and his voice cracked when he tried to sing, even quietly, his favorite song "I'm Sitting on Top of the World."

Here he was.

Beside him, Joy let out a long, long breath. A gentle breeze came through and he heard her whispering, "Oh." Here they were.

Ted looked at his feet, his skin pale against the dark metal. He looked at the rivets lined up across the cord. Eleven feet wide, and just like Joe had said, you could convince yourself it felt spacious. Ted took a deep breath, looked at the edge of the cord, and then looked out. There was the water, there were the lights of Sydney, and there, miles away to the east, was the line the coast made against the sky, the brushing flare of the lighthouse, the darker sky beyond. He shivered—*huuh*—and felt his whole body shake. He could smell salt air as it met the cleaner smell of cool wind blowing in from the south.

"So," said Joy quietly, "this is what it's like to fly."

"Higher," said Ted, "that must feel higher. And faster. But up in the air, yes."

She lay back carefully along the length of the steel, and he mirrored her movement, the top of his head almost touching the top of hers.

"Those stars look pretty good." He tilted his head from side to side, keeping his eyes on the sky. "There's Sirius, and the Cross." Below, Sydney had broken itself into the same patches of light and dark that the foreshore had shown to the ferry—the puddles of streetlamps, the inkiness of parks and gardens, the fireflies of sparse cars moving along streets, the reflections of boats on the water's still surface.

"As long as I know where they are." He could sense her smiling. "You know where I met Joe?" she asked. "Down there under the southern pylons, when they were digging out all that ground, digging down through the years and the sandstone. He showed me the rooms where they reckoned the convicts had been tied up. He showed me a brick with 1789 carved into it—he took me onto the site one day and let me feel the shape of those numbers. Reckoned it was from the old observatory, where that astronomer lived in the beginning. Oh yes," she said, laughing, "he says I make too much of things, thinking about this place, wanting to know all about it, taking its stories on, but he looks a long way back in the other direction. You know, he's even had professors send him articles about what was here, and who."

Leaning out, Ted peered at the land below, erasing the lights, the movement, the development of the place until he could imagine only the smell of a fire and its dull, warm flicker, a wider silence, a wider darkness. He sniffed the air, sure, for a moment, he was catching the smell of wood-burning smoke.

"Anyway," Joy wriggled forward a little, "they kept digging, down and down through the rock. It was amazing how far down they had to go before they could start going up. All the holes they were going to loop the cables through to anchor the bridge to the ground—as if they were afraid it might float away otherwise, like a great big balloon. And then all of a sudden it began, piece after piece in space, working its way up here, higher and higher. I'd seen how it was burrowing into the ground; I'd seen those big cables tying it down. I knew it could take me up into the sky. And here we are. Here we are."

"My mum and me sat down there after the war," said Ted after a while. "It was the day I realized my dad wasn't coming home. Mum'd been to all these offices, trying to find out why they couldn't at least send his body back; it was flu, in the end, after the war was over. I think she thought I understood what was going on, but I didn't give up waiting for him for ages. We sat down there and I watched the water and the clouds and wondered how long Dad might be, and if he'd know to look for us down there, and my mum had a cry. It was a nice spot to sit." He'd always believed he'd seen his first shooting star from the window of the train going home that night, but his mum said he'd slept soundly all the way. "I dreamed of coming back up to the city and waiting. I think I still thought I could just sit there and my dad would turn up, sooner or later."

He straightened himself as a boat made its way from the southern shore to the north, its wake fanning out like the train of a ballgown. All the stories the men had told him about throwing things, dropping things, letting things fall from all this way up—rivets hitting ferries; lunches hitting ferries; not to mention the slightly less tasteful human matter that went, blasé, over the edge. He felt in his pocket for a penny and flicked it, heads or tails, off the side of his finger with his thumb. He wasn't sure what he was tossing for, he just sat watching the coin catch the light as it spun around and around, down into the darkness. He waited—it felt like an eternity—until he was sure he heard it splash. How far would a penny go down through the water? Was it heavy enough to sink? Would it bury itself into the mud, the sludge of the harbor's bed?

"Another thing for the future to find," said Joy. "I wonder if they'll ever trawl for the stuff that's gone over already."

"I wonder if it was heads or tails," said Ted. He was aching with trying to register every moment, trying to squash everything he could see in every direction into his memory. "Maybe we'll see a shooting star tonight—we should wish for something." But sitting there, sitting with Joy, he wasn't sure what he'd wish for next.

"Tell me a story," she said.

Up in the air, against the inky night, he talked about the places he'd found where the bridge showed itself suddenly—the corners you could turn on city streets to find bits and pieces of its cage in the view, and then farther out, on the hill behind the racecourse, or right down beyond Botany Bay; out towards the southwest, out towards the northwest.

"If there were people out there tonight, if there were people with sharp binoculars and steady hands, I guess they'd see us up here, couple of spots on this big smooth thing." Joy sat up a little, lifted a hand and waved towards the four points of the compass.

"I still haven't worked out how it looks so big from some places, and so small from others," she continued. "Even tonight, running along, getting closer and closer, it looked smaller than I imagined it would."

In the pocket of quietness behind their voices, Ted listened to the air around them. He could almost hear the squeak and drag of the stars through the sky—or was it the squeak and drag of the earth turning? It was the sound of the metal's infinitesimal night-time movements, of the bridge pulling itself in a little here, back a little there. Against the soft turn of the breeze that brushed against him every so often, it sounded like a quiet, gentle song.

"Can you hear it, Joy?" He held his hand up as if to pause the air, and the little creaks and moans rose above the ringing of the rest of the silence. "It's bigger than you think, that sound, isn't it? Makes me feel kind of small."

"I think she's just talking to herself," said Joy at last.

"She?"

"She's got to be a she; that big curve. She's going to be so grace-ful when she's done."

"It's going to be big, for sure, pushing itself up and over the top of everything," said Ted. "No one will ever be able to get lost here again—all you'll have to do is climb a hill and work out where the bridge is and orient yourself to that. Feels like you could stand up and scrape the sky . . ." And before he could change his mind, he was on his feet, on his tiptoes reaching up and up and up. He laughed, heard Joy laugh at the same time.

There it was—perfectly timed: their shooting star. He dropped down beside her again.

"I'm glad Joe brought you home." She took his hand again and squeezed it. "You're a grand friend to both of us. You know that, don't you? Joe thinks the world of you, and it's nice to have someone to read with, someone else to look for stars with, someone to tell me more stories. And now, here we are, all the way up here. What a thing to remember, eh, when I'm ninety and you're coming to visit me, all young and spry and busy?"

"It's grand of you both to have me," he said. "Who'd have thought, meeting Joe that day, and it all turned out like this." The knot, the apprehension, in the pit of his stomach gripped and tightened again. Magnificent, yes, but they still had to get down.

On the water below a boat blew its horn and he started and sat up straighter, as if he'd been caught and reprimanded.

"I wonder what the time is," Joy said. "I've no idea how long we've been up here." She flexed her arms, and Ted mirrored the movement. His legs were getting stiff and his feet were getting cold.

"Well," he said, "I guess we should think about working our way down."

"Next time I'm going to come up here and wait all night for the sunrise, see the tracks they say the boats leave on the water," said Joy, adjusting her scarf. "Do you think many people will come up, when it's done? Do you think they'll see any sign we were here?"

"There is something nice about being up high," said Ted, "about getting up as high as you can, to see exactly where you are." As for evidence, some part of him suspected that their footsteps would be set on the bridge's steel as surely as those boats' paths were set on the water—who could hope to be invisible in this most visible of places?

"And then some people jump, don't they?" said Joy, and so simply, as if it was the most natural thing in the world. "I suppose that will happen; I suppose they'll come. Although it seems a shame to do it in such a beautiful place." The city looked so separate, and so inviolable—surely nothing could be big enough to make someone try to jump into it. "I knew a girl who was scared of heights, but she was fascinated by the idea of falling—could almost feel herself being dragged towards the edge, sometimes."

He didn't like this, but didn't know what to say against it that might change the direction of her sentences. He thought about the cold, and the climb down, and their long walk home. He looked out to the east, trying to press every piece of the view onto his mind's eye. Then Joy stood up and it felt like the whole world tilted and swayed; it looked to Ted as if she'd forgotten how to stand, how to be tall. Instinctively he reached out and grabbed her ankle, and the shock of the touch made her stagger, just half a step. The steel seemed suddenly so narrow.

"It's all right," she said and he said, "It's all right," at the same time. "It's all right," he repeated. "I've got you."

She stood very still, very quiet, and he pushed himself up to stand next to her. He could feel the earth falling away from him as he rose taller above the steel. It was terrifying; it was wonderful. He wanted to stay up in the air forever.

She began to sing his top-of-the-world song, holding her hands out to him, and as he took them, they turned in the smallest circle, slowly, so slowly, around and around, singing Al Jolson to each other. They reached the end of the line.

"Dancing through air," sang Ted, replacing the words.

"Or just dancing on air," suggested Joy, and she turned to walk, footlength by footlength, towards the end of the cord. Ted swallowed, followed, found himself leaning out too towards the empty space at its end. "It is kind of seductive," said Joy, pulling back. And they sat, wiggling forward until their feet, their shins, their knees were dangling in space.

Ted shivered. The silence seemed to be growing, more and more of its layers ringing in his ears. Another boat moved across the water below; a bird called out from the shore somewhere, and he caught the smell of smoke again, like the smell of wood burning in Joy's kitchen stove, and looked around for a fire's brightness.

"I'm glad we came," he said, "but we should go now." His hands behind him, he pushed himself up; she was already standing by the time he'd steadied himself. She was leading him now, back along the steel, her feet finding the shape of its curve.

They were halfway down when it happened; he couldn't tell if she tripped, if she took an extra step out towards the emptiness, but she was falling away from him—hanging on hard to his hand as her scarf shook itself free from her hair. It was only two steps, three at the most, and it was done in a moment. But he stood there rigid, his knees locked, his back straight. *I can hold on to her; I can hold her here.* She grabbed his arms and righted herself as one of her shoes—a delicate little thing—fell from her pocket, bounced on the metal, and went down, spinning like the coin, through one, two, three, four seconds and into the water. The scarf fluttered, caught by the wind and almost in reach.

"Leave it," Ted said sharply as her balance shifted and her arm shot out. "It doesn't matter." And then he heard the splash her shoe must have made—so huge that he frowned, and looked down past the face of the bridge to see a spout of water spray white and high above the harbor's dark blue. No shoe, dropped from any height, could have thrown the water up so high—he knew that from all the tools and rivets and bodies and bearings that had gone over the side of the barge. Joy stood against him, shivering, one hand clutching her one shoe so tightly that her knuckles were white.

"I'm so sorry," she said.

His mind was spinning with not really knowing, not really seeing, exactly what had happened.

He said, "But what was that?" And he turned, crouched down, and looked out towards the middle of the bridge through the wide box frames of its struts. The water was calm; not so much as a ripple. "Maybe someone was sitting on the other side," he said. "Maybe they dropped something just as you stumbled—or maybe something else fell off." These seemed dangerous things to put into words.

He tried again. "Maybe it was a bird, diving for something." Which was better. "But there's nothing there now"—to himself. It was as close as he'd come to the frightening, stomach-grabbing moment in his dream.

"What happened, what was it?" she asked, fussing with her hair and avoiding his eyes.

"Something—I don't know—something that could make a huge splash, like a whale," he tried. "I don't know. I didn't know what you were doing." The wind was picking up, and stripes of cloud were beginning to cover the stars. "It's getting cold. We've got to get down. We've got to get home. We've got to go." And he stepped around in front of her and began to walk, looking only at the raised pockmarks of the rivets as they appeared in front of his feet.

They ran back along the beginnings of the roadway—Joy wearing one shoe on one foot, both of Ted's socks on the other, and Ted with his shoes scraping and rasping against his cold bare skin. Ducking through the fence, they skittered down the rough-cut sandstone to the harbor's shore and its great hulking docks, diminished now by the bulk of the thing that was growing overhead.

"All right," she breathed then, standing with her hands on her hips as if she was sizing up something they were about to do, rather than what they'd just done. "All right."

Above them, the caretaker's dog barked at last as they ran past the wharves and their sheds. Dank sandstone walls rose up, the city perched on top of them; there were stairways and alleys cut in here and there, and they stank of urine and something rotten. Men were sleeping all over the city now, makeshift camps in the city's parks spreading farther and farther as more people were turned out of their homes, more people came in looking for jobs. With the certainty of the middle of the night, Ted was suddenly more wary of potential threat, or violence, than he had been of the danger of scampering up hundreds of tons of steel in the darkness. He ran faster, felt Joy striding out to keep up with him, and on they went around the edge of the land and closer, with every step, to home.

In the shadow of one warehouse, he could see a cluster of bodies, a couple of blankets, a drum with the dregs of a fire sputtering in its cavity, and he steered Joy across to the other side of the road—"Shh, shh"—as if they were passing a nursery of gently sleeping children. From nowhere, from the darkness, an old man in a shabby red coat reared up, growling and railing and smelling of drink. He reached out for Joy as Ted stepped back onto the road, pulling her with him, and the old man staggered two steps and turned in at a flight of sandstone stairs that seemed to climb nowhere. Ted pictured him up there, watching their two heads running fast along the road, two points getting smaller and smaller.

At home, in the warm light of the kitchen, with her hair neat again and her sore feet soaking in a basin of water, Joy stirred an extra teaspoon of sugar into her tea, absentmindedly dropping the wet spoon back into the sugar bowl.

"Who was he, do you think, that old man who shouted at us?" she asked. "What do you think he was trying to say? What do you think he saw when we ran by?"

A tall woman with pale hair running through the night, running away from the graceful curve of a rainbow that she'd just conquered; the sky busy above with clouds and wind and stars, and another cloud of water surging up, disturbed below.

"Magic," said Ted. "He thought he was seeing something from an invisible world."

The answer hung in the air, a little large and unexpectedly poetic—an answer that was, as Joe would say, a bit too much.

The quiet space of the kitchen held his words until his chair scratched against the linoleum.

He drank his tea. He stared into the silence. He washed his face and went to his bed. And when he went to sleep, he was too exhausted to remember dreaming anything at all.

Dan

THE FLIGHT attendant's voice shook Dan out of a frantic blurry dream where Sydney and London had jumbled together and he was running to catch a plane, a train, a cab, even a big old sailing ship for a minute. He was stiff, and there was an odd metallic taste in his mouth.

For something that sounded graceful, even ethereal, flying was a brutal thing to do; this long tube of metal, its seats too small, the terrible, infusing roar of the engines. He pressed his temples, willing himself to ignore the rattling pulse of the plane's movement as his view changed from clear sky to the tempting white nothing of clouds, then the jumble of an unfamiliar city, and then the long grey stripe of the runway up close and whizzing by. For half a day he'd been sitting in this strange nowhere of place or time. *At least six months on a boat lets you walk around and breathe real air.* He stretched his legs, laced his swollen feet back into their sneakers, and tried to imagine moving, let alone walking. Whoever was behind him stretched their legs too—Dan could feel the shape of knees, or maybe feet, pressing into the middle of his back. It was almost pleasant, almost friendly. Standing up took an immense act of will, and the plane began to empty at a processional pace.

Ahead on the airbridge, the family from across the aisle still walked side by side in the same formation—father, child, child, mother—their hands linked together. They looked like an up-and-down city skyline.

Dan sniffed deeply; he'd never noticed before how much airports smelled like hospitals. He needed a shower. He needed to change his shirt. He needed a drink, and something to read. He came onto the concourse, squinting against the bright lights, the banks of shops, the familiar brands that appeared in any city, and the food that belonged in other parts of the world. These places, trying to be everywhere and nowhere all at once.

He paused at the bookshop, its light so bright that it looked like it was selling plastic imitations, like the glazed dishes of dim sum and noodles used to lure you into the world's Chinatowns. A pile of the latest children's wizard book teetered almost above Dan's head as the little girl from across the aisle broke free from her family and darted under his elbow to grab at a copy—the whole stack swayed a little—pressing it hard against her chest. "All right," said her mother, "but you'll have to share it with your brother." Dan smiled; he and Charlie had shared books, arguing about who got to take the book home, to put it on their shelf, at the end of each day. He looked at the rows of books: books about September 11, about the end of the world, about actresses' lives, about how to be happy—he needed the drink first.

Hitching his bag higher on his shoulder, he felt something sharp, something cornered, press against him. Investigating, he found a rectangular parcel, in brown paper, with Caro's handwriting on the front. *For the trip*, she'd written, *someone else's story—and he went there too.* It felt like a book—too late for all those empty hours. He tore off the paper as he ordered a beer. It was a cream-colored copy of *Gulliver's Travels*, the last book he thought he'd read with Charlie in some lost set of school holidays. Lilliput, Blefuscu, Brobdingnag, the Houyhnhnms . . . Dan's eye ran across the contents page with its brief summations. Laputa: he remembered Charlie's voice telling them about the floating, flying island, how long they'd spent over the atlas, wondering in which piece of conveniently empty ocean it might appear next.

At the end of the list of places Gulliver had visited was "New Holland." Dan frowned, and looked again in case it was another word that he was misreading somehow. But no, there was Gulliver, going to the very place where Dan was going, the very place in which he and Charlie had sat, imagining themselves setting out in Gulliver's footsteps. How could they have missed that? Maybe they'd never made it to the end of the book (although he thought they had). Maybe the holidays had finished (although he was sure other books had carried on into fresh, new school terms). Maybe they'd lost the book—though he remembered how seriously they took the task of putting the books on their shelves. He could almost picture the spines of the books they'd read running back through years to little-kid stories about wombats and puddings. He flicked through the pages, picking at a word here, half a sentence there. Here was Gulliver coasting past New Holland—yes, he did remember that. Here he was back in England. But then this other antipodean chapter, tucked in at the end. *I began this desperate voyage on February 15, 1714–15* . . .

Perched on a high stool in the bright bar, Dan pulled the beer towards him and took the first, satisfying sip. A long sigh, loud enough to make the man two stools along turn and look at him. Dan smiled, tilted his drink a little. The man didn't smile back, looked at the counter; he looked a bit like the man who'd been at the other end of Dan's row—*Unless*, thought Dan, *everyone looks the same when they're flying too fast over the surface of the earth.* But in front of him was Gulliver, years away from home and probably presumed dead by all his family, finding himself a capacious canoe and making for Australia's coast. His eyes brushed over the lines, following the book's last days and nights and Gulliver's canoe, until they both arrived at *the southeast point of New Holland.*

"It's stories we live by, Danny"—that's what Charlie's grandad said. He'd strung the two families—Charlie's, Dan's—together with stories, the coincidence of this, the sudden twist of that, and a gate he'd made in the fence between their two homes. There he'd been in the war, sending planes out over the very village in Europe where Dan's father—"rest in peace," Gramps dropped in automatically as he did at the mention of his own wife, or his own little girl, Charlie's mother—had been growing up. Why, one of Gramps's planes had probably bombed it once or twice. He'd pull out an atlas and find the very place. There it was, marked with a black spot, as if everything he said was proved true if a name was clearly marked on a map and Gramps could find it. Dan's mother would stand at his shoulder, nodding, and Charlie's grandad would smooth the atlas's page with his hand. "And here we are now, here we are."

Dan's mother understood stories—she'd married Dan's father for his. Dan's father, older than her and with a thick accent that she always attempted when she talked about him. Dan's father, who'd walked out of the mess of Europe after the war, changing his name—his future, he'd said—as he went. She knew little about the place he'd come from, other than what it was called. And she knew little about his reasons for leaving. "When someone is willing to go so far," she'd said to Dan once, "you might not want to know why."

Caro had been intrigued. "You don't know what happened? You don't know why he left? You don't even know his real name?" And Dan would shake his head. Once or twice he'd thought of heading east from England, trying to find out, but nothing ever came of it. If his mum wanted to go, he'd said, he'd take her; for him, his dad was only the faintest outline of a gigantic shape, and the particular smell of a jumper, some cologne, of long-gone cigarettes and coffee. Names came and went in wars, it seemed—and Gramps had reassured him, not long after his dad had died, that half the blokes building the bridge had had at least a couple of names they answered to.

Now, in this bland bar, Dan stared blankly at Jonathan Swift's pages—even Swift'd had a handful of pseudonyms, he thought. Maybe it used to be an easier thing to do. He tapped the book against the bar, as if trying to settle its sentences, and something rammed hard into the legs of his bar stool, shaking him off balance so that he leapt to his feet and the book flopped onto the table, its creamy cover soaking up spots of beer and condensation. On the ground, bouncing against the stool, was a little boy, pale-haired and energetic. Dan turned his head. Did he look like the kid who'd been sitting across the aisle, or did he just look like any kid? The boy smiled and Dan wondered if it was because he'd recognized Dan, or would have smiled at anyone.

"Hi there," said Dan, feeling inappropriately tall as he stood up next to his stool. "Are you supposed to be here?"

Silence as the boy tried to wind his own leg around the stool's long cool metal one. Dan looked around: the sullen man was still drinking two stools along, and there was a nest of Japanese children playing around the potted plants just outside the bar. No sign of the family he thought this kid belonged to—no sign of anyone looking for a missing kid.

"So," he said, sitting down again and feeling no less awkward, "where are you going?"

"To see my grandma," said the boy. "She lives a long way away and I've never seen her before."

Unhelpful, thought Dan. He didn't know whether to ask the boy if he was lost or not—if the boy didn't know he was lost, and was quite happy weaving himself around a bar stool, was it better not to draw attention to the fact, better not to scare him with the idea of it, better to try to head him towards some information booth? Or was it better to keep him in here, in the one place, where someone could find him?

Dan took a sip of his beer, then another. "All right then, what's your name?"

"Dan," said the boy.

"Great," said Dan. "That's my name too." He tried to remember anything he knew about talking to kids, which was nothing, and whether it was against all the stranger-danger codes to offer them something to eat or drink when you found them detached from where they should be and bouncing off your bar stool. *Probably against*, he thought. He reached out a hand—then pulled it back. That was probably banned too. "I'm just going to put my book away, Dan, and maybe we can go and have a look for your mum."

The boy smiled. "My mum's got a new bag," he said, standing with his hand up, ready to be led somewhere, as Dan hooked his backpack over his shoulder. *Okay*, thought the taller Dan. *Okay*. He scanned the bar and the causeway outside again. Still no sign of a parent trawling the crowd, and no sign of the family from across the aisle, missing one. He'd never realized before, but he was slightly scared of children.

"What color's your mum's hair?" he asked.

"Yellow."

"Let's see how many people we can find with yellow hair before we find your mum." They stepped out of the bar, the smaller Dan with a firm hold on the bigger Dan's hand, counting through each yellow-haired lady he saw: "Not that one, not that one, not *that* one."

As they neared the bookshop, the taller Dan caught the sound of a different tone of voice. There was the family from across the aisle—father, daughter, mother—and it was the mother's voice he could hear, asking if anyone had seen "a little boy, blond, please, have you seen him? We were here a quarter of an hour ago." The smaller Dan ran towards her, and before he'd called out—before she could even have registered the sound of his feet against the carpet—she'd swung around and opened a hug for him. There he was, there he was; scooped up and back where he should be. Dan watched the look on her face as her eyes opened, saw Dan, and narrowed a little.

"He wandered into the bar," said Dan. "I recognized him from the plane." Her eyes narrowed further. "I'm sitting across the aisle from you. Going to Sydney."

She smiled then, peeled one arm out of the hug and reached over for Dan's hand.

How formal, he thought, but she didn't shake it, she squeezed it, and the pressure against his own fingers, his own palm, was warm, almost intimate.

"Thank you," she said. "I thought I knew you from some-where—but you know, it's so frightening in a place like this. I don't know what he was thinking—you could have been anyone . . ." Apologizing for the way her eyes had narrowed.

The two Dans raised a hand to each other in a wave.

"See you on the plane," said Dan.

"I'm going to visit my grandma," said the little boy again.

Back in the bar, Dan bought another beer and reopened *Gulliver*, but the words tangled against each other and in the end he leaned back, drinking his way down through the cold drink. What time was it in London? Maybe the middle of the night, maybe the beginning of the next day. Caro would be asleep: he could see her room, its big window and the glow cast by the streetlamp outside. He could almost imagine the rise and fall of her breathing. He closed his eyes. Such a thing, to watch someone sleeping—there was trust in it, and vulnerability. He wondered if she'd ever sat and watched him; he liked the idea. It made him feel safe.

The time in Sydney was even harder to work out, his mind too numb to know how to try. Dan yawned, taking out Gramps's big round pocket watch in case it might still carry the trace of Sydney's time, all these years later. He sniffed—*stupid*—and looked around for an indicator board. He'd be there soon enough, he thought, even if it was another hour before he had to get back on the plane. Finishing his beer, he went in search of the bathrooms.

It felt risky to strip off and take a shower in the middle of an airport; there was something shocking about it. The water pierced the tired bits of his skin, sweaty from sitting strapped into a seat and doing nothing, and as his fingers fumbled with the carefully wrapped tablets of soap, Dan half expected someone to burst through the flimsy cubicle door. But the water was hot, and steamy, and endless, and he leaned against the side of the shower stall, his eyes closed. *Must take up all your attention to have a kid to look after, all the watching and the worrying.* But it wasn't the watching or the worrying, he knew. It was all the loving. He took a mouthful of the water, rinsing it around his teeth, around his gums, and spraying it out like a waterspout.

A decade; he'd been away more than a decade. And Caro was right: no matter how easy he always said it would be to take that twenty-four-hour flight home, he'd never taken it. He cricked his neck to the left, to the right, trying to steam the creases and aches out of it. He was always working over Christmas, and wanting a summer holiday in the northern hemisphere's summer—and if someone suggested New York, or Madrid, or Istanbul, it seemed silly to pass up the opportunity and fly back to Australia instead. He'd got promotions, mortgages, a group of mates he drank with on Fridays and Saturdays. And then there was Caroline. It was easy to stay in London. Never mind his predictable recitative: he should have called his mum more, should have called Charlie—he was good at saying he would and bad at dialing the number. Time slipped by.

His last day in Sydney, sitting at the edge of the harbor, on the steps that led down into the water straight under the bridge and its noise. He could see the shape of his feet, looking paler, smaller, and farther away through the water—Charlie's feet tinier still, her toes wiggling next to his.

"What do you reckon?" she'd asked. "Do you reckon you could dive in from up there?" Her head had arched so far back it should have cut her breath off. It was the one story she remembered her mother telling her, the one set of words through which she could find the sound of her mother's voice.

Dan shook his head again in the shower stall the way he'd shaken his head that day, and drips of water flew out around him. Too high, too far, too scary. He'd been scared enough, if he was honest, about getting onto a plane and buggering off to some city on the other side of the world. How old had they been? Twenty-five, twenty-six; so much an adult, he'd thought, wanting nothing and no one to get in the way of him and the world. He felt younger, less certain, now than he had then—not just because he was undressed and in the middle of an airport terminal. In the end, Charlie had kissed him on the cheek and sent him off in a cab to the airport. "I don't like all that waving and disappearing through barriers," she'd said. "I don't think you can do departures well if you're not going on a ship, with streamers snapping between the shore and the deck. And I've got stuff to do this afternoon."

He'd rung her as soon as he'd landed in London, rung her before he'd rung his mum. It was wrong the way her voice had sounded exactly the same as when she answered the phone from next door—except then they'd been able to hear each other down the line and over the fence simultaneously. She'd sounded so close in that conversation, and in the conversations that followed, dwindling down to fewer and fewer. *You just get busy.* Dry, dressed, he dialed her number again. He had no idea what time it was where she was—he had no idea, really, what time it was here either.

The recording was the same as ever, the same one he might have heard ten years ago, the same one he'd heard in London before he got on the plane. He heard himself leave almost the same message as he'd left earlier in reply—that he was coming home, that it would be great to see her, and bye. Then an afterthought, "And love to Gramps, of course. Tell him I'm waiting for some stories." This time, though, he said his own name twice at the beginning. As if she might not recognize his voice.

Pacing around the terminal, he glanced at the banks of watches and cameras he could buy, the litres and litres of alcohol, the boxes of chocolates that seemed inhumanly large, the multiple perfume shops that all sold the same things for the same prices. He should take something home—some perfume for his mum, some perfume for Charlie, a bottle of whisky for Gramps.

"Do you have anything that smells like white roses?" But that was Caro's perfume, and who was he buying for—Charlie, ahead of him, or Caroline, behind?

The young girl, thin herself in a paper-thin silk dress, frowned at him. "You know the name, sir?" He shook his head.

Walking towards the transit lounge again—it was unbelievable how much he wanted to be strapped back into his narrow seat and on his way—he chose a couple of magazines at random from a newsstand, one hand fumbling for his phone while the other fussed with unwanted change. He redialed Charlie's number without thinking and stood in the middle of the busy concourse, listening to it ring.

"Hello?"

"Charlie? Charlie? Hey, hi, it's Dan. Listen, I'll be home tomorrow—I don't know if you got my messages—and I'm just in Singapore staring at all these perfumes. Do you want me to get you something?"

"Dan?"

"Did you get my messages? I'm on my way. Charlie?"

"Dan. I'm sorry, my phone's been turned off. I haven't listened to any messages for a while. What did you say about perfume?"

"Are you all right, Charlie?"

"Your mother's here—did you want to talk to her?"

His mother? What time was it? "Sure—are you all right?" But she'd put her hand over the mouthpiece; he could hear something muffled, some discussion, and then his mother's voice saying, "No, no, just tell him I'll pick him up in the morning."

"It's an early flight," he said, as if his mother might hear. "It gets in at half-six or something I'll get a cab, really. Tell her I'll get a cab."

"Half-six," said Charlie, sounding like herself at last. "Half-six—listen to you, Mr. Britpop." A long pause. "Okay, so we'll see you tomorrow then?"

"Charlie, are you all right?"

"We'll see you tomorrow," she said again. "It's great you're coming." And the line clicked while he stood for a moment, watching the seconds tick by on his phone. He disconnected at last with the slightest pressure of his thumb, looked back towards the perfume shop—too hard—and then forward towards his gate.

The Russian woman and her father were just going in, the old man frail and hunched in a wheelchair with a hand-knitted blanket across his knees. What had they done to pass the time, Dan wondered, watching the woman struggle with her folder of passports, tickets, documents. Someone from the airline stepped towards the old man's chair, and the woman dropped everything—paper everywhere—putting her hands up: "No, no, please, I am fine, he is fine."

"A certificate, ma'am, you should really have a doctor's certificate so we know that it's all right for him to fly."

"We came through—we came to London. From London today.

There was no problem, there was nothing with this." She was trying to scoop everything off the floor and sort through it at the same time. "*Izvi'nite, pros'tite*, please, please."

"He looks so unwell—we just need a doctor to say it's all right for him to fly. You do understand, don't you?"

The old man, sallow and still until now, raised one hand as if he wanted to interject. His daughter dropped the folder of papers again as she tried to soothe him, to tuck his papery skin back under the blanket's woolly warmth.

"All right," said the flight attendant at last. "Come through here and we'll sort this out—we don't want to inconvenience everyone else." And she took Dan's boarding pass and slipped it abruptly through the electronic reader. "Mr. Kopek, thank you." She paused over the name. "Are you traveling with them?"

"No, no—well, yes, they were on the same plane as me coming from London."

"You're not Russian?"

"No—Australian."

"Good." She blushed. "I'm sorry—I didn't mean that. It's just so difficult with the language and no doctor and . . ." She waved her hands. "Sorry for the wait."

Walking towards the airbridge, he passed the Russians, tucked away to one side like a problem to think about later. He settled into his own seat; Cynthia appeared, settled back into hers.

"Nice break?" she asked, as if they'd both just taken a holiday.

"Nice," said Dan. The now-familiar family filed into its four seats, the smaller Dan asleep against his father's shoulder. His mother smiled across the aisle, raised her hand in half a wave towards Dan, and the plane filled up around them. Clipped into his belt, eyes forward, he could hear the flick of magazine pages as passengers anticipated their next movie, their next designated dinner and breakfast. And then came a sigh, like the sound that came with delayed trains in London's Underground, and people began to realize how long they'd been waiting.

They came along the aisle then, the younger woman, the frail older man, and two flight attendants arguing loudly with a man in a suit. "Without a certificate, Doctor, we really shouldn't let him get onto the plane. Without a certificate from his doctor, he really shouldn't be flying."

"She says he goes to Sydney for medical treatment," the doctor said, shrugging as he glanced at his watch. "She says they have flown this far already."

"But he looks . . ." One of the attendants gestured towards the old man. His skin was dull, his eyes closed, and his breathing shallow.

"Is just cold. Please," said his daughter, "there is a doctor for him in Sydney."

"He's flown this far," the doctor repeated. "I can't give you a certificate without an examination, and there's no time for that—but if he's come this far . . ."

The other attendant sighed. "All right," she said, "we've held everyone up long enough." And turning to the Russian woman: "Do you need help getting him settled? Do you need any extra blankets?"

The woman shook her head. "You are very kind," she said.

"Then let's get going."

As Dan learned again how to put on his life jacket, how to count the seats to his nearest exit, he felt the bustle and attention of the Russian lady settling her father. He could see the furrows of her frown, between the seats, but the expression beneath the frown was exactly that of the smaller Dan's mother when she'd turned and seen her little boy running towards her. And as he watched the Russian woman tuck the knitted blanket high around her father's throat, he thought suddenly, *It's Gramps—that's why Mum was there, whatever time it is. That's why Charlie's phone was off before.* He stared up at the seatbelt sign, bright and bossy, and his breath tightened. He wanted to call again, wanted to know. As the plane accelerated along the runway, he unclipped his seat belt and tried to stand up. Cynthia's hand reached over, making him sit down.

"There's nothing you can do," she said, inclining her head towards the father and daughter in front of them. "I'm sure it will be all right. Poor girl."

Dan leaned his head against the window again as the ground fell away, the asphalt, the city, the shape of the land. The clouds crowded in around him, and he lost the shape of Gramps's face in his memory. This time, he was certain he knew what that meant.

Us going up, he thought, *and Icarus coming down.* There was a painting of Icarus's foot disappearing into the water—Gramps had a postcard of it on his lowboy—and a farmer or two, a whole shipload of people, going about their day, not even noticing the splash. Dan wondered now where it had come from, who'd sent it. It had sat propped up on the little cupboard as long as he could remember, and he would have bet it would still be there. *These days,* he thought, *there'd be thousands of us up in the air in planes, maybe seeing something, maybe noticing something, two wings on fire, plummeting towards the water. Wondering what on earth we'd seen.* His eyes felt heavy; his legs twitched a couple of times.

He was asleep before the flight attendant had made her next announcement.

Inside the Cloud

THE WHITE was thick, heavy, and cold to the point of dampness; a hand held out from a face disappeared altogether and feet faded from view in the dense, still mist. It was quiet, and the clean smell of the air contradicted its solidity: it was ozone, or oxygen, or something pushed through purification.

From above, from some angles, tiny chinks opened to show the sudden sweep of an arm, the rush of running, the collision of a body with something hard, large, unexpected. But there was no noise, just the thick sound of silence.

~

In the dream, William Dawes counted his steps carefully. If he could get his bearings, if he could make out two fixed, distant points, he might calculate his position and work out where this strange space was. He sensed other movement, but could see nothing, and when he called out to hail whoever might be there—"Good morning"; he still didn't know how to say it in the natives' language—the silence swallowed his voice down to nothing. Perhaps he'd been up in the Frenchman's balloon at last; perhaps he'd fallen out, his descent broken by this landscape of clouds.

He stopped a moment, completely motionless, and eased his fingers, outstretched like a specimen of a starfish, away from his face until they too disappeared. It was a surprising relief that they reappeared when he drew his wrist back in towards his body. If he squinted, he could make out the shape of a rainbow through this thick fog, although it seemed a more solid curve—maybe it was the roundness of a far-off English hill, and he had dreamed himself back home.

He took a step back, and another, straining to hear the sound of footsteps, whether they were his own or someone else's, and found his back up hard against something solid. He slid down, crouching, and prepared to wait.

In the dream, Ted Parker was making his way down from the top of the bridge. It had become an endless climb and Joy was so far ahead of him she was already home. The night had ended and the dawn had come up through greys, silvers, until at some point all its color and shape had faded completely and he was left in this blanketing mist, wondering how many more steps he needed to take until his feet reached the ground, reached the grass, reached the shore. One foot carefully in front of the other—he had no sense of how far he'd come, even if he was still heading down or had tricked himself somewhere and made a turn, to ascend again. If he could just get a glimpse of the horizon, of the coast, he could orient himself with the east and know the way home.

He stopped a moment, listening for his own breath, his own sigh, but the whiteness seemed to have leached all the sound from the world as well as its color. He eased his fingers away from his face, their five points flexed like a starburst, and he flinched when they brushed against something smooth, solid, impenetrable. He turned, his back hard against it, his eyes scouring the white space above him for anything—a glimpse of the sun, a star, a lantern on a porch or on a ferry—anything that wasn't cloud. He made himself breathe slowly and evenly: *If this was happening when I was awake,* he thought distinctly, *I'd be scared by now.* He counted beats as he breathed: in, two, three; out, two, three. Slow, easy, gentle, like dancing with Joy on the unfinished half of the arch. *I'm sitting on top of the world,* he sang to his breathing's waltz, but the song made no sound.

He could see it now, above him, as he looked up—the arch, closed and complete, it seemed; a heavier shape against the whiteness that encased him. He laughed, no sound either. Back on the ground after all, but who knew where? Whether it was from fear or anticipation, every bone in his body ached.

~

In the dream, Dan Kopek was outside the plane, the great metal cylinder long gone so that he stood, clumsy but secure, on a cushion of cloud, and wondered how he was supposed to get home now. His arm pushed forward, fingers spread like a firework's flare and as wide as they could go. He watched as he moved them away from himself, saw them swallowed by the white. It felt cold, and clean, and almost wet—he'd have to remember to tell Charlie—and while some sections twirled around him like long, languid ribbons, others billowed, inviting comparisons. There was a boat. There was an angel. There was the great big curve of Gramps's bridge; a little knot of clouds down below even made the complementary geometry of the city's famous Opera House. Dan laughed, swallowing hard when he realized he made no sound. *Some dream,* he thought; *some trip.* He tried to pull a chunk of the whiteness away from itself, but his fingers slid straight through.

He began to walk, in his regular gait at first, and then more cautiously, more tentatively, his hands still lost somewhere out in front of him. Was he walking up, or down, or through? Was there a right direction? Was there a wrong one? He blew, gently at first and then more vigorously as a tiny space seemed to open out in front of him. He was sure there was someone nearby. He was sure that wherever this was, it was familiar. He was sure something was about to happen, and he hoped he'd be able to see whatever it was through the viscous, continuous white.

~

In the space below the southeast pylon of the bridge, Charlie had tried to make herself invisible, speaking only when spoken to and standing back from the digging and the shouting. Every so often, she'd dart forward, grabbing a shot of a hand, a find, a moment. Another yell, and the fill in the first of the honeycomb of holes shook free. *Just like Gramps said*, she thought, clicking frame after frame. Here was the beginning of the lattice through which great steel cables had anchored the bridge's two halves to the ground.

"Long way to go down yet," said one of the workers, and Charlie nodded.

"A hundred and eighteen feet long, and a hundred feet down," she said, and then: "My grandfather worked on it. I grew up with all his stories."

The man smiled at her. "Must add something to being here, knowing we're digging down to where he was all those years ago. Never know what else we'll find while we're here, eh? They found an old brick from 1789 when they were digging round here for the bridge in the first place."

And Charlie smiled in turn. "I know—the old observatory, I guess."

She zoomed in on the man's hand as it rested against a curved block of sandstone. The grain of his skin mimicked the grain of the stone. It was a nice assignment, and it was exciting to see things coming up to the surface again—Gramps'd be even more excited when she told him. She raised her lens—the grain of stone, of skin, lay over the harbor's surface as well, ruffled into the water by the breeze.

"What'd be great," she said, "would be finding some way of being able to dig back through time as well as space, don't you think? So you got moments, not just relics."

"I'll take the relics," said the man, laughing. "I mean, a moment's made an impression if it's left anything behind for us, snooping around years later, looking for evidence and leftovers. A bit of plate, an old brick, the dregs of a fire. We're lucky to dig that stuff up—and if we could find the kind of thing you're talking about, I don't know what sort of camera you'd need to make pictures of it."

Behind her lens, Charlie focused tight on the man's face—right into his eyes—snapping the shot just as he finished speaking. As close as she could get, and she'd no idea what thought lay behind his gaze. On the bridge, two trains passed each other up in the air, their clatter swelling the stream of cars, the voices on the site, the boats on the water. For a minute, it seemed as if all the noise that had ever happened in this place had come back in one deafening roar—machines and tools and men and activity; there was even something like a shot, which must have been a car backfiring somewhere. Charlie almost wanted to cover her ears. Then the trains passed, the traffic dulled; the calls and conversations on the site settled down. She panned back through the last dozen or so shots she'd taken. A couple were good: the symmetrical patterns of the man's hand and the stone, the shadowy space of the first gaping hole that had taken the bridge's weight. But the eyes told her nothing at all. Her finger moved automatically towards delete, but she paused, looking up as she felt a cold wind from the south and saw a bank of cloud shift and obscure the sun. *Keep it*, she thought. *See what it looks like tonight.*

Her hand cupped around the display, her head bent in towards it, she caught a movement from the corner of her eye, and she raised her camera to catch whatever it was in one smooth, reflex action. But it must have been the swing of a tool or the wave of an arm; the site was busy, but there was nothing unusual.

"See that fog come in on the weekend?" she heard someone call below her. "Real pea-souper; I could hardly see to take a step in front of me." Pointing her camera towards the sky, Charlie turned away from the conversation about sea mist and shot at random, to find waiting for her when she looked at her day's work that night a perfect image of the bridge, high and curved, a billowing bank of cloud above, and the blurred streak of a bird, a shadow, cutting down towards the harbor. Must have had it on a slower speed than she'd meant to; she'd let way too much light and movement in. But when she looked through her shots again the next morning, there was no sign of a dive, or a fall.

Tired, she'd thought. *I've got to stop working when I'm tired.*

That was weeks ago now—before Gramps, before everything else. Now, she was more tired than ever before, and the bridge lurked, a mighty and complicated mess.

From above, from some angles, it looked like a dance: the breeze came in from the east and as the whiteness thinned here and there it showed, from a bird's-eye view, the bright spot of William Dawes's scarlet coat, the grey dot of Ted Parker's hat, the blue gash of Dan Kopek's bag. Three men, stepping in and away, with no sense of each other and no fix on where they were. Three men, breathing deep and counting the space between in and out: one, two, three; one, two, three.

Three men asleep in their own pieces of space and time.

In the dream, William Dawes watched as the clouds arranged themselves into the now recognizable topography of Sydney's harbor, and there at the heads a great ship, long-awaited, rose up, all sails and provisions: letters, tea, candles, vinegar, shoe leather, new people. Everything Sydney's heart desired.

In the dream, Ted Parker watched as the clouds arranged themselves into the cords and struts of his bridge, white shapes of men moving on white lengths of steel, and the luminous-white sparks of rivets sailing off every so often like secret shooting stars.

In the dream, Dan Kopek watched as the clouds turned back into the clouds he'd watched through the plane window as he left London; there was the plane's wing, made of cloud itself, and the inside ledge of his window. Leaning forward, he hunted for his own reflection—and when his forehead tapped the hard, thick surface, he pulled back.

There was noise then, high and distinct and separate from the silence. It was air rushing, and each man turned towards its sound—they were facing each other, if they'd been able to see, for a moment, through the white.

From above, from the cloud, something was falling, quick and straight. *It's my comet*, thought William Dawes, *at last*.

It's the next part of my dream, thought Ted Parker. *I'll get to see what happens.*

It's the story about Gramps, thought Dan Kopek, *flying off the bridge and down into the water.*

One, two, three.

The whiteness closed around the end of the movement. The three men paused, stretching and yawning.

The silence held.

Dawes

BY MIDMORNING, the thick mist William Dawes had woken to had burned off, leaving a heavier than usual saltiness that made him lick his lips as if he was parched. He sniffed at the last of the heavy air, trying to place where he'd smelled that smell before. What he should do, he thought, was devise a way of measuring such fog—a funnel, a piece of string, a bottle, and some scales. He'd try it tonight.

In the columns of his meteorological journal, Dawes ruled off his usual notes of times and temperatures, set the journal's loose sheets of paper square, and sat for a moment in the cool dark room of his observatory, blinking a little and flexing his fingers in time with the ticking of the pocket watch. The pages made quite a stack now, days and days quantified in terms of heat and wind and thunder and water. More than a year of full records—more than a year without a comet. And almost exactly a year since the bright flares of the aurora australis had lit up the sky like the cataclysmic interruption feared by Gulliver's Laputans. Perhaps that at least would come around again this season.

To his right, on his desk, other journals lay ready for words transcribed from his conversations with the natives—they were beginning to talk, so long after the British arrival, and under the most dismal circumstances. There was a pox among these natives, yet not among the settlers. A few had been brought in—so ill, so diseased—to be nursed, but mostly the white men had only bodies to deal with, lying on beaches, floating in the water, washing ashore. The Governor had sent special recovery parties rowing around the harbor, to bring them in, to bury them.

The sickness had brought in Boorong, a bright young girl who'd been steered towards the vicar so that he could find out, as the Governor put it, what these people think; what these people believe.

But the vicar was not a man with any "facility for languages," so she'd been passed on to the obliging Lieutenant Dawes, always ready to pick up the tasks that others couldn't manage. Can you map this town? Can you draw this coast? Can you name this plant? Can you explain this weather? Can you count these steps and measure this plain, this gorge, this track? Can you count these steps and tell us where we are? "Can you talk to her, Lieutenant Dawes, discover her beliefs, and share with her our own? Can you introduce her to God?"

His *facility for languages*.

He wanted to ask about the harbor, its trees, its rocks, its habits. And he wanted to ask about *mawn*—that word he'd heard at the end of his long-ago dance, tripping and falling against the sense of something swooping down from the clouds and into the harbor. He'd waited for it ever since, like that comet, and once or twice with such a sense of anticipation that he'd taken himself down to the waterline and stood there as if it would appear at any moment. Once or twice too he'd caught the tail end of a splash—"A fish," said the surgeon; "Just a fish," said Tench—and wished he'd turned a little earlier.

Dawes folded a sheet in half and in half again, down to a long narrow strip. She'd be waiting for him, his student, his new teacher. Leaving the observatory, he looked over towards the settlement's new magazine, a thick-walled room of gunpowder being built nearby, its bricks stamped with the year's date. As the colony's engineer, on top of everything else, Dawes was the officer in charge of artillery and fortifications.

"Does it make you feel safe down here, sir," the surgeon had joked as the magazine's walls thickened and raised, "sitting here with your own cache of powder?"

He passed the hospital, the barracks, the place where lawbreakers' lives were taken, each place now well-established, and each more than a little scruffy and patched. And he wondered which words he and his charge might exchange, what glimpses they might have had of each other's worlds by sunset.

But the exchange was not supposed to be about this place, what was here, or anything that swooped or splashed; it was to exchange Anglican belief for antipodean. And so Dawes heard himself making sentences about the authority of God as it was invested in the King, and the authority of the King as it was invested in the parliament, in the Governor, but not in a way that should imply that anyone other than the King—or God, for that matter—was like God, was godlike. And then there was the star and the birth and the water and the wine and the bread and the body and the cross.

". . . Which brings us to the resurrection," he said at last, drawing a deep breath and leaning back a little.

"Re—" She started to shape the syllables, turning each into a distinct word. And she laughed as she faltered between them, tapping at her own chest then. "Boorong," she said instead. "Mr. Dawes," confirmed William Dawes. They tilted their heads slightly towards each other, these two polite envoys.

Tell me something, thought Dawes. *Tell me anything—any word, any phrase.* He smiled, pointing through the doorway towards the sky. "A god?" And as he spoke the air rattled with an eerie noise, a grating metallic thunder.

The change was immediate, the smile gone and a kind of blank fear in her eyes. "*Mawn*," she said, and like the girl he'd danced with, she made a beak from her hand, held it high in the air, and then swooped it down so it grabbed at her throat. "*Mawn*," she said, but softly, as if she didn't want it to hear her. Were they scared of it happening, of some terrible presence sweeping in—or was it what they hoped would happen, swooping through and wiping the British away like the sun burning off a salty mist?

"This *mawn*," said William Dawes, "this . . ." He made the same swoop with his hand down towards his own neck. "You see it?" Pointing to his eyes. "You hear it?" Pointing to his ears.

"*Naa*," she said, pointing to her eyes, "*naa*."

"You see it," said Dawes slowly, pointing to his own eyes: "*Naa?*"

And she smiled. From his pocket, Dawes took his notebook. "*Naa?*" he repeated, pointing from his eyes out across the room. "To see?" He and the girl nodded in unison. It seemed a nicer word than this swooping, clutching, frightening *mawn*. The girl nodded again as he leaned forward and wrote.

A breath of wind caught a page on the table between them, lifting it quietly, gently, and easing it down towards the ground—his hand shot out, two fingers grabbing at its edge as it hovered on the air. He put it back, square and careful. A pause, and then the same thing again—the page rising, floating, fluttering, and Dawes's fingers snapping it in, putting it down. And a pause, and again—and this time, he heard something as well. She was giggling, her face and her eyes lit up. He put the page down and put the Bible he was supposed to be consulting on top of it as a weight, feeling the next puff of air that was after his paper. Across the table, the girl was quiet, and as Dawes looked up he saw her lips pursed and blowing, softly, softly, before—caught—she pressed her lips together and gave him her biggest smile.

There was no more thunder.

"It floats," he said, smiling himself. "It flies." Flapping his fingers like a bird's wings. And the girl laughed again, nodding.

That night, Dawes began his daily conversation with Portsmouth.

Dear Miss Rutter, of course, and then, *We began to talk properly today*—naa, *the first word: to see. It's the Governor's hope that I can talk about religion—of course, more importantly, about ours. But I have to say we spent most of today laughing, so I will have to be more careful with my parables and apostles in the morning.*

He had imagined it sometimes, coming back to New South Wales, a married man and a teacher; he had even imagined his wife, Mrs. Judith Dawes. But he'd never imagined who he might teach. Now, against the darkness of his little room, he saw who was sitting at his rough school benches. Students like Boorong, with bright smiles and bright eyes and lists and lists of new words that they could teach him—whatever he might teach them. Students who laughed as they made the objects in his world fly.

~

Later, called to account for his time with his young pupil, to provide information for one of the long dispatches prepared over months for whenever a ship might sail back into the world with it, Dawes watched as the Governor's secretary curved his hand in a sweeping arc across a clean sheet of paper. All clear, said the gesture, all ready.

What might go into that letter? wondered Dawes, knowing he still had little to report of the philosophies and beliefs that the Governor wanted to pour forth like confectionery into the cupped hands of London's gentlemen—let alone a comet. *Tell them about the things we see and the things we think we see*, he thought. *Tell them what it is to live with no news from England, from anywhere. Tell them of our strange landscape of poxed bodies washing ashore, and that we've put on a play, with a length of colored paper and a handful of candles in a hut. Tell them how we loved it, how we loved pretending.* For all of which, he knew he was one of the few officers who'd asked to stay longer if he could—there was still so much to see, and his certainty about Miss Rutter was fading as inexorably as an often-caressed picture in a locket.

"Lieutenant Dawes?"

"Sir. I wonder if it might be appropriate to say that we begin to make some way with the language—there are several lists of words coming together now between us."

The Governor's scribe dipped his pen into ink and turned to his master, who said, "We should perhaps wait until we can send the lists themselves. What else?"

"There are the stars, sir."

"But still not that comet of yours, Dawes?" It was getting to be something of a joke.

"I mean the natives' knowledge of stars, sir. If they follow prey through the forests, it seems they use the skies to find their way home. They have names for the Clouds of Magellan that we have taken down already. I am sure no one would mind giving up the words from their lists ahead of their own publications, if it was for some official dispatch."

The Governor slapped at an insect that had perched on his leg. The impossibility of finding things to say when all you really wanted to post home was another long shopping list. Dawes's comet would have been something—if it had ever turned up. The natives' stars were perhaps less important than some pleasing conversion of their souls. But one must send information—always information. He turned to the man with the ink, the pen, the pause. "And have you put down that the natives are harmless, that they avoid those parts we most frequent, that they always retire at the sight of two or three people armed?" The secretary flicked back through his pages, nodding along.

If he stood quietly, William Dawes could still make all the trappings and incisions of this frail little place disappear. The great gashes left where trees had been worried out and pits dug for rocks, for clay. The tents and huts that would only need a single puff of imagination to wipe them away, and the settlement itself, straggling at spots from Sydney Cove and out along the river now to pretty-sounding Rose Hill and beyond. Even the brick walls of the Governor's new house, with its luxurious stairs, its shimmering glass window panes that threw small new rainbows at certain times of the day, its pictures of the royal family brought around the world to impress whoever was found here: it could all be pulled at one end so it unraveled like a fraying cloth.

On one expedition, walking farther west than any Englishman had yet walked in this place and returned, Dawes had looked back across the fifty-odd miles to the coast, towards the settlement, and almost relished its invisibility. *We may all perish, and all evidence of us would be swept from the face of this earth in no time.* Like Roanoke. Even here in the Governor's rooms, he could finish that sweeping away in an instant. It was a glorious daydream, every little piece of change and settlement that they'd made—and made so hard—winding back and back until the harbor was as quiet and as empty as when they'd first come.

"Dawes! Honestly, here I am looking for your opinion, sir, and I find you in the clouds. Now, what knowledge of their beliefs have you managed to extract from this child you are talking to? What does she know now of ours?"

Dawes straightened to attention again. "I'm sorry, sir. I've told her many things about our church, and our worship, but it's mostly laughter that she gives back." Which, he thought, was not altogether a bad trade.

"Laughter." The Governor let out a long, slow breath.

". . . 'graves comma but the body in the'—I think we have something here already?" said the secretary, resting his pen and going on in the formal voice of recitation: " 'And the question has been asked, do the white men go thither?' "

"All right," said the Governor. "So that's all for now—other than that we are here, we are waiting, that we expect at least five hundred men to be sent for the garrison, and that we have had nothing of the world since 1787. I have gravestones for enough of us already, with the parson still waiting for a church. But if I push anyone to build it at the moment I'm afraid there'll only be the funerals of the builders for him to officiate over. And still I have officers who can't row around the harbor without losing their bearings. Even the Judge-Advocate says he has moments of panic wondering where he is." He was talking into a corner of the room, as if Dawes had already gone, and his finger hovered over the point that marked South Head on his map, where men were now posted to scan the horizon for the supply ships the settlement so desperately needed to appear.

Three times he tapped it, as if performing some incantation, before he looked up and said to his lieutenant, "I think that's all?"

And as Dawes made his salute and stepped outside, he heard the Governor's voice—"Read the last back to me"—and the slug of something pouring into a mug. It would be months before the letter could be sent, months before they'd send their next messages back into the world. "Just the section on future state, would you?"

The sound of the secretary clearing his throat rattled and rasped against the air: " 'That they have some idea of a future state appears from their belief in spirits, and from saying that the bones of the dead are in the graves, but the body in the clouds: and the question has been asked, do the white men go thither?' "

Do the white men go thither, thought Dawes, stepping onto one of those presumptuous streets he'd marked out and turning towards the laughing girl and whatever she wanted to tell him today. *The body in the clouds.*

Walking on, he crossed Sydney's precious stream on its flimsy bridge of logs, a structure celebrated as so civilized and settled when it had been installed more than a year before. The stream was close to exhausted. He looked along the shoreline towards his point, his white-roofed building in the distance, and there it was again, that sense of anticipation, of something about to happen, right here and right now—if he could only imagine what. *The bodies in the clouds*, he thought, a little flippantly. *Maybe sometimes they slip and fall.* He shrugged to himself, and ducked inside, sitting down opposite Boorong.

"Mr. Dawes," said the girl, smiling. Smiling back, he took up a pencil, held it at the height of his eyes for a moment, then let it go so it fell to the ground with a clatter.

"To drop," he said carefully. "To fall." He repeated the action.

The girl nodded. "*Yini*," she said, tracing the line of the fall with her finger. "*Yiningmadyémi.*"

Dawes repeated the words, transcribing them as best he could into his notebook. "*Yiningmadyémi?*"

"*Yiningmadyémi*," said the girl. And she pointed at Dawes. "*Muramadyémi*," she said. You let it fall.

Taking a deep breath, William Dawes bent forward and scraped the heavy table across the rough floor. The room filled with a sharp sound, harsh and jarring, and opposite him Boorong tensed and flinched.

"Your *mawn*," he said slowly, replicating her gesture of beaked fingers swooping down towards a throat, and she nodded. He pointed outside to the sunshine. "It comes now?"

She nodded, and then shrugged, closing her eyes and tilting her head. "*Nangadiou*," she said, making a dainty snore.

"I see," he said. "It comes at night too, when we sleep. And it comes with a strange noise." He frowned. "Like a bird?" He pointed to a parrot, its colors looping against the blue outside, and she shook her head.

"*Goo-me-dah*," she said, shivering a little.

"A ghost?" he asked. "A spirit?" Wondering what sound or action he could make to clarify this. "*Goo-me-dah*," he repeated at last, sounding out its syllables. A ghost that comes day or night. He paused, then stood quickly, gesturing for her to follow, and together they climbed the hill towards the British graveyard. "Spirits from the dead?" he asked, pointing to one of the graves. "*Mawn?*"

She looked around, anxious and unsure. Yes. And then she reached over, squeezing the flesh on his forearm and pointing up, squeezing the bone in his index finger, pointing down.

"Yes," he said, "yes: the bones in the ground and the bodies in the clouds—perhaps like our resurrection." He stared at the rows of graves. Early on, when their burials were newer, fresher, some of these graves had been disturbed, opened twice, three times. "Dogs," the Governor had said, ordering their repair. But perhaps, thought Dawes now, his mind stumbling like it was taking quick, impulsive footsteps, perhaps there was something literal about the passage of the bodies to the clouds—*here in my place where anything could happen*. He clicked his jaw, his ears filling with a roar of air: you could think the strangest things.

"The bones in the ground and the bodies in the clouds," he repeated at last, turning back to Boorong. "And the spirits . . ." he began, his hand rising in unison with hers, the two of them swooping down. And they stood together under the day's sun, watching each other in a silence as thick as ocean fog.

Ted

THERE WERE moments sometimes in the middle of a shift, the middle of a day, when for all the noise and machinery and movement around him, Ted was sure he heard the site fall silent. His mum would have said he'd just fallen into a daydream—at least once a week someone had to yell to break his trance: "Oi, Teddy, here." But Ted thought it was nicer to imagine that some kind of synchronized lull, some moment of harmony had come onto this big and busy thing and made a pause, a breath, a nothingness. He never noticed the exact moment the quiet began, only when it was there, thick, and then, a moment later, all the usual sounds crashing in again.

He wondered if the bridge's retinue of artists noticed it, tucked around the site with their pencils, their paints, their cameras; he noticed them more now, after his conversation with the lady under her black umbrella. He'd even taken some of the photographers out on the barge and seen them hoisted up into the creeping structure of the bridge above. He didn't mind the ease with which other people went up into the air so much, now that he'd stood up in that air himself, but he still made the occasional grumble to mask the excursion—heard Joy doing it too.

He wondered if the passengers on the ferries noticed these random patches of quiet as they looked up to see how much further the enterprise was reaching each day. He wondered if the people who lived close to the bridge noticed it—the people tucked into those houses left when great swathes of space were cleared to accommodate its construction, or the children at their desks in the school nearby. Such a racket most of the time; did anyone ever manage to dim it down to background noise? Or was that what his mind had managed to do, when the world fell into silence, just once in a while, and unpredictably?

On some of those nights in the backyard at Joe and Joy's it had been on the tip of his tongue to ask if anyone else registered these stillnesses—but that would be like saying something about the beauty of the thing; the kind of sentence that got stuck somewhere, not quite said. Although, "It's even more beautiful once you've been up there at night, don't you think?" Joy had whispered once under a wash of gripes and boasts and explanations in the yard. It felt dangerous to leave the words hanging in the air.

Then George, the Russian, had said something about his months walking east to the Sea of Japan, keeping warm in winter, about watching the different shapes of snowflakes come down and settle on the pure, clear, whole white, and the rest of the group sucked at their beer bottles and brought up the football match that would be played on the weekend. *He heard*, thought Ted, *he heard what we said—and he said the closest thing he could say to beauty.*

It felt different too walking out now after tea to look at the stars, not least because Joe had given up on his astronomy—"Too many nights staring up for no reason," he said—and now stayed at home to have the teapot ready for them. "Get your shooting stars? Any sign of my comet?" he'd ask as they came through the gate.

It only magnified Ted's sense that they were walking around in a secret.

"You're quiet now," said Joy one night—the "now' a faint indication that she'd noticed something had changed since their climb. "Too cold? Or are you tired?" They were insignificant reasons for silence, back in the context of the here and the now.

Stopping a block or two before the usual loop of their circuit, Ted shook his head. "It's not that," he said. "I don't know. It's just that I feel like I'm still waiting for something to happen—and I thought when we climbed . . ."

"I know," she said quietly. "I thought it would be more too; I thought it would make me feel more." But as he opened his mouth to ask her what she meant, she was already turning for home. "It is colder tonight, though. I could do with an early cuppa."

And there was the kettle, steaming and ready, even though they were at least a quarter of an hour early—as if Joe could always see where they were, and knew exactly when they'd come through the gate.

"Nothing like tea on a cold night," he said. And Ted believed, at that moment, that there must be nothing in the world of Joy that her husband didn't see, didn't hear, didn't know about.

It would be something, he thought, *to have someone who took care of you like that.*

≈

As the winter thickened and the bridge's halves inched closer to each other, Ted's mum still worried about the math for that magical moment of meeting being done half a world away in London by men who'd never seen where the big frame would sit, let alone how its two sections were supposed to join up. She even took the train to the city to see it herself, as if that might somehow make up for the absence of the mathematicians ("Engineers, Mum," Ted corrected her), and pronounced it unlikely that the south side and north side would connect. "When you look at it from this angle, you can see just how squiffy that north side is, can't you? Can't you?"

"I do think this harbor's capable of a miracle or two, Mrs. Parker," said Joy. It was a Saturday, and the three of them had taken their skeptical visitor to the place from where, Joe declared, it looked most like it would line up. "That group over on the north side waiting for the Second Coming—they believed their savior was going to walk right in through the heads."

"I think you're pulling my leg about that too, dear," said Mrs. Parker, taking another of Joy's sandwiches.

"No, no, Mrs. Parker, whenever I went—"

"Have a bit of cake, Mrs. Parker," said Joe over the top of Joy's enthusiasm. And he cut a hefty slice of sponge.

"It's better than a birthday," said Mrs. Parker, looking around for her tea.

Later, on the platform, as the train's engine puffed great clouds of steam around itself, she brushed at Ted's arm and said again how nice it was he'd fallen on his feet with his landlords. "And I guess we must just hope that they take as long as they can to get those pieces joined together and finish the thing off, because who knows where you'll find work next, Ted, or how long that'll take you. And you could do worse than find yourself a nice girl like that," nodding down to the square of sponge Joy had given her for the trip home. "You should see if she's got a sister." She winked as Ted turned scarlet.

She squeezed his hand—an uncharacteristic closeness—and told him to be careful on the water. He could still feel the warmth her fingers had pressed into his palm as the train pulled away and took the tracks' first curve.

Heading home—Joe and Joy with held hands swinging between them, and Ted on the curbside of the pavement like a canoe's outrigger—they stopped at a pool that abutted the harbor's water where a group of the bridge men were gathered. It was a diving contest, a handful of them scaling the high towers, and standing poised, rigid, for a second, a breath, before they tumbled and turned and straightened and disappeared into the water below. Russian George was there, his new wife whispering about the midnight trip they'd made to explore the bridge, and two or three of the other blokes who drank beer in the backyard.

It made no sense to Joe, diving: that a man who spent his working day gripping on for dear life should pass some of his weekend—"Voluntarily, mate, quite voluntarily"—falling off something.

"Diving off," Joy would correct him—and Joe would wave his arms about, saying, "Diving, falling, dropping: makes no difference what you call it, love. It comes down to the same thing." But Joy had promised one of the boys they'd be there to watch him. "He's excited," she'd said, "and it must be exciting to do this, don't you think? Fly through the air?" And here they were, Joe distracting himself with the view out past the pool to the harbor's blue, and a loud conversation about the brilliance of Bradman's batting during the recent English Tests.

"This bloke coming down now went off the top of a crane's rig at one of the docks," someone leaned over and said to Joy. Then, "What do you reckon, Teddy—would you be up for it?"

Ted shook his head, watching the tiny ripples the breeze made across the harbor's surface. "It'd be planes for me if I wanted to get through the air. Aren't they amazing, the way they glide and turn?" They'd had Amy Johnson over the two halves of the bridge a week or so before; now someone was running a book on whether they'd get Charles Kingsford Smith back to the harbor before the arch was done. "It'd be interesting if you could remember what you saw when you were going down," he said at last, to no one in particular, "but I guess you'd be so scared you wouldn't remember a thing." As he blinked, he saw the rush of movement, the flash of blue, from his dream.

"Good job you're on the barges then, mate," said the bloke next to him, bringing him out of his reverie. "Out of the way of temptation—here's another." The diver, his arms held out from his steeled body like a crucifix, had only the tips of his toes holding him onto the deck. Tall, broad-shouldered, with thick curly hair, he looked like a frame frozen from a movie, and then he pushed himself back and away from the tower, legs and arms coming in together like a pincer before he straightened himself out to drop down, down, down like an arrow into the water. The surface of the pool was hardly disturbed. Joy clapped and whooped.

"Wasn't that Kelly?" she called. "Roy Kelly? That one you said dives some lunchtimes round the bridge? He's got the grace of a bird." Joe made a snorting noise. "But look, look, here we go." Her boy, from the backyard—the one they were there to clap for—was climbing the ladder and creeping out to the end of the deck. "I hope he remembers to breathe," said Joy quietly, watching his steps become more and more tentative the closer he came to the open air.

He reached the end of the platform, his toes curling down around the deck as if to remind himself there really was nothing in front of him, and he stood—arms extended but facing out and away from the tower—for almost too long before he seemed to bounce forward, no turns, no twists, and plunge towards the pool.

"Get yourself straight," Ted heard Kelly call from among the audience, a thick towel around his neck. But the boy hit the water with his legs flailing and part of his back flat against its surface. The splash was enormous.

"Eeooww," said Joy, "maybe we shouldn't tell him we saw that." But there he was, dripping and proud in the middle of them in less than a minute, his eyes bright and his towel draped exactly like all the other men's: one of the club now, one of the gang.

"You'd love it," he whispered to Joy. "Like flying, Mrs. Brown, like flying for a bit."

"All I'm saying," said Joe, standing up and making a point of adjusting his sleeves and his hat to indicate that he, for one, was ready to go home, "is that if Bradman keeps making three hundred, the Poms won't get a look-in. Ready, love?"

There was another splash—a flat, slapping noise—as another inexpert diver hit the surface of the pool. Ted and Joy winced at the same time, both back on the bridge, in the middle of the night, when Joy's shoe was lost to the wet darkness. The size of that sound, that splash.

"Terrible," called Kelly from the side, but he slapped the diver on the back and wished him better luck next time—"And get yourself straight, lad"—as the boy climbed out of the pool and made for his towel. The winter sun was dipping towards the horizon, and Joy linked one arm through Joe's, one arm through Ted's, called her last encouragement to the young man they'd come to see, and went out through what was left of the afternoon's glow. She hummed Ted's top-of-the-world song as she went, looking up towards the clouds as though more men might come diving from the sky.

And trusting us to lead her home, thought Ted.

⁓

From below, from some angles, it looked like a dance. Waiting for one of the foremen in the shadow of the southeastern pylon, Ted ruffled Jacko's ears and wondered if he recognized the donor of one of his nicest chops. "A lucky mutt, aren't you, mate?" Twirling the soft fur around in his fingers. It felt like velvet.

On a clear day, the sun would be high: at midday, the bridge cast one straight line of shadow across the water, an exact transposition of where it sat. It was one arch now, its two arms eased together, despite everyone's skepticism, across days and nights of work peppered with temperatures rising and falling, the steel expanding and contracting, and all sorts of other distractions. There was even a whale, surfacing beneath the metal and sending a great spray of water up into the air. "Thought we were in for a bath," said Joe to Ted, who'd missed seeing the waterspout and couldn't work out how to ask someone to describe it so he could see if it matched the nocturnal spray he and Joy had heard.

And then at last, after the drama of an appropriately magnificent thunderstorm, the central joint had eased in, locked together on its pins, the bridge's keystone. "Thank God she's home," said the man in charge of her construction.

"Home and hosed, mate," said Ted now to the dog, glancing up at the darkening sky that had faded the arch's shadow to such a smudge on the water that he thought he might only be remembering what it should look like, and was seeing that instead.

Almost two months since those halves met, and the roadway was now hanging delicately underneath, working its way back out from the center to the two original points north and south. "And a damn sight more exposed that feels than the stuff higher up ever did," said Joe.

"The sense you had, up the top," Joe had said after a beer too many one night when Joy was inside and away from his anxiety, "that you had magnets in your feet, spending so long crawling across the thing, working your way along its steel, so you knew exactly where to stand, and how, and for how long, and how to step away and move." He couldn't have said how they'd all learned that, but they had. "We knew what we were missing when we went from working on the arch to hanging the deck, and we had no idea what was going on anymore."

He'd heard one of the engineers talking about it one day.

"I'm used to the height," Joe heard him say, "you grow with it. But when we started putting in the roadway, well, we only had a flimsy rope alongside, and the steel was only about twenty-two inches across—"

"Which'd be right," Joe confirmed. "It'd be about right."

"—and all studded with rivet heads. Now with the shimmer of light on the water giving it that lovely mackerel surface," the man had said, "it was suddenly all very confusing. I tell you, I felt most insecure for a while and I reckon that was about the first time I felt the height."

"Reckon that's what we all felt too," Joe said, knocking the top off another bottle of lager. The arch was one thing: gentle and elegant, but sturdy somehow. This roadway was just sheer, suspended, midair folly. And everyone seemed more anxious about hanging on as the rivets popped in. "Like we knew we were asking for trouble," Joe finished at last, shutting himself up with a long draught as Joy came out through the back door.

"Maybe that's because a road through the air makes less sense than a curve," Ted had suggested quietly, smoothing the wrinkles along the arm of his jumper as if he could transfer the smoothness to the job for Joe and his mates. Looking up from the barge, the roadway did seem to swing and float, impossibly fine and delicate.

"Like a rainbow," said Joy, hearing the end of his sentence.

"Like the rising sun on an army badge," said Joe.

"Like a big hill floating in the middle of the flatness," said Ted, and Joe mussed his hair as if he was a kid—mussed his hair just as Ted now mussed Jacko's ears.

"What d'you reckon, mate?" Ted leaned down and looked at the steel from a height that was closer to the dog's perspective. "What would a dog think it looked like?"

The dog seemed to consider the question, its head on one side and its gaze as clearly focused as Ted's was. Their eyes followed the movement of different pockets of the bridge's workers, Ted's fingers tapping the time they kept on Jacko's back, and Jacko's tail keeping his own time to the bridge's rhythm. Their noses both caught the first smells of early lunches being cooked up here and there. Their skins, one smooth, one furry, felt the warmth of the spring sun behind the clouds—it was the end of October—and both bristled a little as that warmth disappeared behind a thicker, colder cloud.

And in one of those moments, one of those blissfully quiet moments when everything fluttered down to silence, Ted felt the dog's hackles stiffen under his hand, felt his own frame freeze to tautness.

Someone was falling; someone was falling off the bridge. A mess of movement at the top as his arms flailed, as his body made a desperate, awkward half-somersault. Then a stiffening as the body set itself in a straight line, head through to pointing toes, and the line dropped down to meet the blue. The surface broke, and Ted was sure he could see the body moving, still moving down in the deep, as if there was a light following it, illuminating it somehow.

Ted thought: *That's not where Joe's working—who was it?* Ted thought: *Is he moving too quickly? Too slowly?* Ted thought: *How straight he's stretched himself,* and, *Who else is watching? Who should I tell?* Ted thought: *His splash is going to reach right back up to the deck.* Ted thought: *That's seven*—and was surprised that he'd been keeping a tally somewhere of the men who'd died. Ted thought: *The body's gone down a long way to be under so long*—and then the shouts and calls and the splashes of other men cut across his thoughts as they dived down from the barge he'd left.

He glanced up at the sky, as if a rain of men might follow, glanced behind him towards the foreman, as if he might be shouting instructions, glanced out towards the harbor's middle, towards the place the man had hit, and saw a ferry there, frozen, people pressed against the rail, looking, calling, and a flash of white like a signal as one woman's gloved hands came up to her mouth in horror, again and again. But all he managed to say was the first part of "Oh"—just the very first part of its sound, like a complicated breath.

And then there was the falling man, coming up again through the water, alive. Alive and waving.

All around the site the men stared and cheered, and it seemed to Ted that he was looking straight across the neck of the harbor and into the fellow's eyes.

"It's Kelly," someone called, "it's bloody Kelly." And there he was, looking around as if for the towel that should be there after any dive. From the south side of the shore Ted was certain that Kelly's eyes were bluer now, blue and clear and looking somewhere else altogether.

Above, the clouds parted and the sun flared bright. The dog barked, the foreman called him to heel—and Ted, forgetting his errand, ran down to the shore and looked out towards the barge. He had to rejoin his crew.

Dawes

"TWO DAYS he's been rowing himself back and forth," said the surgeon. "Two days in a little boat from one side to the other." He shaded his eyes from the sun, looked out to the boat as it headed north again, looked out to the other boat, rowing hard to intersect its path. Beside him, William Dawes shaded his own gaze, watched the wake left by the lone rower as it spread wide and blended back into the water's surface. "One of your men too," said the surgeon. "An officer from the *Sirius*. Or a lunatic from the *Sirius* now, I'm afraid. Though I'm surprised there aren't more men reaching the end of their patience and their sanity, after all this time alone—not to mention the scurvy." He sighed, rubbed his eyes. "Were you out on the hunt for him yourself, Lieutenant?"

Dawes shook his head. "Hadn't heard he was missing." Down on the point, busy with his tasks, he was blissfully unaware of a lot of what was going on. The news of a fellow officer stealing a boat and rowing himself back and forth across the harbor nonstop hadn't reached him at all; the news that the settlement had just eaten its last provisions of peas—six months before the Governor had anticipated they would run out—had. They'd been more than two years alone on the east coast of this continent; close to three years away from England itself.

"At least he has the luxury of thinking he's going somewhere, unlike the rest of us," said the surgeon as the two boats collided and the several officers in one overpowered the lone third lieutenant in the other. "Like yourself, sir—on your way somewhere this morning?"

It was a calm autumnal day, quiet and bright, and Dawes had been partway along the seven-mile walk between the settlement and its hopeful lookout on the harbor's cliffs, when he'd come across John White and his lookout of a different kind.

"A good clear day for looking out to the horizon," he said to the surgeon, watching as the subdued officer was planted between two sets of constraining shoulders in their faded red coats.

It was some view from the top of South Head, with the ocean spreading out and running all the way to Valparaiso. Dawes loved it, the size of it, the space of it compared to all the busy nips and turns and corners of the harbor's shoreline. It was like the night sky, vast and available, although not for the appearance of stars or disappointing comets, but for the well-stocked ships that must—surely—appear soon.

The tricks with which this settlement was trying to pull ships across the oceans: parties of men were sent regularly to Botany Bay to check for any arrivals and leave carefully painted signs that they might find—we're here, we're up the coast, sail north, turn left, and you'll find us. A marker at the harbor's heads, and letter after letter sent back by any available vessel describing precisely the location of the harbor's opening, the trickiness of seeing it sometimes. A pyre, and a flagstaff, and then a watch had been set.

Dan Southwell was the watch, out on his own with the weight of the settlement's anticipation pressing in behind him. Eyes peeled, eyes staring, for fleets that didn't come—"Never will," he'd started saying to himself.

At least Dawes, who'd walked out in all directions and had gone farther in most of them than any other white man, looking for rivers that didn't exist, ways through impassable ravines and gorges, anything to get beyond this first plain, thought nothing of a short hike east to the continent's cliffs to take in the breadth of the ocean and bring Southwell whatever passed for news that week. Leaving the surgeon, he pushed on through the bush—picturing himself from above, a single point of red moving along a track that cut the different greens of the bush—and paused as he reached the top of the last rise, breathing the salt of that wide, dark blue, calling his greetings and waving a loaf of bread.

It was enough to earn him Dan Southwell's rating as the kindest man in the colony.

And it was a kind of heaven to deliver news, new conversation; to tell this eager young man about the troubled officer and the perpetual motion he'd set up across the harbor; about another ship ready to sail out with more messages for the world; about a convict's clothes taken by a native as the convict hunted stingrays— and about the stars he was plotting, the weather he was recording, the words he was learning. Southwell had seen the stacks of paper growing in Dawes's room. He'd seen the books, the tables, the almanacs, the instruments with which Dawes was trying to mark out and understand this place, and he liked that every so often he had some private insight into them. It was like watching the magic of a map being copied with a pantograph, one nib tracing over the completed image, while its copy flowed out from the other, inked nib. This place was being written into being, "right before my eyes," Dan Southwell had said one afternoon as another copy of the harbor's dents and curves—the observatory facing the dark north shore—spilled out across a sheet of paper under Dawes's steady hand.

"And they brought him back to shore, in the end?" Southwell

asked now, referring to the renegade rower, breaking off a chunk of the loaf and holding it out to Dawes with a mug of sweet-leaf tea.

"They were trying," said Dawes, sitting down with his breakfast. He suspected there'd been more concern about getting the boat back than recovering the man.

Chewing on the bread, he gazed out towards the west and the one high line of blue hills that sat there, solid and defensive. Camarthen, they'd been called, nodding to another part of Wales. The only thing anyone knew to exist beyond that was the King's arbitrary line—cutting straight down one hundred and thirty-five degrees to mark the western limit of this colony's claim, some nine hundred miles away—and William Dampier's coast, hundreds and hundreds of miles beyond that again to the west.

"How far that way have you gone now, Lieutenant Dawes?" Southwell asked him, swinging around to look past the little settlement himself, past the silver line of the river as it disappeared upstream. "Will you ever get through those ranges, sir? Will you see what's on the other side?"

"We'll get through sooner or later," said Dawes. "And who knows what we'll find on the other side?" It was all jags and peaks and impenetrable trees, as far as he'd been able to go—the one place where even as good a reckoner as himself had struggled to keep count of his steps, keep track of where he was, and where he'd found it impossible to drag his gaze up into the air and imagine the land laid out beneath him. Fifty-four miles from the coast they'd managed in all the times they'd walked out; hardly far enough to change your view of anything.

"You know, Mr. Southwell, I might start studying the clouds instead of the weather they make: another new thing to look at." He lay back on the ground, taking in the sky.

"There are some mornings I think I see sails in the clouds," Dan Southwell confessed. Too many times his imagination had carved their white shapes into tautly rigged canvas, sure that ships were coming—slowly, so slowly—closer to the land, and then watching as they spread and dissipated against the sky.

"Another job for my balloon: looking for your ships—and ships must be more reliable than comets, unless we are truly gone out of the world and forgotten," said Dawes. His head was arched back so that his gaze took in only the blue, the white, the brightness of the morning sun. Land, people—all trace of them were gone.

Dan Southwell had heard about the balloon, and in those long shipless days he confessed to Dawes he'd dreamed about making one himself—the lieutenant hadn't made it sound difficult—and floating over the ocean to find their missing fleet, their missing supplies. Surely that thought must have occurred to the lieutenant too, wondered Southwell, no matter that he always couched his imaginary voyages in terms of mapping, and weather, and other experiments. "But then what's up there, sir—the bodies, you said, from who knows how long . . ."

Listening to the silence of Dan Southwell's hesitation, William Dawes watched a small cluster of clouds drift and adjust while a length of cloth flapped lazily on a line. It billowed to round fullness just as Dawes turned his head down from the sky, so that he thought he saw his balloon again. And he sat up, laughing: the promise of a bit of a breeze, a bit of fabric. How high would he need to go, and how far, to find his comet? Maybe all the way back to Greenwich, where he could land on the lawn and discuss those clearly erroneous calculations with the Astronomer Royal. He could sample some clouds on the way, chart the flight of some birds. He could check the accuracy of any maps against any land below. He could see about those bodies too—maybe that's where the surgeon's mysterious hand and arm had come from, dropped down from the sky in some disruptive storm right back at the beginning of their time in this place. *I've been gone too long*, he thought sharply. *I need to get home.*

He was wondering what he might have said aloud when South-well said again, "But those bodies, Lieutenant Dawes? And those fearsome ghosts that swoop down for your throat? Wouldn't you be scared of all that, up in your balloon?" Sometimes, when they spoke, Southwell saw that his friend's attention had slipped away somewhere, somewhere else. Once, he'd asked him about it, and Dawes had laughed and said he was just up in the air, checking the dent that this south head made between the ocean and the harbor. Now, the birds fell silent and the air felt heavy—*like the roar in your ears when you yawn*, thought Dawes, his mind still far from his friend.

"Lieutenant Dawes, sir," Southwell persisted. "Wouldn't you be scared?"

"The things we believe might be just as frightening to them," said Dawes. "We have our own resurrection. And they have very beauti-ful words for other things—for dreams, for make-believe, for flying through the air like a bird, like a spear: *nángami, búnama, wómera*. Their word for clusters of falling stars is beautiful—*molu-molu*—although they fear shooting stars as terrible portents. And book, they have a word for book now too." The conversations, the lists of words and meanings each knew from the other, continued to grow.

"For book?"

"For book, for telescope, for compass, for reading glasses, for window, for biscuit, for jacket," said Dawes. "For so many things they may never have thought to see. And for us—they call us after somewhere a great way off: *berewal*. They call us *be-re-wal-gal*. We make our way, naming plants and birds and spiders. And the natives walk around us, and name us and our possessions, make it all part of the things they can talk about."

He'd felt better once he knew that the black people had given the white people their own name, their own classification. He couldn't have put it entirely into words, but he'd had moments of fear, before he knew they were tagged as *be-re-wal-gal*, when he'd wondered if the soldiers, the settlement, this little spike of empire might all have been a product of some native imagination, some nighttime dream, like his conversations with the now-faded Judith Rutter. That they were *be-re-wal-gal* made them real, and really here, and for William Dawes at least there came with that a surprising kind of certainty, or comfort.

Turning his head again, he took in the wide blue sweep of the ocean, and sat up a little to watch the sunlight bouncing on the facets and surfaces of the water. There was something transfixing, tranquil about it, and while he listened to Dan Southwell talking—about a couple of whales that had passed, heading north, the possible return of the aurora, the shine of a moonrise he'd seen coming up out of the ocean the previous week—he stood, rubbed vaguely at his throat, and felt himself stepping closer and closer to the light on the water, closer and closer to the edge of the high sandstone cliff where the country began.

It was his name, and shouted, that made him turn back towards the land; the other man must have seen some bird or beetle he wanted to know about, and Dawes felt his face compose itself into what he hoped was a learned look. But it was what was behind his friend, away to the west—it must be in the harbor just down from his own rooms—that caught Dawes's eye: a great spout of water surging up, up a hundred feet into the air, maybe more. He took a step back to steady himself and felt his good leg plant itself so firmly that the land seemed to shudder and tilt—as if he was just newly ashore again and still coping with his sea legs. He took a second step to right his frail, stiff leg and the world tilted again: the shocking gasp, the shocking rush of air when a step is taken and there's nothing in the space where the foot had hoped to stand.

Once before, on that long hike as far west as anyone had gone, he'd bent his head so intently to the task of counting his paces, tracking his own location, that he'd lagged behind and taken one step too far and felt that same sickening lurch of unexpectedly empty air. *If I tripped here; if I fell here; if I died here*—he'd paused, his hands grabbing at a sapling so that he righted himself too quickly and almost toppled in the other direction. *If I died here half the settlement would think I was just the latest to try to walk home.* And he'd sat breathing deep and holding on to the number of paces he'd reached so that he could stand up, walk on as if nothing had happened, and catch up with the rest of the party.

This time, when his hands reached for some useful sapling, some well-placed branch, he found he was scrabbling with grass and grazing the stubble of sandstone. Opening his mouth to call to Southwell, he saw his friend's face working in rapid grimaces and already too far above him. The sea surged and roiled against the cliff below. *Not this*, he thought, *not here*. And, *I want to see what made that tower of water.* His right hand got some purchase on a low shrub; his left foot twisted its toes between two close rock ledges.

"Can you throw something down?" he called up the cliff, and Southwell was back in an instant with the great white sheet that his mind had turned into a balloon not five minutes before. Dawes had an image of himself grabbing at its four corners, its dome swelling with wind and drifting him up, up, and gently up to the top of the cliff. Except, of course, that he'd keep going, keep hanging on, and head west, fast along the harbor to reach the last fine mist of that waterspout.

One heave, another, and he was back on the bluff, his hands stinging and another rip in his uniform's fabric.

"Thank you." He nodded to Dan Southwell, made formal by awkwardness.

The young man nodded back carefully. "You're all right, sir? Your foot? Your leg?"

Patting his shin with more heartiness than he felt, Dawes smiled. "All fine, all here," swinging back around to look at a harbor that lay clear and calm again under the sun. "When you called to me," he said at last, "what was it you wanted to draw my attention to?"

"Your attention, Lieutenant Dawes?" Southwell frowned. "I only called when you began to stumble; your feet were falling so fast towards the cliff, and I called to try to turn you from the steps you were taking."

"So there was nothing—" He paused. "You didn't see—" Another silence, and he eased himself carefully back down onto the ground, the solidity of the flagstaff against his back.

Southwell seated himself opposite, studying the lieutenant's face. Dawes's eyes had shifted to that middle distance again, and he began to speak, slowly and quietly, as if he was feeling his way through sentences for which he didn't quite know the words.

"I think sometimes," he said, "that I spend so much time drawing this place from above, or staring up into its heavens, that some part of me has become stuck up there permanently, trying to put all its pieces together, and I lose myself on the land. That's all this is. That's all this is." And as he laughed, he heard Southwell joining in, kind and friendly.

"Well, you gave me a scare, sir, and I'm glad I could bring your attention back to your feet and the ground." From any other man but Dawes, such talk would sound alarming. But Southwell smiled again at the lieutenant, and proposed another helping of breakfast before he began his walk back along the ridges to the observatory. And although Dawes nodded, and smiled, and took the dish with some relish, he sat gazing, between mouthfuls, back towards the settlement, and forgetting for minutes at a time to chew, to swallow, perhaps even to breathe.

The way his eyes glistened, Dan Southwell said later, they looked almost luminous.

~

"Still waiting?" Watkin Tench asked that night as he sat with Dawes outside the observatory's quiet space. And until he jerked his thumb up towards the comet-less night sky, Dawes wondered how his friend knew of his midday apparition.

"No," he said, "I don't think so. There must have been something wrong with the calculations—nothing I brought from London made sense of it. And of course I'm still waiting for the papers the French astronomer promised me—caught up on our missing ships, I suppose." He drained his mug, hoped the comment sounded wry rather than desperate, and rubbed the map his thumbnail had etched on his trousers back into smoothness. "I expect it's up there somewhere," he said, making a show of standing to end the night, "or something is. But perhaps I'm not the man to see it."

And as he walked towards his room, his blanket, his tiredness made his feet feel impossibly light, as though he really was rising up off the ground, up towards the vantage point of all those maps. Under what word could he describe what he thought he'd seen for his dictionary, he wondered as he settled to sleep—water or spirit? *Badu* or *mawn*?

Perhaps he should row out across the water tomorrow to see if that splash had left any trace of itself or of its cause. How many passes of the harbor would he need to make, he wondered, before he found any evidence of whatever it had been—or before the surgeon came to haul him quietly home.

Dan

AS THE image of thick white mist swirled and faded, Dan's head lolled against the window, hovering just above sleep. He had some sense of his breathing, in and out, slow and gentle, like the rocking of a little boat on shallow water. Now, behind his closed eyes, he was seven again and sitting cross-legged with Charlie on her back stairs, her grandfather above them on the veranda in an old cane chair. It was summer—he could hear cicadas, and he could smell the wet earth in the veggie patches where Gramps had poured buckets of water onto lettuces, tomatoes, radishes. Charlie was picking at a scab on her knee—Dan remembered too, or knew in some part of his memory, that she'd fallen over on the roller skates she'd been given for Christmas—as she wheedled a story out of her grandfather: "Just one more, just one more before bedtime." It was evening, and the light was starting to fade, draining the color out of the end of the day like some shadowy bleaching so that anything real, anything in the landscape, looked like it was only an idea, a monochrome suggestion.

"When I first knew your grandmother," Charlie's grandfather began, "I wanted to fly. The way those planes used to loop and curve over the harbor, as if they were writing a message in the clouds—if you could be quick enough about reading it. Took me years to find out about Icarus; all that time I could've been collecting cockatoo feathers and getting my wings together. Because I reckon if Icarus could get a good enough updraught from a tower in some old palace, I'd've been right as rain and up through the clouds if I'd scampered up to the top of the bridge and launched myself off there. And we were still putting it together then—I could've climbed up bold as brass and gone off the top of it.

"Anyhow, you both know about Icarus—I've told you about him before. And a mate of mine, in the next war, got himself to Greece and saw the place where Icarus flew. A strange spot, he said, built in a valley but raised up somehow, so you could always feel a breeze passing; probably Icarus thought you could trust it to be there when you needed it. He wrote me a letter about it, this mate of mine—silly bugger got himself shot before he could get back home, but it meant a lot to me that he'd gone after the flying boy for me and checked out how he'd done it. A frame of feathers, a high enough spot, and a great big leap into the blue with all your trust and confidence in it. And don't get too close to the sun. That's all—you just had to step off, you know, you just had to step off."

"Like the day you went off the bridge, Gramps." There was a plea, small and singsong, in Charlie's little voice, as if she might trick an extra story out of her grandfather.

"That was a day—late spring, and the water so blue, and that dog barking over on the south. They say I pirouetted like a dancer in the air before I went down through the blue. And all those other blokes diving in and cheering and shouting. Seventh to go in, kids, and the first to survive." Leaning forward to ruffle Charlie's hair. "That did me for flying for a while, of course."

In the dream, the backyard, the veggie beds with their sweet wet soil, fell away to the harbor's blue, and Dan felt himself falling suddenly, falling down through the air towards the water, a man's voice yelling from below, "Get yourself straight, get yourself straight, lad."

He felt something at his belt—a spanner—felt his hand moving up to free it, and felt himself brace for the change of his own weight as the spanner dropped towards the harbor below, the harbor that was rushing up to meet him.

"Tuck your head in, tuck your head in," but instead he turned and twisted, looked up and there was the whole bridge—the slabs of deck that had already been hung, the arch that had met so perfectly in the middle, the pylons, the rivets, the struts, the girders—the whole thing unraveling as if it were a half knitted pullover detached from its needles. Faster and faster until there was just one first section of arch reaching out from Dawes Point, and then that was gone too, and the old houses were popping up like parsley plants, a ferry terminal rearing up on the north shore opposite.

The whole city was winding itself back. The houses went again. The wharves at the quay went. The tram terminus went. The pale sandstone of the customs house went and all the stores around the shoreline. Trees were shooting up as if they were just righting themselves after an accidental stumble, and straight below, a man in a red coat rowed out from Dawes Point in a tiny boat. There were tents, ships with huge white squares of sails rolled into their beams, and masts as tall as tree trunks. And behind that, a great wide silence, the occasional shout, the occasional gunshot, the occasional squeak of a pig or a dog. The water around the boat was the most beautiful sunlit blue.

The man in the red coat looked up, reaching his hand towards Dan as he floated—it seemed—in the air. But instead of pulling Dan down he seemed to rise up to meet him, and then they were both inside some bubble of blue, the bridge was above them again and an ambulance siren—a sharp, modern sound—was cutting over everything, out of place.

Dan turned, a swimmer's tumble turn, although the blueness seemed like air, not water. Straightening, he saw the man in the red coat float gently back to the ground, saw him pointing up, higher. Twisting his head, Dan saw a man with a short grey coat flapping out around him like a cape, like wings, falling towards him, towards him, through him, and away. There were rows of men on the side of the harbor, lined up to the top of the arch where they stood, like weekend divers, waiting their turn for pikes and plummets down into the harbor. But the next movement he saw was the bright tail of a shooting star, not a man, down to the east, down towards the horizon and the ocean. It sizzled and spat a little as it hit the surface, and the silence around it rang—the precise bell of the seat-belt sign being turned off.

Dan's head hit the window and his eyes jerked open.

"Something to drink, sir?" The flight attendant was leaning over Cynthia, a packet of pretzels on her outstretched hand. Dan worked his mouth open and shut, bewildered, parched, and aching.

"A gin—no, some tonic, thanks. And a lemonade . . . and a water."

Cynthia passed the miniature cans and bottles across to him. He'd never felt so thirsty.

"Bad dream?" She was holding out her own bag of pretzels. "I don't like these, if you want them."

"Thanks," said Dan, ignoring the dream, ignoring her question. He wasn't sure how he would have answered anyway. All he could think of was the air above the water, and the thickness of the blue. At least he'd found Gramps's face again, no matter how disorienting it was to dream of falling through one of the old man's stories. Perhaps it was an appropriate homecoming, he thought, being scooped back into the stories he'd thought he was flying away from all those years ago.

He clicked open the can of tonic, nodding towards its fizz, its metallic smell. "This'll be good," he said, raising the glass towards Cynthia. She raised her glass in return, and opened her book again.

Surrounded by white noise, his mouth full of sweat, round bubbles, Dan stared at his watch awhile. His moment of panic about Charlie's grandfather had drained out a little through the dream, through the drink. Now he supposed it was all just due to tiredness, and dislocation, and some strange glitch from making this long and long-overdue trip home.

He thought about Caro's ultimatum—the *here* or *there* that she'd put so politely. Everyone pretended the world had shriveled to the size of a pea with planes and phones and emails and the rest of it, but you still had to choose if you were going to be here, or there. And the distance between the two choices was irrelevant—no one had yet worked out how to be in two places at the one time.

Caro would have had an answer for that: he could hear her voice over the buzz of the plane. "What's the thing where time happens all at once, past, present, and future mashed together? Maybe that would help . . ." He could hear her laugh. No, he needed the eighteenth century, when time and space were different things and people accepted distances, delays. Maybe there'd been a measure of grace in that.

He yawned.

Working his fingers into random pages of *Gulliver*, Dan's eyes kept straying towards the window, towards the night and the clouds, and towards the partial reflection of the two Russians who sat in front of him. Gulliver was leaving Blefescu, Gulliver was showing off his diminutive sheep and cattle to astonished Englishmen at home, but the Russian woman was singing softly, her head bent in towards her father's, and somehow the softness of the notes cut through the mighty noise of the plane's movement and filled the space inside Dan's head that had been pushed empty by the dream. The song was low and sweet; it sounded like a lullaby. His eyes were heavy again, and then *Gulliver* was on the spare seat next to him, closed.

He could feel pressure under his arms, and hands grasping at his shoulders, then he was lifted clear of the water and laid out on a barge, coughing, hacking, with bits of him beginning to hurt. Pain around the top of his legs as if bands of iron had been fitted there. And shards of metal, it seemed, sticking into his body at all angles.

"Strike me," said someone behind him, "it's bloody Kelly. You're a lucky bloke, mate, a bloody lucky bloke. Seven in, one out."

Kelly? thought Dan, somewhere above the dream. *But it was Charlie's grandfather who went off the bridge and lived, and Charlie's grandfather is Joe Brown.*

There was a blur of wind, and he saw himself tucked into a bed in a high, clean room, the arch of the bridge just visible through the window, and the sheets pulled taut around him. His boot leather, which had burst from its soles and pushed up his legs like two too-tight bracelets, had been taken off. The tatters of his clothing, shredded by his impact against the water, had been peeled from his skin. The pain in his back had been defined more properly as a couple of broken ribs. And in front of him, newspapermen jiggled their pencils back and forth as they asked their questions. Dan felt his mouth move and heard an unfamiliar voice, softly, gently Irish.

"I'm often working near the edge of the bridge, and on many occasions I've thought to myself, 'Now, if you ever fall, Roy, you had better make sure that you hit the water feet first or head first.' So when I slipped and fell today, I concentrated on saving my life. That's all I thought about. It was the only thing in my mind: the desire to live. I knew that I was very near death. I hit the water. I went under. There was a roar of water in my ears. My lungs felt as though they would burst. Then I came up to the surface. I was alive, marvelously alive."

"And can you tell us what happened?" Pencils poised in the air.

He was talking about the morning, about the sunshine, about the cloud and the rain that had come suddenly from nowhere. He was talking about the shoes he wore to work—rubber soled, he said, reliable in the dry but downright dangerous in the wet. Which didn't matter mostly—if the rain was too heavy, no one could work. The company didn't like them using rivets when the weather was bad, too easy to break them—too easy to waste them. Anyhow, he'd been lining up a rivet when he lost his footing—as easy as that—and lunged in as many directions as he could, trying for something, anything, that he could grab on to, and feeling himself stagger backwards into nothing, into space, into the fall. Such an easy movement that it must almost have looked like he meant to do it.

"And then I hit the water . . ." The voice paused—Dan was gazing towards the window and its snatch of arch. "Didn't go under very far, and it only seemed an instant from the moment I fell to the time that I was struggling on the surface."

Dan felt a broad smile move slowly across his face and counted the spread of its beam: one, two, three seconds. "Struggling and alive." The newspapermen glanced up, their pencils busy.

"When I hit the water and went under I felt afraid for the first time. During the fall I kept saying to myself that I must fight for my life, but when I was submerged I almost felt that all was lost." There was a heavy silence. "And then I was on the surface again, striking out automatically for the buoy. With almost a shock I realized I was alive. I could have shouted, you know, could have shouted for sheer joy."

And Dan was back in Charlie's yard, back in a childhood summer, sitting on the steps, looking up at Gramps, who'd never sounded Irish in his life.

"You should've been called Joy, love," Gramps was saying, his fingers tousling Charlie's hair again, "after your lovely grandmother."

And Charlie, almost asleep, was smiling, and swaying a little, and Gramps was picking her up, carrying her inside, and sending Dan back to his side of the fence and his own bedroom. As he crawled under the covers, as his heavy head hit the pillow, his eyes closed in that night and opened in the white-noise hum of the plane.

~

Concertinaed into the toilet cubicle, Dan leaned on the narrow plastic bench and stared at himself in the mirror: his brown hair—thin at the best of times—was stuck to his forehead like clammy string, and when he pulled himself up to straighten his posture, his ribs twinged as if he might really have fallen from a great height the day before. He splashed cold water onto his face, his neck, rubbed his wet fingers through his hair. "Just a dream," he told his reflection. His mind was skittering—it felt the way he'd heard people describe panic. Must be the flight, the tiredness, the jet lag, going home. The face in the mirror was too pale—too many summers without proper sunlight; too many days in offices. He splashed again, shook the drops out of his hair; Caroline's name looped through his mind like a mantra. And then *if Charlie's bloody picture hadn't been in front of me, I'd never have . . .*

Backing out of the little booth, he bumped into someone behind him—"Sorry, sorry; *izvi'nite, izvi'nite.*" The Russian woman. Dan felt a drop of water fall from his hair onto the tip of his nose and hang there.

"You are all right?" the woman asked.

"Yes, yes—it's hard to sleep on a plane," said Dan. "And your father?"

"He only sleeps," she said with a tiny smile. "Is better. When he's awake, he asks where is he, where is my mother. I say, I'm her. I say, I'm here. Doesn't matter—is easier." She sighed, rubbed her neck. "It will be good to be there. Australia. Sydney."

"You have family there?"

"The doctor. We are coming for the doctor," she said. "What is it, Australia? Sydney? I don't know what is there."

"Australia? Sydney?" Dan shrugged. "Sydney is a big city. Australia is a big country. Not as big as Russia . . ."

"But what is there?"

"There are beaches in Sydney, and there's the Opera House, and the Harbour Bridge . . . I'm sorry; I've been gone a long time, more than ten years. I don't know what to expect myself."

"A big country, and empty?" the woman asked.

"Dry," said Dan. "Not like your country. I flew over Russia once—lots of rivers cutting through forests. Didn't look like there were any people down there."

"Many people, in your country?"

"A lot less than yours," said Dan.

The woman nodded. "Is nice to meet an Australian," she said, sounding out all the syllables of the long word with particular care. "A long way to fly."

"My friend's . . ." He heard himself falter and pause. "My grandfather used to tell this story about a man from Moscow who walked all the way across Russia to the Pacific and then sailed down to Sydney—in the twenties, I think. Much easier"—he gestured through the one blind left raised to let in the night; the moon was out there, golden, and the tops of clouds—"much easier to go this way."

"And good for my father." She nodded again. "Good for him to go to your country." Another pause, then, "I see you read *Gulliver*." Dan frowned, puzzled. "On your seat—your book. My father says Gulliver went to Australia. I don't know if it was a happy ending." She smiled. "For us, maybe. Is a children's book, yes?"

"I read it when I was little," said Dan. "It was a present when I was coming away." Defensively.

"Perhaps I will read it." The woman smiled again. "I should . . ."

She pointed over the rows of seats, the sleeping heads. "To see how he sleeps."

"Good luck," said Dan. "I hope you like Sydney—and for your father too." The world was burnished through the window; he crouched down, watching the shapes the clouds made, soft and gently moonlit, as the plane skated above them and the woman felt her way hand-over-hand along the aisle.

Thirty thousand feet. At ten thousand feet, people started talking nonsense, making dumb mistakes and miscalculations—that was outside of a plane, of course, with the only oxygen available to them what little was in the air. Higher again, at around sixty thousand feet, an unprotected body's gases would expand—swelling, stretching, rupturing—and then a little higher the body's fluids could begin to boil. What had Icarus done about that, or was that what had done for him, wrongly attributed to the warmth of the sun? Way out in the night, Dan saw the blink of another plane's light, and took in a long breath. Yes, that was as close as those things were supposed to be. Over there; on its own.

He filled a paper cup with water, drank it, and then drank another to wash away the last of his dream. Back in his seat, with *Gulliver* open again, he thought about how he had claimed Gramps as his own grandfather when he told the Russian woman about the long walk across her country. *Is easier*, he thought, echoing her abbreviation. It wasn't like he'd have to undo the misunderstanding, as he had with Caroline. "Did you think he was my grandfather?" He'd feigned surprise. "No, no, a friend of mine's—he's Charlie's Gramps." And he hadn't even blushed.

Gulliver was on his way to the Brobdingnageans, north of New Albion. Dan leaned back, his head angled so he could see the corner of the Russian woman's face, the side of her father's face next to it, whenever he glanced up from his page. The old man's skin was sallow, almost jaundiced; it looked as if he'd already been dried out and preserved, like a Catholic saint reclining for eternity in a glass coffin. It was impossible to think there was any blood flowing. A dab of the face washer, and there was that softly sung lullaby again. Dan shifted his head to see if the old man reacted, but there was nothing: no movement, no blink, no nod.

Four or five times he read the same page of *Gulliver's Travels*—four or five times Gulliver's storm-tossed ship almost sighted Brobdingnag. Each time, at the end of the last sentence on the page, Dan would look up, look between the seats for a moment, and then look back down to the book's words, his train of thought broken.

In the end, the realization came from nowhere. There was no change, no movement, no signal; there was only a moment when Dan thought, clear and sharp, *The old man has died*—and squirmed at the thought, and at not quite knowing what to do about it.

Because what had changed? The man's skin was still a papery yellow. His eyes were still closed. His daughter still sat, dabbing with her flannel and singing her soft song. What had changed that made Dan think anything was different? Nothing he could see, yet the more he stared, the more he concentrated, the more it seemed that he was staring at a body, not at a person, and he began to wonder if he had been watching, but not paying attention, at the very moment of death, and if he might have seen something happen that he hadn't recognized or been able to name. Almost forty years old, and he'd never seen a dead body before. It seemed impossible somehow, given how many turned up on his television set every night, real ones, made-up ones, even hideously malleable animated ones with drawn lines and technicolor blood. It seemed impossible to have reached his age without coming into contact with a corpse. Macabre word. Come to think of it, he'd never been to a funeral either—he had been thought too young to go to his dad's.

He'd been so small when his father died, although he could remember the day of the funeral, his mother in a new black dress that looked uncomfortable, and being left with a friend of hers who told him that his father was in the sky, in heaven. "No, he's in the ground," Dan remembered saying, and he had sat for a long time watching the way a breeze made the leaves of a hedge move, wondering how you would draw the wind. He couldn't remember seeing his father in the hospital, although he knew he had been taken there—there was that smell, that disinfectant smell. He could remember that. And how carefully he'd watched his mother those first weeks after it had happened, as if by paying attention to her every breath, her every movement, he could make sure it didn't happen again.

The soft Russian singing paused for a moment, and Dan watched as the daughter adjusted the rug high around her father's neck. Had she noticed? Or was Dan wrong, and the man still had some shallow pulse, some vague quiver? The woman pushed her father's hair back from his head, and Dan was sure he caught the tiniest twitch of the man's eyebrow in response. Of course he wasn't dead. Of course she wasn't sitting there singing to a body. And of course there was nothing odd about his never having seen a cadaver. Who did these days? Who had to?

He had no idea how long he sat there, his chin propped on his hand as he stared at snatches of the two people in front of him, waiting for a sigh, a yawn, an exclamation. In the end, he dragged his gaze away and fished around in his bag for one of the magazines he'd bought, flicking idly through its pages to register a headlined word here, a piece of a picture there. There was a photo of the spot in the Botanic Gardens where Charlie's grandad always took them for picnics—Dan supposed it was a pretty popular view, straight across the harbor and past the Opera House to the bridge. There was a photo of the beach he and Charlie had played on when they were little, the blue of its water so saturated the page itself looked almost wet. It seemed as much an omen as the great big billboard picture of Charlie's he'd seen in the Underground. Of course the old man was just sleeping. And there, tucked away at the back of the magazine, was a black and white picture of the harbor taken from way up in the air—sixteen thousand feet, the caption said. The points and pokes of land were almost solid black, and the pale color of the water had been polished to silver white by the early-morning sun and the length of the film's exposure. In the middle of the shot, like the most delicate filigree or tracery—like Gramps's *gold to airy thinness beat*—the curve of the bridge, still recognizable from so high up, from so far away, threw a perfect shadow of itself across the water. Dan smiled. Somewhere in his place in London, he had a card with this picture on its front.

They'd been sitting under the bridge when Charlie had given it to him, five, maybe ten minutes before he'd caught his cab to the airport and London. He folded the magazine to a single page's width, smoothing his hand across the picture. "Bird's-eye view," Charlie had said, "up there with Icarus—in case you forget what it looks like." *Safe at 16,000 feet—wings still intact*, she'd written on it. *You can use this to guide yourself home if you get lost.* Funny how he remembered the lines; he hadn't thought about the photograph itself since he'd tucked it into his pocket and come away.

The seat in front of him shuddered a little as the Russian woman turned, pulling her legs up underneath her and changing the angle from which she was soothing her father's face.

Dan looked up to follow the movement, and there was the old man, exactly as he had been.

Exactly.

Yes, thought Dan, *he is dead.* There was no question, no emotion, no catching the moment of a soul sneaking out. The man was no longer a man; the daughter must have known; and Dan saw, just for a second, what the nothing after death really was. Nothing. He saw the daughter push up her sleeve, check her watch, and he thought, *She's waiting, she's waiting for something before she tells anyone.* His own watch told him they were almost four hours out of Singapore—almost halfway to Sydney.

The plane was dark and still, most people asleep or staring at their screens. *Maybe if the plane is more than halfway to Sydney,* thought Dan, quite distinctly, *it will keep flying with a body on it. If the plane is less than halfway, maybe they make it turn back.*

The woman's hand kept up its rhythm, down to the water bottle, up to the forehead, down to the water, up to the face.

What a place to die, thirty thousand feet up in the air and stuck in this cold metal tube, thought Dan, although it hardly mattered, he supposed, in the instant of its happening. *Whatever it was, it must have been peaceful, or I'd have noticed.* He felt his shoulders flinch a little: that goose, that grave. *Wouldn't I have noticed?*

At last, when a flight attendant came through the dimness with brimming beakers of water, Dan reached over and took two. "The old man in front," he said, "I don't think he's—I think you should . . ."

She leaned over, placed her hand on the old man's shoulder and pulled it away almost immediately. "Excuse me," she said to the daughter, "are you all right? I'll try to find you a—" And she disappeared back along the aisle. In the space between the seats, Dan watched a tear run down the woman's face; it had reached the line of her jaw by the time a voice came over the intercom asking for a doctor. She was Caro in the cab, on their way to the restaurant from the Ferris wheel on his birthday. She was his mother, years ago, before his father died—but never, Dan realized now, never that he saw afterwards. There was more in this quiet stream of tears, thought Dan, than any loud or elaborate sobbing. This was pure hopelessness, or exhaustion, or resignation.

On the other side of the empty seat, Cynthia stirred a little in her sleep, her feet shifting under their blanket.

He expected more noise, more activity; he expected them to turn the lights on in the plane, or to make some official announcement. But everything was very quiet, very slow somehow. A man came from another seat somewhere, pressed his finger to the Russian man's wrist and shook his head, and someone unrolled some kind of first-aid kit. The Russian woman pushed herself farther back into her seat, pressed herself against the window, away from the commotion. There was movement, but only for a few minutes, and then the body—not the Russian man anymore—was picked up and carried towards the back of the plane, wrapped in a blanket. *They must have somewhere they put them*, thought Dan. *They must be prepared.*

Another voice cut through the darkness. Was there anyone on the plane who spoke Russian? But no one raised their hand this time, and the Russian woman stayed sitting, smaller, in her seat, the blanket pulled over her knees.

"I don't think she's all right," said Dan to the next attendant who passed. "Isn't there anything—she spoke some English before; we talked about rivers and books." He didn't know if he should try to talk to her again, or should leave her, just sitting, with the now-empty seat beside her.

The flight attendant shook her head. "We'll do everything we can when we get to Sydney," she said. "There'll be someone waiting to meet her there." She frowned. "But are you all right, sir? Is there anything I can get you?"

"No, no," said Dan quickly. "No, it's nothing to do with me; I'm fine." It sounded more flippant than he intended; he'd just wanted the Russian lady to know someone was thinking about her.

Between the seats, he tried to catch her eye, to smile, to make some acknowledgment of something. But the woman's eyes were closed tight, whether she was sleeping or not. *To have come this far*, thought Dan. He wondered if she'd be able to stay in the city she'd been sure would help her father. He wondered if he should give her his number—not that he'd be in the country for much more than a week—or his mother's number, or Charlie's.

He wondered if it really was Charlie's grandfather he'd been worried about at the beginning of the flight, or if it had been some presentiment about this old man who'd died above the world and in front of him. He closed his eyes and saw nothing but tired darkness, suddenly aware that he was rubbing the palm of one hand with the fingers of the other, but gently, rhythmically, like the light touch of a face washer or a handkerchief. His own skin felt smooth; his own skin felt warm.

Ted

IN THE days after Kelly fell—or dived—Ted kept falling back into that moment. Coming in on the ferry, something would disturb the water's surface and he saw again the waterspout a man could make when he hit the water from a hundred or more feet up. Walking by the workshops, someone would shout, and he heard again the calls that had followed Kelly's line through the air, through the water. Brushing against some softness—a cushion, a curtain, the next door cat that wandered in sometimes—he felt the velvet of Jacko's ears between his fingers, felt the dog stiffen, himself stiffen and saw a man in the air and dropping down, one, two, three seconds and into the blue.

At home, Joy clipped any mention of the incident from newspapers and magazines, reading aloud the columns where Roy Kelly had talked about the accident. A couple of broken ribs and his boot leather jammed fast up around his thighs—they were his only injuries. And the papers said he was smiling; the papers said he was laughing: "'I am often working near the edge of the bridge,'" she read, "'and on many occasions I have thought to myself, "Now, if you ever fall, Roy, you had better make sure that you hit the water feet first or head first." So when I slipped and fell today, I concentrated upon saving my life—'"

"'Upon'?" Joe cut in. "'Concentrated upon'? Kelly? That's fancy newspaper talk that is. Poor bloke probably couldn't speak for trying to breathe."

"'—upon saving my life,'" Joy continued. "'I hit the water. I went under. There was a roar of water in my ears. My lungs felt as though they would burst. Then I came to the surface. I was alive, marvelously alive.'"

"Marvelously." She paused. "Now there's a word." Caught up by the story, by the moment, by the miracle, she made Ted tell her again and again about seeing it—couldn't believe Joe had missed the fall, the surfacing, the messy rescue when Roy Kelly was again almost drowned by someone's enthusiasm in trying to drag him out of the water. "Away on the other side," she kept saying. "Of all the days to be away on the other side of anything."

Joe shook his head, muttered, "Too much, too much." Which Ted heard, but didn't acknowledge.

"'Marvelously alive,'" Joy read again. "How magnificent to feel marvelously anything." She took a deep breath, her fingers marking her place on the page.

"'I tried to clutch something, but there was nothing there to clutch and down I went. I turned a somersault—'"

"I guess that bloody diving came in handy after all," from Joe.

"'—and then I remembered that I must concentrate upon—'"

"Upon again?" Joe scoffed, swishing water around the sink, flicking the dishcloth over the dish rack.

"'—upon entering the water either headfirst or feet first. I waved my arms and screwed up my body in an effort to do this. I began to fall down feet first and I almost felt satisfied. I clasped my right hand over my nose and my mouth. And then I hit the water. Unfortunately, I was not quite upright, otherwise I don't think that I would have been hurt at all. I did not go under very far, and it seemed only an instant from the moment I fell from the bridge to the time that I was struggling on the surface. Struggling and alive.'

"Struggling and alive." She sighed. "It's like something from the movies, isn't it? I'll never be able to look at him the same way again. I wonder if he'll keep diving, when he gets out of hospital? Wonder if he'll go back to the bridge?"

It was evening, and a cool breeze was coming up from the water. Outside, in the garden, leaves and petals rode the current of the strongest gusts, and Ted paused, a stack of clean plates in his hands and his eyes distracted by a flash of white roses shaken free from their stems. The petals lifted a little way, and then, becalmed, began to float back down to the ground, tiny parachutes, or shards of dislocated cloud.

"I should pick a bunch of those to take round to his wife," said Joy, catching the end of the movement. "What a thing, to be told your husband had fallen, to be thinking the worst, even if it was only a second before you found out he'd survived."

"Do you think they'll give him the money, even though he fell off and he's alive?" Ted hadn't meant the question to sound so blunt, but if you fell off, if you died, your family got some kind of compensation, a hundred pounds or so. Which was a peculiar kind of accountancy or reckoning, now that he thought about it.

"An envelope of pounds couldn't buy you much of a miracle," said Joy, "and I guess Kelly's already had his one of those."

She smoothed the newspaper and stepped back into her recitation—the moment Kelly described as his worst: "'When I hit the water and went under I felt afraid for the first time. I could hear nothing, see nothing, and feel nothing except the terrific pain in my side from my broken ribs. My brain was not functioning. And then I was on the surface again, striking out automatically for the buoy. With almost a shock I realized that I was alive. I could have shouted for sheer joy.'"

Ted smiled, remembering the relief of the moment after Joy's body had wavered on the arch; the exhilaration of Kelly, coming up for air, coming up to breathe.

"Miraculous," she said, "whatever you think about the flowery language, Joe. We think it's miraculous, on this side of the kitchen." She nodded at Ted. "Better than Smithy, better than Bradman, and even better than that Second Coming that never came."

Ted laughed; he liked it when she made these jokes about her own extremity.

But Joe was shaking his head. "I'm not saying it's not tremendous Kelly's alive; I'm not saying it's not extraordinary. But you know—" He paused to shrug. "There it is, done now, and all those 'upons' and 'sheer joys.' In any case, they say he'll be back at work in next to no time."

"I just think it's irresistible." Joy was staring into the garden, watching the wind brush its colors across the green. "You wait, it'll be told again and again. It'll be the story everyone knows. It'll be bigger than the bridge itself."

Joe shook his head again. "Nope, the bridge is the big story—always has been, always will be. A year's time, two, when the thing's open and we're all rushing across it, no one'll remember Roy Kelly and his miracle. No one'll remember when it wasn't there, let alone what it took to make it. We'll be doing well to remember the names of the boys who didn't survive."

〰

Later, lying in the bath with his ears under the water, Ted thought about the end of the fall, about what Roy Kelly had said about being under so much water you could see nothing, feel nothing, hear nothing. In the bath, lying still, everything was magnified. Small sounds from around the house—from its pipes, its other room, its other people—pressed into the water and grew. A series of heavy clunks that was some nearby piece of plumbing. The sound of footsteps reverberating on the other side of the hall. Joe's voice, distorted into roundness, sending next-door's cat back into its own garden.

Imagine if the harbor had worked the same way, amplifying all the sounds of the bridge, all the sounds of the city, all the sounds of the boats to and fro and up and down the river.

It would have been blue, he thought, *all blue, and that's what I could see—that's what I thought I could see in his eyes, when he came up, when he looked straight across to where I was standing.* How much space had been between them? It was maybe half a mile, Ted knew, and yet he was certain that his eyes had met Kelly's and that he'd seen their new bright color.

He'd told no one about this and now, coming up above the bath water and ducking underneath again, he wondered if it would wash out of his mind sooner or later. Probably not, he reasoned, if, like Joy said, the story kept being told. And probably not if, the next time he saw Kelly, there were two blue eyes looking at him, that moment, trapped.

In bed, one book forgotten under the pillow, Joy's copy of *Gulliver* open facedown on the floor, Ted lay, tensed in the night's darkness, toes pointing as far forward as they could and fingers taut on the mattress next to him like two arrowheads. He was Roy Kelly, tucked under the tight corners of hospital sheets, his ribs aching, and his skin weeping where his boot leather had been disconnected from the meld it had made with his legs. Joy said you could see the bridge from the roof of that hospital, from some of its windows. Ted was Roy Kelly, hobbling out of bed in the middle of the night, up to the roof, to check it was still there, the thing he'd defeated, the greatest dive he'd made. He was Kelly, leaning against a rail, picking out the darker arch against the dark night sky. He was Kelly, making an ordinary step and finding himself, extraordinary, in the air. He was Kelly, diving with blue above and blue below, and nothing but blue in between.

He was asleep.

Outside in the night, an owl called twice, three times, over the rattle of a window. Inside, Ted had stepped straight into the dream that had stalked him, an air gun heavy in his hands, his body stiff against the punch it made when he let its pressure meet the rivet, and all the bits and pieces of the bridge tightening and firming around him. His feet were planted, sure, on the metal framework and the light line of rope that marked out one boundary of the air in which he might stand lay taut across his back.

Below, in the water, something shifted, and as he bent towards it—it looked like a gesture, like a wave, but he couldn't see anyone there—he stepped out somehow, under the rope, and there he was, in midair. And down on the grass under the bridge's heavy southern pylon a man stood, fussing at the ears of a dog and looking up at the disturbance. Looking up towards his flight.

That was the first second, and he knew immediately—he must have been practicing this dive in his mind for years—that if he could fold himself into a tuck, he could use the force pushing upwards to flick himself straight, feet first, head up. *Bend in the middle, bend in the middle, and use the wind rushing by to turn yourself—like the motion of a clock's pendulum. If you can move your body fast enough, it will generate its own momentum.* One chance, bend and straighten. *You've got one chance to bend and straighten.*

That was the second second.

The world blurred into blue, green, blue, red, blue, grey, blue, blue. He felt his hand move towards his nose, his mouth, trying to protect them from the surge of the harbor's water.

That was the third second, and he was awake, his body still trying to fold itself, to flip from falling head first to feet first, his stomach clamping the covers tight. There it was; there it was at last, the dream whose pieces he'd been catching, the dream whose story he'd scrabbled after. He'd dreamed Roy Kelly's fall—been dreaming it for years.

Turning onto his side to face the wall, he traced the shape of an arch, a rainbow, a rising sun with one finger. It should mean something, he thought, but he was buggered if he knew what. Still, there he was, smiling in the dark because he'd seen, at last, this familiar, fleeting sequence of images, and he'd seen for the first time the whole picture they made. *A dream, just a dream, just a dream,* he thought in time to the ins and outs of Joe's snores from the other side of the wall. As if that one moment had been waiting for him, somewhere, all along.

He traced another arch onto the wall. *But what about seeing yourself standing somewhere else in a dream, when you're in another person's body, looking at yourself standing down on the grass with a dog?* He rolled the other way, wriggled himself down a bit to look out the window.

"Lucky to have the job," he heard his mother saying, "that's all there is to it. Wherever it is, and whatever you're doing, you're lucky to have the job. Don't make it more than that." Eyes closed; eyes opened; eyes closed; eyes opened. And somewhere in between—he wasn't sure if it was outside or inside his head—he saw the bright and speedy streak of a shooting star.

Almost asleep again then, he fell into a deep dark-blue space that he recognized, for the first time, as the lowest point of that fall.

On the other side of the wall, Joe's snoring stopped at last and Ted pulled his blanket a little higher towards his chin. *I'm sitting on top of the world,* he thought, and then, *Just flying through air, just flying through air.*

～～

It was only a few weeks before Roy Kelly came back to work, presented with a medal—"gold," said someone; "bronze," said someone else—inscribed to mark the miracle. There were rumors he'd been given a watch too. Ted looked for it, new and shiny, on the boilermaker's arm—he looked for the new bright blue in Roy Kelly's eyes. But he never seemed able to get a clear look at either and, as the right angles of the suspended deck spread themselves back from the middle of the curve towards its landlocked ends, he saw less and less of the miraculous diver altogether.

Less and less, then, of all the bridge boys; the backyard beers wound down at Joe and Joy's. The job was rounding up, finishing off, and the stories the men told each other now on the rare nights they did still gather had turned away from where they'd come from and what they'd done to wondering what they might do next. The deck met the ends of its arch; the pylons took on their slick silver granite coating; the road came in layers of asphalt, concrete; the last of the sixty thousand gallons of thick grey paint went onto the steel.

One last man fell, and died, and a team of painters was dispatched to clean his blood off the granite.

The noise dulled and the bustle stilled. The barges stopped coming and going. The workshops sat silent. And the bridge looked like a whole bridge as the city adjusted to its shape, its size, to the way it could insinuate itself into so many different views and aspects. The tallest thing in Sydney's profile, the thing that came closest to the clouds.

And Joe, it seemed, was right. As plans for its opening hatched and bloomed, the memory of the structure's evolution dimmed a little every day. It would be just another road that people walked along, already impervious to the time before, when it wasn't there, and to everything that had happened in between. It would be just another road that people walked along, up in the air, between the blue of the sky and the water, as if it was nothing at all.

But sometimes at night, the dream still blinked on and off inside Ted's mind, and once, watching a ferry's path across the water, he imagined standing where Kelly had stood, standing like a diver with his toes curled over the edge of the steel, ready to push himself out and away and into the air. It was the buzz of an aeroplane that broke his daydream; men with newsreel cameras getting ready to make pictures of his bridge for the world.

For three weeks, they tested it with every weight and strain they could think of—could it withstand winds of a hundred miles an hour? Could it withstand a change in temperature of more than a hundred degrees? Could it bear the weight of ninety-six railway locomotives, jammed in buffer to buffer?

It could.

Standing below by its southeastern foot, Ted watched the light change. If he stood long enough, he might see the precise angle of the sun that threw the bridge's reflection perfectly onto the water, might see the creeping shadows of dusk as the air darkened almost to the darkness of the frame itself, right round to those early-morning stripes the night's boats left behind. Overhead, the engines rolled on, one by one, paused, waited, and then began to roll off.

As they puffed out of the sky and back onto the land, Ted crouched down again with Jacko, both listening to the machines' fading thunder. It was an awkward squat—his feet often still felt like they were planted on the barge, suspended over the harbor's movement. He supposed he'd get used to dry land again, after a while. Funny too to think of this land being under cover now, protected from the sky and all its weather by the roof of the bridge. Funny to think that the sky above it that he'd gazed at as a boy, the sky taken in by Joe's patient astronomer, was blocked out completely, that the rain would have to find its own sneaky chinks and crevices to get through to the grass that would grow, smooth and obscuring, over all the disturbance of the bridge's site and foundations. The long tubing tunnels that had snaked down a hundred feet into the land, into the bedrock, to hold the two halves of the arch apart from each other with that intricate web of cables, had been filled in, disappeared and buried as if they never existed.

"Another layer," said Joy that night. "Something for the next lot to dig up, like Joe dug up that old brick." And it was funny, thought Ted, that the past could be set up for the future as quickly, as easily as that.

Joe leaned back, blocking a shape in the air with his hands to show off the size of the brick. "All those years buried," he said, "buried and forgotten; they think it was a keystone, you know—not just a regular brick, but the keystone for an arch." He smiled a little. "Still wish I could overhear what they talked about, with their nips of rum—probably gardens and gossip and all the same stuff we talk about now." He raised his cup towards Joy, towards Ted, and then, "There's work going out at the airport, Russian George says. Said we should head out tomorrow, see what's happening. You'll stay with us, Ted, no question. And we'll see how George can fix us up for something to bring in the shillings."

Ted smiled. It hadn't occurred to him that he might leave—hadn't occurred to him that he might have to. He was halfway through rereading *Gulliver* with Joy and he wouldn't have wanted to break off in the middle—Gulliver, after all, was about to reach the flying island of Laputa. Again. Such a little piece of conversation, and such a big thing resolved; he turned his smile from one to the other.

"It'd be something to be near the planes," he said. "About the only thing that would make up for not seeing the bridge all day." There was a rumor that Smithy would fly by when it opened, and Ted wanted to make sure he knew when to look up, and exactly where, to see that sleek tube of silver.

~

In the mash of plans for the bridge's opening, someone had suggested that the families of the bridge's dead men walk across first.

"There's not so many of them as would slow down the ceremony," said Russian George.

"But it'd be a bit depressing," said Joe. "Reckon they should be aiming for jubilation, shouldn't they?"

"Send Kelly across," said Ted and Joy at the same time.

"Miraculous," said Joy.

"Marvelous," said Ted. You couldn't do better for jubilation or celebration.

But it was a band of the workers who led the way in the end, a banner slung out in front of them, and only slightly held up by some trouble with a man on a horse, his sword glinting in the sun. Ted and Joe, in step in the middle, were so far from the edge that the view was invisible and they might have been walking along any landlocked boulevard.

Still, it was extraordinary the way it reared up, opened up, to receive you. Approaching along the road from the south, the height of the arch seemed to disappear altogether—foreshortened, one of its artists might have said—so that all there was to the bridge was the boxy rectangle of its frame directly overhead. And then you were in it, in the guts of it, looking up through the crosshatching of cords and struts to the blue and the sunlight above. Flags flicked their color in the breeze from the summit of the arch, and an occasional plane, higher again, turned a metallic glint towards the ground. Inside, in the center, it was enormous; Ted almost lost his footing with his head thrown back to take it in, and the line of workers behind him was ready to walk on over the top of his pause.

"Come on, Teddy, keep it moving," someone called, "and watch how your feet are falling." There was a rumor—no one knew if it could be true—that the vibrations of them all marching in step could bring the whole thing crashing down with a great splash into the harbor.

But it looked so graceful, so elegant, the way its two lines curved, one larger, one smaller, the way that web of steel jumped between them, linking, tightening, and holding, no matter how the footsteps fell. And all around, the cheering, and the noise: from the sound of it, all of Sydney had been pulled into this great big thing, this great big magnet. *No chance of hearing her talking to herself today*, thought Ted, wishing he could touch just a bit of her steel, feel its smoothness, its strength.

In the crush of the crowds—they said more than a million people had pressed into the city—Ted lost sight of Joe, made his way into a pub, reckoning on one drink before he headed home. The barmaid smiled, nodding her head towards the bustle outside. "You part of all that?" she asked, and Ted nodded, too proud not to say he'd marched over with the first band of workers.

Her eyebrows raised. "That'll be something to tell your grandchildren one day."

The cold bubbles fizzed inside his mouth; sure, there were stories he could tell. And he told her about walking for work from the beach back when he'd begun, about the graceful curve made entirely of straight lines, about the view from the top in the dead of night, the city's lights thrown over the land below like a blanket of sparkling jewels.

"You're the poet of the bridge," she laughed, and he laughed too.

"Tell you the best one," he said, and he started the story of Roy Kelly's dive, that throwaway line beforehand as his spanner had fallen—"S'pose someone'll be going over sooner or later"—and the sharp retort, "Don't be so damn silly." He gave that line to Russian George, thickening his voice into a suitably round accent and apologizing for the "damn."

And then it was the day, it was the hour, and he was telling the story as Kelly himself—he knew what the water looked like, rushing up, as well as he knew what the man looked like, rushing down. How many times had he seen it, in its pieces, awake and asleep, over the years? "Then I came up to the surface, and I was

216

alive, marvelously alive." The woman's chin in her hand, her eyes shining.

For the rest of her life, thought Ted, *she'll tell people that story: how she poured a drink for the man who went off the bridge and survived, how she had a drink with him the day it opened.*

"What's your name, then?" she said, taking the empty glass as he pushed it across the bar.

He thought about it a moment, made a play of counting the coins for his next drink in the palm of his hand. Ted Parker wasn't the name of a hero—*and neither*, thought Ted, *was Roy Kelly. Bit too Irish*, as his mum would've said. He placed the coins on the bar towel, stacked carefully, biggest to smallest, in a heap. "Joe Brown," he said.

The name of the best man he knew, tied up and part of the best story he'd ever told.

"Have this one on me, Joe Brown," the barmaid said, pushing the coins back towards him.

~

There was no work on the planes; not much of it anywhere. In the end, Joe found a postman's round and Ted went to the train yards, watched all the engines coming and going across the knitted pattern of the tracks. Every so often, he hopped onto a carriage and ran down to see his mum; he'd stay for lunch, sometimes for dinner, and if there was a full moon rising at the right time, he'd walk down to the sand and watch it pave its way across the water. Never stayed more than a night—he said he missed home when he was away from it, and his mother didn't seem to mind that he didn't mean this place where she was.

On the way back, he took the underground train through the city, loving the moment when it reemerged into the sunlight and headed on over the bridge to the north side. It was strange being back on it, and the noise and push made by one engine seemed so small, so insignificant compared to the scores of them he'd watched line up for all those tests. But then the whole thing did seem smaller now—and people did walk across without even noticing where they were. The only stories he heard men telling were about missing the last ferry north and how—miraculously—they could make their way home across the water. That was as much of a miracle as they wanted.

But sometimes, through the train's window, he thought he caught a glimpse of something—maybe fluttering, maybe floating, maybe falling. Sometimes it was a bird, turning with the wind. Sometimes it was the glint of a plane's metal skin, higher up. Sometimes it was less distinct, a shimmer, a curl in the air below. His neck might crane this way, then that, his eyes trying to dodge the angular grey struts and bands of his bridge. And once, with the window open, he was sure he caught the sound of a great splash in the water, sure he felt a spot of its wetness on his cheek. Once, with the window open, he was sure he heard shouts from the quieter shore that now lay below. Once, he was so sure he'd seen something he'd left the train as soon as it stopped on the north shore, walking back along the bridge's footpath towards the south and peering down into the quiet calm of the harbor. A boat puttered past, a little girl in the stern, craning her neck to look up at the enormous shadowy thing blocking her sky. She waved at Ted, both arms high above her head, and Ted waved back as her boat disappeared below the deck. Shaking his head at his fancy, he started the long walk back to Joe and Joy, the water dipping in and out of view as he made his way along the river, cresting hills every so often and turning back for glimpses of this bit of the city, to the south, this bit, to the east, or an illusory curve or cross brace of bridge.

Later, lying in bed, he tried to understand how something like that might work. If Joy was right and Roy Kelly was a miracle, then you'd expect him to leave something of himself behind—but would you expect there to have been hints about the moment before it happened? He supposed these were the sorts of thoughts you could only have when you were half asleep, but if something happened somewhere, if something singular, unexpected, happened in some particularly malleable place, maybe it couldn't help but leave a trace—or alert you to its coming. People sat and waited for miracles, so there had to be signs that they would come. People went back to the spots where extraordinary things had happened, so there had to be evidence left behind.

He thought about the boats' wakes so clearly visible at sunrise. Everyone took them to mark the tracks of things that had traveled the night before. But what if they were the routes—the curves, the turns, the jibes and tacks—that some flotilla of boats was going to make that day, the next day, whenever? He liked that; it felt like a kind of magic calligraphy, a map coming into focus from an invisible world, the way photographs were said to appear on their blank sheets of paper. All you had to do was work out how to translate its message. And a man falling down into the water—surfacing, alive; really, that could only be the punctuation.

Dawes

WILLIAM DAWES flicked through the pages of words and sentences, adjusting a sound here, a dash of punctuation there. There were so many pieces of conversation in his little books now, all woven around a new vocabulary. The laughing suggestion, "*kotbarabáng*: he will cut," from one woman as Dawes had carefully shaved her husband's face; the discussions about washing taken to the vicar's wife, about trying to get fleas out of jackets, about drinking tea, bathing in the morning, about the same word being used for ships and islands.

There were prefixes and suffixes that changed a tense from past to future, that changed the number of people you were talking about, that changed the outcome of the action you were about to undertake. Because how you talked about rowing somewhere was different if you intended returning alone or with someone else in your canoe. And how you talked about being beaten differed if two of you had been hit by someone, or three.

The intricacies were extraordinary; so many things still to learn. Yet here were pages and pages of words: winds, constellations, fish, trees, plants, and body parts. And beneath them all, on some pages, he could make out fragments of this coastline, that inlet, sketched in faint pencil.

This collection of knowledge for his laughingly proposed compendium, and he had made a start on a dictionary. No alligators or comets, but twenty-odd pages of new words—Eora words; Kamarigal words; Darug words—although its alphabet was jumbled so that *L* came after *W* and then the whole notebook gave way to more lists. Names of people. Names of colors. Names of fruit. Still, "Mr. Dawes *búdyeri káraga*," they said.

"Mr. Dawes pronounces well."

Taking up his pencil to add another phrase—"here we are, talking"—he mulled over the best way of transcribing its sounds, its syllables. "*Galu píyala*," he tried; "*ngalu píyala*." The different weights and inflections of moving a single sound to a slightly different part of your mouth; he loved trying to pitch the letters perfectly, place them perfectly, catch their smallest intonation or their subtlest emphasis. "*Galu? Ngalu?* We two are talking to each other. We are talking. *Ngalu piyala*."

Almost eighteen months lay between this day and the stumble he'd made at South Head, eighteen months since that sensation of the world falling away, the sight of that great jet of water streaming up. The longed-for ships had come—their ratio of ailing convicts to supplies all the wrong way round at first, so that the harbor seemed awash again with dead bodies, but white this time, not black. News of the world had come—wars and illnesses and political revolutions. And then more ships, and more people, and more stories, and a summer so hot that bats and birds had fallen from their perches, unable to hang on. Another infernal image.

A whale had come too, frolicking and spouting off the observatory and making Dawes wonder if it was a whale he'd seen, all that time ago—a whale that, somehow, no one else had noticed.

Through all of which, Dawes kept talking to his native neighbors, through the convivial times—one woman insisting on delivering her child as close as possible to the Governor's house, as close as possible to the house of the man some of them called "Father"—and the conflicted ones—when the Governor had demanded revenge for the murder of his gamekeeper: two natives to be taken prisoner, the heads of ten others brought in bags to be displayed, as admonition, as deterrent.

The strange negotiations Watkin Tench had undertaken, talking the total down to six prisoners, of which, he suggested, some might be "set aside for retaliation," while the rest, "at a proper time, might be liberated." Very well, the Governor had agreed, although if six prisoners could not be taken, "they should be shot."

That strange expedition, Dawes among its men, wishing he'd refused to go, and saying so, first to the vicar and later to anyone who would listen—irrespective of the dangerous insubordination of the statement. He'd needed this new phrase then: "*Ngalu piyala.* We are talking to each other." Surely we don't decapitate the people with whom we have these conversations? They're living with us; their children are living with us; they are having their children among us. He'd needed more of the light, vital words that he knew now: *badaya* for laughter, *gittee gittee* for tickle, "*poerbungána*: take my hand and help me up," or the particular song to be sung when a flock of pelicans passed by.

Tench had shaken his head over his friend's stance. "There will be more to this," he'd said. "It will send you home, whatever you've said about staying, whatever you've told the Governor, the Astronomer Royal, about all the work that still needs to be done and you being the only person who might do it. It will turn this point of yours over entirely from science to gunpowder."

And whatever warm words he listed, whatever jokes and friendships he made, there were other questions Dawes could ask now, in his new language.

"*Mínyin gulara eóra*? Why are the black men angry?"

"*Inyam ngalwi* white men. *Tyérun kamarigal.* Because the white men are settled here. The *kamarigal* are afraid."

"*Mínyin tyérun kamarigal?* Why are they afraid?"

"*Gúnin.*" The guns.

The guns, thought Dawes now, pulling free the pages that held the last month's weather and the list of the girls who were teaching him their language. His hand hardly paused as it passed over that still-blank sheet that he'd headed up so optimistically—*Report of the Expected Return of the Comet of 1532 and 1661 in the Year 1788*—more than three years before. He still looked, every night, so committed to scanning the heavens that Sydney's newer residents—who knew him less, who found the distance he let his many occupations create between himself and the rest of the settlement inexplicable—made their own jokes about his tasks, his passions, and laughed that this busyness rendered him invisible to mortal eyes.

Then let the immortal ones see me, he'd thought sacrilegiously when someone told him of this. All that time he'd spent imagining himself—his eyes, his gaze, his comprehension—up in the air: better up there than embroiled in a mess on the ground.

He straightened his records and inventories again. Sometimes he wondered if there was a way of arranging their points to make not a dictionary but a different sort of map, one with more layers, more dimensions, than foreshores, tracks, and river courses. A different picture of this place, and underneath it all the accompaniment of that sound, that rushing of air, of wind, of water, of something, and the constant sense that if he'd been able to turn, just once, a little sooner, or later, or farther, he'd have caught sight of something extraordinary—even if it was only from the corner of his eye.

His dreams of comets—the one he still sought, and the apocalyptic one from Laputa with which he confused it sometimes in the dead of night—intermingled with what he knew now of *goo-me-dah*, dead bodies, the nasty diving *mawn*, or that local belief, learned so long ago now, about bones in the ground, bodies soaring to the sky. And these dreams collided with his memories of stumbles and falls, like the day on the harbor's south head.

"*Mikoarsbi*: his foot slipped."

At least now he dreamed in two languages, his and theirs— patiently plodding dreams of consonants and labeling; fast inter-locutory dreams about who was saying what, in which language, and what it meant, and who might understand. While Watkin Tench dreamed that his manuscript proved word for word the same as the manuscript delivered by John White. While John White dreamed of the terrible omen of his name in a fledgling settlement: "More Indians with blue eyes," he'd confess quietly to Dawes when he'd spent another night watching another settlement fail, another batch of white men disappear.

"*Mímadyimi*?" Dawes would say cheerfully against their night-time fears. "What's the matter with you?" No wonder the new-comers muttered that they wondered where he was sometimes.

This place had always been a place of imagination: the remnant of the idea of a Great Southern Land presumed to exist to balance the globe; the remnant of the idea of verdant grass and cool water promised by Captain Cook, by Sir Joseph Banks in that mythical "Botany Bay." People were still imagining it from the other side of the world, even now when real things had been claimed and named and classified and published. One optimist dreamed for it a vast and bounteous future, complete with Art and Industry and a mighty bridge spanning the harbor—which would have sounded as fanciful to the people who lived in its shabby settlement as the gossamer bridge Dawes had proposed years before to the surgeon.

At least he'd leave a bridge of words between the new people

and the old, thought Dawes, and everyone could keep talking if
he was sent home. Some part of him trusted he would stay, simply
because he knew how to say a long time: *tarími.* "*Tarimíba inyam
ngalawaba.* I will live here a long time; I will stay a long time."
And he knew the native name for this place—Warran. But if they
did send him home, the words would stay, like the tracks left by
those curled vessels that carried his interpreters to the observatory's point and back, little stripes of movement laid onto the
harbor. Because perhaps he never would find his way back again, if
this really was a place of lost pathways and indistinguishable inlets
that could shift and move like Laputa. All those officers who still
got lost in the coves closest to the settlement—still unable, after
almost four years, to tell which was which, or where they were.
And now there were convicts who believed that China was a scant
one-hundred-and-fifty-mile walk to the north; some had set off
for its promise.

If this place was as malleable and mobile as that, then at
least his translators—Boorong, Balinderri, Nanberri, Wauriweeal,
Berangaroo, Djalgear, Pandul—might help him pin it down, and
his brightest star, Patyegarang, who not only taught him her words
but was learning to read his own, could act as its envoy, its bridge.
She'd refused his English at first. Why should she learn his words,
she'd argued, when he understood so perfectly what she was saying
in her own? But his books had fascinated her—When would he
read to her? Would the vicar read to her instead if he had no time?
Now she read their pages herself. Some nights, their lessons lasted
so long that she was still there when Dawes went to take the temperature of the sunrise. Some nights, they talked so long that she fell
asleep where she sat, muddling the words for candle, for blanket, in
her tiredness. And when she crossed the harbor in her small canoe
in the morning, he stood watching the line its course etched across
the water's surface, like a pathway etched onto a map.

If he did find a way back, with the embodiment of his now-faint image of Miss Rutter—Mrs. Dawes—he'd make his balloon and take them both, his wife and Patye, up through the clouds and into his bird's-eye view of this place.

"William Dawes." Standing behind him in the doorway, Patye. "William Dawes." She nodded towards one of the big ships, lolling on its anchor in the cove.

"Not yet," he said. "I don't know yet if I sail home or not. And if so, I don't know when." He shrugged, and she shrugged in return, picking up a book from his desk, flicking through its pages, and pausing here and there when something caught her eye. "'The word, which I interpret the "Flying" or "Floating Island" is in the original "Laputa",'" she read, slow with care, and, "'I ventured to offer a conjecture of my own, that "Laputa" was "Lap outed"; "lap" the dancing of the sunbeams in the sea, and "outed" a wing.'"

"So well, you read so well, Patye," said Dawes as she smiled, put the book down, and sat herself on a chair. "Nothing more?" And she shook her head, pointing to the doorway: someone was coming along the path.

"Come in, sir, come in," said Dawes, falsely hearty, but the man waved the words aside—no, he wasn't stopping, just passing to say that the Governor would decide who stayed, who embarked in the next weeks, and that if Lieutenant Dawes had any good word he'd like put in or spoken . . .

But Dawes waved the offer aside in his turn. "The Governor will decide," he said simply. He was doing good work—had done so much of it in the colony's life: that surely stood for something. "In the meantime, perhaps my friend here could read a little for you, that you might tell the Governor of her progress?" He scanned his pile of books and papers for something more appropriate than *Gulliver*, pushed the Psalms towards her. "Maybe one-thirty-seven, the Lord's song in a strange land?"

But Patye demurred, squirming a little in her seat, ducking her head and sitting awkwardly on her hands.

"No?"

The messenger made his salute. "I will leave you with your lessons, sir," he said at last. "I hope you're able to continue them when the ships sail."

"If not," said Dawes without hesitation, "*wellamabaóu.*" He smiled, enjoying the man's blankness. "I'm sorry, that's *I will return.* This language is becoming so familiar to me now."

In the stillness that followed the man's departure, he opened the Bible to the Psalms, pushing the book towards Patye. "'They that carried us away required of us a song, and they that wasted us required of us mirth,'" he read, his finger moving across the words as he spoke them. *Badaya, badaya*: to laugh so heartily, it almost hurt. "You wouldn't read, Patye? You wouldn't show the Governor's man how much you knew?"

"I was—" She dipped her head to one side, ear touching shoulder.

"Bashful," he said. "*Wúrul?*"

"*Wúrulbadyaoú.* Ashamed," she said carefully. "If I didn't say it well." She paused a moment, then: "There was more talk of going away?"

"And of returning." He smiled again, watching as she made a great show of pushing his books, his papers, out of his reach, before she stood and moved towards the open doorway, holding out her hand.

"Ah, Patye," said William Dawes, puffing the air out of his cheeks. "Perhaps you're right—no more words for today." And he let her lead him from the room's darkness into the thick brightness of the day. He looked up as automatically as ever but no comet. Of course it was years too late, invisible at noon, and now lost, he supposed, somewhere in the greater space of constellations and orbits.

At the edge of his little firepit she crouched down, gestured for him to crouch as well. "Here," she said, "here," patting the ground next to her. And he sat, clumsily, his stiff leg straight, his good leg crossed beneath him. His mouth filled with the fire's smoke, and he looked so long at its light that bright discs stayed in front of his eyes when he finally blinked. There was the tide, curling against the rocky shore below, and, following exactly the same beat, Patye was holding her hand up to the fire, warming its skin, and pressing that warmth into William Dawes's own hand, cradled and upturned in his lap.

It was the rhythm of the gesture he noticed first, the way her movement mirrored the in and out of the water. And then the gesture itself, the transfer of warmth, like comfort or a gift. Her face turned towards the fire, she was looking at its heat, not at her friend, and Dawes found himself staring through the flames, the harbor, the whole scene now imprinted so clearly on his memory, as the fire's warmth traveled to his hand, to the center of his hand, through hers.

"*Ngalu piyala*." She turned from the fire, smiled at him. "*Ngalu piyala*: here we are, we two, talking." Then her gaze went back to the fire.

Watching the surface of the water, his eyes and mind suddenly tired, he felt the rhythm of her hand against his again and again, heard the low, soft sound of her breath like a breeze through the fine needles of the she-oak or the last hiss of a wave as it ran out against the shore.

To the east, towards the harbor's southern cliff, a white seabird swooped and dived down to the water, then another, and another, each catching the sun so their feathers glistened like satin or lustered china.

"*Molu-molu*," said Patye, and she shivered.

"*Molu-molu*," Dawes repeated.

Yes, they were like a shower of shooting stars: her terror, his beauty. The clouds above sat smooth and square, like the sails that had haunted Dan Southwell's dreams—Dan Southwell, back out in the world somewhere. Dawes wondered what shapes he saw in the clouds now, wherever he was, on sea or land. Maybe the shape of the harbor's high northern head that he'd stared at, waiting, so long. "And this?" He nodded towards the fire, her hand, his hand, the triangle of warmth she was making.

"*Buduwa*," she said. "*Buduwa*."

"You warm your hand by the fire and press the warmth into mine? *Buduwa?*"

She nodded, but it sounded softer to him the next time she said it: "*Putuwá*."

"*Buduwa; putuwá*." There it was again, the closeness between the sounds of different letters, and yet what different parts of your mouth you needed to make them. Such a friendly word, warm and generous: he wished it had an equivalent in English.

Watching and waiting as she paddled her small canoe across the water, William Dawes rubbed hard at his eyes until bright flares like the fire's imprinted on them again. Looking up to the wide blue, the last glint of his fingers' pressure flashed across his vision, but there was nothing falling from the sky; of course there never had been. It was a dream, a fantasy, a misapprehension snuck in through some chink in his imagination.

Walking slowly, he circled the observatory, up to the ridge and between its trees, and down again to where the colony's defensive little magazine sat, its bricks strong and sturdy. He leaned forward, patting its keystone and tracing the date etched there—*1789*—with one finger. His hand was as golden brown as its sandstone now, the texture of its skin as lined and ingrained as the rough rock. And the keystone's promise had been right: 1789 had given way to 1790, to 1791. There would surely be a 1792 as well, and then another year, and another, whether or not William Dawes stood in this place long enough to see them.

Buduwa; putuwá: he must write that down. Soft as a rose petal—he'd carry it like a poem. His own keystone.

Dan

ARMS HIGH above his head, fingers locking them into an arch, Dan winced at the bouncing and buffeting of the plane's wheels against the runway and the sudden drag of a speed that belonged in the air meeting the still solidity of the ground.

"Welcome to Sydney," said a disembodied voice, and he saw his reflection smile in the window. Cynthia stowed her book; the family across the aisle began counting jumpers and toys, and the Russian woman reached between the seats to touch Dan's arm lightly.

"Welcome home," she said. "It looks very beautiful."

He nodded towards the window in acknowledgment and saw the vast airport tarmac covered with lines and numbers, instructions in different-colored paints, the points of different-colored lights, like a map drawn directly onto the surface of the land.

"Well, more beautiful away from here," he said. "But thank you. I'm sorry you came so far and . . ." He glanced at the empty seat next to her, uncertain what to say.

"Is no matter now." Her face was blank.

"And I wondered, could I give you my mother's phone number, if there's anything . . . ?"

She shook her head slowly. "Welcome home," she repeated, and gestured for him to join the slow-moving queue.

Where would they take her father, he wondered as he began to walk: through the front door of the plane, like a passenger, or through the back, like a piece of cargo? He closed his eyes, let the push of the other passengers carry him forward. He was aching to be anywhere but inside this aeroplane.

The floor of the airbridge squeaked and bounced, fragile— almost implausible—after the heavy certainty of the plane. Dan felt his legs shake a little against its movement, his feet bracing as he took each step.

"Got to find your land legs," said Cynthia, moving ahead of him. "Another flight survived."

Barking, thought Dan, and laughed. Perhaps he had become Charlie's Mr. Britpop after all.

In the cavernous arrivals hall the man in uniform seemed to spend too long comparing the photograph in Dan's passport to the tired face in front of him.

"You've been away a long time?"

"Been years now, yes."

"And you're in the money game . . ." Glancing at the immigration card. Dan shrugged. "Guess everyone is now, one way or another," said the man, stamping a blank page in the passport so hard that everything in his cubicle shuddered. "Even the wife wants an investment property." And he shrugged in return.

Dan smiled. "Good luck with that then," he said.

Below him, in the baggage hall, people slouched against empty carts, peered at the black bags on the carousel that all looked the same, reached out to pat the dogs that combed the hall, sniffing and snuffling. "So sweet," he'd heard a woman say once as a dog busied its nose against the outside pocket of her case with increasing interest. "Sweet," the officer had agreed. "Particularly if it's only

a lamb sandwich that he's interested in. Mind if we have a look?"
And the woman had paled. Years ago, he'd seen her—wasn't even
sure which airport it was now—yet sometimes she came to the
front of Dan's mind and he wondered what had happened to her
and why he'd thought of her. So many people you saw in a day,
but she'd lodged in his memory, surfacing every so often and still
so clearly delineated that he knew he'd recognize her if he ever saw
her again.

Coming through the last customs check, he caught sight of himself here and there, in metal surfaces, in glass ones. He hoped people
would suck in their breath and slap his shoulder and say, "Mate, you
still look the same," or, "But you haven't changed at all." *That'd be
nice*, he thought. *That'd feel good.* Then the glass doors that gave way
onto the arrivals hall showed how his shoulders slumped, and as he
pulled them up, he glimpsed, through his own reflection, a man
holding a square of cardboard with his name written on it. Dan
Kopek—his dad's made-up name. "For wealth," his mother always
laughed at the irony, "for riches." *There could hardly be two of us.*

"I think you're waiting for me?" The wheels on his case were
having trouble taking corners, lurching as its weight tipped and
weaved through the crowd. "I'm Dan Kopek, but I thought my
mother . . ."

"They called a car this morning to take you to the city, to Charlotte Brown's address in the city." The man rolled the cardboard in
on itself, impassive. "You want to ring them to check?"

"No, no." Dan righted the awkward case. "As long as you know
where I'm going." And he followed the man out into the morning,
the sweet warm spring air rushing up against him. His shoulders
loosened a little: birthday air, right temperature, right weight, right
brightness. A group of girls passed, thin and honey-brown in summer dresses, their voices loud with Caro's accent. *She should have
come with me*, he thought suddenly. *It would have been fun to show*

her all my places. It would have been great for her to meet Gramps. Showing her off, he thought out of nowhere: *I'd like to have shown her off.*

In the car, he took the backseat and slouched as he watched the buildings and busy streets pass. There was more traffic, and there were bigger cars. More freeways too, ribbons of concrete flying off where he remembered slow lanes and the stop-start of lights.

"Where's this place we're going?"

"Middle of the city—one of those new apartment blocks. You been away long?"

Long enough not to know about new apartments in the middle of the city. Every second image through the window showed cranes, or hoardings, or deep pits waiting to be filled. Disoriented by the route, he thought for a moment the car was heading in the wrong direction, and was about to say something when the city's skyline appeared from the crest of a hill—recognizable enough, even with its new spires and heights—and he leaned back again. He wondered why he'd never found a correspondingly familiar view of London. He knew pieces of it—Big Ben, the Eye, the dome, the Battersea Power Station—and he could count off the bridges along some of the river's reaches, but he couldn't have drawn the shapes of glass and steel running alongside any section of the river the way he thought he could here, even if this city's topographies and connections were blurry in his mind. Sydney set itself up like a stage; maybe London, so much older and more organic, didn't like to pose so much.

He closed his eyes, back above the rows of rich sandstone cliffs and buttresses that he'd watched during the plane's descent. Their color had been high, exaggerated by the early sun like the colors in the city were now, and any water tucked between them had turned to quicksilver as the plane crossed them. The first time he'd seen that happen was the first time he'd flown anywhere—a holiday when he was a kid, with Charlie and Gramps. Where they'd been going, he'd forgotten; all he could remember was how astonishingly big the country had looked, and Gramps's stories about the "poor buggers sent out to map that with a bit of flour and a compass and off to try and measure the lot." He'd seen quicksilver water. He'd seen their plane's shadow skating fast over the land's surface. He'd seen mountains and valleys, and ridges lined up like stored scenery with empty space behind—there was something comforting in the fact these things had still looked the same this morning.

Eyes open now, the city itself looked like a cardboard cutout of shapes and blocks, with nothing behind its facade but that space, or a drop, or maybe even the edge of the world. One of those tricks your mind could play—he glanced up towards the clouds, their picture-book shapes nothing like the complex landscape of crevasses and peaks and spots of rainbow he'd just flown through. How quickly, how easily, you could move from above to below.

When he opened his eyes again, he was deep in the city's canyons, horns blasting and cars cutting in front of each other, all haste and self-importance. A bunch of kids—the girls looked so young, which made Dan feel old—tumbled out of a bar, headed for a convenience store with bright lights cutting the bright morning and shelves heavy with milk, candy, dailies, and glossy magazines. Straining to read the newspaper posters, to see what was happening in the world, Dan's head jerked against the window as the car swerved and the driver swore.

"Jesus—sorry." One of the girls had lost her footing, falling into the path of the car and jumping back, wide-eyed and gasping. The driver pulled into the curb and Dan wondered for a moment if he was going to check that the girl was all right, or abuse her for being in the way. But, "It's this building," he said. "Just ask at the desk and they'll buzz you up."

"How much do I . . . ?"

"Taken care of. Just ask at the desk and they'll let her know you're here."

More than a decade ago, in his taxi to the airport, Dan had imagined Charlie walking back to her single room in the hollow of one of Sydney's grubbier inner-city streets. *Nice that life's going well*, he thought as the heavy glass doors opened automatically to let him in.

The elevator pushed up far enough and fast enough to make his ears pop twice, the hall beyond its smooth doors quiet and sepulchral with thick, dark carpet and too many mirrors. He looked left, right, left again, heard a door click somewhere, and saw a line of light widening in the gloom.

"Charlie?"

"Down here. I'll just hold the door open so we don't lock ourselves out on top of everything."

"On top of . . ." Trying to turn his case into her doorway, hug her, and make some proper greeting, and then it seemed as if the wall had fallen away from her apartment and he was about to be sucked off the edge of its dangerously high floor. He staggered against the vertigo, his arm reaching for the sofa.

"Bloody hell, Charlie," he said. "Look at your bloody view." It reached across the air his plane had just breached, out towards the thin line of purple-blue hills that rose up from the city's plain, eighty, ninety kilometers away or more. Between this here and that there, the city poked up glass and metal and steel. Angular shapes caught the morning sun and gave way to the colors and shapes of cheek-by-jowl living intercut with trees, water, road. So many windows up so close; so much space so far away.

"Your heights thing," she said. "Sorry." She watched as he steadied himself and took half a step forward, unsure of how to get back to some kind of greeting. In the end, he stepped back again and balanced on the arm of the lounge.

"This is some place you've got. It's good to see you. I didn't know which perfume to get. How's Gramps?"

"Don't worry about the perfume. You should call your mum, let her know you're here." They were frozen, awkward, in the wide, light room, and the silence lasted a little too long. Then, "Good flight?" asked Charlie, but her voice was flat.

Dan rubbed his eyes. "Weird flight," he said, blinking. "Near-death experience when another jumbo cut underneath us just out of London. Spent the transit stop looking for a lost boy's family. Then the old man sitting in front of me died halfway to Sydney. And I was having the weirdest dreams—Gramps's story, you know, diving off the bridge; I don't know where I thought I was, or what I was thinking. I was him, but it wasn't him. I don't know." It sounded nonsensical, disconnected and abbreviated like that.

Charlie shifted her weight from one foot to the other, and the silence thickened again. "Do you want a shower or something?" she said finally, crossing into another room and coming back with a towel. "You'll feel better when you're a bit less scruffy." That was more like her voice, and she threw the towel at him, smiling at last as his hand jumped and caught it. "Have a shower. I'll make coffee. Then we can talk. Bathroom." She pointed away from the wall of glass.

Pulling his shirt over his head, he could smell the cake of soap he'd used in the airport. He shook his limp hair, peered at himself in Charlie's mirror, wished she'd said, "But you still look the same, you haven't changed at all," as if those phrases would have had some extra power, like spells or incantations. Leaning closer under the bright yellow light, he clocked the freckles, the lines, the pastiness of his skin after so many British summers. The marble bench was cool under his hands, against the tops of his legs. *A few days ago*, he thought, *I was on a Ferris wheel with Caro, and then Charlie rang, and then I saw her photo in a tube station on my way to work, and now*—he squinted—*and now I'm here.* He rubbed at his eyes until he saw flecks of silver, purple, blue behind their lids, and when he opened them again he almost swooned. *Like I saw her yesterday. Like this is nothing out of the ordinary. I don't know where the fuck I am.*

Standing under the running water, he was almost split in half by the shower's pressure, full and hot. He could feel every muscle in his shoulders, his neck, his back, could feel himself letting out a long deep breath that he didn't remember taking in. He was in Sydney. It had been a long flight. Everything would be fine. Maybe Gramps was fine—maybe it had turned out to be nothing. Good to be here, wherever here was. Up in the air and Charlie on the other side of the door. It felt like home. He turned the tap to full cold, wincing against the water's icy needles—hadn't done that for years. Every day until he left for England, he'd finished every shower with the cold tap on full, icy water pricking his skin. It was a nod to summer, to cold showers after long swims, but in England the showers never had enough pressure, the summers never had enough heat. He'd never even been tempted to try. Here, in Charlie's bathroom, he adjusted the taps without thinking. It really did feel like home.

She was sitting at the table, facing the window, her coffee in front of her and a second mug at the seat opposite. "So you don't have to look at the view," she said, pointing. "Better? Find everything you need?"

The coffee was strong, dark, and hot; it ate into the roof of his mouth as he took too big a gulp. Turning a little, he braved a glance at the window and what lay beyond.

"Don't you find it distracting?"

"I'm not here that much," she said, blowing across the top of her mug. "Your mum rang, while you were in the shower—she's coming over, be here lunchtime or so. We had a late night, that's why we thought we'd send someone to pick you up instead of coming ourselves. I thought your mum could use a bit of a sleep-in." The quiet push of her breath across the coffee. "Of course I still see her all the time; and yes, she lets me know how you are . . ." This in response to some question playing across his face. "Anyway, so Gramps," she said. "Turns out," another long pause. "Gramps, yes, he passed away last night—we were just back from the hospital when you rang."

Dan felt his throat tighten and his eyes water, and the coffee seared another line from his mouth down into his chest. *I knew*, he thought, *I did know. And I should have . . .*

He was crying properly now, and he rubbed hard at his eyes with his sleeves, like his six-year-old self. *Caro was right: I wanted to be here. And now she'll never meet him, never hear him tell his stories.* Which seemed suddenly the worst and loneliest thing.

He swallowed again, a mouthful of the dry, locked-in air, and reached over, unsure whether or not to take Charlie's hand. "Charlie," he said, leaving his fingers near hers, on the table but apart. "Was it—did he—I'm so . . ." He saw himself standing too close to the space beyond a train platform, saw the silver bullet of another plane closing fast and near, saw the dull grey skin of the Russian man, his stillness.

"Pneumonia; he was pretty frail the last couple of winters. Even stopped walking down to the bridge in the end, although he managed every day till last year. And then he stopped getting out much at all. At least he wasn't in the hospital long—he didn't like being there at all. Your mum kept trying to work out ways we could kidnap him, but she's—well, your mum's not as young as she used to be either. These years since you left, mate—" an iciness nipped at the end of the clichéd word, "it's a bloody long time. Still—" She finished her coffee. "Good that you're here now."

"The night you rang: Caro had just told me I should come home—she thinks I should work out which side of the world I want to be on." He tried to smile, surprised by how much he already wished she was with him. "And then I spoke to you, about Gramps. And then the next morning I was standing opposite a poster at the tube station and I realized it had one of your photos on it. Gramps and Mum'd think it was a sign." He shrugged; she mirrored his movement. "One of those photos where you were trying to flatten the bridge out, shoot straight along the front so you lost the arch altogether. You still shooting it, Charlie? You ever find a way to get up there?"

She glanced at her watch. "We could walk down now, if you want. Easy there and back before your mum gets here. I've tried to walk down most days since Gramps stopped." Glancing at her watch again. "I just need to call a couple of people, if you want to . . ." She waved towards the sofas, her other hand already reaching for the phone.

Dan stood, took a couple of steps towards the window, his eyes watching the changing size of his reflection rather than anything on the other side of the glass.

The morning sun, risen directly behind the building in which he stood, was igniting the glass in the windows that faced him; he could almost feel the movement of the Earth as it turned towards the huge warm ball and piece after piece of the city lit up. Below, people were moving into their days—some jogging, some walking, some with their arms raised for taxis.

At the west-facing wall, Dan pressed his toes against the glass and worked his gaze down. Someone was crossing against the lights, too slowly for the traffic, although Dan realized after a moment he was only imagining the honking and the yelling from this entirely silent and sealed room. All he could hear was the hum of an air conditioner and the low mutter of Charlie's voice. Poor old Gramps; poor Charlie, obviously struggling, the way she skirted around it, away from it. He wished he'd had something better to say. Tipping his forehead to touch the window, keeping his breathing slow, he

ASHLEY HAY

watched as a man at the lights hit the pedestrian button again and again, so impatient that he finally looked up, way up, in exasperation. Dan was sure their eyes met.

He took half a step back again, lowered himself down to sit, trying to pick out buildings where he'd worked years before, buildings where friends had lived, probably didn't anymore. He leaned forward and looked north along the street.

But there was no trace of the bridge, obscured as it was by a nest of skyscrapers, metal and shiny reflective glass. It seemed wrong that the city's panorama could be missing its most identifiable piece. No matter how far he moved, he couldn't bring it into view, and he straightened at last, staring at all the windows and walls in front of him, wondering if this was Sydney at all—it could be anywhere. He lay down, his fingers patting the carpet's pile, and he wondered what Charlie meant exactly about his mum not being as young as she was, and his eyes closed, heavy.

"Dan?"

Sitting up too fast, his feet jerked against something hard—a table, the frame of a chair—and his hands pushed him up out of sleep. Brown carpet. Cream sofas. The huge thick window next to him. A complex light shade hanging from the ceiling above. For a moment—a breath, maybe long enough to count to three—he had no idea where he was.

"Dan?" A hand on his shoulder and he turned to see Charlie there as the world slithered back into place, back into time. He squeezed her fingers, felt the pressure of the warmth they returned. "Where'd you go?" The ice had gone out of her voice, and she kept hold of his hand, smiling. "I've got so many things to tell you."

"About Gramps?"

"Kind of. Come on—let's get out before you fall asleep again." And as she pulled him up, he steadied himself against her, gave her the hug he'd missed on the way in.

240

"I'm glad I came," he said.

Going down in the lift, he tried again, and failed, to piece together the shapes and turns of the streets that would connect where they were to where they were going. *Dear Caro*, he thought, imagining a postcard, an email, a text, *You'll be pleased to know that Sydney's streets have rearranged themselves while I've been away so it's not just London that I can't pin down. I'm walking with Charlie; I came too late; I wish you were here.* The higher sun shut his eyes into a squint as soon as he stepped outside, narrowing the tunnel of space he could see, and he strode out fast to keep up with Charlie's pace.

When they were little, when they came into the city, sometimes by ferry down the river, or by a train that clattered across the famous bridge, Dan and Charlie played a game, imagining everything disappearing, winding back to a Sydney that was only dirt tracks and rough tents and penned pigs and cows, not roads and pavements and smelly exhaust fumes. Gramps started them on it, telling them what the space had looked like around the bridge's big footprints—all through the industry of its creation, and then back further, back to tents, and trees, to British men in red coats, some with guns, some with compasses and telescopes, and then back before that again. Then Charlie began reading about remnant places, like the sand dunes below Kings Cross that people remembered from four or five decades earlier, when work on the bridge began. And it had kept them busy every trip after that: "Maybe this was a swamp; maybe there would've been great trees here; reckon you'd have had a view out forever from the top of this hill." Charlie took to hunting for parts of the city where what had been there was still allowed to poke through—the waterline at the end of the Botanic Gardens where you could stand on the bumpy sandstone ledges with your feet in the harbor's coolness, the bushy reserves beyond the zoo and

Middle Head on the opposite shore, still thick with birds and ango-phora, lizards and eucalypts. She sought out the little markers the city put down for other things that had changed or disappeared: the discs that marked the line of Circular Quay's foreshore as it had been in 1788 when the British came ashore; the pretty fingers of metal and glass that laid down the line their stream had taken, that one channel of running water that had dictated their choice to come here in the first place, and to stay.

Stepping over one of these markers now, Dan said, "Remember when we worked out we were walking up in the air?" Two little kids, each holding one of Gramps's hands, and he was telling them that what was left of the stream was now buried deep beneath their feet, that the level they were walking on now would have been up in the air for the first convicts, the first soldiers, the first few ladies.

"Our feet up around their ears maybe," he'd said. "Our feet walking up in the air." Over the Tank Stream, around the line of the harbor, the city that day floating above whatever place the city had been one hundred, two hundred, thousands of years before. "Did we get lost? I can't remember. We had a picnic, down by the harbor—and there was something else, wasn't there? I always meant to ask Gramps what else happened that day."

"I can't remember," said Charlie. "But I remember that thing of walking on air—that felt miraculous," she said as he went to take a step forward off the curb into the empty street and her arm flew across, blocking his chest. The light had changed; the traffic was coming. She hooked her arm through his, pulling him into step. He'd forgotten how tall she was, possibly even taller than him, if they turned back to back and both stood up straight, competing six-year-olds again. Long dark hair pulled back and perennially tanned skin. She looked great, hadn't changed at all.

"Like the people who were waiting for Jesus to walk across the water between the harbor's heads," said Dan. The way Gramps told that story, some days Dan and Charlie thought it really might have happened, back in the impossibly distant past of Gramps's youth, and that he himself might even have seen it.

"Another of Gramps's miracles," said Charlie, steering them left around a corner where Dan was sure they should have turned right. His feet braced against the steep slope of a hill, and by the time he looked up to orient himself they'd reached the huge buttressing wall that fed the roadway onto the bridge. There was a basketball court, tall skinny kids leaping high for the ball, higher for the hoop. Beyond its fence, with a heap of ratty plastic bags at his side, an old man in a tattered pink coat rocked back and forth on a bench, his eyes milky, his skin caked with dirt.

"Been here for years," said Charlie, heading towards him. "As long as I've been coming. Seems to be so many more of them now. And you think, you know, he must be someone's brother, someone's mate—don't they wonder where he went?" She reached down, put a handful of coins onto his stained cardboard plate. "I don't know: I reckon most people don't even see them anymore. This bloody government."

"Caro gets twenty pounds turned into pound coins every payday," said Dan, "and walks along The Strand giving it to"—he pulled himself up against the word *beggars*—"guys like this." He wasn't sure he'd ever handed over twenty pence, let alone a pound. The noise of movement on the bridge, eight lanes of traffic, the clatter of trains north and south, surged above like a thundering cloud; a door in the bridge's ramparts opened and a line of people in matching grey jumpsuits came out in single file and disappeared into another door a little way along.

"Maintenance?" asked Dan.

Charlie laughed. "You *have* been away a long time. Come on." She led him around the last sweep of road that delivered them under the bridge's Meccano to the place where it pushed itself out from its ramp of land, its ramp of road, balanced its weight on its one great big hinge, and leaned out to straddle the water and meet itself coming over from the other side.

The morning he left, they'd met here, at the bridge's southern feet, before sunrise, Charlie adamant they should find the old secret ways up and onto it, to start Dan's last Sydney day one hundred and thirty-four meters up in the air.

"Best view of the city," Gramps always said. "Best way to remember it, from above, with the sun straight out to the east, the light coming up through all the silvers and golds, and the harbor starting to wake up. That time of day, you can see where all the night's boats and ships have gone; their wakes leave lines etched on the water, and from up on the arch you can see them all." But in the night's last darkness, the bridge a greater and heavier darkness above them, Dan had shaken his head, declaring himself happy to watch the sunrise from the grass instead.

"Heights," he'd said simply, sitting down with his bag at his back.

"We'll regret this," Charlie had said as the light made the silvers, the yellows her grandfather had promised. "We'll regret not having this story to tell."

And Dan, shaking his head again, had said, "Don't like heights, and there's nowhere to leave my gear." Didn't tell her he'd climbed up one New Year's Eve years before, with some girl whose name he'd forgotten, then as well as now—if you drank enough, he'd discovered, even vertigo could fall away. Didn't tell her that, and didn't tell her he'd seen the wakes of all the boats hanging on top of the water, like Gramps had said. It was funny how the things you hadn't said stuck in your mind as clearly as the things you had. They probably all seeped out sooner or later, the stories that had been misplaced, buried or kicked aside, waiting to emerge, as likely as not, with a new set of emphases and meanings. It was like look-ing at old packets of photographs, and the way the images you'd chosen as your favorites, as the most important at the time, were almost always supplanted by some detail tucked into one you'd almost tossed out years ago. Recast now; redefined.

So Charlie had shrugged, and they sat, and the sun came up, and the day came on, and they made their way through the morn-ing under her grandfather's bridge.

"I always wanted to see old footage of it being built, shot over days and days and days but from the same place, so you could speed it up and see it drawing itself onto the empty space." She'd laughed. "Remember that old book Gramps had? The vicar who took a photo of it every day from his window, and then talked his way onto it, him and his camera? Imagine if he'd taken his photos at midday—Gramps's dive might have left a fleck you could see. I always thought he should have set those photos up like a cartoon flip-book, so you'd go from empty space to the great big bridge as you flicked through. I might try to do that one day, if someone will let me near a building that's big enough and grand enough while they're making it."

A city the size of London gave birth to new skyscrapers of all different shapes and sizes all the time. And each time he'd seen one reaching higher and higher, Dan had thought of Charlie, wondered if she'd ever found her building. He watched her now, bounding across the road towards the park, its grass greener than he remem-bered it. The name had changed too, with an older, softer word—Tarra—added onto the Dawes Point he remembered. He followed Charlie along the path and over the verge, and there was the harbor, the same deep blue, the same geometric shapes of boats, the same in and out of trees and land and roofs running ragged out towards the back of South Head and its lighthouses, which he remembered from the day he flew away.

"I did some work down here when they started excavating the cable tunnels." Charlie was crouched down against a sandstone arch that jutted up through the grass. "Remember the stories about how they tied the two halves of the bridge back and then eased them together? Remember the stories about the cables being slackened off and the great storm that blew up while they were trying to do it and the two halves touching in the darkness, although they told everyone it happened the next day so they could clap and cheer and think they'd seen it?"

Dan squatted beside her. He wasn't sure what he was looking at, a wall with rows of holes drilled into it, like the game he and Charlie used to play where you dropped colored discs into rows of slots, or like a card cut to hold different strands of thread or wool.

"Do you see?" asked Charlie. "The cables ran down from the end of the arch, fed through these holes, and then down to the anchor point a hundred-odd feet below. There are pictures of the men down there, standing in these wet sandstone shafts, and the huge steel cables running alongside them. They must have felt like they'd crawled into the guts of the planet. It was great to be here when they found all this: it was great to be able to shoot this bit of underpinning."

Dan said, "Can I see the pictures?"

"Sure—they're back at the flat."

"That's some flat," he said again, and this time she almost blushed.

"It's a bit posh, isn't it? But I like being able to see out to the mountains, and I like living up in the air. And I like that it lets me see the river winding away, and sometimes I like seeing the city without the bridge. I was spending so much time down here, and so much time trying to get Gramps to tell me all his stories about it so I could write them down and remember them for him, I was starting to have arch-shaped dreams."

"Thought you always did," said Dan. It was the geometry of their childhood, and each time he'd heard himself telling one of its stories, Dan had imagined Charlie doing the same. There was a power in them; they were stories that people listened to, and remembered.

On the water below, a boat tacked and jibed, its white sail disappearing briefly as it went about and then flaring blindingly bright again in the sun. "But I guess you wouldn't want to lose those stories." A pause, cluttered almost at once by cars and a siren, the blare of a ferry's horn.

"When I was working down here," said Charlie as the noises fell away, "someone told me there were hundreds of bridge workers whose names were lost completely, never written down. Like Russian George, who Gramps used to talk about, who walked all the way across Siberia to the coast and ended up here—I looked him up and there wasn't a record of him."

"I suppose Gramps must be written down somewhere—the miraculous man who fell off and turned it into a dive." From above, among the rhythmic thunk of tires on the roadway's joins, the circular clatter of the two tracks of trains, Dan registered a different noise, a metallic shunt, percussive, repetitive. The people in grey jumpsuits were making their way along the bridge's underside, and it sounded to Dan as if they must be walking on the metal frame in shoes made of metal themselves, like the armor-plated feet of a suit of chain mail. "What *is* that?"

"BridgeClimb," said Charlie. "Fabulously successful, fabulously popular—they attach you to the bridge with this nifty metal clip, and you climb up one side of the arch to the top, cross over, and come down the other side, all without ever being unsecured. Been going eight or nine years now."

Dan laughed. "Gramps's dream for us realized. Did you ever get him up there? He'd've loved that." From the water's edge, a loud group came sprawling up the hill. They were in their fifties or sixties, some in regular day clothes, some more dressed up, with a bride and groom at their head and bottles of champagne being passed around. Dan smiled, but saw Charlie stiffen as one of the party stumbled backwards towards them, steadying herself on too-high heels as she framed a picture of the group with her camera.

"You're shooting into the light from here," said Charlie, but too quietly for the woman to hear. "You'll get nothing but dark shapes, and most of them moving." Standing to offer herself as a photographer, she collided with the woman, who had stumbled again, and fallen this time, with a thud.

"Oh," she laughed, "well, that's enough to take your breath away." She took Charlie's hand and hauled herself up.

"I said you're shooting into the light from here," said Charlie. "I can take it for you if you want." And she took the woman's camera and raised it to her eye, shaping the air with her other hand as if it might mold and still the scene.

"I wouldn't worry about trying to get them to stand still, love," said the woman, dusting her bottom, her hands. "We're all color and movement today."

Charlie clicked, paused, and clicked again—three or four times in rapid succession. The last frame caught the bride's skirt flaring as she turned to laugh, her face in the sun, and Charlie smiled, passing the camera back to the woman who stood now, her shoes off, more carefully balanced on the grass.

"I hope you like them," said Charlie. "I hope your friends will be very happy." She watched as the woman stepped back onto the path, a little too tentatively, and headed off with her party. "Something nice about pictures of moving people," she said then, sitting down again next to Dan. "A bit smudged, so you can't really tell if they were there or not. The space around them looks more permanent than they do."

Dan narrowed his eyes: everything looked more permanent than people this morning, but he suspected that that was more to do with jet lag. That truncated version of his flight home that he'd thrown down for Charlie almost as soon as he was through her door—it suddenly felt as if he'd made a perilous journey around the world, rather than an easy and comfortable one. Maybe it was traumatic; but it must be less traumatic than having your grandfather pass away. *Dear Caro*, he thought, *I've come too late and the sun is bright. The place looks real but it looks like the people might disappear in an instant. I miss you.* Overhead, another batch of grey-suited climbers clattered along the bridge's underbelly, the jingling and rattling of their safety clips drawing Dan's eyes back up towards them and away from his train of thought.

"Okay," said Charlie at last. "Okay. So I bought myself a ticket for the climb pretty early on—wanted to check it out to see if they might let me take a camera up sometime; ordinarily you can't take anything with you. They even make you take their handkerchiefs, not yours, and they make you strap them to your wrist so they can't fall off or blow away. I came in, put on the suit, walked down the road—where you saw that lot—and climbed up the first stairs to the gangway beneath the road deck. Even being on it, feeling the metal under your hands, being so close to the rivets, to the shapes, being able to smell it somehow . . ." Her laugh was low and round. "I know, it sounds a bit religious. But all those stories, Dan, he'd told us all those stories.

"And we start to climb and the guides are telling us this and that: how much metal, how many men, straight bits making big curves, all the stuff about the design. Up these ladders, your head poking up between lanes seven and eight of the cars, which scared the shit out of me, and up, and up, and then you're out on the arch, standing on top of it, sky and birds and clouds above. A big wide staircase of steel curving up towards the sky. Just like Gramps

ASHLEY HAY

said. I started humming that song of his: 'I'm Sitting on Top of the World.' Felt like there should be a sound track of that playing somewhere. The funny thing is, when you're standing on it, you're still looking around as if you should be able to see the bridge somewhere else in the city, like you in the flat this morning. And you're trying to look in every direction, work out where everything is—it feels so different when you're up in the air, you know."

And Dan nodded.

In a tree beside the road below, a kookaburra began to sing, its satisfied gurgle following the shape of the hill to where Charlie and Dan sat, cross-legged, and looking east, one waiting for the other to continue.

"They always sound like they're practicing vowels," said Charlie as the bird hit the end of its trill. "Trying to get their beaks through the *oooo*s and the *aaaah*s. I'd miss them, I reckon, if I was away for ten years. Anyway, there we are, four hundred feet up in the air, having our photos taken by the guide, and they start to tell the story of the man who fell off the bridge, dived into the harbor, and survived."

"They start talking about Gramps." Dan grabbed her shoulder. "That's fantastic, Charlie; must've been strange hearing it up there though, thinking that all these people were going to know about it now."

"Weird." She nodded. "Weird because they keep calling him Vince Kelly. Not Joe Brown." Talking across Dan's frown, across the hand he held up towards her words. "But of course, it's a great story—off the road deck and getting himself into a straight dive, and coming up with a broken rib and his shoe leather up around the tops of his legs. It's a great story."

She reached for her bag, pulled an envelope out of its side pocket, held it out for him. He could feel the regular shape of a photograph inside it before he'd opened the flap. *Kelly*, he thought,

250

sounding the name over and over. He was looking at a picture of a small disc, rose-gold against the palm of a man's hand. "'To celebrate his preservation from serious harm,'" he read aloud. "Is it a war medal?"

Charlie laughed, but the sound was colder than it should have been. "This is the medal presented to Mr. Vincent Kelly—also known as Vic; also known as Roy—to commemorate his surviving—miraculously—a fall from the Sydney Harbour Bridge, as he did seventy-seven years ago, on 23 October 1930. The man who owns it now showed me—he collects stuff, memorabilia, and a magazine wanted me to shoot him for something the afternoon after I'd done the climb. So I went, started telling him this story, you know, my grandpa, the stories you grow up with, making conversation, this new Kelly in my head, not knowing what to think. And halfway through—I hadn't mentioned a name—he smiled and said, 'Mr. Kelly, Mr. Kelly,' and showed me this little plastic bag with a medal in it. It was so small, sort of fragile, but I thought it looked like a war medal too."

Dan's hand was waving now—"Kelly, his name was Kelly?"—as the dream he'd had during the plane's endless night firmed and fixed in his mind.

Charlie nodded. "Seems that the man whose medal it was had died ten, maybe twenty years ago now—maybe more. It felt warm, you know, like it'd been in the sun, or pressed against someone's skin. I probably thanked him a bit too enthusiastically for showing it to me. Then I caught a bus to Gramps's place and asked him who this Kelly was."

Her grandfather, sitting in his favorite chair, by his favorite window, the one that gave a glimpse of the water, of the bridge's arch. Her grandfather, shuffling into the kitchen to put a kettle on for tea, wanting to hear all about her morning. He'd been waiting for her, he said, to report in on the climb. "How'd it feel, love? What did it look like up close? What kind of people went with you? And this bloke who started it up—what was he like, Charlie? What an idea. What a champion idea to get off the ground."

Reaching for the milk, measuring the sugar, stirring it round and round in the hot brown liquid until she couldn't feel a single one of its crystals crunching under the spoon, Charlie felt as if time had slowed to a fraction of its regular pace. She set the cup down in front of the old man, set the two biscuits he liked with each cup of tea just as carefully on his saucer. And she tried to think of a way to ask him what she wanted to know.

"They tell stories while you're climbing," she said. "They have these little headsets so you can hear the guides all the way up. They tell the story of the only man to go off the bridge and survive." She didn't pause, her eyes fixed on her teacup, not wanting to see what his face looked like. "But it's not you they talk about, Gramps; it's not Joe Brown. It's a guy called Kelly. And I met the man who has the medal that was presented to you—to him—the medal with the line about preservation from serious harm. The medal you reckoned had been lost in the garden years ago when you came back from the war."

The regularity of sounds; a teaspoon against a saucer, the suck of the warm fluid. These were probably the oldest and most familiar sounds in her life. She glanced up, quickly, to see if she could see her grandfather's eyes. But his head was down, concentrating on his tea, and his hand was as steady as ever when he lifted his cup again to his lips.

"I only ever said it might have been lost in your gram's garden, Charlie Brown," he had said at last, pushing the wet biscuit crumbs he'd dropped into one neat pile on the Laminex table. "Lot of things got dug over and buried in those beds. Lot of things sprouted and grew there too."

He stood up, but tentatively, as if the floor had begun to shift and undulate under his feet. Charlie watched as he braced himself at the window. He rarely looked old—spry in his ninety-odd years—but a different shadow sat around the profile of his face, and she wasn't sure if the breaths she could see in the movement of his shoulders belonged to tiny gasps, or small tears. Then he straightened himself, straightened a stem or two on the plants on the ledge, and fussed with a dead leaf here, a trickle of water there. Her tea was cold before he finally spoke.

"Do you remember the rosebushes in that garden, Charlie Brown?" There was no clue in his voice that this might be a new or different story. "Do you remember that great white rosebush that grew in the middle of the bed? I always meant to take a cutting from that one—why didn't I do that, before I left? It had the most beautiful perfume, like perfectly warm sweetness, and the petals felt like velvet. Truth and innocence, your gram always said that's what white roses stood for. She carried them at her wedding, you know; there's a picture—she looked gorgeous, of course—and her arms are just full of these big white roses, so rich, so huge, you wanted to bite into them." Leaning against the bench, as if he was balancing against the rocking of a ship. "The day she got married."

On the harbor, a dozen yachts chased each other along avenues of wind—Gramps pulled the window against its movement, and the room jolted with an immediate silence. It was a long time before he turned back to face Charlie. She was holding her breath without realizing, and her chest began to ache before he spoke.

"Well then," he said, "so you've met Mr. Kelly, in a manner of speaking. He was a great diver, Charlie; they said he went off the top of a crane into the harbor once, and we saw him at the pool one afternoon. He was elegant, so elegant. And it was nothing short of miraculous the way he got himself straight before he hit the water the day he went off the bridge. To have been looking at the right place at the right time, love, and after such a long time of waiting . . ." He rubbed his face as Charlie frowned.

"Waiting? Gramps, I don't know what—"

Her grandfather turned, his fingers rubbing a line from his eyes out to his cheeks, stroke after stroke. "Charlie Brown, Charlie Brown, what else was in that wonderful garden? The lemon tree— do you remember? And the tomatoes and the sweet peas? And that pit with the ashes from the fire, thick silver dust that never seemed to overflow—I thought that was some kind of magic, but maybe it just used to blow away into someone else's yard. The nights we'd sit out the back, us boys and Joy, everyone full of stories. The nights we'd walk and look at the stars. I was a young bloke then, love, and everything felt possible."

More silence then; Charlie hardly dared to move for fear of disturbing whatever journey her grandfather was taking. His eyes were closed now, and he was humming to himself, very softly. *I'm sitting on top of the world* . . . When he did open his eyes, he was looking through the room, the day, through Charlie herself, to another time, another place.

"The highest thing I ever dived off was a board at the beach, scared all the time; so scared I could hardly remember it as soon as it was over. I didn't dive off the bridge, love, you're right. But there are lots of reasons for telling stories, and I've seen that one so many times . . ." He paused. "Have another cup of tea?"

Her grandfather, silhouetted against the light as he refilled the kettle, flicked its switch. "Never thought I'd get used to this newfangled thing," he said. "I still miss the old stovetop one we'd set on the combustion stove. Do you remember that, Charlie? Do you remember your gram's old house, the combustion stove, the rosy-pink kettle?"

And Charlie, sitting very still on the other side of the kitchen, had said of course she remembered the house, the stove, and was about to confirm the kettle as well when he cut her off.

"You take things on for people, love." His face was turned away from her, but his shoulders had slumped a little, and he was rubbing hard at the back of his head with one hand. "It wasn't that I jumped out of my world and into someone else's—it was my world; they were my stories. The first story your mother ever told me—she was a little girl, just four or five years old when I got back from the war—was about how I'd dived off the bridge and survived . . . and survived." He stilled his busy right hand with his left one, and stood awhile, the fingers of one hand rubbing at the palm of the other. "Did it matter that she thought it was me?" And Charlie's grandfather, stepping back to the kettle and its cheerful whistle, spread his hands, palms up, appealing, and almost smiled. "Did it matter that you thought it was me, Charlie Brown? I mean, whichever man it was, to fall, to survive, that's still some story."

He made the new tea, the same ritual she'd watched him complete through all the years she could remember. He set down the cups, pushed the biscuits towards her first, watched her closely as she chose one, dunked it, testing its sogginess, and then picked it up and ate it quickly before it disintegrated.

"That's my girl," he said quietly, "I always figured someone would find out—someone would, you know, call me on it. But I'm sorry it was you, love, and I'm sorry it was today and this way. It was only you and your mum I pretended to—no, and that barmaid the day the bridge opened. She gave me a free drink for it too." His smile flared again.

Charlie glanced down at a little pile of grass growing between her leg and Dan's: her right hand had been snapping off blades of grass, turning them like rings around her index finger, flicking them away, starting again. "And then," she said, raking her fingers through the stems, "then he said this thing. He said: 'We'll always say we're someone else if we think it will help someone, if we think it'll help someone we love.'" And she smiled a screwed-up kind of smile.

Dan's frown deepened against the day's brightness; even sitting down, he was so tired he felt unsteady, as if he was at sea. The story that had marked out their childhood, the story about miracles and flying, leaping into the unknown, the first story he'd told Caroline, let alone anyone else, and it belonged to another family? A family whose name he'd dreamed about, somewhere over the earth, on his way home? He blew out a long, slow breath—"That's some thing, that's some thing to do"—and turned to Charlie, not sure what to think, or say, about his own appropriations. Her face was still, so close to blank that she looked almost unfamiliar, but her eyes were glassy with tears and he reached out and took her hand to stop it shredding away the grass. "I'm sorry, Charlie, and that he died—so sorry for you—the rest, the story . . . I don't know what to say."

She shrugged again, squeezed his fingers and let go. "If I hadn't done the climb, or if there wasn't a climb, how would I ever have heard that story? Maybe it was in a book somewhere, but I never saw it—I suppose I never went looking for other versions of the stories that came from Gramps."

Out in the harbor, a tubby little ferry turned its nose east: Dan picked out the letters of its name—it was the *Sirius*—as he wondered what he should say next. "Did he know this Kelly? Did he even see it happen?"

Charlie nodded. "Yup. Yup. He knew Kelly. And he saw it. Was standing here, near this pylon, and looked up and saw a man—saw Kelly—lose his footing, turn a somersault, and fall down into the water. Three seconds, he said—" and her fingers clicked their beat the way Gramps had counted them out whenever he told the story. "And then Kelly came back up to the surface, 'marvelously alive'— wasn't that always the phrase?"

"Marvelously alive." Dan nodded in turn. "That was it." He was trying to move his eyes smoothly through the space between the bridge's deck and the water so that it took precisely three seconds. It seemed incredibly slow. He was trying to remember the rest of his dream.

"And it was bizarre, you know: I didn't really think about why he might've done it, not straightaway," said Charlie, her head still nodding in time, Dan saw, to the passage of seconds. "I just told him that it *was* a great story. It was a great story, made us feel so proud when we were kids that we knew the person who'd done that, and made us feel like amazing things were possible. He said that was good. He said that was what he wanted. He said that was all." She stopped nodding, just for a beat or two, then started to shake her head from side to side. "The thing is—"

She paused as a batch of joggers went by, as if she didn't want them to hear, and her voice was so low when she spoke again that Dan had to lean in so that his head almost touched hers, just to catch her words.

"The thing is," she said, "he'd borrowed some other stories too."

Ted

"WANT TO hear the story, Ted?" In the cavern of the hangar, Ted pocketed his spanner and wiped his hands, ready for the next tale they'd brought down from the sky.

The group of boys who'd flown had come back full of some place crumbling beneath them. "Roads, buildings, bridges," said one. "You should've seen the steel move, Teddy," said another. "Curled up and folded like an overcoat." Giving his shoulder an extra clap because they knew he was making hard work of it since his mate's accident.

Ted went over the machine again—bolts, gears, fuel—listening as the boys calmed down, headed out of the hangar, took themselves off to celebrate another run. There was a letter from Joy in his pocket, and he wanted some quiet before he read it. It was the first one to come since Joe died. He wished his boys hadn't shot out a bridge that day—or wished they hadn't told him. Or wished he didn't take bridges so personally. Still.

The envelope was miraculously soft and clean against his grubby hand; he let it lie in his palm, testing its weight before he opened it. There was a soft smell too, and the fragile petals of a white rose slipped out into his lap. He scooped them up, let them flutter down again, and then turned them one by one as if part of the letter might be written onto their clean, blank surfaces.

I went up the bridge's pylons today before they closed them, Joy had written. *I wanted to remember how big the city looked spread out over the plain, how little all the houses looked, and the cars, and everyone in them. I'm not as fit as I used to be, so the climb was hard, harder than I remember when we climbed the arch, but then you always said that was just like one long easy hill crest. There was no one up there, but it was a pretty grey day. The wind smelled salty, bringing the sea in from the coast. I thought I'd send you a rose to put wherever Joe is—I don't suppose I'll ever be able to visit him so I'm glad you were there. The world feels too big with all this, Ted, so make sure he's got this bit of the garden, would you?*

He curled one of the petals around his fingers, the other hand holding fast to the page.

After a quarter of an hour or so, I heard someone come out onto the lookout behind me—a biggish bloke, thick hair and a nice smile; I thought I recognized him; thought he might be one of the bridge boys that used to come for a beer in the yard. He'd such a fancy watch on, and the bluest eyes: you know, I reckon it was Roy Kelly, coming up for one last look himself. The mountains looked so blue, Ted, and the ocean out in the other direction. There was a storm coming in, big banks of dark clouds rolling closer and closer and changing all the colors to steely grey. And this man and I sort of followed each other around the pylon's walls, not quite catching up to one another. I tried to remember which section of the arch we'd climbed onto. Do you know I couldn't even remember which side it was—east or west, front or back? It must have been the east. Did we see the beginning of the sunrise?

He held the door open for me when I was done. And he smiled and said, After you, Mrs. Brown. I don't know; I didn't

*want to ask him who he was in case it wasn't Kelly—I wanted
to be able to send you that story and think that it was him. It'll
be good to see you, Ted, when this is over and they let you come
back round the world. It'll be good to have you near again.
They might have the lookout opened again by then, and we can
go up and wait for the miracle man. Write to me about where
Joe is, and when you leave the flowers for him. He always said
you'd bring his watch home for me if anything like this happened. It will be good to see you, to hear all your stories.*

There was no signature, as if she'd just decided that was enough
to write, and folded the paper, once this way, once that. Then,
before she sent it off, she'd sketched that familiar arch, the stripes of
steel that suspended its deck, the salt-and pepper-shaker shapes of
its pylons. Maybe she thought that was signature enough. Counting through the rose petals, Ted wondered if she'd mind if he kept
one for himself: he could see the whole backyard—him, and Joe,
and Joy, and summer—in its tiny triangle.

On the floor next to him, Joe's things sat in a bag. "Take the
watch," Joe had said at the end, "take the watch and get it back to
Joy, will you? And tell her the good stories from all this, not this,
not the end." And, "Take care of her, would you? You know how
much she makes of things." His voice had trailed into a cough.

The next time he'd spoken it was as if he was back in the backyard with the bridge boys, slugging cold beer, his breath faster, and
his hand reaching out for his wife.

"Joy? Where are you, Joy? Can't see you for the darkness—we
need a shooting star, love, or that comet, at last." The words had
sounded strangled, as if they must have hurt. "Where are you,
love? Joy?"

So that Ted had reached out himself, patted the seeking hand,
and said it was all right, it would all be all right, said that Joy was

here—"I'm here"—as softly, as gently as he could. And watched as his friend's breathing slowed, and slowed again, and stopped.

The letter in his lap, Ted rubbed his thumb across the watch's glass, not velvety like the rose petal but still so smooth it was almost soft. He watched the speedy sweep of the second hand awhile, fascinated that it could move so quickly when he knew how long some minutes, some hours, could be. Compared to the watch's sheen, there was so much grease ingrained into the lines on his hands that his skin seemed to have disappeared completely.

All those years of working up in the air, out over the harbor, and the silly bugger had slipped from a scaffolding, falling not far at all, and that was it. The first thing Ted had thought was that there must be some way of trading Roy Kelly's fall for Joe's; there must be some way of making that Joe's miracle. If only Ted had known how to do it, and if only Ted had seen Joe's fall, the way he'd seen all those fragments, those premonitions, those leftovers of Kelly's. Kelly's miracle, in that faraway place with its water and its sandstone and its impossibly blue sky and white clouds. Joe's accident, in some loud tangle of men and engines and blood and dirt.

Lying back in his bed later, Ted closed his eyes and saw the bunk above become a big hunk of steel rising up into the sky above his head, the way he'd watched cranes floating huge girders and braces and bits of deck and track up to become the bridge's shape. Why had it never occurred to him that one might drop? Why had it never occurred to him, on the barge beneath, that something might fall? Now, in this night, with Joe's things nearby and the letter from Joy in his pocket, the fear of some great big remembered beam crashing down, squashing the life out of him, set him shaking all over. *Not now*, he thought, *not after all this*.

He pulled his breathing back to slowness, tracing the curve of the arch on the top of his blanket—a decade since it was finished and opened, and he could still draw such accurate pictures of its shapes, its structure, by heart. These were the most familiar topographies he had—the bridge, and what was planted where in Joe and Joy's garden. He recited those rivets, those plantings, like a spell, a mantra, running through them each night as he teetered against sleep.

But when the sleep itself came, he stepped straight into the same old dream more often than not: the bridge, the day Kelly fell. He knew it was that day in particular by the bands and puffs of grey clouds that covered the sun around midday. Except now it was always Ted perched up in the air—and perched high on the arch's peak, another three hundred or so feet up from where Kelly had stumbled. It was Ted turning and pausing and lining up his flight, Ted easing through the blue air down towards the blue water, Ted going down, down, down into the darkness and then turning again to surge back up to the surface and emerge, just as the sun did, "marvelously alive."

And the man standing watching on Dawes Point, fiddling with Jacko's ears, was the old swaggie in the faded red coat who'd reared out of the shadows that night he and Joy came down from the arch and ran home. Faded coat, shining eyes, and a look of puzzled wonder on his face.

~

He'd meet her, he said, off the ferry at the quay, but he was early, and wandered west around the cove, finding himself under the bridge—the southeastern foot, just down from the spot where Jacko's kennel had been, just down from the spot where he'd met Joe. Where he sat, waiting, looking out across the water, smoking a bit, because he did now, and wincing a bit every time a train rattled through the air above him. Out over the water, a gull circled, swooping and diving and climbing back up into the sky. It was the right kind of movement for a coat flaring behind a falling man,

262

but you could always trick yourself into thinking you were seeing something normal instead.

The sensation of falling through air—he'd asked Kelly to describe it, the one time he'd seen him after his famous fall. But all Kelly could say was that it had been fast, so fast, and that if there was a sound, well, he didn't really know, but maybe it was like a huge gust of wind.

How strong would the wind need to be, wondered Ted, *to carry you up instead of down?*

Kelly had done a better job of describing the mechanics of his somersault, the one chance you had to use the speed of your fall and jerk yourself around so your feet were facing down. To have the presence of mind to think that; to know how to make your body do that. Joe should have practiced falling after all—maybe such a little drop needn't have killed him. Ted closed his eyes, pictured himself in the air, clenching at the pivot of his stomach, kicking himself over and down, down, down. There it was; there was the dive; there was the moment. And something did splash into the water as he got to the end of counting three and looked up at the pure blue of the sky. Probably just a fish leaping, a bird swooping, or something tossed in from a boat. But still, there it was, there it was, like an echo in this place.

The harbor's foreshore bustled around him, and he swung between the sense that he'd been gone an irreparably long time, and that he might have been here yesterday. It was good to be home at last. Walking around the city's streets, trying to remember its geography, he'd felt like an observer walking in an unfamiliar land, as though the space he knew best was playing tricks on him, keeping him at bay. But he'd taken care to keep out of the way of the bridge until this morning, trawled through his mind for all the corners and crests that might reveal it unexpectedly, and stayed away, his head down as an extra precaution. He'd imagined coming up the rise to find her sitting there—even earlier than him and filling in time herself. But the little park was empty and he sat there, looking at the birds, the water, the headland out to the east, alone.

He thought about Kelly's flight, about the softness of Jacko's fur, about running into Joe here in the fading light of that long-ago evening, about all the stories in the backyard, and walking out to look for comets, for shooting stars. He thought about his smaller self, sitting here while his mother cried; thought back further to Joe's astronomer.

All the watching and waiting that had been done here.

A dog barked, and the round sound of a couple of boats' horns cut across the top of it. The watch in Ted's pocket lay heavily against his leg and he took it out and wound it automatically, shining its silver edges on the cuff of his shirt. Another quarter of an hour. He lit another smoke and walked back towards the wharves, his breath quickening as the ferry emptied and Joy didn't come.

"Joe Brown?"

There was a man standing behind him, a smooth suit, a hat; he had a satchel of some kind in one hand and a little girl, pretty blue frock, held fast to the other.

"I'm . . . I don't . . ."

"You're Joe Brown? Your wife said you'd be here. Well, I'm sorry, we tried to get in touch. Mrs. Brown, she's been fighting this terrible flu—she's over in the Mater—and they've been passing little Grace around us neighbors. My name's Caldwell, three down; we moved in after you went away last time. Must have been just before Gracie was born—four years ago now? Coming on for five?"

"I think there's . . ." Ted was peering at the man's face, the man's mouth, as he spoke, trying to make sense of the words—or trying to make them say something else. From the corner of his eye, he saw the sun catch the little girl's hair so that it shone gold, and as he looked down towards its brightness, she looked up, quickly, shyly, and she smiled.

"This must all feel awfully strange, but the doctors . . . they say Mrs. Brown . . . well, you wouldn't have met little Grace before, would you? But it's good to have you home, Mr. Brown. And I'm sure it'll give Joy the boost she needs." He touched the brim of his hat in a fake salute. "You're a man with some gift for living, Mr. Brown. Your wife told us about your fall up there—" his hand vaguely raised towards the famous bridge "—and anyone who could get through years of flying for the Poms, well . . ." He nudged the little girl forward towards Ted. "She's a good girl, this one, and glad her daddy's home." A too-hearty smile. "Get everything back to normal now." And he tipped his hat again.

All the sound had been sucked out of the world—or out of Ted's head at least. He heard himself saying small things about the capabilities of doctors, about the prettiness of the little girl's smile; heard the man saying small things about getting to work and having them all over for a cuppa when Joy was better, was home. Then he saw the man walk away, saw the little girl's face looking up at him, saw a bird curl and dive again out over the water. It must be some trick, some surprise—the little girl was fussing with the ribbon in her hair. And what had Joy told this bloke, that Ted was Joe, that Joe was the man, the one man, who'd dived and survived? That Joe had spent his war flying, not just filling and fixing those planes? That Joe had come home?

The morning sun disappeared behind a cloud, illuminating its edges: Ted could see a ship in its big white shape—wondered if the little girl might see it too. "So, Grace." Grace. The little girl smiled, sat down, and he sat down next to her.

He could feel the watch ticking in his pocket, tapping at his flesh. Say something; say something. The man in the suit had reached the road—turned back and waved. Grace, polite, waved back, then turned and took Ted's hand. "Mum says you know how to fly," she said, looking up, and he saw she had blue eyes, wide, clear, blue.

All right, he thought. He pulled the watch out again, its flat silver back glinting in the sun—just on midday. "Would you like to walk across the bridge, Grace?" he asked, squeezing her hand and feeling it squeeze back, warm. He had no idea where his words were coming from, or what he might—or should—properly say next. "Walk over and see your mum? I could tell you a story while we went—tell you a story about making this bridge. What do you reckon? Want to hear it?"

She squeezed again, and smiled. "I've never walked up in the air there before. Mum always said we'd do it when you came home and you'd show me where you flew. But is it high? Will I be scared?"

"Come on, then," he said. "It's great being up in the air, on top of the world. Don't you want to see what happens?"

Dan

"THEY WALKED along Cumberland Street and up the stairs onto the bridge," said Charlie. "Ted Parker made it look like he was tap-dancing up the stairs, and my mum showed off the way she could twirl so her dress flared out. He told me he wasn't really sure what he should do, just knew that he should get to the hospital and see Joy. So they started to walk and he told her about building the bridge—about men hanging on with their toes while they climbed up, about cooking sausages on a shovel for lunch, going to the loo in a paper bag and watching it sail through the air and just miss a ferry. He said he just wanted to make her laugh; said she had a laugh somewhere between Joy's and Joe's. Halfway across he started the story of flying off the bridge, and she knew it better than he did, correcting his details and telling him he'd somersaulted at the top; down for three seconds; into the water; and then surfaced again . . ."

"And how bright the daylight seemed when he came up," said Dan. "That's the bit I always loved. So much glare he had to squint to stop the rest of the city disappearing." All the places he'd seen this happen—birds, sails, even figures could disappear on widely lit plains. Every time, he'd thought of Gramps. Every time, he'd thought it was magic: with enough light at the right angle, you could make a whole city disappear. Now, sitting in this first morning of being home, looking around at the harbor's edge, so clear, so familiar, it occurred to him that the opposite might also be true, that every so often the light would touch something the right way—a slightly brighter beam, a slightly different angle—and you'd not only get some unexpected glimpse of it, you'd feel like you were seeing it anew.

They sat there, eyes crinkled against the glare, imagining the little girl who was Charlie's mother, the man who would become her grandfather, dancing across the grass, on their way up to the bridge.

≈

Ted Parker held the girl's hand tight. He'd always been slightly scared of children, but the look on her face, he thought, *half Joe, half Joy*, and shining with the moment: that she'd known her father was coming home. And that she'd known her father was the man who could fly. She was smiling, skipping, taking a look at him every so often as if she wanted to make sure he was real. He caught her eye in one of the smiles, and watched it expand into laughter. *Anything*, he thought in that instant, *I will do anything to keep you safe and smiling*.

He'd never felt so sure of a thing before.

Their feet followed the line of the bridge, began to take the ups and downs of the hills on the other side. Ted wondered if he'd remember the way to the hospital, but the streets unfolded in front of him like a marked map. He hated hospitals, hated their sharp smell—more since he'd sat through the end with Joe—but when he felt Grace pull back as they neared the building he knew somehow that it was his job to make this easier for her. *Light and easy*.

In the door, up the stairs. "Don't worry," he said quietly. "Everything's fine—I'm here." Saying it for himself as much as for her. He'd never held a child's hand before—there was such trust, such confidence in it. Like holding Joy's hand to the top of the bridge—and as he remembered this, they reached her bed. She looked diminished, sleeping under the taut white covers, and he began to sing, just gently, just quietly the words he and Joy had made up for his favorite Al Jolson song.

". . . just dancing on air, just dancing on air."

Grace was in his arms, her head snuggled against his shoulder. *This is what I came home for*, he thought distinctly. *This is what I will do now.*

He settled himself in a chair, settled himself to wait as the sunlight danced around the room's walls and the world and the day turned.

"Sometimes, when I was away," he whispered to Grace, "I thought I'd forgotten what your mother looked like."

And the little girl smiled and said, "But she's beautiful, isn't she?" And Ted nodded.

"Sometimes, when I was away," he whispered, "I thought I was forgetting all my stories."

"I could tell you, if you do," whispered Grace. "I know them all."

Ted laughed. "I'm sure you do."

Joy stirred a little, her eyes still closed. He'd never seen her sleep before, Ted realized, and now she was down so deep that for an instant—now—and now—he thought she might have stopped breathing and he had to lean closer, closer, to pick up any slight movement she might make. Was she dreaming? Did she know they were there? He held Grace and felt her breath against his hand: she was sleeping now too. He didn't dare move. Through the window, he could see the crest of the bridge's curve, and he sat, and waited, and wondered what might happen next.

It was afternoon when he woke, startled by a sound, a movement, so sudden that he thought for a moment he'd stepped from one dream into another. Grace fiddled with some pencils at his feet, and Joy's eyes were opening slowly, and looking a little, and closing again. He saw their blink, their gaze, before he was awake enough to remember where he was, what was happening.

"Joe?" she said at last, and Ted felt himself shudder back into his own time and place.

"I'm here," he said, reaching out to smooth the sheet across her shoulders. "It's all right, I'm here."

"I knew you'd come," she said, eyes closed again, smile soft. "I wrote to Ted to bring you home, and I knew he would."

"Ted would do anything for you, Joy," said Ted. From the other beds came sounds and movements, but Ted was sure there were only three people in the room, possibly in the world—himself, Joy, and Grace. He watched as the little girl crawled up onto the bed, snuggled herself in between her mother's arm and body.

"She likes this," said Joy, kissing her fast on the top of her head as Grace giggled and beamed.

"Good," said Ted. "I can do that."

"And she likes tomato on her toast in the mornings."

Ted nodded.

"And she likes stories, so you'll have no problem with—" The end of the sentence disappeared into a hacking cough that sounded as if it might turn her inside out. But she pushed away the water Ted held out. "Think it's too late for that," she said, and he was sure, from the look, the smile she gave him, that she knew exactly who he was. "It's all right," she said then, patting his hand. "I knew you'd come—you're the man who can fly."

And Ted smiled, held her hand, and watched as she slid back into sleep. *All right*, he thought. *Well, all right. I'd better get Grace home.* And as they turned to leave, he leaned forward and kissed Joy's forehead—perhaps he'd always wanted to.

"It will be lovely falling in love with you again," he whispered.

~

"She only lived a few weeks," said Charlie now to Dan, "and then, said Gramps—said Ted Parker—who was going to take care of my mum after that? So he took her on, still answered to his own name but also answered to Joe's if people used it instead. He was pretty defensive about that, said that half the blokes who worked here had been working under two or three names, said that he'd been reading about soldiers who ended up having three names and four lives, said that even Mr. Kelly had been Vic and Vince and Roy. Didn't seem like such a big thing, he said.

"And he kept going back over the story of your dad walking into the west, making his name up as he went, on a letter here, a document there, and that was all there was to Kopek, he said, and none of us had ever minded."

Ted Parker, buying a bunch of white roses in the supermarket, had turned to Charlie and said out of nowhere: "I did love your grandmother—she and Joe, they were my family too. And I did mean it when I said it'd be something to fall in love with her again. I thought I might have had that chance. But still, but still . . ." Handing over the money for the flowers, taking a gulp of the air around them and shaking his head at their want of perfume. "Your mother and I, we didn't do too badly together; she never knew, if that's what you're wondering, and it meant the world to me that she told me, before she got sick, what a good father I'd been."

The main thing, her grandfather had said, was that it had never occurred to him that he wasn't Grace's dad, or Charlie's grandfather, and that they weren't a family. "And he did make a joke about it one day," said Charlie. "Said he'd always wondered if I'd rather have been a jazz player than a cartoon character."

"Charlie Parker, Charlie Brown," said Dan. "I suppose that would've been all right either way." He squeezed her shoulder with a hug. They were walking back from the bridge, down towards the quay, the rows of wharves, and the pavement was thick with tourists.

"Let's go up by the mouth of the old stream," said Charlie, steering him through the crowds and across to the wide forecourt whose fountain marked the place where the settlement's first, quickly exhausted stream had splashed into the harbor. There were the birds, the frogs, the echidnas, the lizards in bronze; a curling curve suggesting rocks; a curling curve suggesting leaves. "Do you remember how Gramps used to say they'd been peeled off one- and two-cent pieces," she said, "and that's why they were all brown?" She leaned forward, her fingers just touching the very top of the water. "It must have been so pretty with the ferns and the she-oaks and the lilies along here." She flicked drops of water onto the fountain's surface, watching them catch the light and disappear. "What do you think—about Gramps? What do you think about it, Dan?"

Dan slid his hand along the bronze skin of a goanna, his fingers registering the hard metal that formed it while his eyes followed the texture of its skin, scaly, and a little baggy, but certainly reptilean. There was nothing like this in England, he thought. *They must have looked monstrous.* He wondered how long it had been since a goanna wandered through this part of town. He wondered what he wanted to say to Charlie.

"Well," he said at last, "I'm not really one to talk about appropriating—sometimes when I tell the story, I say it was *my* grandfather who flew." He watched her carefully, but she barely reacted, her fingers still toying with the water. "We all borrow things, don't we? Nudge the truth a bit now and then. But he was a good grandfather—for me, as much as for you. And there's no harm in it, is there? It doesn't change anything we think about him. It doesn't change how much we loved him, does it?"

"Love," she said, her own hand molded around the smooth

bronze stone on which Dan's goanna sat. "We never talk about that, do we. I don't mean"—fast, across a kind of fear that fell on his face—"anything soppy. I just mean family, us that way. I missed you, Dan, I really missed you. I'd do things, and see things—stuff happens, you know, and there are certain people you want to tell about it."

The things he might have told her. Dan thought of random moments with Caro, of holidays and nothing weekends, of flying over the Matterhorn, of the light under the Waterloo Bridge and the way that one little cloud had shone, illuminated, on his birthday.

"I should've rung home more, talked to Mum more, talked to you—I meant to. I was always promising myself I would." The water around his fingers now felt silky; it would be lovely, he thought from nowhere, if it was big enough to submerge him. He could lean all the way forward into it. He could wash away his tiredness, wash away the flight, wash away all the things he'd meant to do or say and hadn't. It felt like that kind of space. "It's not even that you get busy," he said. "It's just—it was never quite—never quite the right time. And I always knew I could just fly home if I wanted to." He shook his head. "Poor old Joe."

"Poor old Ted," said Charlie quietly. She was very still, her only movement her fingers flicking at the water again. Her grandfather: their best friend, the person who had filled them up with stories and adventures, who'd taught them, if nothing else, that it was perfectly possible for them to fly—however they wanted to take that. She'd done better than him at that, thought Dan; photography against banking wasn't much of a contest. Gramps's mantra: "Anything you want to do, anyone you want to be." They hadn't realized how literally he knew that could be taken.

And Gramps had been right to invoke Dan's own father: fleeing a country, picking a new name, ending up in a life that held his mum, him, in a whole other piece of the world. When he was young, it had never really mattered to Dan who else his father might have been, and as he got older, his dad dead years already, he hadn't wanted anything other than to hold on to what little he remembered. His mother had nodded. Gramps had nodded. As he'd said to Caro, he'd happily take his mum to the place his father had come from, if she ever wanted to go. But he wasn't that interested in knowing more himself.

"So I figure," said Charlie suddenly, "that it's like the Second Coming—those crazies waiting for Jesus to come through the harbor's heads. The way Gramps told the story, sometimes it was just a story, sometimes Gram had been there, had seen it happen herself. Sometimes Gramps had been there too—and sometimes it was just something he'd heard someone talking about that might happen one day."

Her face scrunched up a little—Dan thought it was against the glare of the sun, then saw the tears on her cheeks. "I know it doesn't matter," she said, "I know it shouldn't change anything. But I did mind about the flying. I minded that it wasn't him, that he hadn't done that. I started imagining these little threads running away from his words—him telling us, and us telling someone else, who passed it on to someone else, and one of those threads might have led right back to Roy Kelly or Vince Kelly or whatever his name was. What would he have thought?" Her fingers kept busy, brushing back and forth, back and forth, across the water, making tiny waves, and her shoulders shuddered as she sighed from somewhere low and deep.

"The last few years, Gramps got into this history stuff, all the old Sydney stuff, settlement and the British, and then, later, the bridge. He was really taken with it. I thought at first it was just that he wanted new things to talk about, new stories to tell. Towards the end, he said it was because Joe Brown had always been interested in it, and he wanted to do it for him. We found some fantastic stories—the day someone thought they saw an alligator here; the day someone said they'd found gold here." She laughed. "And then there were whole days when nothing had been written down—no record of anything in a journal or a letter." As if Sydney might have skipped that twenty-four hours altogether—or something so impossible had happened that the whole settlement had united around it in silence.

It was Charlie's weather-journal photos that had piqued her grandfather's curiosity; where Dan had asked what she was trying to show, or prove, her grandfather had understood them. "You're looking for overlaps, coincidences, aren't you, love? Bits of time between now and then that are the same?" It had taken a while, but he'd finally found a picture of the old brick dug up when the bridge's foundations were being built. "Just keep going down through the layers and you'll find intersections," he'd said, sliding it across the table towards his granddaughter.

"And remember when you dug this out, Gramps? And you took Gram down to see it?"

"First day, pet, yes . . ." And only later, after, Charlie realized how little he'd told her about where it had been found, and what else had been there, and what kind of day it had been, no matter how many times she'd asked.

"They reckon it was from the old observatory," her grandfather had said, "and I thought that was pretty right because it was such a good place to sit and watch—there were blokes over by that pylon saw that dive off the bridge, and sometimes when I went back there, after the war, I felt I could just about see it myself. Powerful bit of time when someone flies instead of falling."

Riffling through Charlie's photos as he spoke, he'd settled one on the top of the pile, tapping it square. On the left of the picture, a record of the weather one spring day in 1791—the wind coming in from the southeast before the sunrise of a cloudy day, with a little rain at noon. On the right, a series of narrow panoramas of the same day, more than two hundred years later—the cloud in the morning, the rain at noon—taken from the site of the old observatory where those first eighteenth-century readings had been made.

Charlie held the stack still in her grandfather's hands: in the center of the modern midday, something had jarred and blurred, marring the image—she wondered how she hadn't noticed it before. But as she frowned, her grandfather pulled it up towards his eyes, adjusting his glasses.

"Well, well," he said, "there it is. There it is."

"And he asked me if he could have it," said Charlie to Dan. "The first one of my pictures he'd ever asked for. He put it on the lowboy with that postcard of Icarus's foot disappearing into the water—remember? The dive. He said it was the dive."

Sitting beside the imitation stream, Dan ducked his head a little lower to look back to the bridge. "Kelly's dive," he said. Kelly with the soft Irish accent, snapping himself into a somersault, or in a high hospital bed aching where the boot leather had been peeled from his thighs. Kelly, with the newspaper men pinning his words with their pencils. Should he tell Charlie he'd dreamed all that? Should he tell her that those old tin-can phones were still whizzing stories between them, even around the world? Maybe it was like climbing the bridge without her, a story not told, a thing not explained.

"Do you reckon we could climb it?" he said. "Not with that clipped-on mob, but just on our own?"

"They'd have us for terrorists," said Charlie, laughing. "There are security blokes patroling it now. But there's some bloke lying in a hospital who tried to BASE jump from it in the middle of the night, except his chute didn't open. He's been in hospital months now; I thought about asking him if I could photograph him—is that too macabre? I'm thinking about starting a new series of shots—him and that amazing German woman, the paraglider who got sucked up into the clouds in a storm. It took her higher than Mount Everest. And she survived. Did you read about that? And the Frenchman who's planning to freefall from forty thousand meters? All these other versions of the body in the clouds."

"The what?"

"The indigenous people who were here before the British, before us, I guess, they believe that you come from the clouds when you're born, and that when you die, your bones stay in the ground but your body goes back up. It was one of the first things the British learned from them when they arrived. the bones in the ground, the body in the clouds." She picked at one of her fingers while Dan waited for her to go on. "Sometimes, I realized, Gramps did tell the story about diving off the bridge as if it had been somebody else, and once he said he wondered if it was possible to move differently through the air in this place because there'd always been people here who believed that that was what happened—when you began to live, as much as when you died." She pushed her hair back and it flickered against the wind. "Different kinds of resurrection, I guess. It's a wonder he didn't have me driving him around the harbor to sit and wait for that Second Coming. Gram did sit there waiting, for a while, you know. That story was true."

She looked at her watch, at the sky. "We should keep going, get back for your mum," she said, on her feet with a hand out to help pull him up. He felt her take his weight as he pushed himself away from the ledge he'd been sitting on, and wished he could just fall against her and sleep for a while. So far, so tired, and now he was confusing her grandfather's face with the Russian man's, pallidly inanimate and floating in front of his eyes. And Caro, Caro's face seemed to have slipped away completely—he gagged a little, horrified, then made himself picture her building, her front door, her flat, and there she was, safely inside. Two in the morning in her world: he pictured her asleep, then wondered if she might be awake, wondering about him, staring out of her window at other windows, lit and dark. Funny, for a moment it was the view from his window he imagined for her, and for the first time he thought what a safe and warm thing it would be to know she was sitting at home—in their home—waiting for him.

Overhead, high in the blue, came the faint buzz of an engine and Dan and Charlie both looked up to see an aeroplane cut straight through the middle of the cloud, creating a precise stripe in its wake that brushed the sky back from white to blue—the reverse of the usual jet stream. Dan arched his head further back so as not to lose sight of it, almost overbalancing against the angle. "I've never seen anything like that before." But the cloud was recovering, spreading straightaway and softening the sky's color until it had returned to white less than a minute later.

"I guess it happens all the time," said Charlie, rubbing at her own neck, "and we just don't notice it."

His eyelids heavy, his gaze just ahead of his jolting steps, Dan followed the sound of Charlie's voice south, back towards her place. Her heard her say the word "orphaned" and realized she was talking about herself. He imagined the two of them now, from above, their heads bobbing along like mobile markers on a map. Such a paucity of family webbing out around them: his mum; a few second cousins; a great-aunt on Charlie's side whom Dan couldn't now place as springing from Joy, or Joe, or Ted. Two single points, moving together along a street: in his mind's eye Dan was floating high above the image of their walk, clearing the tops of buildings and heading for the sky.

They reached a curb and Charlie pulled Dan back as he made to step off into a stream of traffic again so that he bumped into someone next to him.

"Sorry, mate," said Dan. The man shrugged, his fingers busy

on his mobile phone while his eyes stared at Dan's face as if he was trying to recognize him—not as someone in particular, but as any sort of person at all. *What do I look like to you?* thought Dan, foggily. *What are you seeing?*

Turning back towards Charlie, he saw another man come along the pavement opposite. He was older, dressed in decrepit layers of clothing and cradling a torn plastic bag. A brown dog bounced at his ankles, its tail high and happy.

Neither dog nor man paused or registered the traffic, and at first Dan didn't see what had happened, only that something was suddenly caught under the wheels of a car coming around the corner—a taxi, sleek and silver, and in the backseat a woman, thrown forward by the sudden stop, frowning and cursing as the car, shockingly, lurched forward again, through screams, and stopped.

The dog freed itself, made for the gutter with a terrible swagger, and took two or three steps before it realized it was injured, it was in pain, and it sank onto the concrete, unable to move any farther.

It yelped then, but only once, heaved itself up again somehow, staggered, lurched, fell. There were so many screams cutting across its broken body, and then a terrible, nasty silence.

"I didn't know if that was a person or a dog," said someone next to Charlie. "Not that one would be better than the other."

"I did not want to see that," said Charlie quietly.

Dan closed his eyes, seeing the furry rump trapped under the wheels, the way it had wriggled itself out and assumed—it knew how its paws worked, how its legs worked—that it could just stand up and walk away. He swallowed the taste of vomit, his breath bubbling horribly in his throat.

The old man was crouched down next to his pet among a forest of legs, three or four people on mobile phones.

"He'll be right, mate," said someone, but Dan wasn't sure if he meant the old dog or the man—and wasn't sure that it was going to be true of either of them.

In the backseat of the cab, the woman looked around blankly, uncertain of what had happened. Her eyes scanned the people on the pavement, caught sight of Dan—who raised one hand, wanting somehow to acknowledge her, to soothe her—and moved on. The cab driver took off his glasses, rubbed his eyes, and accelerated away before his hands were back on the wheel. "That woman," said Dan, "she looked like the Russian woman on the plane." He wasn't even sure if this was true, but he wanted to give Charlie something to think about that wasn't what she'd just seen. "She said she thought Sydney looked beautiful when we landed this morning. We talked about reading *Gulliver's Travels*—I was thinking about when you and I read it, when we were young, but I couldn't remember if we'd ever finished it."

Light and easy; the thought came out of nowhere.

"I did not want to see that," said Charlie again, stepping off the curb as the lights changed in their favor. "Come on, let's go." Stepping wide around the huddle on the footpath that was the dog, the man, the misery of it all.

"I mean," said Dan, running on, wishing he could stop and knowing he was making something worse now, not better, "it's not much of a story to bring you, a man dying on a plane, and then his daughter running over a dog in front of us. If it was her; if it was—"

"No," said Charlie, stopping his words and balancing his gait as he weaved a little next to her. "But Gulliver's better. Maybe we can start reading the same books again, just on different sides of the world. Then we can argue about what they mean and whether they're good." Smiling a little, leading the way.

Dan smiled too, but he read books with Caro now—sometimes simultaneously, sometimes ones she'd just finished. And sometimes, just before they slept, she read him a page or two of whatever she was partway through, and he'd drift into a different sleep with the sound of her voice and its words like waves turning a little pulse against a shore. That, he thought now, was one of his favorite things about being with Caro. And there were never any arguments about it.

Reaching Charlie's building, reaching its elevator, Dan leaned back against the mirrored wall and let his eyes shut properly. His body felt even heavier as the cabin pushed up from the ground.

"Here," he heard Charlie say as the door opened, and he watched again as a triangle of light spilled again into the dark hallway from her opening door. "Here you are, I'll make another coffee—try not to think about it."

His tiredness had reached a pitch somewhere between drunkenness and nausea, and he leaned in towards her bathroom mirror, splashing handful after handful of cold water onto his face.

"Dan? There's coffee." His cup on the side of the table away from the view.

He took another too-big, too-hot gulp. "So my mum," he said, the skin inside his mouth tingling. He was trying not to think of the heaviness in his head. "You said she's not as young—"

"No, no, she's fine—I didn't mean you should worry. Just that she'll be a bit more lonely. She was visiting Gramps, Ted, almost every day, and I'm away a fair bit, and you're . . . on the other side of the world. She's fine." Charlie nodded. "I took some pictures last week, in the hospital. Here—I made some prints for your mum."

There was Ted Parker, wide eyes gazing out across the rooftops of the city view. And there was Dan's mum, her hair a little darker, her face a little thinner than how Dan always pictured her, and her first pair of glasses tucked high on the top of her head. She was smiling; she was squeezing Gramps's arm, she was happy. She was reassuringly herself.

There you are, thought Dan. *They didn't matter, all those years on the other side of the world.* But he knew that wasn't quite right.

"What did Mum say about the whole Ted thing?" he asked then, tilting the photo towards the light.

Charlie smiled. "Not a lot. Said it didn't change the person Ted had been and all he'd done for us. Said I was going to have enough loss to deal with without losing him before he died. And she did say, incidentally, that she'd never believed the story about flying off the bridge, was always terrified it'd make you want to climb up there and give it a go. I told her you'd piked out the last morning you were here, when we'd promised each other we'd climb up and see the sunrise. I didn't tell her you'd gone up there years ago with some girl . . ." Seeing the look of surprise on his face, she said, "Somebody told me at a party once."

She pushed another pile of photographs towards him: the cable tunnels from the bridge's foundations, with other slivers of its size, its structure, its setting framed up in other shots. The men who'd found the old stone, she said—"the men who'd really found it"—had found a ring in the wall nearby and made up some story about it being a place where convicts were chained. "But it must have been the observatory, William Dawes's observatory, and Ted and Joe were much more taken with the idea of him than with the idea of convicts and shackles and big heavy bolts."

Her index finger tapped at the side of one of the prints, touching its corner and bouncing back from the small pinprick it made. "Some guy, William Dawes," she said softly. "Out here on the *Sirius* to watch for a comet that doesn't come, and then all the things he gets busy with in the meantime—stars and maps and words and treks. This lovely description of it being Dawes's job to amalgamate all the courses each person reckoned they'd walked during a day when they were out on an expedition, the coordinates of their compasses, the number of steps they'd taken. They said he could do it almost without interrupting a conversation."

Charlie had dug for this other, older man as far as she could, running up against the wistful letters of historians, writing as the bridge was being built, about how sad it was that someone like him should almost have slipped out of view altogether—so few papers, such little evidence. That place under the southeastern foot of the bridge—which Dawes had called Point Maskelyne, for the Astronomer Royal, to acknowledge the role of astronomy in the beginnings of Sydney—had ended up named to honor him instead. And then Dawes Point had had its earlier, gentler name brought back alongside it: Tarra. His name, and the older name, back in conversation. Someone had found the lists of words he'd collected from those first conversations he'd had; someone had found his meteorological records from that first observatory—the journals that Charlie had used for her photographs. But most of what he'd left, the ideas and information he must have generated, had disappeared from view.

"Then again," said Charlie now, clicking open the folder on her computer that held all her weather images, "there were those who said at the time that he wasn't always visible to mortal eyes, so maybe he was always going to fade away, a little mysterious. 'Not visible to mortal eyes': I think that was one of Gramps's favorite lines."

Dan watched the images dissolve one into the next; the blues and whites of the weather, the neat newspaper type of the modern forecasts, the careful handwriting, sepia, in ruled columns, of the eighteenth-century records. It was particular handwriting, handwriting that had been concentrated on. *Violent thunder. Pleasant cool breeze.* Days when the sun was *somewhat obscured.* Days when the sun *shone through the haze. Sea breezes. Hailstones.* Sometimes a *shower of small rain.*

"I imagined things to tell him in the end—I didn't think he'd mind. I read about those early French aeronauts who went across the Channel in their hot-air balloons and I imagined William

Dawes dreaming of building his own balloon and flying over this place he was mapping. I read about the Englishman who came up with the first classifications for clouds, a decade or so after Dawes was here, and I imagined Dawes staring at the shapes of clouds, wondering how they might be classified, and wondering about the stories they might hold. I read about the settlers and the Eora dancing, and I imagined William Dawes dancing slowly down by the water. His handwriting always reminded me a bit of yours." She zoomed in on one of the columns of sepia text on her screen. "Like it never changed from the handwriting you learn at school." She zoomed in again so the letters blurred and fuzzed. "Just the next round of stories, I guess."

Dan finished his coffee, stared at the brown sludge in the bottom of his mug, the same color as the journal's text, as if its shape might hold something for him. He snorted; he'd be visiting Cynthia's clairvoyant next.

"My stories aren't so great," he said carefully. "Death and near-death experiences from a weird trip home. And then, that dog." He felt like he should apologize. "I don't think you need those stories in a week like this." Straightening to smile, maybe to pat her shoulder or touch her arm, he caught the flick of something dark in one of her photographs and leaned towards the screen, his hand up to stop her clicking on to the next image.

"Yes," she said, "that's it. That's the one Gramps liked. I never see the movement straight off—but you're right, there it is, in the middle. Right day. Right time. That's the one he said showed the fall."

"It's the strangest thing," said Dan without thinking, without knowing exactly what he might say, "but flying home, I dreamed I saw the fall—Kelly's fall; I even knew his name was Kelly. And then I dreamed I was diving in myself, like it was a competition. Like it was deliberate. The strangest thing," he said again as the picture on the screen began to fade and change. "I don't know what any of it means—especially not this morning."

"That's what he meant when he said he'd seen it before and after," said Charlie slowly. "Ted Parker said he was dreaming of that fall for years before it happened, and after too."

The screen went blank, came up again in a different series of photos: the middle of the city, the middle of the day, and Charlie must have been high above one of its parks, her camera up around the level from which Dan had imagined them earlier, all the people below reduced to the shorthand of round heads and streaking busyness.

"Color and movement," he said.

"I was trying to work out how we must really look, smeared across time and space," said Charlie. "What traces we must leave." She laughed. "I keep coming back to the same story." And she pushed the empty cups farther across the table so that Dan could get closer, find the angle that resolved each hurried blur into the single, sharp moment his eyes expected to catch.

"I got one of those pedometers at an office Christmas party," he said, rubbing his eyes. "Wore it for a week or so—we all got one, and everyone was fascinated by how far they'd gone, or hadn't gone, compared to what they'd expected." Remembered not knowing the length of his own stride; remembered all their abortive attempts to try to count each step of the most mundane excursion without the machine. Front door to tube. Office chair to elevator. No one, as far as he could recall, had ever managed to pay attention from one end of their journey to the other. "What I thought would be better though was if, instead of just counting the steps you took unreliably, because one girl left hers on her desk all weekend and came back to work on Monday to find it claiming to have taken a hundred and sixty steps in the meantime—if it could draw you a track of all the places you'd walked that day, or that week, or that year. You'd have all these lines heading out in all sorts of directions, and I'd have the same path trodden over and over."

"Not fair to compare us," said Charlie. "You go to the same place every day, sit at the same computer, do your job, move money around. I go to different places, look for different pictures. But the lines I was making to the bridge, to Gramps's place, to the hospital would be so heavily inked they would have saturated any paper by now." She looked up towards the tall glass windows as the light fell a little: the sun had gone behind a cloud. "Remember flying back from that holiday with Gramps when we were kids? Remember the way the water lit up like quicksilver as the sun hit it and we flew over the top?"

Dan nodded. "I was thinking about that this morning. I was thinking about that when I was flying in, when we came out of the clouds and I could see the ground for the first time."

Charlie's hands were up, her fingers spread like stars and her thumbs hooked together, the way a child might make the shape of a butterfly. She flexed her fingers like its wings, watching the pale shadow thrown by the movement.

"And remember we saw the plane's whole shadow gliding across the ground, so small, and so fast, that we got scared at how high we must be, how fast we must be going?"

"No," said Dan, trying to mirror her movement with his own hands, struggling to latch his thumbs together, to re-create the fireworks shape his fingers had made in that thick, white dream. "I remember the shadow but I don't remember being scared—and you had the window seat."

"You had the window seat. You saw the bridge when we came in past the city."

He shrugged, wishing his fingers would flap like Charlie's instead of arching like claws. He was sure he'd been sitting in the middle—sure Charlie had always scored the better view.

"I always thought that was why Gramps gave you his watch," she said then, "because when you saw the bridge that day, you said you always thought of him flying from it—that you thought of him, whenever you saw it, even when it was only in a picture."

Dan unlocked his thumbs, took the watch from his pocket, and slid it towards her. "I don't remember that," he said again, "but I found the watch in my bag when I was coming home. I always meant to give it back to you. Ted Parker's watch." Aiming for ceremony and forgiveness.

"Joe Brown's watch, really. Joe's. My other grandfather's," said Charlie. She rubbed its silver on the leg of her jeans, adjusted the time for Sydney and laid it on the table so its tick reverberated. And she watched it for a moment, her hands tucked up at her mouth as though she'd been caught halfway towards prayer. She looked at the watch, looked at Dan, and began to rub her hands against her jeans. He could hear the purr of her skin against their fabric. Then she reached out and took his hands in hers so he could feel the warmth from the rubbing.

"The best thing I learned from William Dawes," she said. "There was a word here, when he came: *putuwá*. 'I warm my hands by the fire, I press the warmth into yours.' Nothing like it in English," squeezing the cups his two hands made in hers, "but out of all the things he saw and did and found here, and all the things that happened, I reckon that's the pick." She let go, rubbed her hands warm again, and reached back across the table for his. "All the last night with Ted we kept this going—he said Joe and Joy used to do it, but they wouldn't have known there was a word for it, and one from right here, in this place. He remembered one night before the war in particular: they were out looking for a comet and Joe Brown had warmed Joy's hands that way as they stood there in the dark." Warming and holding. Warming and holding. Then, "I'm sorry you came home like this—Gramps, and the other plane, and the old Russian man, even that poor dog." She was tracing a line on the tabletop that looked like a section of coast, with inlets and streams, coves and capes. A curve in towards the west, an offset stub like a flourish at its end. "He turned us into cartographers, Ted Parker, convincing us every story was a point on some map. I stare and stare at all the different points and coordinates until I can see the connection. But it's good you're here now. It's good you're here."

She smiled, and Dan smiled in reply, rubbing his palms together for warmth, and pressing them onto her smaller, finer hands to soothe their restlessness.

Dawes

REACHING TO support himself as he went below, William Dawes felt the sharp sting of a splinter driving into his palm—winced and cursed, trying to see where it was. The belly of the *Gorgon* was dark and dim as she prepared to leave for England, and the contrast between these shadows and the hard December daylight outside flushed Dawes's eyes of their sight for a second or two, maybe three. Blinded, he paused, right-hand fingers tentatively feeling around his left-hand pain—maybe to relieve it, maybe to pluck the offending spike free—and for the same two seconds, maybe three, the darkness seemed to have swallowed most of the harbor's sound and movement too.

William Dawes, still, alone, and quiet, preparing to sail back into the world. All he could hear was the faintest sprinkling of a piano's notes—softly keyed, halting, and jarringly out of tune. Except the piano had been taken to a house upstream, he thought, so if this sound was a piano, it could only be an echo or a memory.

It was Tench who stumbled against him, coming out of the day himself and blinking against the internal gloom. "My last sentence set down," he said, waving a satchel of papers, "and dull it sounds at the moment: on the thirteenth of December 1791, the marine battalion embarked on board His Majesty's ship *Gorgon*, and on the eighteenth sailed for England. I'm hoping for something a bit more—" he paused, and seemed to bite at the air in search of the right word "—literary once we get under weigh. I wonder which latitude we'll have reached by the year's end?" He clapped his hand on his friend's shoulder and propelled him back to walking. "Come on deck?"

Nodding and stepping, Dawes pulled the splinter free, rolling it back and forth between his fingers. "I do wonder if I'll ever see this place again," he said, knowing how unthinkable that would sound to almost every other man on board, all happy to be heading home. "It feels a little more fixed now, a little more permanent. It feels like it's here to stay."

Tench leaned back against the wall. "I don't know if I'd go that far," he said, "although it has defied the presence of John White and the weight of Albion." He'd spent the previous week looking at grazing fields here, vegetable patches there, declaring this maize crop successful, that tobacco promising, that wheat problematic. And always the want of water, the ongoing want of water.

Back in the light, the two men leaned against the ship's roll and gazed across to Sydney. From offshore, from some angles, it looked as if William Dawes's old daydreams of the whole place unraveling back to nothing might have started to come into effect, whatever his sense of its fixedness.

"Four years, give or take," said Tench, his eyes moving from the shadow of his own shape on the surface of the water to the town beyond. "And look at it—a few old huts scattered around, and the dried-up squares of some abandoned gardens. Your observatory, with its magazine and battery, still looks the most substantial thing we've got. Although now, of course, the instruments sail home with you, and your place is left to its guns."

"A different sort of watching and waiting for it now," said

Dawes. And *gwara burdwa*: the wind has fallen. How long would he be able to think in this other language?

Leaning out from the ship's rail, he nodded towards his point, his little white building, the line of trees still standing along its ridge, the water turning slowly against its rocky shore. "We've seen some seasons," he said, straightening up, "years in and out, the stars, the nights, the aurora." Through the glare, he could make out some movement against the white walls of the observatory, like letters trying to settle onto a page. Squinting, leaning out farther again, he smiled: they'd come to watch him in farewell. He wondered who would teach them now, and who they would teach—the surgeon, the vicar, the other officers and office bearers, whoever would listen. He hoped the conversations would keep going; he would send them more books when he reached England.

When I reach home—and there was Miss Rutter, smiling, a white rose dropping from her fingers. It had been so long since he'd seen her.

Raising one arm in a wave, he saw them gesture in return and smiled again. "They have this word, Lieutenant," he said to Tench. "*Buduwa—putuwá*. It means passing the warmth of your own hand, your own skin, into somebody else's. A pretty word, don't you think? It makes me feel the paucity of English."

Tench shook his head. "Your idealism and your optimism, sir." But—"*Pu-tu-wá*"—he sounded the syllables out to himself. "Where will that sit in your great project?"

Fashioning his hands to mark out a block, Dawes said quietly, "My keystone, sir, my keystone," and his friend followed his gaze back onto the land and up to the white wall and its busy figures.

"Of all of us," said Tench at last, "I suspect you're most likely to come back here, to see how it turns out."

Here was the pull, the turn of the water—everything ready to be off and away.

But Dawes shook his head. "There'll be something waiting for us in the world that changes all the things we think we'll do," he said. From inside this harbor, as he knew so well, there was no sign of open ocean or clear horizon, let alone what was happening somewhere else and how that might press in against you. At first that had felt isolating; now he wondered if it had been protective.

Either way, such thoughts weighed heavily on some men and not at all on others—such as the captain who'd arrived with his load of convicts just four or five months before, who'd brought not a single letter, newspaper, journal, or report from the world. Desperate for some information, a story, an inkling of anything happening elsewhere, Tench had rowed six miles out to sea to greet the ship, only to discover its ignorance.

"I never thought about the matter," the captain had said, as he stood a moment, rubbing at his head, suggesting that perhaps Britain was at war with Spain. Tench leaned forward for his every word. Had he heard that? Was it Spain? And if so when, and where, and why? The captain had rubbed his head again. He couldn't honestly remember, he'd confessed, and couldn't remember what the trouble was about—if, indeed, there was trouble at all.

"I cannot wait," said Tench now in a voice that strained itself through clenched teeth, "to be completely consumed by news and gossip and the events of as many people and places and happenings as possible." And Dawes saw him disappearing under pages and pages of paper, so hungry for every detail they held.

Below the observatory, a kingfisher began the low and guttural gargle of its laugh, pushing up into its vowels, its *aaa*s, its *eee*s, its *ooo*s.

And will I hear you again? Dawes ducked his head, trying to catch a glimpse of its creamy feathers and seeing, instead, the gentle and continual rearrangement of the audience outside his old quarters. Already his old quarters—already the place where he no longer lived.

I saw a girl on the shore, the day we sailed in, he thought, *and now she—or her sister, or her friend—stands up a little higher, with her own sisters, her own friends, and we can hail each other in words we all understand. They named us* be-re-wal-gal; *we come from* bere-wal. *And now*—he raised both his hands high as the order came for the ship to make sail—*now we head back to that great way off.* He waved. The group by the observatory waved their reply.

Beside him he heard Tench's laugh and turned to see him also waving and grinning towards the shore. "Mr. Darwin," he said. "I was thinking of Erasmus Darwin and his poem about the 'Visit of Hope' to our lost little place. Art and Industry. All those 'broad streets' he imagined—that you'd surveyed. All those 'tall spires' he dreamed—that you'd laid onto the Governor's plans. All those 'dome-capped towers' and 'bright canals,' and his 'proud arch, colossus-like,' binding the 'chasing tide'—ha! Imagine the size a bridge would need to be, to close that gap." His finger etched the line from south to north. "Some span next to our huts and our canvas!" And his head tipped back with the exclamation as Dawes followed his gaze, up into the limitless cerulean that arched above Point Maskelyne and then out to the east, to the path their ship would beat.

Beyond those heads, beyond that blue, lay wars and revolutions, new presidents and constitutions. Inventions had come into being while he'd sat by this harbor that would change how big, or small, the world seemed—the meter, the steamboat, the semaphore machine. He would see Judith Rutter, would tell her of all that he'd found on the other side of the world—"and this word, you see, *putuwá, putuwá.*" He would marry her and see the birth of their son, another William Dawes, who would have his father's eyes for the stars, who would become an astronomer known himself for a luminous gaze—no disappointing comets among his son's scientific record.

He would be proposed and passed over to return to New South Wales as engineer, as superintendent of schools. He would become, instead, the governor of Sierra Leone, making another journey back to England from there with incantations from another language tucked among his papers: charms for friendship and a divination for recovering from illness. More words, more new words. He would end his life an old man living in the Caribbean, engaged in the last years of a long fight against slavery. Arguing for bridges, for conversations, between different groups of people.

Across the years, he would hear of this place becoming Australia, another new name. He would hear of those westerly hills—now breached—renamed from Carmathen to the Blue Mountains. And he would hear of his own little point changing its name again and again, the Astronomer Royal well and truly displaced.

He would hear of Sydney Harbour sprouting big mansions—there was even an aviary in one, although to augment what shortage of birds, he would never be able to imagine—and of so many ships coming and going from so many parts of the world. A normalcy of food and post and even places of science—a botanic garden, a museum, and a new observatory, upstream, at Rose Hill. He would talk to Patye for the rest of his years, but he would never hear of her again, not in letters, in memoirs, in published reports or official dispatches. And his image of her would fade—as his image of Miss Judith Rutter, of his father, had dimmed in just four years—until he wondered if he might have imagined her, with the alligators, the roses, and the swooping, diving ghosts.

And yet, at the end, he would ask a young girl who sat with him to remind him again of that beautiful word. "It was for warmth, my dear, and friendship. Patye? What was that word? Is it you?" And the girl would say, "Hush," and, "I'm here, sir," and, "Yes, sir, it's me, Patye." Pressing his hand with the warmth from her own, saying whatever he wanted to hear.

And his old observatory, given over—as Tench had predicted—to the settlement's defenses, would have its ground dug to hold the bones of executed criminals, its ground dug again to quarry stone for buildings that echoed the plans Dawes had drawn and were designed by the man who did indeed propose raising a bridge—Erasmus Darwin's bridge—from the little observatory in the south across to the north. Imagine that, a great bridge in Sydney, where much was once made of a few logs laid down to ford a diminishing stream. It was there too, of course, in the end, the proud arch, its foundations burrowing down through the ground on which William Dawes had stood, had lived, had watched and waited. Even his comet would blaze across the sky at last—not here, but over England, over the northern countries, and more than two centuries late.

All this was tucked into the future as William Dawes looked away from the sky to the diminishing size of a rowboat, moored in the shallows and rising and falling on the tide. His own breathing fell in time with its movement, and in its lull, he caught the edge of something solid from the corner of his eye, as if someone had drawn a thin black line across the blue.

Creaking and heaving, the *Gorgon* made her way east, the harbor sliding by and punctuated by coves and inlets, beaches and islands.

"And still there are those," said Tench, watching the way his friend's eyes ran across every curve and outcrop as though transferring them onto yet another map, "who can row around here and not know where they are."

Dawes shook his head, indicating the names of each place as if nothing could be simpler: "Warran, Barawoory, Woganmagule, Walla-mool, Carragin," and, on the north shore, "Booragy and Kuba Kuba and Garángal."

Glancing back towards the cove, he saw a white bird dive deep and come up sharply, a fish flapping in its beak, and remembered Patye's *molu-molu* and, further back, his band of workers and the bare structure of his observatory. Across the ground, spilling down to the waterline, lay that length of canvas that would be pulled taut across a frame, painted up with a mix of linseed and lead, and fitted to become a roof that he could open to the night. Perfect; just as William Dawes had imagined, and just as his French astronomer had endorsed. The men had reached down, Dawes among them, and taken the sides of the canvas as if it was a vast quilt for a vast bed—they had lifted it, and without any discussion had flicked it up, like laundresses hanging a sheet to dry. The canvas had cracked, arched into a perfect dome with the winter breeze beneath it, and then it had settled, fluttering, just for a moment. *My balloon, my magnificent balloon.*

Now, in his mind's eye, the material flicked again and again, with him caught under its big safe bubble of air, rising up—although beneath him, he saw, was not the blue, the gold, the green of water, rock, and bush. He was floating over a map inked black on thick creamy parchment, as if he were part of one of his own illustrations.

"—and on to Burrawarra and Tarralbe," he finished his recitation for Tench, pointing towards the harbor's southern headland and beyond, as the color came back into the world.

"And what will you do with it, your great accumulation of words and numbers?"

Dawes laughed. "You could have my vocabulary for your own publication, and everybody wants the maps, and I still have to write up my Report of the Expected Return of the Comet of 1532 and 1661 in the Year 1788." His eyebrows raised at the ongoing joke of it. "I don't know, Lieutenant Tench. There'll be more than enough work to do when we get back there; who knows which stories they'll want us to tell?"

"I liked the idea of your cyclopedia, everything from alligators to zoology, with *mawn* and *molu-molu* in the middle."

Molu-molu and *mawn*: his beautiful shooting stars and his terrible swooping spirits. "Thank you, sir," said William Dawes. "Whatever happens, I've got the beginnings of it." A project for his old age, perhaps, when he was an old man come back to this place and its conversations, his papers stacked in their trunks and ready, at last, to be pieced together.

The thumb of his right hand pressed into the palm of his left, but it wasn't the splinter's itchy scar it sought; it was warmth, it was exchange, it was *putuwá*.

Gliding on, the *Gorgon* turned and tacked towards the heads. It had almost reached the last place from which the settlement was visible, and as Dawes leaned and strained towards the smudge it made on the land, he saw again some sudden streaking movement. A body. A balloon. A bird. He had no idea. He blinked, and the movement, the settlement, had gone, left to other people now, and to all the new stories and maps and discoveries they would make.

Whatever was happening here, it would continue after he had gone as it had before he arrived.

Spinning on his good leg, William Dawes looked out across the opposite rail. Between the heads, north and south, lay a dark blue stripe of water and a lighter one of sky—on and on, all the way to Chile, had he been able to see that far.

Into the blue, he thought, *and on we go, back into the world.*

Out of the Blue

THEY WALKED down to the bridge after the funeral—unsure what else they should do, where else they should go. In the pub that sat under its bulk, they raised their glasses to Ted Parker and his stories, to Joe Brown and his family, to William Dawes and his little piece of land.

"And to Caroline," said Charlie.

"To Caroline," said Dan, raising his glass again. "She was right to make me come."

"I thought it was my billboard that did that." Charlie smiled. "And to you, Dan Kopek, my friend. Thank you for coming." A lull fell around Charlie's words and they sat awhile in its silence, Dan's eyes staring through the empty air in front of them and Charlie with her grandfather's watch cupped in her hands like a scoop of water. The edge of her face glanced in and out of its silver as if it were reflected in the smooth surface of a pond or a pool.

"But I've been thinking," she said, "that you should keep this. Not just"—she put up one hand to stop his objection—"because he gave it to you, but because of the story. You had his dream; coming home, the night he died, you had his dream. I never have. I can take a picture that might have the memory of that fall in it, but it's you who sees it there—you and Ted Parker. I only see it when someone points it out. I went looking for new versions of it—making pictures for the journals; finding stories about bodies in clouds. You've got the original."

"But you're always part of the story, Charlie." The watch sat between them on the table. "And you wanted the watch—it's yours, please. You always wanted it. And it belongs here."

She shook her head, placing the smooth silver circle into his hands and closing her own around them. "It's yours. It's your story now."

~

The last conversation she had with her grandfather, a gossipy show on the television above their heads and him railing against the way everyone wanted these stories about people they didn't know, instead of paying attention to their own. "Work out what your story is," he had said, clutching her hand. "Don't get distracted by all these others. You and Dan, you know some good stories—make sure you both tell them."

Squeezing Ted Parker's hand, warm and gentle, one last time, Charlie let the silence sit. The next time he spoke, his hand still in hers, it was Joy Brown he asked for. And Charlie, her eyes closed, had said, "Shh," and, "Don't worry."

Said, "Shh, it's all right."

Said, "I'm here, I'm here; of course I'm here."

~

"Will you come back again soon?" asked Charlie as Dan cradled the watch, uncertain, in his palm. "All this," waving her glass towards the harbor, "and your mum, and, you know, the rest of us—will you bring Caro to meet us at last?"

He had a strange flash: him and Caro tucked into Gulliver's

canoe and making for the New Holland coast through a thick white sea mist. "Of course," he said, coming out of his reverie. "She always wanted to come, but you know me. Disorganized—or careless, as Gramps would say."

"Useless." Charlie brushed at the side of his head, but gently, so that the end of the gesture cushioned his cheek for a moment. She held his gaze. "It's right, what you're doing, going back—you know that."

He smiled, tilted his head in the slightest nod. *Work out what your story is*, that's what Gramps had said. And Gramps was his story. Charlie was his story. Caro, now, was his story. And Gramps was right—those stories held you together, gave your skin shape, like muscles and bones. He'd willed them together, just as Joy Brown had willed him into her family after the war. You could always do it, if you had some stories, some places and memories, to glue you together. No matter how you came by them.

Dan took a mouthful of beer. "Anyway, tell me, what happened to William Dawes, sitting out there, writing down words and waiting for his comet?" He pointed towards the grass beneath the bridge.

"Died in Antigua, in the 1830s, with a trunkful of stories—piles of journals and letters and reports and notebooks, I guess. Most of it was destroyed by a hurricane, and then one of his relatives got rid of the rest."

Dan said, "He needed his own Ted Parker—or his own Joe Brown—to keep telling the stories, even if it meant things got borrowed now and then."

"He got them, Joe and Ted," said Charlie. "They all found each other in the end. But I don't know if he ever saw his comet—no one did till 2002, and then it was over Japan, over England, not down here."

"They're not much, comets, compared to meteor showers," said

Dan. "You expect them to streak across the sky but they just hang there, really—like still photos, not movies." He hoped Charlie wouldn't take that the wrong way. "I mean, I saw one, one weekend in England, a few years ago now . . ." He heard the words come out before he knew what they were going to be. "The night I met Caro—we were camping in Kent; it was spring and there was a comet, this silver streak." And as he said it, he could see it, a silver streak glowing against a dark night sky. It was beautiful, beautiful. *All this time*, he thought, *and just saying it was enough.*

"Of course you saw it, Dan," Charlie laughed. "Of course you did. That's a story worthy of Gramps."

Through the pub's window, the light was dropping from sunshine through shadow to the thick velvet of a storm. A group of tourists, ranged against the harbor's backdrop for someone's camera, split apart under the first drops of rain, darting towards the awning the bridge provided as the thunder began to growl. The sound of the traffic fell away—a bird called; another answered. And the old man Charlie and Dan had seen sitting by the bridge's shadow the first morning Dan was home shuffled past, bundles of plastic bags in each hand. Draining his glass, Dan nodded towards him. "Heading somewhere before it rains."

It took two minutes, maybe three, for the rain to reach its full intensity, and by then it was coming down so heavily that the air was thick with silver.

"Well," said Charlie, "wherever he ended up, I reckon William Dawes must always have dreamed of here: four years in a place like this, and it must have been beautiful too. I always imagined him leaving Sydney, trying to hang on to all the new words he'd learned, the new things he'd seen. I always imagined him at the end of his life, thinking about his observatory, and this point, the color of the sky, the color of the water. It's the perfect place to see things from, don't you think?"

Sitting quietly with Ted Parker, pressing a cool cloth to his forehead, warmth into his hands, coaxing small sips of water into his throat, she'd kept up a stream of stories for him. All she'd wanted was for him to know that she didn't mind—didn't really mind—about the stories he'd borrowed and refashioned and made his own. "I was thinking about the day Nipper Anderson went off the bridge," she'd say. Or, "I was thinking about how far Russian George walked to end up here." Or, "I was thinking about William Dawes, counting his steps from Sydney Cove to the coast, seeing new birds and spiders and shooting stars. Hearing a new language for the first time—that nice word," pressing her grandfather's hand, "that one he must have liked best, *buduwa*." She talked all the way through her own childhood, through as much as she knew of her mother's, through all the things she remembered—or imagined— about Gramps's own early life, Ted's, Joe's, whichever. She saw a tall ship sailing through the mist in the harbor one morning, and she made that a story for him, as if it had slipped through time. She saw the splashes made by fish jumping in the harbor and took sentences about them to him too, as close as she could get to that impossibly high splash he'd been seeing all his life.

"Do you remember that day," said Dan, breaking her train of thought, "that day he brought us down here with sandwiches and a picnic, and he told us about those great big safety nets they had strung up when they made the Golden Gate Bridge?"

"And he said if they'd had those things here he'd never have gotten to fly."

In some corner of Dan's mind, a stagnant pool of jet lag still lingered; he had moments of feeling he was still caught up in the air somewhere, his feet straddling tiredness and turbulence. Between the dislocation, beyond the vivid dreams from the flight, and beneath the constant line that Ted Parker's story of flying off the bridge had drawn on his imagination, there was some shuffle of movement—a moment, a color. He couldn't quite shake it free from wherever it had lodged.

"That day," he said slowly, "that day we came when we were kids, the first time, with a picnic: did we see . . . did we think we saw . . . ?"

Across the table, Charlie began to frown. "I can't remember—there was a bird, wasn't there? Something about a bird?" She was rubbing her finger around the rim of her glass, teasing out fragments of its clear ringing sound. And then the noise firmed and thickened, rising and falling so that it seemed sometimes to fill the room, sometimes to fall away, and sometimes to spread out across the wet afternoon's air. "Listen," said Charlie, but her finger was poised above the glass as the harmonic went on, swelling and rising. "It's coming from out there. It's the bridge."

They were almost skipping when they left the pub, on the edge of running as they crossed the road and headed for the grass, hand in hand, six years old again. Above them, odd drops of water found chinks between the pieces of steel, rounder, larger than the rain that fell easily, uninterrupted, from the sky. They stood with their faces up, trying to catch the isolated drops and listening to the long, strange chime that suspended itself between the steel, the wind, the water.

"Gramps always said she could sing," said Charlie, both hands up towards the bridge as she blinked in the wet, "said he heard it the night he climbed up with Joy, the day the arches joined, the day Kelly fell, the day he met my mother and took her up in the air."

Lightning, a blanket of it, spread wide and white across the sky, and out towards the east a single fork speared down to the horizon. Dan heard Charlie catch her breath, and thought, *It's something to be here—and it's beautiful.* If he went away now, he knew he would always need to come back.

And then he saw it, just below the bridge's deck and beginning to float, to fall. Count to three, and it would be gone.

He grabbed Charlie's hand again, spun her around. From above, from some angles, this looked like a dance.

"Look," he said. "*Look*."

It's happening. It's happening. It's always happening.

Acknowledgments

Certain parts of this book were inspired by real moments and real people. Some of its incidents, some of its conversations, derive from incidents and conversations that someone took the time to record. There was a man called William Dawes who came to Sydney with the First Fleet to look for a comet. And there was a man called Vincent "Roy" Kelly who fell from the Sydney Harbour Bridge and survived. But this book and its people and its coincidences are the stuff of imagination.

The first epigraph lines are taken from "Musée des Beaux Arts" copyright © 1940 and renewed 1968 by W. H. Auden; from *W. H. Auden Collected Poems* by W. H. Auden. Used by permission of Random House, an imprint and division of Penguin Random House LLC, and Curtis Brown, Ltd. All rights reserved.

The epigraph reference to the body in the clouds—and the book's title—comes from Governor Arthur Phillip's letter to Lord Sydney on 13 February 1790 as reproduced in the *Historical Records of New South Wales*, vol. I, part 2 (1978).

Most of the indigenous words used in the text come from William Dawes's notebooks, held by the Archives & Special Collections of the library at SOAS, University of London, and reprinted here with their permission. The call number for this material is MS 41645.

A small number of words and phrases collected by other early British visitors and used here are drawn from Jakelin Troy's *The Sydney Language* (1993).

Dawes's journals are now available online at www.william dawes.org and the spellings and accents used in the novel are based on these transcriptions. However, the letter ŋ has been transcribed where it appears in the novel's text as "ng," as in Jakelin Troy.

The words collected by William Dawes—and by other officers and settlers—come from a number of language groups and dialects, including Dharawal, Darug, and Gundungurra. Thanks to Frances Bodkin for talking to me about this, and about the ways the different accents of the British influenced their transcriptions of these words.

The extant correspondence between Dawes and his Astronomer Royal, Nevil Maskelyne, is part of the Board of Longitude papers in the Royal Greenwich Observatory's archive held by the University Library, Cambridge, and recently made available via the Cambridge Digital Library. Dawes's weather journals, rediscovered in 1977, are held by the Royal Society in London.

The poem referred to by Watkin Tench (p. 293) is Erasmus Darwin's "Visit of Hope to Sydney Cove, Near Botany Bay."

Text attributed to the Reverend Frank Cash (p. 85 forward) is taken from his *Parables of the Sydney Harbour Bridge: Setting Forth the Preparation for and Progressive Growth of the Sydney Harbour Bridge, to April 1930* (1930).

The newspaper article regarding Roy Kelly's survival of a fall from the road deck of the Sydney Harbour Bridge (p. 205 forward) was published in the *Sydney Morning Herald* on 24 October 1930.

Conversations between the bridge builders—and anecdotes told by them—were in some cases inspired by Richard Raxworthy's incomparable oral history, *Sydney Harbour Bridge Builders* (1982), and by *The Construction of the Sydney Harbour Bridge*, a video released by the Institution of Engineers, Australia, that combined a 1969 interview with one of the bridge's supervising engineers, Frank Litchfield, with footage shot by Henri Mallard in 1930 as the bridge was completed.

Thanks to Maria Richardson who talked to me about the Mater Misericordiae Hospital in North Sydney where Kelly was taken after his fall. And to Paul Cave, the founder of BridgeClimb, in whose collection of memorabilia the medal presented to Vincent Kelly "to celebrate his preservation from serious harm" is now housed. I had the chance to see it during an interview for a story published by *The Monthly* in August 2006, and that moment, like the story of Kelly, did prove to be "something that lodges deep in the imagination."

The line "like gold from airy thinness beat" as remembered by Dan (p. 70), and by Ted (p. 90), is from John Donne's "A Valediction: Forbidding Mourning."

The quote on page 108 is from Dannie Abse's poem "Watching a Cloud" from *New and Collected Poems* by Dannie Abse, published by Hutchinson. Reprinted by permission of The Random House Group Ltd, and by permission of United Agents LLP on behalf of the estate of Dannie Abse.

In terms of artworks, the sketch of the bridge under construction referred to on p. 89 is inspired by Grace Cossington Smith's *Study for The Bridge in-curve* (1930), held in the National Gallery of Australia. Antony Gormley's stunning *Blind Light* (2007)—an installation the artist describes as comprising "a chamber 11 metres by 9.5 metres by 3.5 metres high, filled at 1.5 atmospheres of pressure with 7000 lux of light and a density of purified water vapour such that if you hold your hand out in front of you, you can't see it"—was on show at London's Hayward Gallery between

May and August 2007, and inspired some of the ideas of what it might be like to find yourself standing in a cloud (p. 151). The postcard on Ted's lowboy (p. 162) is inspired by the painting that also inspired the Auden poem quoted in the epigraph: Pieter Bruegel's *Landscape with the Fall of Icarus*, held in the Royal Museums of Fine Arts of Belgium in Brussels. And the postcard Charlie gives Dan as he leaves Sydney (p. 201) is inspired by David Moore's image *Sydney at 16,000 Feet* (1966), held in the Art Gallery of New South Wales.

The compendium of information drawn from First Fleet journals which refers to days of "no extant record" (pp. 275) is John Cobley's *Sydney Cove 1788* (1962).

Thanks also to Steve Offner, Gail MacCallum, Hannah Westland, Ali Lavau, Clara Finlay, Angela Handley, and Jane Palfreyman. Thanks too to Jenny Hewson, Alice Whitwham, Sarah Cantin, and Judith Curr. And to Nigel Beebe.

This project has been assisted by the Australian government through the Australia Council, its arts funding and advisory body.